A strange, sharp sensation smote Lyrralt's left shoulder, so hard it knocked him to the floor, slicing into his bones.

He gasped as though his lungs had emptied of all air.

Sensations too varied, too contradictory to assimilate, flashed through his muscles, across his skin. Heat and cold, pressure from within and without, pain and pleasure. Blissful pain, as if his flesh were being peeled from his body.

Lyrralt opened his mouth wide and screamed in agony . . . and joy.

Saga

From the Creators of the DRAGONLANCE® Saga

THE LOST HISTORIES

The Kagonesti
Douglas Niles

The Irda
Linda P. Baker

The Dargonesti
Paul B. Thomson and Tonya Carter Cook
Available October 1995

DragonLance® Saga

**The Lost Histories
Volume 2**

The Irda

Children of the Stars

Linda P. Baker

DRAGONLANCE® Saga
The Lost Histories
Volume Two

THE IRDA
©1995 TSR, Inc.
All Rights Reserved.

Cover art by Larry Elmore. Interior art by Jeff Butler.

First Printing: June 1995
Printed in the United States of America.
Library of Congress Catalog Card Number: 94-68140
ISBN: 0-7869-0138-1

9 8 7 6 5 4 3 2 1

TSR, Inc.
201 Sheridan Springs Rd.
Lake Geneva, WI 53147
U.S.A.

TSR Ltd.
120 Church End, Cherry Hinton
Cambridge CB1 3LB
United Kingdom

Acknowledgments

To all the following friends and family, who have been with me along the way, part of who I am and what I write, a very special thank you:

My sisters, Laneta and Lisa, and my mother-in-law, Gerry, for putting up with me

My bosses, Gene, Gardner, and Jean, without whose understanding and support I could never have finished this book

Ann Zewen, my first editor, who gave me the courage to begin and continue

Carolyn Haines, one of my first writing instructors, for giving me belief in myself when she said of my short story, "You can get this published!"

Jan Zimlich, teacher, editor extraordinaire, and the voice of my conscience, thanks for holding my hand and cheerleading and saying, "You're going to finish this if I have to kick your butt the whole way!"

Margaret Weis, for inviting me into the wonderful world she created, giving me my first chance, and for her gracious support and advice

Patrick McGilligan, my editor, for patience beyond the call of duty and for all he's taught me

Last, but not least, I dedicate this book to:

My mother, Lena, who has also been father and friend and supporter, and who likes *my* fantasy writing although she doesn't read fantasy

And my husband, Larry, with all my love and gratitude, for the 2 a.m. sessions, for thinking everything I write is wonderful, for being my champion, and because he "don't wanta hear no negative waves!" I couldn't have done it without you!

Prologue
Song of the Ogre

The Keeper of the History of the Ogre stood alone and unassisted on the platform, though she was as ancient as the stone walls of the castle. She had buried the bones of all her friends, of her children, and still she lived, because of the Gift, which she alone possessed.

She opened her mouth, and it came, the Gift of the gods. A voice as pure and clear, as bright and beautiful, as stars shining in the darkness of a night sky. The ribbon of sound pierced the air. The words wove the History of the World, of the Ogre, firstborn of the gods.

By the hammer of the gods, the universe was forged
* from chaos.*
From the sparks of the anvil, the spirits were scattered,
Cast to glimmer and dance in the heavens.
From the forge of the gods, the world was wrought,
Playground of the gods.

The spirits were singing, their voices like starshine,
Shining like the gods themselves, pieces of the heavens.
The gods looked upon them and found them most
* wondrous.*
The gods looked upon them and coveted their souls.
The world shuddered.
Battlefield of the gods.

The High God looked down upon what his god children
* had destroyed;*
His wrath was mighty, his pain transcendent.
From the fire of his anger,
From the divine breath of Takhisis,
From the heart of the flames, the races were born.

Takhisis, Sargonnas, Hiddukel, gods of the Dark,
Made the stony Ogres.
Gifted with life, gifted with beauty,
The Ogres turned their faces earthward.
Children of the stars.
Firstborn of the gods.

Paladine, Mishakal, Those of the Light,
Made the willowy Elves.
Cursed them with goodness, cursed them with virtue.
Those of the middle, Gilean, Reorx, Gray gods all,
Made the plodding humans, set them to serve.

Watchers of the darkness are the mighty Ogres,
Cast down to rule the world from the lofty mountains.
Hair colored of the shadows, eyes like the moon,
Fairest of all and truly immortal.
Singers of starshine, masters of all created.

Rulers of the low ones; the animals, the elves, the
   humans.
Within our hearts, all dreams are dark.
Within our souls, all pain is pleasure.
We turn our faces upward.
Born of the stars, chosen by the gods.

Chapter 1
A Good and Perfect Gift

"My dear, you know that magic, beyond that necessary for daily needs, is forbidden to all but the Ruling Families."

Lord Teragrym Semi, eldest of the five Ruling Council members of the Ogres, considered by many in the royal court to be the most powerful, plucked a piece of fruit from the bowl sitting at his elbow.

"Yes, Lord, I know. But . . . there have been exceptions."

Eyes cast down, the young Ogre who kneeled before him allowed her voice to trail off. Her eyes, so strange and black, stole upward, then back down too quickly to give offense.

Teragrym pretended to examine the fruit, searching the fuzzy red skin for blemishes, then tossed it back into the bowl with a sneer. He did not deem it vital to mention that the punishment for disobedience of the law was death. He assumed she was willing to risk death.

Magic danced in the air about her, well concealed but barely controlled. Powerful enough so that he could sense it without casting a "seeing" spell. Just that feeling, coming from one not of a Ruling Family, was enough to condemn her.

Her fingers twitched, and he imagined he could see the spell she was longing to cast dancing between them. It would probably be something spectacular, designed to impress. No doubt she knew more than just spells of fire and water, of mischief and play.

For a race renowned for its beauty, she was striking and exotic, dark where most of the Ogres were silvery. Pale of flesh where the norm was emerald and indigo and raven black. Her black eyes were almost elven, and there was a warmth to the gem-green paleness of her skin that reminded him of the pale-pink flesh of humans. It was an almost repellent mixture and strangely compelling.

With her billowing robes spread about her in a perfect fan, she made a fetching picture. A perfect, ripe flower, offering herself. "You are very beautiful. Young. Healthy. Well placed at court. You could make a brilliant match. Be secure. Why do you risk telling me this?"

"I can make a match for myself, yes," she whispered. "Or my uncle will make one for me, and himself. Perhaps it would even be a brilliant one, with a well-suited family. But I do not wish to be some family's adornment."

Teragrym snorted, almost laughing in her face. This particular Ogre did not strike him as being malleable enough to be anyone's adornment.

"I would never be allowed to learn magic as I wish to." She glanced up, smiled with beguiling sweetness. "Please, Lord, families have been known to take in someone who showed promise, who could be of use . . . who would vow undying devotion in exchange for . . . considerations."

"Yes," he agreed. "That is true. At least, it was, before the clans were united by the council. Now . . . " A great many things had changed in the time since the Ruling Council had gained power and the king's supremacy had declined. "But now, I think such a person would have to convince me that I need a mage in my household who is not of my clan."

"My lord, you toy with me." There was sharpness in her tone, carefully controlled disapproval. Perhaps even a hint of anger.

He responded with mild rebuke, thin-lipped lechery. "Did you expect there would be no obstacles?"

"I will meet any test you see fitting!"

He laughed, delighted in spite of himself. With a nonchalant flick of his wrist, he cast a spell. Wordlessly, so effortlessly it was mocking.

A snarling, slavering thing appeared at her elbow. A creature of shadows and decay.

She flinched, edging away from the vision. With the slightest effort, she snuffed the enchantment, using a powerful "dispel."

Her triumph was short-lived.

"That is no proof of worthiness."

"Lord, set me a test. I will pass it!"

"But, my dear, that *is* the test. Prove yourself." Before she could protest or question, he motioned for his assistant, indicating that the interview was over.

"Send for Kaede," he ordered the aide who scurried to his side.

She almost protested. Her long, thin fingers twitched. Her chin came up. At the last moment, with obvious effort, she bowed. "Thank you, Lord Teragrym. I will provide suitable proof." As she rose, smoothing the folds of her robe, she said softly, "Proof of worthiness."

He waited until the heavy stone door had slid silently closed behind her, leaving him alone in his audience hall.

The room was small but high ceilinged, ornate, plush. Teragrym breathed deeply, allowing the pleasing surroundings to relax him as he motioned his aide closer.

"Watch her," he told the young Ogre. "I think she could be dangerous."

* * * * *

"The Prince of Lies will speak to you," the High Cleric said. "Or not. Accept you. Or not."

Lyrralt nodded, not trusting himself to speak, for surely it would be unseemly to reveal his excitement, his agitation, before the altar of Hiddukel, the dark god of gain and wealth.

He had been preparing for this moment of being judged worthy or not worthy for all of his young life, for perhaps two hundred of his three hundred years.

To a human savage from the plains, it would have

been many lifetimes; to the long lived elves, a fraction of a lifetime. For an Ogre, it was a pittance of time.

The High Cleric was placing the bowl of scented water before him, folding away the light robe she'd brought.

The room was devoid of furniture save for the altar, a huge block of marble bearing the broken scales, symbol of his god, and the small chest on which lay the garment, symbol of his hope. There was no carpet on the floor, no hangings on the walls to insulate the chill of stone.

Lyrralt rubbed his bare arms and stared with open envy and longing at the High Cleric, at the delicate runes marking her emerald skin. They marched from shoulder to wrist on both arms, symbols of her devotion, symbols of Hiddukel's blessing.

The High Cleric faced him one last time before leaving him to his test. "Let Hiddukel set the runes rightly," she said softly, bowing her head, both to him and to the altar. Then she left him alone in the cold, dim room.

He took a deep, deep breath, told himself he was not cold, then knelt on the cold marble floor and bowed low, palms open and exposed.

Lyrralt took up the silver bowl which sat at the foot of the altar, sipped of the scented water. He rinsed his mouth and spat delicately into a smaller bowl carved from bone. He dipped his fingers in the water and touched the liquid to ears and eyelids. Then he scooped a handful of the cold liquid and splashed it on his shoulder and upper arm.

Ritual complete, he was ready to ask Hiddukel's blessing.

He closed his eyes, concentrated with all his strength, and prayed. "Please, Mighty One, Lord of Fiends and Souls, Prince of Lies, accept me as your servant."

He paused, feeling nothing but his clammy, wet skin, then squeezed his eyes even more firmly and prayed even more fervently. He promised undying devotion, unquestioning obedience. He glanced at his shoulder. The indigo skin was unblemished, perfect.

He prayed and he pleaded. He made promises. He bowed until his forehead was touching the floor. The water evaporated from his skin, but he felt no response from his god.

It was not fair! Lyrralt rocked back on his heels and sat, palms on thighs, breathing heavily with the exertion of his entreaties. He had wanted only this for so long, neglecting his duties on his father's estate, shirking his responsibilities as eldest son and older brother.

He had thought of little but the things he would gain as a cleric of Hiddukel. The esteem, the advantage, the wealth. Oh, the benefit the robes of the order would give him once his father was dead and he was master!

A strange, sharp sensation smote his left shoulder, so hard it knocked him to the floor, slicing into his bones.

He gasped as though his lungs had emptied of all air.

Sensations too varied, too contradictory to assimilate, flashed through his muscles, across his skin.

Heat and cold, pressure from within and without, pain and pleasure. Blissful pain, as if his flesh were being peeled from his body.

Lyrralt opened his mouth wide and screamed in agony . . . and joy.

As quickly as it had come, it ended.

He sat up, shivering but no longer cold. He touched his shoulder. There was no pain, but his perfect skin was flawless no longer. The bone-white runes, stark against his dark complexion, marched in three rows across his shoulder.

The door opened, and the High Cleric entered, followed by others of her order, and they gathered around him, exclaiming happiness and welcome. The High Cleric sank to her knees beside him and gazed at the markings on his shoulder.

"What do you see?" Lyrralt demanded.

She smiled at his impatience and ran a fingertip across the sigils. "Many things. You have many paths you may follow, young Lyrralt. Many possibilities."

"Tell me."

"I see a beginning. Hiddukel shows . . . " She lifted an eyebrow, impressed. "The Dark Queen. Perhaps you will be called upon by the Dark One herself."

Lyrralt shuddered to think of being honored by Takhisis herself, Queen of Darkness.

"No, perhaps it means only darkness or death to a queen. A dead queen. It is not clear."

"But we have no queen!"

"Hiddukel will guide you," she admonished gently and continued to examine the runes. "There is family here. Someone close. There is mischief. Revenge. Success."

The High Cleric motioned to one of the others, and

he brought Lyrralt's robe.

As Lyrralt stood, he asked, "It's not very clear, is it?"

"Never in the beginning, but the Prince will guide you."

* * * * *

The lamps danced in the mine, bright pinpricks of light stabbing through darkness as thick and black as ink. The timbers that shored up the walls and ceiling creaked, and the rocks they held back groaned, singing a song eerie and sad.

"The slaves say the earth is crying for the gems and stones we take out of it."

Igraine, governor of Khal-Theraxian, largest province in the Ogre civilization, smiled indulgently at his daughter, Everlyn. In the dim light, he could barely see her, but he knew her eyes were dilated with excitement, her deep-sea complexion darkened to emerald.

Only child, pampered, spoiled, raised in the brightness and cheer of one of the finest estates in the mountains . . . He couldn't explain why she preferred the darkness, why she preferred the rocks and minerals his slaves dug out of the earth over copper and gold and polished gems.

He glanced up at the ragged rocks just inches above his nose. His race had lived in the Khalkists from the beginning of time, choosing as their rightful place the lofty mountain range that divided the northern half of the continent of Ansalon. The mountains spread downward from the Thorad Plain, home of the wild humans, to the tip of the forest of the elves.

Khal-Theraxian, built on the southernmost arm of the Khalkists, was only a few days' ride from the heavily wooded edge of the elven forests. At one time, it had been a bustling center of trade for those dealing in stolen elven goods and elven slaves. But that was many generations ago, before the riches under the ground had been discovered, before the firstborn had realized that the good and gentle elves made poor slaves and the malleable humans made excellent ones.

Igraine's ancestors had worked the mines of Khal-Theraxian, had perhaps even stared up at this very ceiling, for this particular passage was a very old one, just recently reopened and reused. Perhaps they, too, had stared overhead and wondered if the ceiling of rock would come crashing down upon their heads.

The tunnels were dug by humans, sized for humans, not the lofty Ogre masters who towered over them by at least three hands.

Although his nerves danced, Igraine didn't show any worry or concern. A governor had to set an example. He didn't quake in the face of a slave uprising, nor when caught in the midst of a mountaintop blizzard. And he did not show how the creaking and singing of the rock in the depths of his most productive mine made his skin tighten and crawl.

Everlyn glanced up at him, her even white teeth a slash in the shadows, her silvery eyes aglitter.

Despite his unease, he returned her excited smile with one of pride. Beautiful and spoiled and fearless. Her emerald skin and her willowy stature might be from her mother, but her spirit was from him. If not for her, he would never have ventured so deep into the mines.

The dark, dank place with its low ceiling was fit only for slaves, for the humans who chipped away the rock and brought out the gemstones, the best in twenty provinces. Some gems were as large as their small-boned hands, better even than those from the elven lands to the south.

"The earth sings louder and louder as we go deeper," said the harsh, grating voice of one of the human slaves, the one who called himself Eadamm. He was a strong man, just approaching middle age for a human, perhaps almost thirty, which seemed a child to Igraine's seven hundred years.

Igraine knew the slave because he had pale hair and eyes as blue as the summer sky and because the slave brought Everlyn samples of the rare rocks and stones of which she was so fond.

"I don't think it's safe."

Igraine glanced at the slave sharply. Had there been a note of anger in his voice? Of surliness?

The human had already turned away, raising his lantern to lead the way deeper into the low tunnel. Whereas Igraine had to stoop to fit, Eadamm was able to walk with head held high and shoulders straight and tall. Even Everlyn, who was tiny for an Ogre, was bent.

"We found the bloodstone back there, Lady," Eadamm told Everlyn, pointing toward an irregular oval of midnight blackness, a hole in the dark.

Everlyn started down the sloping tunnel toward the opening.

"Lady, it's not safe." Eadamm glanced back at Igraine for support. "The rock shifts and groans constantly. We've been bringing out the rubble and looking through it for stones." He pointed to the littered floor.

Without hesitating or even glancing back, Everlyn disappeared into the blackness. Her voice floated back to them. "I want to see."

With a grimace, Igraine followed. Light flared in the room ahead, blinding him for a moment.

Magic in the tunnels wasn't wise. Besides ruining the vision of the slaves, who had spent so many years below ground they could barely see in the brightness elsewhere, there was something not quite safe about using magic so deep underground, as if the very earth were trying to spoil the magic.

He went forward quickly into the light, bumping his head on the low ceiling. "Everlyn . . . " His warning trailed away as he stepped through the opening. His daughter had set a small fireball to sparkling in midair, illuminating the small cavern.

"Isn't it wonderful?" She paused to look back at him. She leaned against the far wall, pushing and prying at a large chunk of rock. "Look at the bloodstone I've found!"

Eadamm paused beside Igraine, blinking in the sudden brightness. "I'll get a pick, Lady." He set his lantern on the ground and retreated. His voice echoed back into the small chamber as he called to one of the other workmen.

His words sounded like gibberish to Igraine. Before his eyes, the fiery orb bobbled. The jumble of rocks that served as walls seemed to move with it in the flickering light. His daughter's magic made his skin squirm.

"Ever—" The breath was sucked out of his mouth by the grinding of stone against stone. The ceiling was moving!

Everlyn screamed as the wall before her shifted, leaned inward as if pushed by an unseen hand.

Igraine leapt toward her. Pain lanced through his arm and side as something struck his shoulder, knocking him backward. Dust flooded into his nostrils, his mouth. Jagged rocks, torn from the ceiling, rained down on him. Through the crashing of stones and the creaking of timbers, he could hear his daughter crying out.

Eadamm grabbed him and pushed him out of the path of a huge crush of ceiling. His head struck hard against something as he fell out of the small room.

Sparkling dust and pebbles rained everywhere. The floor tilted. Igraine clung to the wall, feeling the stones shift beneath his fingers. He could hear Eadamm calling for Everlyn, could hear her answering, her voice threadbare with fear.

He pushed to his feet, heart pounding. As he stumbled toward the sound of Eadamm's voice, Everlyn's magical light went out. Her cries fell off abruptly, leaving him alone with fear.

The cries of the slaves, screams of pain from farther in the direction of the main tunnel, joined with the groaning of the earth.

A moment later, Eadamm was there, a hand under his arm, trying to help him move, his lantern casting wavering shadows through the haze of dust. Eadamm shouted for help. Slaves crowded into the passageway, pushing and shoving and crying out with fear.

The sickening scent of humans, unwashed and afraid, of blood and grit, Igraine sucked into his nostrils. His head ached, a huge throbbing alarm like bells between his ears.

"We must get out," Igraine rasped, tasting blood and dirt. He passed his hand over his forehead and eyelids, hoping to clear his vision. His fingers came away wet and sticky.

"Lord, no!" Eadamm thrust his lantern into Igraine's hand and snatched up a timber almost twice his own height. "She might still be alive!"

Igraine could barely hear the words the slave had spoken, but from Eadamm's actions, he understood.

Eadamm wrestled the thick log under one of the sagging beams overhead. When he bent to pick up another timber, another slave hurried to join him.

The huge, rough-hewn log Eadamm had braced against the ceiling trembled. Pebbles and sand sifted down. The ceiling bowed with the weight of the earth above.

Another rumbling from deep in the bowels of the mine was followed by the crashing of rock. Farther down the passageway, a slave screamed.

The slaves crowded in beside Igraine were the best miners in the Khalkists. Irreplaceable. Worth too much to risk.

"There's no time!" Igraine grabbed Eadamm and pointed up. On cue, more rock vibrated and fell. The rumbling from deep in the mine sounded again.

"Everyone out!" Igraine raised his voice to be heard above the sounds of the mine and shouted the order again. He wished for Ogre guards to help, to get the stupid humans moving in an orderly manner, but there were no guards in the mine, only a couple stationed at the exit for show. It was a matter of pride for the whole province that Khal-Theraxian's slaves were so well-conditioned, so well-behaved.

Bobbing specks of light began to recede from the

cramped passageway, back the way they had come, as the slaves began to obey. But some of the slaves stayed where they were. Under Eadamm's guidance, they were already methodically digging away the stones that entombed Everlyn.

Igraine grabbed the nearest human and shoved him roughly toward the safe end of the tunnel. "There's no time. Get out now! All of you."

He led the way out of the passage, back the way they had come, climbing over boulders and rocks that had not been there before.

The long walk toward safety was a journey of darkness and fear punctuated by falling rock and death cries from behind, deeper in the mines. Igraine's head throbbed, and his ankles protested. The tunnels through which they passed had been distorted by the movement of the earth, were twisted, jumbled, blocked. With every step he expected that the ceiling would crash down on him, blotting out the pinpricks of light from the lanterns ahead.

He stumbled and would have fallen but for one of the slaves. The man, bent and gnarled from years of toil in the mines, smelled horribly of human sweat and sweetly of human blood.

Igraine shoved away the helping hands, stood on his own. "How much farther?" he asked. Dust sifted down from above, sparkling in the lantern light.

"Just ahead, Sire." The slave pointed.

Igraine saw that the light that was illuminating the motes of dust wasn't from his lantern, but came from the warm yellow glow of Krynn's sun. "Make sure everyone gets out," he mumbled, hurrying toward the exit.

Sunlight bright as molten gold stung his eyes as he stepped into the fresh afternoon air. It seemed hours ago that he had entered the dark, gaping hole in the mountainside.

The slaves were coming out behind him, looking as stunned as he felt. A handful of the group that had accompanied him, cousins and staff and guards, saw them coming out of the mine and hastened to meet them.

It was a lovely fall day, air clear and crisp, sky blue and unmarred by clouds. His entourage wore bright splashes of color, red and blue and green silk. He could sense their agitation, hear their voices lift in excitement as they saw him.

He must be a sight: clothes torn, face bloodied, eyes hollow and distant. In a moment, they would descend upon him. He couldn't bear the thought of facing their distress, their questions, the crying of the old aunts who had raised Everlyn after her mother had died.

He turned back to his slaves, to count how many had not escaped the mountain, to see that the injured were looked after. He realized immediately that some were missing.

"Where's Eadamm?"

The humans nearest him shook their heads. Of those who were just emerging from the mine, who had been in the rear, three refused to meet his gaze. They stood with eyes cast down, shoulders hunched as if waiting for a blow. Finally one mumbled, "He stayed behind, Lord, to save the Ogre."

The one in the middle elbowed the speaker hard. "He means 'the lady,' sir. 'The lady.' "

"Yes, Sire, the lady. I meant no disrespect."

Igraine backhanded the man, knocking him against the walls of the mine. So Eadamm had gone back, disobeying his orders.

Igraine, governor of the district of Khal-Theraxian, had built his reputation on his handling of slaves. On his *ruthless* handling of slaves. The king had given him position, land, a title because of it. Igraine never allowed a slave to break a rule, to show disrespect, to shirk his duties, to disobey an order. Examples had to be set.

His personal honor guards came rushing up the path from the meadow, exclaiming, bowing. One grabbed up the slave Igraine had struck and dangled him by his arm.

"Lord, what has happened?"

"Where is Lady Everlyn?"

"Are you harmed?"

The questions came at Igraine too fast and thick to answer, and he turned and waited until the rest of the group was within hearing distance. He didn't want to tell what happened more than once. "There's been a cave-in. Everlyn is . . . lost." He steeled himself for the cries of anguish.

Naej, who had been mistress of his estate until Everlyn was old enough, who had been mother and mentor and friend, covered her face with her hands.

"Sort out the slaves," he told the captain of the guard. "Make sure they see to their injured. Find the foreman and see how many are lost." Igraine's face hardened. "And find out how many stayed in the mine against my orders. These three knew of it. Keep them separated from the others." If the ones inside the mine died, these three would be used to set an example.

Behind him, a feminine voice started a song of sorrow for Everlyn, a melodic sound without words that was eerily like the grating of stone against stone in the tunnel. Naej whimpered, and another voice, this one masculine, joined the song.

Igraine whipped around, intending to tell them to shut up, to leave. He knew he would have to sing, to mourn, but not yet. Not just yet.

Naej had uncovered her face, was opening her mouth to sing. Instead she cried out, the O shape of her mouth going from anguished to astonished and delighted. "Everlyn!"

He wheeled to see six figures emerging from the entrance to the mine, one tall, five short: Everlyn and the five slaves who had remained behind to save her.

She was alive! Walking, albeit unsteadily. One sleeve was missing from her tunic. The hem hung in shreds around her slender hips. Both knees, scraped and bleeding, showed through rents in her pants. Her long hair was sticking out in tangled lumps. Her dark skin, bloodied at temple and shoulder, was coated with gray dust.

Igraine had never seen a more beautiful sight.

For the second time that day, pandemonium erupted around him as his guards, his entourage, his slaves, rushed to aid those who had just emerged from the mine.

Igraine plowed through them, stepping on Ogre and human alike to get to his daughter.

She threw herself into his arms, tears streaking the dirt on her face. "I thought I would never see you again!"

He squeezed her tightly. "I thought I would never see you," he said gruffly.

Naej, brushing at the dirt and small rocks tangled in Everlyn's long hair, said as she had when her charge was a child, "Let's get her home, Igraine."

Before Naej could lead her away, Eadamm stepped forward and bowed. "Lady . . . This is for you." From the front of his shirt he produced the rock Everlyn had been trying to free from the wall of the tiny room.

It was a bloodstone, smoky and black—so dark it seemed to suck in the light and hold it—and shot through with globs of carmine. It looked like huge drops of blood had been trapped inside. Too ugly for jewelry, too soft to be useful in making tools, bloodstone was mostly used by minor magicians for show. With the casting of a spell, they made the red glow and throb like fire. This piece was the size of a potato with three thumb-sized pieces like growths protruding from one end.

Everlyn laughed, taking it as gently as if it were an egg, with much delight. "It will always remind me of how I felt when I saw the light of your lantern burst through the wall of rocks."

Eadamm bowed to her again and started away, but Igraine stopped him. He motioned for his guards to come forward.

"Put these slaves under arrest along with the other three."

Everlyn looked up from the gray-black rock. "Why, Father?"

"They disobeyed my order to evacuate the mine."

Eadamm met her solemn gaze without lowering his.

"I understand," she said, softly, regretfully.

* * * * *

Igraine, governor of Khal-Theraxian, sat alone in his office, the only light coming from the glowing coals in the fireplace. He had moved his favorite chair, the one covered in elf-made cloth, next to the huge, floor-to-ceiling windows that overlooked his estate.

Solinari, the silver moon, overwhelmed her sister moon, Lunitari, bathing the garden and fields and distant mountains in pale light. Igraine's eyes saw none of the cold beauty spread before him, not the nodding heads of fall flowers, not the mountain peaks already beginning to display their snowcaps.

A tap on the door interrupted the silence. A shaft of light cut through the room as a guard opened the hall door and peeked through. "I've brought the slave, Lord."

Igraine murmured an incantation, and several candles leapt into flame. A small fire hissed and crackled into life in the fireplace. "Bring him in."

The guard gestured to the human who was waiting in the hall, then withdrew when Igraine motioned him away.

Eadamm came into the room. He was clean, wearing clean though threadbare shirt and pants. Only his hands, bruised, scraped raw, and bound with chains, showed the signs of the afternoon's events.

Igraine regarded him in silence for several minutes, during which the human stood without moving, his gaze fastened on the windows and the view outside.

"There is something I would like to understand," Igraine said finally, noting that the human didn't flinch when he spoke, didn't fidget in the silence that followed.

"I have always prided myself on being a fair master." He saw, finally, some emotion on the face of the slave, a flitting feeling that he didn't know human faces well enough to recognize, but perhaps he could guess.

"A fair master," he repeated more firmly. "Harsh, but fair. My laws are harsh, but none of my slaves can say they don't know them. Therefore, if they break them and are punished, it is their own fault."

Again the twinge of expression, quickly suppressed.

Igraine continued. "But I understand their infractions. I understand the taking of things, for I, too, wish to have more. I understand the shirking of hard work. I understand running away. All of these are things which a slave thinks and hopes will not be discovered. I understand breaking rules when one does not expect to be caught. But what you did . . . "

If Eadamm understood that he was being offered a chance to respond, perhaps to beg apology, he didn't show it.

"You knew that by disobeying my orders, you were condemning yourself." Igraine said. There was just enough question in his tone to allow Eadamm to dispute him if he wished.

He didn't. "Yes, Lord, I knew."

"Then this I do not understand. A runner thinks only of the freedom of the plains, not of the capture. You knew you would be caught."

"Yes, Lord."

So vexed he could no longer sit, Igraine stood and paced the length of the windowed wall, then turned swiftly to face Eadamm. "Then explain this to me!"

In the face of Igraine's agitation, Eadamm lost his

calm. "If I had not disobeyed your orders, Lord, the lady would have died!" he almost shouted. Then he controlled himself. "The lady has been kind to the slaves. She has . . . "

"Continue."

"She has a good heart. It would have been wrong to let her die."

"Wrong?" Igraine tasted the word as if it was unknown to him. He had used it many times, in many ways, with his slaves. "Wrong to obey me?"

For the first time since he'd entered the room, Eadamm looked down, casting his gaze to the floor as a slave should.

Rather than being pleased that his slave was finally cowed, Igraine wished Eadamm would once again look up, that he might see the expression on the ugly human face. "You knew you could not escape. You knew the punishment would be death."

"Yes. I chose life for her."

Igraine sighed. He sat back down in his chair. He waved his hand in dismissal and turned back to the view of his estate. He heard the door open, then close.

As soon as it closed, Everlyn stepped into the room from the porch. She stood, flowing nightdress silhouetted in reverse against the night.

"You should be in bed," he said gruffly.

"I couldn't sleep. Father," she whispered, her soft voice tearful, "could you not *choose* to let *him* live?"

Chapter 2

Destiny's Song

The audience hall glittered as if it were filled with burning stars, ashimmer from gilt embroidery on fine robes, gems dripping from throats and fingers and wrists. The flames of hundreds of candles danced in glass lamps etched with the symbols of the evil gods, reflected off the gold and silver of ceremonial daggers, and still the huge room was not illuminated. Shadows clung to the corners, filled the three-story-high ceiling.

The scent of heavy perfumes from a dozen provinces plaited and twined, choking the air, battling the aromas of melted candles, spiced wine, warm sugar cakes and succulent human flesh wrapped in seaweed and baked to savory tenderness.

The clamor of a thousand voices, the ring of goblet against goblet, had quieted as the Keeper of History stepped forward to the front of the throne platform and sent the Song spiraling forth to mingle with the glitter and the scents.

Khallayne Talanador paused on the first landing of the huge southern staircase and allowed her eyes to half close so that only pinpricks of light sparkled through, a thousand-thousand, four-pointed, multi-colored pricks of light dancing against her lashes.

The sweet, siren voice of the Keeper, singing the History of the Ogre race, lulled Khallayne into almost believing she stood alone instead of in the midst of the best-attended, most brilliant party of the season.

As the Keeper sang, her elaborate, flowing gown shifted and shimmered around her feet. The many scenes embroidered on it, exploits of past kings and queens, glorious battles, triumphal feasts, exquisite treachery, seemed to come to life.

Khallayne's gown was a copy of the Keeper's, with shorter sleeves to allow her hands freedom and fewer jewels worked into the embroidered vestrobe. But where the Keeper's gown had a multitude of scenes, hers bore only one. The depiction of Khal-layne's favorite story danced about the hem, the tale of a dark and terrible Queen. First she was alive and vigorous, then dying, then rising up from the shards of her burial bones, her subjects quaking before her.

She had come to be known as the Dead Queen, sometimes as the Dark Queen. She had ruled in the early times, when the mountains were still new. It was told that she was more beautiful, more cunning and clever, than any Ogre ever born. Suspecting that the nobles about her were scheming, she had her own death announced, then waited in the shadows to see who would grieve. And who would celebrate. The purge was quick and glorious; the Dead Queen left few alive to mourn their executed brethren. Three of the present Ruling Council families, all unswervingly loyal to the Dead Queen, had come to power during that time, replacing those who had not sung the funeral songs quite loudly enough. Khallayne had loved the story since childhood, admiring and aspiring to such perfect cunning.

The last sweet notes of the Song ended, but Khallayne remained where she was, held in place as if mesmerized by the shimmer of the Keeper's gown, by the old story she knew by heart.

She could remember a time when she was a child, before her parents' death, when the Keeper had walked, albeit a little unsteadily, to her performances. The Keeper had been ancient even then. The Ogres were a long-lived race, so near immortality they were practically gods, but even they had marked limits. For the good of the whole, no Ogre was allowed to live to the point of being a burden, not even the king. None except the Keeper.

For her extraordinary talent, she was allowed a rare privilege. Now, elite honor guards carried her everywhere in a litter, waiting in the background while she sang the History of the Ogre.

The guards, puffed with pride and importance, flanked the Old One now, and escorted her through the elaborately carved private exit behind the platform.

From where Khallayne was standing, she watched the honor guard give way to guardsmen who had been standing in the shadows, just out of sight. As the last one turned smartly and disappeared, she saw that his brown tunic was emblazoned with a blue diagonal slash down the arm, the uniform of the Tenal clan.

There, whispered the dark voice of her intuition. *There is the thing you seek.* Khallayne touched the beaten copper crescent pinned to the lapel of her tunic.

"Thank you, Takhisis," she whispered. "Thank you." Her smile rivaled the glitter of the party for its brightness.

She stepped back into the pale shadow between the wall and a huge stone column and murmured softly the words of a "seeing" spell. It was a risky thing to do, casting in this room, where someone might be sensitive to a flutter of power, but she felt rash and exhilarated now—now that she knew how invincibility would soon be hers.

The roar of hundreds of voices muted to a whisper. Her vision faded until her surroundings became only a soft focus of brown and gray.

Below her, on the floor of the great hall, the pinpricks of light that were enchanted gems sparkled like embers. A hazy aura surrounded those who wore spell-enhanced finery. Such simple spells, like lighting candles and starting fires, were the kind of magic allowed anyone, regardless of position.

The auras that fascinated her were much different. She sought the magic of the most powerful nobility, the ones who were allowed to progress as far as their natural abilities permitted. Across the room, Lord Teragrym, for example—his was a seething aura of darkness, a great power.

She smiled, tasting the triumph to come.

"Looking for something, Khallayne?"

She tensed, then relaxed as the playful tone of the words was made clear through the distortion of the spell. The voice was filled with biting cynicism, yet still warm and sensual. It could only be Jyrbian.

She turned carefully, slowly allowing the "seeing" to seep away, colors and sights and sounds returning to normal. He was exactly what she required, perfect for her plans.

"Good evening," she said.

Jyrbian bowed, smirking, managing as only he could to be both admiring and sarcastic at the same time.

"Good evening, Khallayne." Lyrralt, older than Jyrbian, bowed more sincerely than his brother. He didn't come forward to take her hand, but stayed back a step, his eyes tracing the fine slave-embroidered brocade of her gown.

As he stared in astonishment at her, she stared back, then broke into a wide grin.

Never were two brothers more alike in some ways, yet more different in others. Jyrbian and Lyrralt bore the same dramatic coloring, skin the dark blue of sapphires, eyes and hair like polished silver. The similarity ended there. Lyrralt was tall and lean, where Jyrbian was shorter and more muscular. He was also quiet while Jyrbian was brash, furtive where Jyrbian could be demanding, fierce and directed while Jyrbian played and joked and smirked.

Instead of his usual tunic, Jyrbian wore the sleeveless dress uniform of a soldier, form-fitting silk with bright silver trim.

As subdued as his brother was flashy, Lyrralt was

wearing his simple white cleric's robe. It was decorated with dark red embroidery that looked like drops of blood. His only adornment was a bone pin with the rune sign for his god, Hiddukel, burned into it, also in red. The formal robe, with its one long sleeve hiding the markings of his order, gave him an appearance of mystery and dignity.

"I didn't realize this was a costume ball," Khallayne teased.

They had been playmates in childhood, before her parents had died, before the Ruling Council had reclaimed their estate for distribution to a worthy courtier, and she had been forced to live with cousins. Since her uncle had bought a place at court for her, she had learned that the two grown-up men were very like the little boys she fondly remembered. She and Jyrbian had become friends again. Lyrralt was more difficult to gauge.

They reacted to her teasing just as she'd expected. Jyrbian grinned, spread his arms for her to better see his uniform and the strong muscles it emphasized, while Lyrralt frowned. "This is not a costume," he reprimanded gently.

"Oh, no," Jyrbian said with a biting tone. "My brother has been blessed by his god."

Lyrralt tugged at his long left sleeve proudly, symbol of his acceptance as a cleric of Hiddukel. "Yes, I have, more than you know. You could have chosen this path, too. But you are irreverent to a fault. Playing at being a soldier instead of applying yourself to something useful."

Jyrbian scowled. "I do not play, *brother*. Just as you do, I look to the future, and I see what is coming. I see what will be needed."

Khallayne stepped between the two, forestalling further disagreement. It was an old argument, one she'd heard many times in many guises. Lyrralt thought his brother useless and frivolous. Jyrbian was ever scheming, jealous of all that Lyrralt, as eldest, would inherit.

She spoke first to Lyrralt. "I didn't mean to tease. You know I'm proud of you." Then Khallayne turned and laid her hand on Jyrbian's bare forearm. "What do you mean? Are you implying that the clans are going to be allowed more warriors sometime soon? There's been no increase since—since—"

"Since the Battle of Denharben," Lyrralt supplied. "Before our parents were born."

No Ogre house had made war on another for centuries, at least not openly, not with soldiers. Once, it had been every clan for itself. Smaller clans had been forced to ally themselves with larger ones to survive, until they grew strong enough to attack their allies. It was a perpetual cycle. But since the Ruling Council members had solidified their position with the strategic use of economic reprisals and land redistribution to their supporters, they had managed to limit the number of warriors a clan could have.

Feuding between the clans had become more subtle, and positions as warrior and honor guard had become prestigious and rare, passed down from parent to child the same as land and title. A warrior was born to status, not hired.

"There have been rumors," Jyrbian said mysteriously.

"I should have you thrown from the parapets!" she laughed. "You know something you don't want to tell. Besides, you've never really trained as a warrior."

"No one's trained as a true warrior anymore," Lyrralt scoffed. "They're all just honor guards who play with swords and pikes and practice marching in perfect rows. Even the king's guard is mostly show."

"You're wrong, as usual. I've watched them train." Jyrbian twined his fingers with Khallayne's and tugged her toward the stairs, talking as he moved. "True, I haven't practiced at marching. But I promise you, my other skills are not lacking."

Khallayne allowed herself to be drawn away, leaving Lyrralt behind. She couldn't imagine what gossip Jyrbian must know if he thought warriors would yet again be in demand.

Animal herders were all that were necessary for the raids on human settlements. And the raids on the elven lands, deep in the forests to the south, were easily handled by thieves. The things that could be stolen, beautiful carvings and thick, lustrous cloth, could not be matched anywhere on the continent of Ansalon, but the elves themselves, with their stoic demeanor and their unwavering devotion to goodness, made terrible slaves.

"Jyrbian . . . " She touched his forearm. Hard muscle rippled under his indigo skin. "Come and eat dinner with me. We'll go up on the parapets afterward and look at the stars. I have something to tell you. And something I'd like you to help me *do*."

Laughing at her with his pale eyes, Jyrbian slipped his fingers under her sleeve and stroked the soft flesh of her wrist. "You're the most beautiful woman here tonight," he whispered, "the most beautiful woman in Takar."

She laughed. Khallayne knew he'd probably uttered the same words to every woman with whom he'd spoken since the party had begun at sundown; certainly he had said them to her every time they'd crossed paths for the past twenty years. And as she had answered for all those years, now she answered smugly, "I know."

"We do make a perfect pair," he murmured, holding up her hand, admiring the darkness of his wrist against skin the pale green of sea foam. "Like day and night. Unfortunately . . . I hope you will forgive my bluntness, but there are more important dinner partners in the room. As my brother is so fond of reminding me, I must be mindful of my duties—and my fortune." He brought her hand up to his lips, kissed her knuckles, then wheeled away smartly.

"Jyrbian . . . !" Left standing on the stairs, Khallayne watched in disbelief as he bounded down the steps, his long silver hair, braided warrior-style, swaying back and forth across his shoulders.

Khallayne's fingers twitched, itching to be at work in the air, inscribing some terrible spell.

"He's trying to get a special assignment from the Ruling Council."

Khallayne had forgotten Lyrralt was nearby. Absentmindedly, she tucked her hand into the crook of his elbow. "I don't understand how you can tolerate him sometimes," she said coolly, watching Jyrbian's progress through the crowd. "You know sooner or later, the thought will occur to him that the easiest way to 'make his fortune' is to inherit it."

Across the room, Jyrbian joined a group of Ogres standing near the steps to the throne platform. A young woman dressed in a fancy tunic immediately took his arm.

The words of a spell, one they had used when they were children, which made the skin sting as if nettled, leapt to Khallayne's lips. She had not thought of it in fifty years, hadn't used it in a hundred, but it would be very interesting to see whether Jyrbian could be as charming if she sent it spiraling through the air. She could almost taste the words, then forgot them as Lyrralt spoke.

He faced her with a mock look of remonstrance wrinkling his forehead. "My father's minor nobility and wealth isn't enough to suit Jyrbian. He's aiming much higher these days. And so far, all it has gotten him is an errand that will make him miss the slave races next week."

"What errand?"

The closeness of her body, the warmth of her breast against his arm had the effect she desired.

Lyrralt covered her hand with his and leaned closer, answering as if he were not aware of the words. "Some fool errand to Khal-Theraxian for Lord Teragrym."

As he said "Teragrym," she turned her face away, afraid that he would see the change in her expression, in her smile. Surely she must look like a wolf, ready to pounce. "Yes, I've heard talk," she said, "about the governor of Khal-Theraxian. Something about a new method of working his slaves that has increased production."

She composed her expression, molding it to a flirtatious one. Tucking her hand securely into the crook of Lyrralt's arm and lifting the heavy hem of her robe, she started down the stairs. "Is that Teragrym's youngest daughter with Jyrbian?"

"No, that's Kyreli. She's not the youngest. She's

the one who sings so well. I think Teragrym is hoping she'll be the next Singer."

Khallayne's brows pulled together in a frown that had no playfulness about it at all.

The Ogres made a song for everything. They sang for happiness, for sadness, for rain, for sun, for cold, for heat. They raised their lovely voices in song for the most important thing and for nothing at all, and even the gods paused to listen. Hunters charmed the beasts with the beauty and grace of their voices; slavers lured their prey into shackling their own hands.

Khallayne was irritated by it all. For she of winsome ways, of quick mind and daring beauty, could not sing. She had hair that was like silk pouring through a man's fingers, eyes that could beguile the most hardened heart, a magical power so natural and strong she dared not expose it. But she could not sing. Her singing voice had all the beauty, the charm, of a stone door scraping over a sill filled with grit.

Lyrralt stopped as they reached the bottom of the stairs. He leaned close and lowered his voice as if imparting a secret. "Have dinner with me. I've got something to tell you that's much more exciting than rumors of warriors."

She considered him from beneath her eyelashes. Maybe he knew something of Teragrym's interests in Khal-Theraxian.

She smiled and took his arm once more, settling in against his warmth, and leading him toward the far end of the huge chamber that contained the dining area.

They circled the king's table, off which nothing

could be eaten. It was there purely to be savored, relished, for admiration of the "flavor of the appearance."

"Have you ever wondered from where this curious custom comes?" Lyrralt asked as he slowly walked the length of the table, admiring the rare ghen blossoms cooked in honey and floating in wine, sea darts and other fish, brought all the way from the Turbidus Ocean, swimming in spices and gingerlike leaves.

"No, I haven't." Khallayne followed him, barely noticing the complementary arrangement of scent and texture and color.

As she filled a plate with juicy, broiled scrawls and bread dripping with honey jelly, she asked, "Did you notice earlier, when the Keeper left the stage, that Tenal guards were waiting in the hallway?"

Shaking his head, Lyrralt placed something on her plate that resembled a delicate blue flower.

"I was thinking that perhaps it means one of Tenal's sons or daughters has been named as successor to the Keeper. She's well past the age when the Song should have been passed on."

Though he tried to cover it, she saw that Lyrralt had made the connection she'd hoped he would. He furrowed his heavy, silky brows in surprise. They found an empty table against a wall, somewhat isolated from the other tables, and dispatched a slave for wine.

"I thought it especially odd," Khallayne picked up the thread of their conversation with false nonchalance. "Because I felt sure one of Teragrym's daughters would be chosen. . . . "

"So was Jyrbian." Lyrralt grinned suddenly. "And

he's pursuing the wrong daughter! He had big plans for tonight . . . I think I'll wait until tomorrow to tell him. The look on his face will be—"

"Oh, I think we can do better than that." Khallayne sipped her wine, savored the tartness on her tongue. "Much better."

Lyrralt paused, goblet halfway to his mouth, staring at the gleam in her black eyes. He'd never seen an expression so wicked, so alluring. Excitement and foreboding surged within him. The runes on his shoulder burned as when they were new. "Is this why you wanted Jyrbian's help?"

"Yes. But I think you'll do a much better job."

She paused. "I've got an idea," she purred. "A perfect idea. It will get us both what we want."

Lyrralt drew his chair close, leaned toward her. "And what is it *you* want?" He could feel the heat of her body. "It's never seemed to me that you strived for the usual things—position, nor even gift of land or a home outside the castle walls. When Jyrbian and I heard you were coming to court, we thought you'd seek to regain your family estate from the Tenal clan. But, unless you're even more devious than I imagined, I haven't seen any evidence of it."

She smiled and touched the rim of her goblet to his. "Thank you, sir. I *am* even more devious than you imagine. But land is not what I desire. What I have learned in my three hundred years is that land is a transitory thing, easily given, easily taken away on a whim. I seek a more permanent reward."

"And you will tell me. Perhaps tonight as we walk the parapets?"

She stared at him, speculatively, and slipped a hand underneath the edge of his sleeve.

His eyes widened as her fingers crept upward on his skin. When she touched the edges of the runes, he trembled.

"Wouldn't your order be extremely pleased if you obtained the sponsorship of Lord Teragrym?"

"How?" He drained his goblet without taking his eyes from the movement of her hand under his sleeve.

"Very simple. I think we can get our hands on something Teragrym wants very much. And we can do it so that Jyrbian would be blamed, in the unlikely event this . . . redistribution was discovered."

For a moment, Lyrralt was too stunned to speak. All the blood had drained from his face, rendering his skin a dull grayish hue.

But Khallayne knew she had him—a fish swimming lazily along, complacently, agreeably, right into her net. His mouth was even hanging open in an oval, like a fish gasping for air.

"The runes spoke of this," he whispered.

Her hand froze, then the tips of her fingers twitched on his skin, on the spongy runes just above his elbow. "Of what?"

He gazed at his sleeve. The runes engraved into his skin were the gift of his god, a sign that his piety had been accepted. Even more importantly, they were a gift *to* his god. For a race as beautiful and as proud of its beauty as the Ogres, to allow their flawless skin to be marked and scarred was a sign of absolute devotion.

The first markings were not usually shared with those outside his order. Few were privileged to view the first communications of Hiddukel with a disciple. Later, when his arms and hands were covered with markings, he would wear sleeves that exposed his forearms and wrists, as the High Cleric did.

"The runes spoke of many things. Of destiny and revenge. Of position and power. And there was a reference that I didn't fully understand, until I saw you tonight. To a dark queen."

"But I don't understand. I'm not a queen."

"Your gown, Khallayne. The decoration on your gown, of the Dead Queen. And there's more. The runes speak of family and revenge."

She slowly withdrew her hand from beneath his sleeve, scraping her nails along his skin as she moved. There was a humming in her mind, as of bees around a field of flowers, and a cold prickling on her skin. She whispered. "The Dead Queen . . . That settles it. We're going to steal the Song of the History of the Ogre from the Keeper and give it to Teragrym."

Chapter 3
Theft of History

"We'll need something of Jyrbian's. A bottle, a container of some kind. A charm, or a jewel. I'll find a slave who knows in whose apartments the Keeper is staying, one we can trust not to tell."

So easy. It had been so easy. Lyrralt, though obviously stunned, had not questioned her directions.

He had pushed away his plate of half-eaten food, followed her from the noisy audience hall, and gone, quickly and lightly, in the opposite direction, toward the southern end of the castle, toward his and Jyrbian's apartments.

The hem of her gown whispered softly on the stone floor as Khallayne escaped the din of the party. She went down, descending into the service passageways of the castle.

As she entered the bustling kitchen, she lifted the hem of her gown off the floor, stepping over a puddle of grimy water. The room was smoky from the huge cooking hearths, humid with the steam of boiling kettles and pots, the uncirculated air choked with the nauseating scent of humans.

Not one of the slaves looked up to meet her quick scan of the room. Just as well. Their ugly pink faces were as disgusting as their scent.

Khallayne snapped her fingers at a small, scurrying slave who wore a serving dress with little grace, as if it were stitched-together cleaning rags.

The girl bobbed a quick but respectful curtsey. "Yes, Lady. May I help you?"

"I need Laie."

The girl glanced back over her shoulder. "Laie is . . . occupied, Lady. May I serve you?" She dipped another curtsey, again quick and nervous, betraying her fear far more than did the quake in her voice.

"Occupied? What do you mean?"

The woman bobbed again, never raising her eyes from the tips of Khallayne's soft leather shoes. "She is—" She glanced behind her for support and found none. "She is . . . "

"Stand still and tell me where the slave is!" Khallayne snapped, irritated by the bobbing woman and the overpowering smell of so many unwashed slaves.

"Lady, Lord Eneg is in the kitchen!"

Khallayne made a sound of irritation, at last understanding what the mumbling slave was trying to indicate. An Ogre would have to be an outcast to have not heard of the appetites of Eneg.

Khallayne had used Laie many times before, to spy for information, for errands she wanted kept secret. As slaves went, Laie was brighter than most, a wellspring of information, and she knew to keep her mouth shut. If Eneg killed Laie, another would have to be found and trained. "When did Eneg take her?"

"Only just a moment ago."

Good. There might still be time. It was rumored that Eneg enjoyed playing with his victims.

Khallayne gathered the hem of her gown up above her shoes. "Take me to him."

Still obviously nervous, the woman led Khallayne to the back of the kitchen, through a low door, and into a long, narrow, dark hallway. A supply passage, Khallayne supposed, built for the smaller, shorter human slaves. It was very different from the wide, sweeping hallways in the rest of the castle.

Khallayne had to duck as she stepped through the doorway into a room. A moldy, sweet smell of sweat and the coppery, decaying scent of human blood greeted her as she stepped over the threshold.

Khallayne spared barely a glance for the room, which was outfitted for Eneg's sport. The important thing was, Laie was still alive, kicking and whimpering as she tried to pull free of Eneg's grasp.

With a menacing scowl, Lord Eneg turned around as the door banged into the wall. His emerald skin was splotchy and blemished, so dark it was almost black, glistening with moisture and blood.

When he saw who the intruder was, his expression became a leer. "Have you come to join me, Lady Khallayne?"

Khallayne shrugged, shaking her head. She didn't

see how he could stomach the small, low-ceilinged room and the awful stench. The foul odor of the kitchen was a spring morning compared to the rotting air concentrated in this small space. "I require the services of this slave."

The scowl returned. "Get another!"

Laie renewed her struggles to free herself.

Khallayne studied him for a moment, ignoring the slave, then said sweetly, "Lord Eneg, this slave belongs to me. If I had to train another, I would be very displeased." She rubbed her fingers together, holding her hand up so he could see that the air around the tips of her fingers glowed slightly with the beginnings of a fire spell.

Eneg growled, a rumble deep in his throat so menacing that the slave in his grasp screamed and yanked her hand free. She stumbled and tripped the few feet to Khallayne and fell.

Khallayne gestured toward the whimpering woman. "Surely another slave would suit your purpose as well as this one . . . "

Eneg took a step toward her. The determination he saw in her face changed his mind. He waved his hand dismissively. "Take her. Send another from the kitchen."

Khallayne swept back down the low hallway without waiting to see if the woman would follow. No doubt the slave was eager to escape from the hot, fetid room.

In the kitchen, Khallayne pointed at the first slave she saw, a young man no larger than Laie. "Lord Eneg requires your services." She pointed back down the hallway and escaped into the passageway outside the kitchen.

Laie came stumbling behind her, trembling with fear, stinking of Eneg's playroom and blubbering her thanks for being saved.

"Hush!" Khallayne said irritably, as the slave thanked her for the fifth time and tried to kiss her hand. Khallayne dipped her hand into the tiny pocket in the lining of her vest and produced a small coin. She held it out so that it was visible in the dim light, but pulled it back before it could be snatched by the slave's eagerly outstretched fingers. "Do you know which apartments house the Keeper of History tonight?"

Eyes fastened on the dull copper which Khallayne turned slowly in her fingers, the slave nodded. "No, Lady, but I can find out. A tray was sent up earlier."

Khallayne closed her fingers over the coin. "Then do so. But first, go to your quarters and wash, then meet me here. And quickly, or I'll give you back to Eneg!"

Tense and irritable, heart thudding with anticipation, Khallayne hovered in the shadows of a cavernous doorway until the slave returned.

She was wearing a clean shift and her short, straw-colored hair was mostly combed. "The lady Keeper is staying in Lord Tenal's guest apartments, Lady." She curtseyed and thrust out her hand.

With a smile, Khallayne put the copper coin into her palm without touching the slave's grubby pink flesh. "Fetch a tray of food, whatever the Keeper prefers, from the kitchen."

The slave's odd-colored blue eyes grew round and large with fear at the suggestion that she return to the kitchen.

"If anyone asks, say Lord Teragrym has commanded it. And if Lord Eneg chooses you again, simply tell him you belong to me," Khallayne told her. "Remind him I don't want to have to train another slave."

Khallayne shook her head as Laie vanished. In the time it took an Ogre to mature from child to young woman, human slaves went from babies to old and useless. But no matter how old or young, they were worse than children. Slow and dumb and witless, even one supposedly as bright as Laie.

Lyrralt was waiting for them at one of the side exits to the audience hall, leaning against the stone wall.

"The Keeper's in Tenal's wing."

Lyrralt nodded, eyeing the slave who stood half-concealed behind Khallayne.

Motioning for Laie to proceed, Khallayne and Lyrralt started along the passageway, nodding to other guests as they went. "What did you bring?" she asked.

Lyrralt patted a pouch hanging from his belt, bowed once more to an older lady as she eyed the two of them curiously. "Crystals from Jyrbian's collection."

Once they were upstairs, in the second-floor hall and away from the strolling party guests, they followed Laie until they rounded a corner and found her peeking around the corner at an intersection. "This is the hallway where the apartment is," Laie whispered, pointing ahead. "There are guards."

Khallayne smiled, both at the roundness of the slave's eyes and at the way Lyrralt's arm tensed under her fingers.

"Do we kill them?" he asked.

"It's all right. I expected them." Feeling less calm than she allowed herself to show, she drew away from him and took a deep breath. She closed her eyes, concentrated, and, as in the audience hall, the sounds and smells of her surroundings grew blurred and hazy.

Lyrralt gasped.

Khallayne knew that he was feeling the surge of magical power she was drawing about her like a cloak. She trembled with the power of concentration, murmuring words she had wrested from the memory of a human wizard. Her hands came up, for a moment covering her face as if masking it, and she uttered the words again, lips moving silently.

Lyrralt gasped again. The slave whimpered.

Khallayne opened her eyes. Where Lyrralt had stood, now there was almost nothing, a disquieting disturbance in the air, a warm, scented breeze as if a ghost had brushed past.

"What have you done?" Lyrralt's voice, stunned, fascinated, whispered from the nothingness.

"A spell of . . . of distraction, I suppose you would call it. If we make no sound, the guards won't see us."

"It makes my eyes hurt."

"Yes, there is a small bit of aversion to it. It makes the illusion easier to maintain." Turning to the slave, she murmured, "Laie?"

The woman was crouched back against the wall, her eyes so round and large it seemed they might burst from her head.

"Laie? Go down the hall. Tell the guards that Lord Tenal has ordered a tray sent to the Keeper. When they let you through the door, make sure to leave it open long enough for us to slip inside."

With obvious effort, the slave controlled her fear. "But, Lady, what if they won't let me through?"

"They won't stop you. Just make sure you keep the door open. Now, go!" Khallayne, who had stepped closer to the woman, gave her a shove.

The slave almost squealed with fright, but she moved quickly, looking back over her shoulder as if she were being pursued.

It went as Khallayne had said. The guards leered. One lifted the corner of the linen napkin to inspect the tray, but they allowed the slave through. Laie paused just inside the heavy wooden door, holding it open with her foot while she pretended to balance the tray. She felt a spectral puff of air, then another, flit past.

One of the guards took the tray from her and placed it on a nearby table. "The Old One sleeps," he whispered. "Leave it here and go."

The slave nodded gratefully and hurried out.

The Keeper's room was as lavish as anything Khallayne had seen since arriving in Takar. Two smoldering torches cast the only light, imparting flickering shadows more than illumination. Even in the smoky dimness, she could see the opulence of the slave-carved wood furnishings, the gleaming mirrors on walls covered with lush tapestries. She was sure, had she been able to examine it in daylight, that she would have found the thick carpet on which she trod to be elf made.

With a whispered command, the distraction disappeared and Lyrralt was visible.

"This . . . " she breathed, leaning into Lyrralt in the near dark, pressing her mouth close to his ear,

". . . this is how I will live someday."

"Perhaps we both will." For a moment, his hands hovered near her.

The Keeper was asleep on a low couch near the hearth.

Khallayne had never seen an Ogre so aged; most accepted an honorable death long before the years advanced to such fullness. She stared at the Old One's face, lined and seamed with wrinkles, as Lyrralt stirred up the dying embers and started a small fire in the fireplace.

From his pouch Lyrralt produced a clear crystal sphere and two faceted crystals, one a double-pointed amethyst, the other a perfect sapphire as dark blue as his skin.

"I wasn't sure which would be best," he whispered, holding them out for Khallayne's inspection.

She chose the crystal sphere, the plainest of the three.

Lyrralt would have backed away, but Khallayne caught his wrist and pulled him close to the Old One. "Kneel here."

Lyrralt burned to ask what she was going to do and how and where she had learned such things. He watched carefully as Khallayne placed her hands on the Keeper and whispered words that to his ears were unintelligible.

Khallayne placed the sphere on the Keeper's mouth. For a moment, it seemed as if it would roll off, then it caught and rose, floating less than two fingers above the Old One's lips as if suspended on the soft exhalations of her breath.

Lyrralt whistled soft and low in admiration.

Khallayne moved to the end of the couch and

stood over the Keeper. She fixed Lyrralt with an intense, unwavering gaze. "I'm going to try to use your energy in addition to my own," she said. It won't hurt you, but you may feel . . . tired. After I begin, make no noise, speak no sound, unless you wish to lose it forever."

He nodded.

Khallayne cupped her hands around the Keeper's head. She opened her eyes wide and concentrated. The currents of power flowed through the room, tugging at her gently.

She *had* performed the spell many times, but never before on one of her own kind. Now that she could feel the papery, withered old flesh between her fingers, she wished she'd risked the working of this one, just once, on an Ogre.

Gathering her concentration, striving for confidence that suddenly seemed to be ebbing away, she murmured the words of the spell and sent the pulsation outward. The Keeper moaned softly and rolled her head as if feeling the touch of Khallayne's magic, then was still.

After a moment, while Khallayne held her breath and waited, a soft, throbbing light began to materialize between her hands. Careful not to allow her exhilaration to overcome her, she raised her arms slowly, tenderly, feeling the pressure against her palms, the thrill of magic coursing through her fingers and arms.

Then Khallayne pressed her palms together lightly. The incandescent light shifted, surged, began to stream into the crystal sphere.

It appeared to Lyrralt that the Keeper's head was suddenly filled with light, flowing from her lips into the crystal poised above. Power filled the room. The air smelled like the coming of a thunderstorm.

As the crystal sphere became more radiant, filling with a golden rainbow of light, the Keeper grew darker and darker.

Even after the light had gone from the Keeper and was imprisoned in the pulsating sphere, Khallayne remained standing over the Keeper's body for a long moment. Then she plucked the sphere out of the air and away from the Old One's mouth.

Lyrralt felt the sudden release like a jolt to his nerves. When he was free of the tug of the spell, he felt a terrible urge to speak.

Clinging to furniture for support, Khallayne edged away from the Keeper. Though she trembled with the weight, she held the pulsating sphere up in the air.

"The Song of History," she whispered in a tired voice as Lyrralt climbed to his feet and joined her. "It's done."

He took the sphere gingerly, and carefully turned it in his hand, holding it up toward the fire to see the light pierce it through. "How wonderful!"

Khallayne sank onto a stool. "Yes, wonderful. This is the legacy that's been stolen from us. Kept from us by greedy nobles."

* * * * *

Khallayne gazed out the large window in Jyrbian's apartment, eyes roving lazily over the twinkling lights of the city below, refracted and splintered by the beveled glass. How boring, how sad, she thought, to be staring out of one of those houses, looking up enviously at the twinkling lights of the castle.

She, however, was where she belonged, and for a moment she gazed at the dozen miniature reflections of her own face in the panes of glass. The myriad Khallaynes smiled back at her wearily.

"Are you going to tell me how you did it?"

Lyrralt sat on a low stool in front of the fire. He cradled the sphere between his palms, watching the light twist and twine through it. "Are you going to tell me how you did it?" he repeated.

"Magic," Khallayne answered, her voice unconcerned, barely conversational.

He turned and saw from her broad smile that she was teasing him.

She joined him, kneeling on the floor and taking the sphere from his fingers.

"I know it's magic. Where did you learn to do it?"

She turned the sphere over and over in her hands, then used the edge of her vest to polish it. "From human wizards."

"What?"

She lifted her chin defiantly. "I took the knowledge from human wizards who were slaves in my uncle's household."

When he offered no condemnation, she continued. "I was always much quicker to learn magic than my cousins. When they were still playing with sticks and dry leaves, I could light a fire, boil water, float objects.

"When I was ready to progress, my tutors told me I had learned as much magic as was allowed a child of my station." The sphere lay forgotten in her lap as she balled her fingers into fists.

"I didn't like being told no. I didn't see why I

should be restricted. There was a slave on a nearby estate. I knew she was a mage because the lord there was a friend of my uncle's, and he had bragged that he held her there by keeping her daughter as a hostage. I made a deal with her.

"For her knowledge, I agreed to free her daughter. The spell I used to steal this"—she indicated the sphere —"was one of the things I learned from her. I've spent many years draining the magical knowledge of human mages."

"You freed a slave!" Lyrralt gasped, more aghast at that revelation than any other.

"Of course not," she said coolly, standing and taking the sphere to the window. "I didn't have to, once I learned this spell."

On the sill beneath the etched glass was a collection of crystals and spheres and rocks, all arranged neatly, sitting in brass holders or dangling from silk thread. She took a larger crystal, placed it in an empty stand, and laid the Song of History in its place. "What do you think?"

Among the grouping of more colorful rocks on the sill of Jyrbian's window, the sphere was plain and unremarkable. He slipped an arm about Khallayne's waist. "He'll never know it's there. Unless we're discovered and have cause to reveal it."

Chapter 4
A Friend of Treachery

From his position on the receiving platform, Lord Teragrym motioned for Jyrbian to sit on the level below in front of him. It would not do to have the younger Ogre tower over him.

In the presence of Teragrym, Jyrbian's joviality and brashness was dampened into watchful respect. Teragrym, who had kept his seat on the Ruling Council longer than any other because he was not careless, observed that Jyrbian bore watching.

Jyrbian sat, bowing before and after he had lowered himself to the floor, feet and lower legs folded under his thighs. With a negligent flick of his wrists, he arranged the vestrobe he wore over simple tunic and pants into a fan of cloth. The movement showed surprising grace for one so large and appeared totally unself-conscious, as if he did it without consideration for his appearance.

The audience room into which he had been received was not large, but it was opulent. Thick carpets warmed the stone floor. Painted screens and tapestries and heavy curtains left almost nothing of the stone walls visible. The furniture was sparse, consisting only of a stool for Teragrym, a low, heavily carved table at his elbow, and a writing desk farther back on the platform.

Jyrbian glanced surreptitiously about, taking in the luxury, the understated elegance. He could imagine himself quite easily in a cozy setting like this.

"My daughter has mentioned to me that, aware of my interest in what is happening in Khal-Theraxian, you have volunteered to make a visit there and report back to me."

Jyrbian smiled, then modified the expression. "Yes, Lord. I would be pleased and honored to be of service."

"And what would you expect in return for this service?"

Jyrbian's pulse accelerated as the answer leapt to his throat: power, prestige, wealth, permanence, but he didn't voice that thought. "I ask nothing, Lord. I'm honored to simply serve."

Teragrym smiled. The younger one stared down at the patterned carpet and appeared deferential, but Teragrym knew the avarice in his soul, the envy in his heart. Teragrym, too, had been a second son, brighter and bolder and more worthy than his firstborn brother. "There is a hunger in you, young

Jyrbian. It is not so well disguised as you think," he added when Jyrbian's head came up with whiplash speed, his silver eyes a mere hint of evil in the darkness of his face. "The journey could be dangerous."

Teragrym was about to add, "Very dangerous," but Jyrbian interrupted. "I know about the attacks on the mountain trails."

"That report was for the Ruling Council exclusively. How do you know?"

Jyrbian merely shrugged. "There's always talk."

Teragrym's estimation of Jyrbian increased a notch. "Very well, so you know of the attacks, which seem to be increasing in our mountains. Will you, therefore, take a company of guards with you?"

"I would not be likely to inspire the governor's confidence riding into Khal-Theraxian surrounded by guardsmen. Besides," Jyrbian scoffed, "I am as well trained as any guard. I will go alone. Or perhaps as one of a small party. I know someone who is acquainted with the governor's daughter. Perhaps we might pay a social call."

"I approve." Teragrym nodded slowly. "Surely there is something you would ask? Such service should not go unrewarded."

Jyrbian shook his head. He had thought it through carefully before he came. If he asked for something specific, that would be all he received. If he didn't specify, there would be no boundaries on what he might receive, should his errand prove worthwhile. "If the lord would feel me deserving of reward, naturally I would be honored. But I would also be honored simply to be of service."

Teragrym smiled again, almost as if he could read the calculations going on in Jyrbian's mind. "Very well. I accept your offer to serve. And I'll expect you to report back to me—and only to me."

Jyrbian nodded stiffly.

"I need to know—" Teragrym paused, considering. "I need to know *everything*. Be observant. I want to know what Igraine is doing to increase the production in his mines. I need to know if he says anything that could be considered treasonous."

"Treasonous?" Jyrbian shifted forward, poised eagerly for what would come next.

"That is a rumor we have heard. But whether it is exaggeration or truth . . . " Teragrym shrugged. "The line between acting for the good of all and the good of oneself is sometimes subtle. Sometimes it is the same thing. I must have enough information to judge for myself. I must know what is said, and what is not said."

Teragrym waited a moment, scrutinizing Jyrbian, then dismissed him.

Jyrbian was so excited he could barely maintain his poise until he was out of Teragrym's sight. The reward for such a task should be excellent indeed! As he exited into the hallway, he was beaming so broadly that the female Ogre who was waiting to enter paused in surprise in the doorway.

She watched him until he turned a corner, and hesitated even a moment longer.

"Kaede?"

Teragrym's voice snapped her back to the present and into the room.

"To what do I owe the pleasure of this visit?"

Kaede bowed and sank to her knees, knowing how Teragrym hated having someone loom over him. "Lord, forgive my unannounced arrival, but I have come to ask a favor."

"What sort of favor?"

Kaede clasped her hands in her lap to cover her agitation. "I have come to ask your permission to right a wrong that has been done my family."

* * * * *

Lyrralt paused inside the door of his apartment. He lit the candles with a few words and a flick of his wrist. His rooms were larger than Jyrbian's but located on the far side of the hallway, so he was without windows.

He had spent his morning walking the cold hallways of the castle, listening in on conversations, joining groups of Ogres to exclaim in dismay at the news. The Keeper could not be awakened. She lay as if dead, but breathing, and no one had been able to rouse her. He had started for Khallayne's rooms but wound up in his own instead. The Ogre female with whom he'd passed his night after Khallayne pleaded tiredness was gone from the room, leaving not even a trace of scent, less of memory.

He possessed no wall hangings to brighten the dark room. He owned no carpets on his floors to dispel the coldness that emanated from the very bones of the old castle. He preferred things that way. He preferred the severe beauty of the gray stone walls, the stingy light, and he filled his space with beautiful, delicate things instead of expensive ones.

On an ornately carved table against the back wall was a marble water bowl. He lifted it carefully, rinsed his mouth, and spat into a smaller bowl exactly like it. He dampened his ears and eyelids.

Shivering in the cool air, he slipped out of his long robe and replaced the garment with a sleeveless praying robe, then settled before the fire to pray, to ask for guidance, to learn what Hiddukel, God of Wealth and Accumulation, thought of his impending good fortune.

* * * * *

Khallayne was dreaming of magic, of spells so powerful that her mind could barely contain them.

"Khallayne, wake up! Wake up!"

The voice penetrated her consciousness, jarring her awake even as a hand on her shoulder shook her. "Wake up!"

She opened her eyes to the warm, golden sunlight of a fall morning.

Silhouetted in the light, Lyrralt was leaning over her, his face in shadow. "Wake up," he repeated.

Groggily, she covered her eyes with her hand. What time was it? Had he been there all night, in her apartments? Then she remembered that he hadn't and why he hadn't. He had wanted to stay, but she had talked him out of it because she had wanted to distance herself from him.

"Are you awake?"

The question finally got through to her, and she sat up, pulling the down coverlet up over her breasts.

His face, now that she could see it, was a study in displeasure, brow pulled low, eyes narrowed and dark.

"What is it? What's wrong?"

"They discovered the Keeper this morning. It's all over the castle."

Her heart gave a thump. She fought the fear she felt, remembering the steps she had taken to protect herself, thinking quickly that she must order Lyrralt from her room. Get him as far away, as quickly as possible.

The last thing she had done, before they had slipped away from the Keeper's apartment the night before, was work a "masking" spell, a kind of camouflaging of her presence. But the essence of Lyrralt, the magical scent that a really good mage could find if he or she knew how, that she had left. Just in case. "So?"

"They can't wake her. It's like she's dead, but still breathing."

"Do they suspect magic?"

"Not yet. Everyone seems to feel that it's an illness, or that she's simply so old. But they will figure it out, won't they?"

She relaxed against the pillows, the cover spilling off her shoulders, exposing her lovely skin. "What do you mean?"

His fingers clenched. He longed to drag her from the soft bed and dash her head against the wall! "You've done something. Something to lead them to me!"

"Of course I haven't," she protested immediately. "Why would you even think such a thing?"

He walked to the fireplace and murmured an incantation. Small flames licked up from the embers and rapidly grew to a small, crackling fire. The runes on his shoulder, and the new figures below on his arm, itched. "I have been warned of treachery."

Khallayne reached for her robe, slipped it on as she climbed out of bed. The silk kimono was cool and soft on her skin and very pleasing to the eye.

Despite his anger, Lyrralt's gaze was drawn to her, which irritated him even more.

She stretched, reaching for the ceiling. "Don't be ridiculous," she said lazily. "We're perfectly safe. The Keeper won't wake. No one will ever know what we did, except Teragrym. And he will never tell." She shrugged, watching the way his eyes followed the movement of her breasts under the loosely wrapped robe. "All the others were like this. After I took what I wanted, they slept. Then they died."

She opened the door of a wardrobe and selected one of the tunics hanging within. "Now all we have to do is wait. After she's dead, the History is ours to bargain with."

He was across the room in an instant, his fingers squeezing her upper arm until he could feel the hardness of bone beneath the flesh. "That was a pretty speech, but I'm not convinced. Hiddukel does not lightly offer his counsel! Be warned, if I am suspected of this crime, I will not go to the dungeons alone! And you have more to lose than I."

Despite the pain, she didn't wince. He could have pinched the limb off and still she would not have allowed him the satisfaction of seeing her show pain. "But you're being foolish to think I would risk telling anyone. There is too much to lose. Too much to gain. Be warned yourself, I do not take lightly to threats!"

She stopped and glared at his hand. A moment later, a sharp pain shot up his arm. Lyrralt snatched his hand away and stepped back.

She pushed so close he could feel her hot breath on his face. "Do not touch me so again!"

"My apologies." He grinned, admiring her in spite of himself, shaking his hand to ease the stinging of it. He executed a mocking little bow and slammed the door loudly as he exited her bedroom.

* * * * *

The morning sun was up over the castle wall, the last of the bags loaded onto the horses, when Khallayne strode into the courtyard.

Jyrbian paused to watch her as she came down the steps and across the flagstones, leaving Lyrralt to finish checking the saddle and packs on their horses.

"Are we ready?" she asked, tossing her saddlebags across the rump of her gray gelding.

Lyrralt, squatting to check the hooves of his horse, stood up so quickly that the animal shied sideways. His gaze locked with Khallayne's, his brow furrowing with surprise and anger.

"*I've* been ready since sunrise." Jyrbian said. "We'll leave as soon as everyone is here."

Without taking her eyes from Lyrralt, she asked, "Everyone?"

"You know Briah, don't you? She's going, and her sister, Nylora. And Tenaj and those two cousins of hers. I can never remember their names."

As if summoned by their mentioning, the remainder of the group came trooping down the steps, bright laughter and conversation rumbling up into the morning sky. They were a polychromatic lot, with skin tones ranging from almost as pale as Khallayne to deep sea green. All shades of silver hair, from Briah's bright mercury to the cousins' soft pewter, were also represented.

With Jyrbian distracted, matching everyone up with their horses, Lyrralt sidled around to Khallayne.

"When did *you* decide to join this expedition?" she asked, her voice cold and disapproving.

"When it occurred to me I would be safer away from the castle for a while."

Khallayne caught up her horse's reins. "There is no place you'd be safe if I truly wanted to implicate you!" she hissed. "I included you because I thought we shared a common interest. A common goal."

Lyrralt smiled at the others but said to her out of the corner of his mouth, "I became disturbed when the Keeper didn't die in a day or so, as you said she would. Now I find you leaving the city with my brother." He held out his hand, offering to assist her in mounting her horse, thinking how much he would instead like to pitch her across the horse and watch her brains spill out onto the flagstones.

Khallayne pushed his hand out of her way and mounted without any help. "I planned since the night of the party to visit Khal-Theraxian. Jyrbian provided a convenient means to get there."

"Are we riding, or are you going to talk all day?" Jyrbian interrupted, riding toward them on his huge stallion. "At this rate, we'll just clear the city gates by nightfall." He reined the horse around and headed toward the southern gate.

With a quick glance at Khallayne, Lyrralt mounted. Lagging as the others went ahead, he guided his horse close to hers.

After a moment, she sighed. "Lyrralt, the Keeper will die. No one will ever know we stole the History.

"And even if the truth is discovered, Jyrbian will

take the blame." She turned her unblinking gaze at him, her eyes as black as a starless night, yet as bright as starshine. Slanting, alien eyes. Depthless, ruthless. "I think you'd be glad to have him out of the way. I'm sure he wouldn't hesitate to do the same to you."

The corners of his mouth twitched. "I'll be watching you," he said simply, without rancor, before he cantered ahead.

The castle of Takar was set high on a mountainside overlooking the crescent of city wrapped around its base and the open valley beyond, site of many of the Ruling Council's estates.

Before the Battle of Denharben, Takar had been one of four cities in which the king resided. He had traveled between Takar, Thorad, Bloten and Persopholus, giving equal time and attention to each; and for a time, after the Ruling Council had solidified its position and taken power in the king's name, its members, too, had kept up travel between the cities. But the key to their power had been the relocation of their enemies to the outlying districts, where lesser properties were located, while ownership of the best provinces and estates went to their strongest supporters. Takar had been the main seat of power ever since.

As the travelers descended through a series of switchbacks, the magnificent view of the valley and the purple mountains in the distance slowly disappeared, and they entered the city proper.

Passing through a magnificent stone archway inlaid with bronze panels depicting battles of old, they rode into what the commoners covertly called "the hostage district." It was so called because the council, in another step toward gaining control, insisted that the families of the rich and powerful occupy

their city homes year round. The homes, fashioned
of stone with high garden walls of mud brick, were
nearly as magnificent as the private quarters in the
castle, and certainly more roomy.

Lyrralt rode ahead, joining Jyrbian at the front of
the group.

The populace had long been awake by the time
they rode through the city, which was filled with the
bustle and noise of everyday trade. Takar's wealth
lay in commerce, the trade of riches from the surrounding areas, ore and gems from the mines, food-
stuffs from the rich valley farms, slaves from the
faraway plains.

Near the southern wall of the city was the huge
coliseum where games and slave battles drew Ogres
from miles around. It loomed, blotting out the sun, a
massive bowl dropped down among the dwellings.
The group shivered in its enormous shadow as they
passed.

Then they were through the southern gate and
into bright, golden sunlight.

For over two hours, they rode south along a ridge
overlooking the Takar Valley, then they veered to the
east and up sloping trails. This led them into the
forests and higher ridges, where they would make
camp for the night.

Their companionable chatter silenced the twitter
of birds and sent small animals scurrying through
the thick underbrush.

* * * * *

R'ksis emerged in stages, skittering out into the
sunlight, then dipping back into darkness. Each

time, she stayed out longer. Finally, clinging to the shady side of the trees, she remained above, but not far from the mouth of the cave. No disr wanted to leave the dark, cool safety of its underground home.

The world outside was thick forest. Golden leaves overhead filtered the bright light. Scrubby bushes and a thick carpet of decaying leaves lay underfoot. The boulders that hid the entrance to the subterranean home had a coating of gray-green fungus. R'ksis scraped some off with a crescent-shaped claw and stuck the appendage in her mouth.

She spat it out. Compared to the rich, moldy taste of such food from beneath, it had little taste. It was sun-spoiled. It was not what she and the others had braved the surface for, anyway.

R'ksis sniffed, testing the air. Blood. Sweat. The odor of horse and Ogres hung in the air, scenting the forest. "The Old Ones," she nearly hissed, motioning for the males to come forward.

They stayed inside, in the comforting darkness. When she motioned again, they hissed and clicked their claws against the rock walls. "Light bright. Too bright. Hurt eyes. Sun too warm," they protested.

With an oath, she left them, knowing they would follow.

The scent of the Old Ones thinned as she moved through the forest. She adjusted her course. By the time she'd picked up the trail once more, the ten males had caught up. They had taken the time to roll on the ground, camouflaging their pasty green flesh.

She nodded her approval, then quickly flung handfuls of leaves and dirt across her own body.

"Food," G'hes, the oldest male, clicked and hissed,

sniffing. He sounded much more assured now.

"Old Ones!" She bent, scooped up a large rock and crushed it in her claws, as she would crush the Old Ones. The Ogres were an ancient enemy, thieves who lived above, yet forced their slaves to tunnel into the mountains—not to make homes, but to rob the earth.

"Old Ones taste good?" The youngest member of the party asked eagerly. S'rk was the only one of them who had never been above before. He stood completely upright, taller than the others, his compact body taut with excitement and fear.

The others hissed their pleasure. Ogres tasted even sweeter than the tunnelers, the slaves of the Ogres.

It took almost an hour to find the source of the lush blood scent. As they walked, trees and boulders thrust up through the earth's surface, and dense patches of undergrowth, where the sun broke through the canopy of leaves, passed by unnoticed. It was all featureless terrain to eyes accustomed to the lush darkness of the underworld, to the beauty of dripping caverns.

As the scent of the Old Ones grew unbearably thick, G'hes, the oldest male, chortled, "Tribe be pleased."

"First, catch," she warned him.

* * * * *

Jyrbian ranged from the front of the procession, where Lyrralt rode silent and morose, to the back, where Khallayne did the same.

He joined her for the third time in as many hours, asking the same question he had before. "Why so glum? Isn't this a beautiful day for a ride?" Then he loped ahead once more when she refused to talk with him. Then Tenaj called, "Quiet!"

They obeyed at once, because Tenaj was the hunter of the group, the one who spent long hours on the trails, in the forests.

Jyrbian waited for Tenaj to catch up with him, motioning the others past. "What?" He mouthed the word, making not a sound.

Tenaj glanced down the trail, the way they had come, then into the forest. Except for the unnatural quiet, which could easily be caused by their passing, everything appeared normal.

Except for that sense of someone—something. Not watching exactly, but *waiting*.

Tenaj shook her head. "Something," she said quietly. "I don't know." She rubbed the back of her neck. "Maybe I should ride back a ways, just to check things out."

"Not too far, okay? There've been a couple of attacks on hunting parties on this trail. I don't think we should get too spread out along here."

Nodding agreement, Tenaj reined her stallion around.

She kept her hand on her sword as she rode toward Takar. The forest was too still, showing no signs of life, even though the party had passed by several minutes before. It made her jittery, and her horse, already half-wild, skittish.

Then she went around a turn, and there was the reason. Disr, four of them, on the trail! They blinked their pale, watery eyes. Dirt and leaves stuck to their slimy flesh. Probably more of them in the shade beyond, she thought. For a second, they gazed at her, eyes blazing with hatred and hunger. Then there was noise from the forest, and the dense, compact bodies moved in unison.

Tenaj turned and ran. "Disr!" she screamed, as soon as the others were in sight. "Disr! At least five of them!"

Khallayne was in the rear. She slowed her horse as she heard Tenaj yell and half-turned in the saddle.

· From the left, something hit Khallayne's arm. Something dense, but slick and large. Her breath left her lungs. She felt numbness shoot through her shoulder and arm. She cried out as the ground came toward her face with startling speed!

She struck the hard, packed earth, then glimpsed something dank and dense, with claws and a compact body, moving impossibly fast. Horses' hooves danced near her eyes. Pain shot through her thigh, as if a knife had just ripped the flesh.

Screams sounded from above and in her own throat. Fear, warning, pain! An even more frightened scream came from a horse. The slimy thing, smelling of vinegar and rot, was upon her, tearing at her flesh. Everywhere it touched, pain.

Through the confusion, she heard someone scream her name. She heard a war cry, terrible yet reassuring. There was frenzied movement above her. Then away from her.

* * * * *

The Old One surprised them! The scent had been so strong, they hadn't sensed the Ogre female on the trail. At a hiss from R'ksis, the group divided, scuttled back into the forest, and pursued, dropping to all fours for speed.

As they flanked the Old Ones, the scent of food was overpowering. The voices of their prey were raised in alarm, the hooves of their mounts sending a fear-filled vibration through the packed earth.

Leading her group, R'ksis attacked first, using the momentum of her speed to launch herself at the first Old One she encountered. The Ogre's body was knocked from the saddle, falling heavily to the ground.

With the battle lust of the young, S'rk was upon the stunned Ogre in an instant. He ripped at the leg of the creature, opening the flesh. Ripped again with his jagged fangs.

The Ogre screamed, flailed weakly at her attacker, then collapsed. To R'ksis, the sound of her enemy's pain was as welcome as home; the scent of the warm, steaming blood was sweet.

A terrible screech rent the air as S'rk reached again for the fallen Ogre. R'ksis glanced up to see a large Old One leap to the ground. A male, from the looks of it, drew his sword as he jumped. Another Ogre, the one from the trail, joined him.

The very sight of them infuriated her. Meal forgotten, R'ksis jumped up to meet them. Her nostrils flared as she caught the scent of Ogre sweat, of fear. And then the Ogres were upon her!

R'ksis swiped at the bigger one, claws extended to their full range. But her reach couldn't match that of the Ogre's sword. The blade struck her a glancing blow, bouncing off the natural armor plates covering her shoulders.

The Ogre attacked again, swinging his sword in a low, whistling arc. R'ksis rolled and dove between the two attackers, slashing at their legs. They wheeled with her, and the female's blade sang in the air above R'ksis's head. She backed away as they split, trying to flank her.

All about her were the sounds of battle. The hissing and clicking of attacking disr. The scream of a wounded animal. The hiss of a dying disr.

The Ogres attacked in unison, and R'ksis ducked beneath the swinging weapons. The female changed her tactic, lunging forward with one foot and thrusting with her sword. R'ksis stumbled back, falling out of range of the sword.

Two of her males were dead, their bodies crumpled in the sunlight. But across the path, G'hes was closing in on a female Old One, his long, sharp tongue tasting the air in anticipation.

S'rk joined the fight, leaping in from the side.

R'ksis heard the female Ogre's sword bite into the thick covering on S'rk's back. He rolled and came to his feet, eyes clenched with pain.

R'ksis met their assailants alone, protecting S'rk with her body. She stumbled backward, avoiding a sword thrust, would have fallen but for S'rk. His hands were trembling. She could smell the sharp odor of disr blood.

"Run, youngest! Run far!" She pushed him, just as the male Ogre swung. The blade, wicked and gleaming, missed her, missed S'rk. Then, incredibly, reversed its direction, slicing back. The edge, as sharp as disr claws, bit into S'rk's throat. The youngest one gurgled, gazed up at her as he fell.

Just as she saw the life dim in S'rk's eyes, she heard G'hes's death cry, saw him fall, clutching at his chest. Before the Ogres could attack again, she screamed a wordless warning of retreat to those of her pack still standing. Then she blended into the forest, so quickly that the Ogres couldn't respond.

* * * * *

Topsy turvy, the sky tilted, trees growing sideways.

Khallayne saw Jyrbian battling a nightmare, a thing with armor plates on its rubbery, four-legged body, with eyes as red as Lunitari. It reared up on its hind legs and stood as an Ogre, met him with hissing and clicking, like a beetle.

Jyrbian swung with his sword. Blood, as red and thick as any Ogre's, spurted from the creature's neck. It choked and crumpled. Another creature, standing near Tenaj, darted a panicked glance about, then melted back into the forest.

The sky tilted sickeningly again. Khallayne remembered no more.

She woke with dirt clogging her nostrils and the smell of something rotten mixed with her own blood. The hands that were turning her over were not gentle, and pain throbbed dully in her shoulder, thigh, and arms. Voices, warped and only vaguely recognizable, filtered through to her mind.

"Careful."

"How bad is it?"

"Don't touch the slime around the bites! It's poisonous."

"Tenaj, Levin, stand guard."

"We need to get moving. There may be more."

This voice she recognized as Briah's, and she struggled to sit up. But hands held her down.

"How bad?" another voice insisted again.

"Can you heal her?"

"Yes." The hands probed the wound on her thigh, sending bursts of pain like glass shards rocketing up her leg. "But there will be a price."

She gasped aloud with pain.

"Do you understand, Khallayne? Do you agree? There is always a price from the gods for a healing."

At last, she knew the voice, knew the hands. She opened her eyes and stared into the face of Lyrralt.

"I can heal you if Hiddukel grants it, but there will be a price. Sooner or later, he will ask something of you and you will have to give it. Do you understand?"

"Just do it, Lyrralt!" Jyrbian snapped. "Do you think she has any choice?"

Now Jyrbian's face, shining with sweat, eyes glazed, exhilarated with battle lust, came into view. "That thing ripped her leg open almost to the bone. If she doesn't bleed to death, the disr poison will kill her. Get on with it."

Khallayne caught the sleeve of Lyrralt's tunic, remembering the feel of the runes on his skin. To whom would the price have to be paid? "I agree."

He laid his hands on her and raised his eyes to the sky, lips moving. He twitched. His fingers tightened, then relaxed.

The pain surged, worse than anything she'd ever dreamed. As she opened her mouth to scream, she felt her flesh ripple, join, torn edge against torn edge, and begin to knit.

Chapter 5
Passing of the Gift

The estate of Lord Igraine, called Khalever, after his daughter, was different from any Jyrbian had ever seen.

"What is it? Do you feel it?" he murmured to Khallayne, who rode behind him, her arms linked around his waist.

The creature in the forest had killed her horse, and since no one had wanted to turn back, they had been taking turns riding double.

Khallayne shook her head. "I don't know." Peace, quiet, contentment were the words that came to her.

There were sounds aplenty, wind in the trees, bees, birds, a door slamming, the nickering of their horses, and the welcoming neigh of one of Igraine's animals, but quiet was still the sense of it. Quiet . . . but something missing . . . She looked about uneasily, puzzled, as her fingers clutched Jyrbian tightly.

At the end of the long drive stood the main house, tan stone decorated with insets of pinkish shale around the sparkling windows. Gently rolling fields of grain stretched away toward the hills, verdant and lush in the summer sun.

Lord Igraine, governor of Khal-Theraxian himself, came out onto the wide porch to greet them. He was small for an Ogre, a good two hands shorter than Jyrbian, and simply dressed. His skin was a rich green. His eyes crinkled as he smiled, welcoming them to his home. "It is always a pleasure to have visitors from Takar. How was your trip? What is the news of court?"

Nylora and Briah both spoke at once of the attack in the forest and Jyrbian's bravery in dispatching the danger, of the death of Khallayne's horse and the hardship of riding double, of the Keeper's sudden sleep.

Igraine smiled through all of it, turning his head from person to person, seemingly fascinated.

As he listened to each person in turn, Igraine gave them such attention that each felt all-important. His demeanor was compelling. Jyrbian had to study the technique, for surely anyone could learn to feign such intense interest.

"How terrible!" Igraine pulled a sad, shocked face when told of the Keeper. And, "I hope you are not too badly shaken," when told of what had happened to Khallayne and her horse.

The group grew silent as they waited for Khallayne to respond. Though nothing had been said, the silence between Khallayne and Lyrralt had grown increasingly uncomfortable over the last three days.

"I'm fine," she said, then, because everyone still waited, she added, "Lord Lyrralt healed me." She could barely say the disgusting words.

"A healer!" Igraine's gaze settled on Lyrralt, on the robe with one long sleeve. "A cleric of Hiddukel. Honored Sir, you are welcome in my home."

Lyrralt's expression was smug.

Jyrbian's frown drew his brows almost together.

Igraine made an expansive gesture that included his house and the surrounding areas. "You are all welcome in my home."

The chatter started immediately, Nylora and the cousins exclaiming at the loveliness of Igraine's estate and about parties and such at court. Khallayne cut through the babble without raising her voice. "You are the news of the court, Lord Igraine. Everyone is talking of your new prosperity and wondering how such a thing is possible."

The crinkles around Igraine's eyes grew even deeper as his smile broadened. "Lady, I should be glad to tell you all." He bowed low over her hand as she passed by him and entered the large foyer.

Jyrbian glared at the back of her head and imagined his fingers closing around her lovely neck. It wasn't that he minded her bluntness with the governor, but that she had said such things in front of all the others! Such matters should be discreet. And *he* wanted to be able to report back to Teragrym, without word-of-mouth stealing his thunder.

At the same time he admired her agile mind, her smooth tongue. He wished he could extract both from her head, slowly, painfully. "I, too, would be interested in hearing your story," he said quickly, wiping the perturbed expression off his face for the benefit of his host.

"Yes, of course. Come inside." As Igraine turned, a lovely young woman, tiny for an Ogre and unusually delicate, stepped into his path. He caught her hand and drew her through the door. "Meet my daughter, Everlyn, who is really the beginning of and the reason for my tale."

Jyrbian knew his eyes widened and his smile came alive, but he was unable to control his reaction to the sight of Everlyn.

She was as delicate as a flower, as bright and unblemished as the purest of crystals. Her eyes were the silver green of sunlight sparkling on a clear water, her shining hair almost too thick against her small face. Though she was at least two hundred fifty years old, he guessed, fully grown, the top of her head barely reached his chin. Even more intriguing, she smiled with an expression unlike anything he had ever seen in his life, an enigma he could not solve.

Jyrbian bowed low. "If I hear no story at all, this trip will not be a loss."

Instead of the ardent response he expected, she smiled mysteriously and glanced away from the intensity in his eyes, murmuring a thank you for the compliment.

Playing the part of gracious host, Igraine led them into a large, cool room outfitted as an office. With its heavy oak walls, it would have been dark but for the gallery of tall windows that looked out over the back of the estate. The ceiling was painted the color of the night sky, and silver had been worked into it in the pattern of the constellations of the gods.

As everyone exclaimed at the beauty of the room and asked how the slaves had created the decoration, Khallayne strolled along the windows and gazed out toward the mountains that ringed the perimeter of Igraine's property.

Careful to make sure she was unobserved, Khallayne whispered the words to a "seeing" spell, shivering as the power rose up and skittered along her nerves. As the power took hold, she realized what it was about Igraine's estate she found so disquieting. Her mouth fell open.

"What is it?" Jyrbian asked. He had Everlyn's hand tucked firmly through his arm and was leading her along the windows, admiring the view. He had come up behind Khallayne.

Khallayne was so surprised, so astounded, she spoke without taking note of Everlyn. "Where are the wards?" She gestured outside, toward the estate. "There are no wards, nothing, to prevent the escape of the slaves. There aren't even any guards!"

Jyrbian scanned all that was visible through the tall windows, but he didn't really need to confirm her news. She was right. That was what felt so odd about the place! No guards.

Although Igraine's personal wealth originated from inheritance, it was well known that the largest part of his income came from his mines, which lay north of his estate. The majority of his guards would naturally be stationed in the mountains. But Jyrbian still expected to see at least a handful of guards around the grounds. Honor guards in fancy dress, if nothing else. Or slave guards, especially near the slaves' quarters. Yet there were none. None as far as he could see.

Another oddity. The slaves' quarters were not usually so close to the main house. But he could see the stone huts of the slaves—with glistening thatched roofs, not the miserable, ugly hovels he expected. These were clean, almost picturesque, set against the backdrop of slate-gray mountains, green fields, and blue sky. Beside several of the dwellings, humans worked with rakes and hoes in tiny gardens. Human children, their grotesque little bowed legs bare, played in the nearby dirt. A snatch of human song, low and unlovely, carried on the breeze.

It seemed almost profane.

"You are admiring my estate?" Igraine spoke from behind them.

Jyrbian started, wondering how long the Ogre had been standing there, how much of their observations he had overheard. "We were noticing that you do not guard your slaves, neither with wards nor sentries."

"Because my slaves are happy here. They do not require wards, magical or otherwise."

"Happy?" Khallayne sampled the word on her tongue. Slaves were not happy or unhappy. They were simply slaves. "How is this unusual state achieved?"

"It has been the best kept secret in our world." Igraine laughed. "I will share what I have learned if you truly seek knowledge. But I caution you, what I say will not be easy to understand at first. It will go against many of the things you have been taught, many of the things you believe. You must be willing to listen with an open mind. An open heart."

He looked first at Jyrbian, then at Khallayne, waiting for their signal to continue.

Jyrbian wanted to learn all he could for Teragrym

and then shut his ears, hear no more. He nodded for Igraine to continue, as did Khallayne.

"Very well. What I have learned is this." Igraine pushed open the tall windows before them, and a breeze cooled by high mountain snows wafted in. "Choice."

Lyrralt, who had joined them, looked puzzled, Khallayne felt sure Igraine was toying with them. They stole glances at each other to reassure themselves they had heard correctly.

"All beings, be they Ogre or human or elf, master or slave, have choices."

"You joke with us, Lord," Jyrbian said, careful to keep his voice respectful. "Of course, we have choices. What has this to do with your prosperity?"

"You do not understand." Igraine noticed that most of the group had drifted over. "Come, sit down. Let me tell you the story of how this happened. Then you will understand what I mean." He herded them toward the circle of chairs around the fireplace.

When they were settled, he told his story, speaking in a solemn and poignant voice of the mine, of the groaning and crying of the earth, of the death cry of his daughter, of all that had happened to tear the blindness from his heart. Overcome with emotion, he paused for a long moment. When he continued, his tone had changed into one of bitterness and self-recrimination. "In my selfishness, my greed, I ordered the slaves out. The sides of the tunnel were still shifting, the ceiling still falling. They were too valuable to risk."

"But that was a rational assumption," Nylora protested. She was seconded with nods from most of those present. "What else could you have done?"

"I could have tried to save my daughter, as one of my slaves did. In spite of my orders, he rallied the other slaves. With bare hands, they held back the sliding rock while others ran for beams to shore up the roof.

"They braced the beams with their bodies while he dug me free," Everlyn said softly and shivered. "It was terrible in that little space, with the rocks pressing down on me. The air was choked with dust. I could feel blood on my face." She shuddered.

"All this simply because Everlyn wanted to mine a piece of bloodstone for herself." Igraine pointed at his daughter, frowned sternly, but the frown gave way to a bittersweet smile.

Khallayne looked around at the others' rapt faces. They didn't understand.

"Bloodstone? What is that?" This from Briah.

Igraine pointed to a hand-sized chunk of rock in a brass stand on the mantel. "A rock. A plain rock, too soft for building, too ugly for jewelry. Who but Everlyn would even want one? Who but my strange daughter, who collects such rocks and stones!"

After glancing at Everlyn for permission, Khallayne reached to pick up the bloodstone. It was the size of a potato, smoky, so dark it seemed to suck in the light and hold it, and was shot through with fat streaks of red that looked like drops of blood.

It was, as Igraine had said, quite ugly, shiny, as if had been polished, but rough to the touch. Khallayne offered to pass it to the others, but only Jyrbian held out his hand.

"I myself am a collector of crystals," he said, turning the rock in the light.

Everlyn smiled shyly, took the stone, cradling it in her small hands, and again glanced away from the interest shining in his eyes.

"This is the first time I've heard of slave disobedience bearing good results," Briah said sharply.

Lyrralt struggled to comprehend the story, trying to piece together the meaning of it. He realized there was more to it, something else Igraine was waiting for them to grasp. His arm throbbed, the runes tingling, a grim sensation. "There's more," he said, almost in a rasp.

Igraine nodded. "I couldn't understand why a slave would disobey so flagrantly, why he would choose the life of another over his own."

Lyrralt made the leap before the others. "You didn't destroy him," he guessed.

Khallayne and Jyrbian both looked at Igraine with amazed expressions. Igraine smiled back. "How could I?" he said simply.

"But he disobeyed," Khallayne protested. "The penalty is death."

"He saved the life of my only child."

"But the law—"

"Eadamm saved my life!" Everlyn interrupted hotly, a fierce expression on her face.

"Shhh." Igraine quieted her. "It is not easy to understand."

"No, I don't understand," Briah insisted. "The slave disobeyed, no matter the consequence. If he was not put to death . . . " For a moment, she was quiet, pondering her next words. "If he was not put to death, then you broke the law. Your broke the law on behalf of a slave."

"I did not break the law."

"Then the slave was executed?"

"I sentenced Eadamm to death at my whim."

"And your whim has not yet transpired?" Jyrbian guessed.

"No. And I doubt that it will. Eadamm not only saved Everlyn, but when I spared him, he proved a natural leader. He organized the other slaves. In one month, they took as much ore from the low mines, as many gems from the high mines, as they previously had in two months."

"Doubled?" Jyrbian breathed deeply in disbelief. "Your production has doubled?"

Igraine had told the story before. He had seen the same expressions flit across the faces of his neighbors, his relatives, his guests. First anger, disbelief, then awe and finally greed.

"There's more. When I saw this happen, I tried an experiment. I loosened the restrictions on the slaves. I gave them tiny freedoms, inconsequential things, and again they worked harder. They produced more. This summer, I allowed the huts and the gardens you can see from the windows. In the meantime, my profits have *tripled*."

Now avarice gleamed at him from five pairs of eyes—all except Lyrralt's and Khallayne's.

Jyrbian thought of his family's land, much like Igraine's, though on a smaller scale: lush farmland backed up to cliffs and mountains riddled with mines, many of them unplumbed. To triple the output! He thought of Ogre cities built entirely of the valuable green stone shot through with tans and grays and pewters, which came from the rocky hills like those behind his home.

"We must have refreshments," Igraine said, changing his tone and standing. "Everlyn, why don't you take everyone on a tour of the house? I'm sure they'd like to see our excellent examples of elven sculpture."

Lyrralt glanced up and found Igraine's gaze fixed intently upon him. Lyrralt suddenly felt the runes on his arm dance feverishly.

Dutifully, Khallayne stood to join the others, but stepped through the tall windows onto the porch instead. The sun was setting, the land beginning to take on the shadows of darkness. Toward the slave huts, the sparkle of lantern light came to life.

It took a moment for her to understand why the lantern glow seemed so out of place, then she realized that on her uncle's estate the slaves were not given lanterns in their quarters. At nightfall, if they weren't working, they were expected to rest for the coming day.

As she stood there, breathing the fresh, cool air, a silhouetted figure eased out of a door at the other end of the gallery and into the shadows of the yard, a woman slave with a shawl draped over her head.

Trying to see where the woman went, Khallayne didn't hear Igraine slip up behind her until he had touched her arm. "Are you not hungry, Lady?"

She started, then relaxed, smiling apologetically. "I was only admiring your estate, Lord. And noticing how odd it seems to see lights in the slave huts."

"Yes, it is. But they appreciate having a little extra time for themselves in the evening. And the amount of oil they may use is rationed. In the end, I gain more than I lose."

She looked pensively at the lantern-lit windows again before turning to him. "What you're doing is very dangerous, isn't it?"

He raised an eyebrow.

"In Takar, I've heard things said," she continued. "They're jealous of your success, and perhaps a little afraid of it. There are some who say the number of runaway slaves has increased dramatically since you began your program. We were warned to be careful on the trails."

"But you experienced no trouble," he admonished gently, "not from slaves anyway. And believe me, I have not had a runaway since last summer. You know how the court is for starting rumors. Perhaps others cannot control their slaves. If so, surely it is no concern or fault of mine?"

He certainly was persuasive. She had to grant him that. "Yes, of course, you're right."

"Lady Khallayne, many have come to hear of my success. They go away changed or confused or even angry. There is very little in between. Yet I had the feeling you were mostly disappointed with my explanations."

"Lord, I hope I've given no insult—"

"None," he said. "But I have the feeling you didn't really come here for the same reason as everyone else anyway."

"Really? Why?"

"Well," he admitted, laughing. "Lord Jyrbian did tell me you do not own an estate. Of what use would my management techniques be to you?"

He walked off into the shadows and seated himself on a long, low settee. "Come." He patted the soft cushion on the seat. "Tell me why you have come so far to meet me."

Everything about him, his voice, his open manner, his beguiling tone, the way he sat patiently, quietly waiting, invited her to confide in him. She strode to the settee and sat down beside him. "Truthfully, Lord—"

"Igraine," he interrupted. "Just Igraine."

For a moment, she was taken aback by such familiarity, but there was nothing insincere about Igraine. "Igraine." She tried the word and found the sound of it, like its owner, forthright and comforting. "I did come to hear your tale, to learn how you've become so successful, but I had thought . . . "

He waited in silence for her to continue. She felt his entire attention was hers.

"I thought the reason for your success would be magical in nature."

He straightened.

She felt a thrill of triumph to have startled him.

"Magic! You thought I had increased my profits by magic?"

"I . . . hoped," she admitted. Tensely she waited for his reaction.

"Jyrbian did not say you were of a Ruling Family."

"I'm not." She drew one leg up on the settee so that she could face him. "But I know a lot. And I want so badly to learn more. I think I could be so—"

She stopped when she realized what she'd confessed. She tensed as he looked her over, as his lips moved. The scrutiny of the spell he cast passed over her like fingers on her skin, on her very bones. The sensation lasted only a moment, then was gone.

"Yes," he mused. "Very powerful. Well, Khallayne . . . My methods for running this province are not magical. And I am not of a Ruling Family, but as governor I have been allowed some leeway. I will be glad to teach you what I know."

In the minutes since they had started talking, the sun had set. Khallayne knew he couldn't see the sudden rush of blood to her cheeks, the dilation of her pupils, but surely he could feel the heat, hear the pounding of her heart. "You will?" Then immediately, "Why?"

He stood, reaching down to pull her up. "As you said, there are those who do not appreciate my ways. I believe there are dark days coming, for me and for all the Ogres. I think an ally such as yourself would be most beneficial."

"What would I have to do?"

"Help me spread the word. Help me change the world. Be my friend. I can use someone as powerful, as persuasive, as you."

He sounded almost insane. She had never encountered anyone like him before, and she wondered if perhaps he were using some sort of spell to influence her, because, lunacy and all, she wanted nothing so much as to do as he said.

"I don't think the world needs changing, but I do want to learn the magic."

Igraine clasped her shoulders and smiled at her.

"Perhaps I already can help you," she continued. "With this warning. As governor, you report to Lady Enna, correct? And the profits of the province must be tithed to her?"

Igraine nodded.

"And the other ruling members might be . . . threatened by your success?"

Again he nodded.

She leaned close and said in an almost-whisper, "Then I think you should know that Jyrbian has come at the behest of Teragrym."

* * * * *

Jyrbian looked up and frowned as Igraine strolled into the dining room with Khallayne on his arm.

He was already in a sour mood. Everlyn had brought him to the room and introduced him to the large crowd of visitors and relatives. She had bustled about, ordering extra plates and more food.

He had invited her to dine with him, had deliberately saved the chair beside him for her, even glowering at Briah when she tried to sit in it. But Everlyn had disappeared through the door to the kitchen and never returned.

Now it appeared that Khallayne had been in private audience with Igraine. His scowl deepened.

"Oh, how lovely," Khallayne exclaimed, detaching herself from her host so that she could walk to the head of the table and look at the elegant dining table that dominated the room. It appeared to be built of translucent ice.

"It's very old, from a time when my family traded in elven slaves." Igraine said.

"Is it made of crystal?"

"Can you imagine an entire city made like this?" One of the females Everlyn had introduced as an aunt beamed proudly at Khallayne.

As the two of them launched into a discussion of elven architecture, Jyrbian pushed away his uneaten supper and joined Igraine.

"Lord Igraine, if I may be so bold? This slave who saved Everlyn . . . "

"He is an extraordinary human." Igraine took up the conversation with only the slightest prompting. "It is from him that I have learned everything."

"I would like to meet this extraordinary slave."

"I would, too."

Jyrbian looked around to discover Lyrralt standing behind him. He grimaced, but before he could tell his brother he wasn't welcome, Igraine answered, "I'd be pleased to have you both tour the grounds and meet Eadamm. Of those who have come to visit and to learn, there are always those who see beyond the obvious. I hope this time it will be you." Igraine bowed and left them standing there, wondering to which of them he had spoken.

"And me? I always see beyond the obvious, too," said a lovely voice behind them.

They turned to find Khallayne lounging against the sturdy elven chair at the head of the table. Her heavy, dark hair looked like coal against the crystal, and her black eyes glittered as if lit by candles.

* * * * *

The slave named Eadamm was unlike any human in Jyrbian's experience. He had never seen one who bore himself with such pride and audacity. He had none of the hunched look of a slave waiting for the next command. He stood tall, shoulders back, and his gaze met Jyrbian's squarely, without flinching.

"It's almost as if he doesn't consider himself a slave at all," Lyrralt murmured.

Jyrbian, who usually was offhand with slaves as long as they performed their tasks with a minimum of efficiency, found the slave's attitude unsettling. "A slave wearing decoration?" he questioned, pointing out the black-and-red stone wrapped in silver hanging from a silver chain on the slave's neck.

"It does seem a bit frivolous," Lyrralt agreed.

Despite his misgivings about the slave, Jyrbian was impressed with the quality and quantity of raw gems being processed from the mines. Igraine's fields, also, were thriving. What could this philosophy do for his father's estate?

He glanced speculatively at his brother, who had edged away and was standing near Everlyn, listening as the slave explained their mining procedures. He sounded unbearably pompous. Yet Everlyn was smiling at him as if his words were as fascinating as thoughts from the gods.

* * * * *

Later that evening, Jyrbian lay in bed and remembered the slave and the way he held Everlyn's attention. Jyrbian didn't seem to be able to coax more than a pleasant but detached smile from her.

He pulled the rope over the bed, which rang a bell in the kitchen. When the night slave entered his room hesitantly, minutes later, he was standing beside the window, naked, the moonlight shining on his magnificent skin.

* * * * *

Lyrralt, too, could not get the slave out of his mind. He could almost hear Igraine's persuasive words. "Think of it, Lyrralt, a choice. A true choice. Decide for yourself what is right or wrong. Good or bad."

In the privacy of the room he'd been given, he opened the vial of water, rinsed and spat, touched ears and eyes.

Worse even than Eadamm's face, the whispered words that none of the others had heard kept returning. When Igraine had seen that the sight of Eadamm and the happy, confident slaves had intrigued him, had puzzled him, Igraine had whispered, "Free will, Lyrralt, such as only the humans who live on the plains have. To choose even which gods you will worship!"

He banished the memory and prepared to pray, to meditate.

There was no warning. No buildup of itching and tingling. The searing agony branded his flesh, speared him with instant pain. He writhed on the cold stone floor and cried repeatedly the name of his god until it was over.

When sanity returned, and he could move his arm without torment, he sat up. It was several minutes before he dared look down at his arm. To his surprise, there was only one rune. Even with his novitiate's eye, he had no trouble reading the augury.

It had only one meaning: Doom.

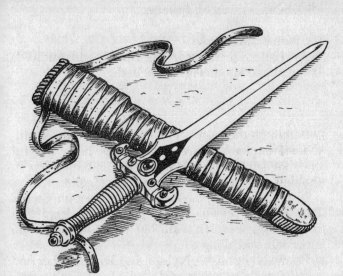

Chapter 6
Magic to Spill Men's Blood

On the morning they were to start for Takar, Khallayne slept late. In her dreams she found herself alone in Igraine's audience parlor. As she looked up at the constellations on the ceiling, they began to spin, moving faster and faster, until the pinpoints of brilliant light became magical threads, streams of silver, gushing across the sky. Her feet drifted upward.

The embroidery on her tunic, which depicted an inferno, ignited. She could taste the smoke, smell charred skin, singed hair. Then Jyrbian was at her side, and Lyrralt, and Briah, smiling as their faces melted, as their flesh dripped in globs onto the floor. And still the constellations swirled, visible through the flames and smoke.

And she, whirling in the flames, untouched, laughed and laughed and laughed.

*   *   *   *   *

Although the members were the same, the group that started back to Takar was not the noisy, playful one that had left three weeks before. Subdued, lost in thought, they rode the steep path single file.

Instead of taking the faster route, through Therax Pass, the way they had come, Jyrbian had decided to return by a western trail that wound around the mountain and along a high ridge.

Briah and her sister, Nylora, and Tenaj and her two cousins rode together and spoke in low whispers. Jyrbian, Khallayne, and Lyrralt rode apart, alone with their thoughts.

The roar of rushing water drew them forward and upward. The sound at the beginning of the steep trail was just a distant hissing, but it grew louder and louder as the trail leveled and foliage thinned, becoming scrubby plants and tufts of grass.

Right beside the waterfall, the sound grew deafening. The rushing water threw a rainbow of spray into the air, then fell away into the valley, a silver ribbon snaking its way through the fields. Stands of green-and-gold grain rippled gently in the breeze.

Khallayne, riding in the middle of the group, reined in her horse and sat staring at the magnificent view before her. One corner of the fields, all Igraine's land, was bisected by the river. Farther to the north-west, out of sight, was the manor, and even farther were the mines.

She had been to the mines, riding with Igraine. There had been no special magic at work there, just the usual activities of slaves, the starting of cook fires, the wielding of common tools, jewels laboriously dredged up from the bowels of the earth. Those were mostly mundane tasks, which was disappointing, but the things Igraine had begun teaching her, spells of higher cunning than anything she'd stolen from humans, unusual wards of defense, were special. And there would be more. Just as soon as she could, she would make arrangements to return.

"What do you think of it?" Jyrbian stopped beside her, interrupting her daydreams.

"It's breathtaking."

"I didn't mean the view," he said acidly. "I meant Igraine and his ideas."

"I don't know. It's . . . They're . . . " She was stalling. She knew exactly how she felt. Igraine's ideas were at best dangerous, at worst treason.

Lyrralt stopped beside them. "What if everyone decided to act in this fashion? What would happen, Khallayne? Our world is built on order. To each, his place. To everything, its reason. What will it mean if everyone chooses to behave anyway he or she pleases?"

"For myself, I think I like the idea of choice." Jyrbian nudged his horse on. He would prefer to be alone with his thoughts of Everlyn; he intended to ask for her when Teragrym offered him a reward for his services.

"You don't know what you're saying!" Lyrralt snapped.

"Yes, I do." Jyrbian reined in. "And I know what I would choose for myself."

"You mean *who*, don't you?" Khallayne asked.

"Women and sex!" Lyrralt snorted with disgust. "You think of nothing else!"

For a moment, Jyrbian stared at his brother with something like astonishment, then he shrugged and raised his eyebrows. "What else is there, Brother?" When Lyrralt didn't respond, Jyrbian shrugged and twisted his face comically, the old expression of cynicism returning to his eyes.

Khallayne didn't laugh. For just a moment, just before Lyrralt had broken the spell, the expression on Jyrbian's face had been something she'd never seen before. For just a moment, he was alien to her, a handsome stranger whose face shone with pure, sweet emotion, totally devoid of hunger and greed.

"Let's move on. I want to make time to stop at the Caves of the Gods," Lyrralt said, ending the conversation by turning his back on both of them and riding away.

The Caves of the Gods were one of most visited landmarks in the southern Khalkists, located at the highest point on the Therax Ridge, where three trailheads met.

From that wide, well-worn section of trail, travelers could head down along the north face of the ridge and continue deeper into the Khalkists, or go down along the south face to Takar, or even farther down the mountainside and out across the plains to where the eastern arm of the southern Khalkists wrapped the ancient city of Bloten in a protective curve.

The Caves of the Gods were little more than a squiggle of trails honeycombed in the mountain. But the caves had three entrances near the trailheads, and inside, the paths formed a circular maze, all interconnected, all leading eventually, some way or another, back to one of the three mouths. The mouth by which one exited, upper, middle or lower, foretold the answer of the gods to one's prayers.

It was from the mouth of truth, the mouth of success, that the attack came.

Lyrralt had walked far back into the cave, away from the soft voices of his companions, until all he could hear was the monotonous drip of water and his own soft footfalls in the dust. Travelers and pilgrims over the centuries had carved niches into the soft stone and left charms, talismans, icons as evidence of their passing.

Finding a place where cool air seemed to flow from the rock wall, Lyrralt had stuffed his torch into a sconce and stood, watching the light flicker on the stone and the gray smoke waft away into darkness.

It was then he heard the voices—the whispering, rumbling voices of many—of humans.

He hurried back the way he had come, shouting a warning. He turned the wrong way twice and had to backtrack. By the time he dashed into the midmorning light of outside, slaves were leaping from the upper mouth of the cave. Shrieking men and women streamed from the ridge.

Khallayne had been rubbing her horse with a bit of old blanket when the animal screamed in anger and pain as a rock struck its withers. It lashed out with its hind legs, sending her flying backward. As she landed on the soft clay embankment across from the caves and slid down, chaos exploded around her.

Howling humans leapt off the clay embankment above her and charged the party from the opposite

edge. Lying on her side, gasping for breath, Khallayne first felt an urge to laugh.

There were probably ten of the enemy, men and
women as ragged and tattered as the lowliest sewer
worker, so scrawny that their legs and arms looked
like sticks draped with dirty flesh. The weapons they
flourished were simple farm instruments, hoes and
rakes and shovels, makeshift pikes and crude clubs.

Across the path, Briah leapt astride her horse as
one of the slaves swiped at her, leaving bloody
gashes down the horse's shoulder and Briah's leg.
Khallayne's urge to laugh was stifled by disbelief
and a rush of fear.

As the ragtag army ran toward him, Jyrbian reached
back with both hands, drawing the sword he wore
strapped across his back. Standing nearby, Tenaj followed suit, leaping to Jyrbian's side.

The others in the party were trying to control their
mounts. The animals were kicking, bucking, wheel-
ing in circles. The pack of humans turned as one
toward the two who stood alone, Jyrbian and Tenaj.
The ring of steel made Jyrbian's heart sing as he met
his first attacker, an ugly, scarred male with a pointed
iron spear that might once have been part of a gate.
The sound was followed by a gurgle of death as Jyrbian easily parried the first thrust and slit the slave's
throat.

Lyrralt regained control of his mount, leapt astride
it and, drawing his mace, rode toward the clump of
slaves, slashing right and left.

Struggling to regain her composure as another
human leapt from the embankment above, Khallayne managed to kick out and trip the man. They
rolled, a tangle of arms and legs and heavy wooden

cudgel. Although smaller, the slave was strong from years of toil in Ogre mines. He managed to end up on top of her, but his first blow was clumsy. The club grazed Khallayne's temple.

She didn't allow him another chance. She yanked her dagger free with such force that she split the scabbard, then she plunged it into the man's ribs. The man's blood gushed over her hands and onto her belly, soaking her tunic. Bright red. Slippery. The salty scent of copper filled her nostrils. The human's face, looming above her, looked comically surprised, then life drained from his brown eyes and he slumped.

Shuddering, Khallayne pushed him away and crawled to her feet. The fighting was all around her, the clang of sword against metal, the war cries of the attacking humans, the neighing of an injured horse, the scent of blood and the sour sweat of human slaves. Human fear.

Lyrralt, no longer astride his horse, was conspicuous in the melee, swinging his mace in wild, whistling arcs. He was doing little real damage, but holding back the attackers.

Jyrbian and Tenaj stood back-to-back. Nylora, Briah, and the two cousins also fought with their backs together. All wielded swords stained with blood. The ground was littered with the bodies of humans who had stupidly ventured within range of their practiced blades. The remaining slaves were ranging and scuffling about the two groups, threatening.

"Khallayne, do something!" Lyrralt shouted, gesturing toward the embankment above the caves. At least ten more humans could be seen approaching, thrashing their way through the scrub and trees.

She knew what he was asking, but it would mean

exposing herself . . . The others would realize her power. And would die knowing anyway, if they were outnumbered.

Something boiled inside her. Something bubbled with excitement.

One of the humans stabbed, and Briah jumped to block him. Her wounded leg refused to bear her weight and, as she slipped, a woman slave swung her weapon with all her might.

Briah screamed and fell with the long spikes of a farm rake buried in her body. Trying to aid her sister, Nylora would have fallen also had one of the cousins not stepped in to close the gap and yank her back.

Breath coming in short, painful gasps, Khallayne gripped the bloody handle of her dagger. Fury, the flame of temptation, writhed inside her.

"Khallayne, now!" Lyrralt shouted, pointing toward the embankment with the tip of his mace. At the last moment, he lashed out viciously with it and gutted a slave rushing toward him.

Despite her fear of being exposed, she shivered in anticipation. The squirming inside was a thrumming in her blood, a music pulsing in her veins. Pleasure, almost carnal, slithered across her skin. She spoke the words that leapt into her throat and flung her hands out.

Lyrralt's attackers burst into flame, so suddenly that the two humans had no time to scream. Lyrralt was almost engulfed. His mace was scorched, but then he managed to jump backward and roll away from the flame licking at his hands and arms.

Khallayne saw Lyrralt only dimly through a wall of rushing wind. Her vision clouded by blood and smoke, she flung out her hands and spoke the words again. The incantation seared her throat.

The slaves who had started to scramble down the embankment were thrown back by a wall of fire.

Vision and hearing still impaired, Khallayne threw out her hands again, this time sending a fireball slamming into the embankment. Shards of gray rock and red clay went flying. Another spell was bubbling in her throat when something barreled into her and knocked her down.

She scrabbled for her dagger, sensing the handle against her palm through a haze of fury. She came up fighting, the words to another spell forming on her lips, bare fists striking out, only to realize the person she was hitting was Jyrbian. What she had heard through the roaring in her ears was his voice shouting her name.

She collapsed into his arms, gasping and spent, but also exhilarated.

Jyrbian supported her in the crook of one arm, his sword at the ready, but the few slaves left alive had fled. "Whatever you did," he said, his voice husky with admiration, "it worked."

She said nothing, simply looked up and met Lyrralt's gaze as he came over to them.

"Are you harmed?" Lyrralt asked.

She managed to shake her head and push herself away from Jyrbian.

Blood was running off the bodies of the dead, pooling on the hard ground. The woods at the edge of the clay bank were charred, little trickles of fire still licking the dry leaves. Above the caves there were three lumps of charred black that vaguely resembled human forms.

The only sound came from Nylora, who had knelt

beside Briah's body and was moaning. She touched her sister's lifeless body at the forehead and throat and wrist, desperate to find some sign of life.

It was obvious to the others that there was none. A row of neat punctures, encircled with blood, ran diagonally across Briah's chest.

Nylora looked up and saw Lyrralt. "Heal her," she pleaded. She paused and touched the hole over Briah's heart. Her fingers came away red and sticky.

"I can't," Khallayne heard him whisper as he went over to Nylora.

"You saved Khallayne," she accused Lyrralt.

One of the cousins leaned over and caught Nylora's arm to pull her up, but she resisted. "You saved Khallayne! I saw what she did. I saw her use magic!" she screamed. "If you don't heal Briah, I'll tell everyone!"

Lyrralt dropped to his knees in front of Nylora and grasped her bloody hands. "I can't," he said with anguish. "The gods have not yet granted me such power."

She jerked away from his grip, moaning, "This is what comes of Igraine's free will."

"These weren't Igraine's slaves," Jyrbian said gently, holding out his hand to help her stand.

"What does it matter *whose* slaves they were?" She slapped his hand away and pointed at Jyrbian. "This is what comes of it!" She threw her short sword at him, but the weapon thunked onto the ground harmlessly.

Lyrralt looked around. There was blood all around him, on his hands and his clothes. He could taste it in the air. The rune on his arm throbbed. He had to struggle not to give in to the whisper "Doom," while they tried to console Nylora.

Lyrralt stared at Briah's body, his fingers clasped over his left shoulder. Khallayne gazed only at the scorched earth across the path.

Jyrbian took charge. Only Tenaj was unaffected, alert and aware of the possibility of further danger.

"We need to round up the horses," he told her. "The slaves may have run, but that doesn't mean they won't come back."

Briah's horse had been killed, and the others had disappeared into the forest. With a curt nod, Tenaj strode off, calling for Khallayne to help.

Once found, the horses were nervous; precious time was spent calming them, while Jyrbian grew more agitated, sure that the group would be attacked again.

"I'll put Briah's body behind me," Tenaj said.

Jyrbian shook his head. "No. I want the strongest fighters mounted separately, in case we're attacked again."

Soon they had checked each mount for injuries and were ready to move. Eyes tearstained, Nylora took up Briah's sword and the heavy rings from her sister's fingers and climbed to her feet. "It's Igraine's fault. It's his fault Briah is dead. And when we get home, I'm going to make sure everyone knows what he's doing! I'll make sure everyone knows everything!"

Khallayne, her expression stiff, mounted without bothering to glance at the hysterical Ogre.

Chapter 7

If This Be Treason

A gong pealed, sonorous and stately, and five doors opened simultaneously onto the raised platform of the chamber of the Ruling Council. Five council scribes, stiff and formal with importance, entered onto the platform, carrying their writing trays before them.

The audience, seated in semicircular rows ranging from the foot of the platform to the back of the room, placed their right hands over their left on the floor and bowed low over them. The most important families, or their representatives, were seated in the front, with the ranking members kneeling beside the center aisle.

The room was full, the back rows crowded, as it had been since the Keeper had died the week before. Each morning, as many Ogres as possible crowded into the chamber, hoping to hear an announcement about the History.

The scribes took up places behind the low tables of the council, but remained standing.

After another sounding of the gong, four of the five members of the Ruling Council—Teragrym, Enna, Narran and Rendrad—entered from opposite doors and took their places at the long, low tables, leaving the center seat open.

A moment later, the final member, Anel, entered from the center door and joined them. Her family held the king in traditional safekeeping and, therefore, she was the leader of the council.

As a group, the five members sank to the soft linen cushions that protected their knees from the floor. Their elaborate robes fanned out in circles of bright color about their bodies, silver embroidered with white, palest yellow, bird's-egg blue, a dark burnt umber the color of plowed earth, and, in the center, the leader, in a plain, unadorned red the color of rubies.

"Who is the first petitioner?" Anel began the council's official business with the ritual question.

"I am, Lady."

A soft gasp went up from the audience. The speaker was not an aide, but Lord Narran himself. "I bring a matter of government security before the council, and I ask that the chamber be cleared."

Again a sound went through the audience, a barely voiced groan of disappointment. The council frequently met behind closed doors, but normally not on an audience day. However, the audience rose to go, filling the room with the sound of rustling cloth.

When they were alone, even the scribes gone, and all the doors closed, Anel turned to Narran. "What, my lord, is so important as to warrant that kind of drama?"

"This morning, I was given information which I feel we must act upon immediately, Lady."

Anel dipped her head slightly, granting permission for him to continue.

"Is it about the History?" Rendrad asked.

Narran shook his head. "No, it's more serious than even that. I believe Igraine, governor of Khal-Theraxian, is responsible for the slave uprisings that have troubled us of late."

Enna half rose from her cushion. Though Igraine had been appointed governor by the whole council, Khal-Theraxian was in her domain. Her own winter home was in the province, not far from Igraine's estate, and she was supplied with a healthy percentage of the levies. "Narran, you go too far! I know you've been jealous of Igraine's improved production, but—"

Narran, too, rose, his yellowish green complexion growing dark. "I do not—"

"Enough." Anel cut through both their angry voices with just the one softly spoken word. When they had both subsided, she spoke to Narran. "Have you evidence to back this claim?"

"I have details of what he's been doing. Once you've heard, I believe you will agree that he is committing both treason and heresy."

Enna clenched a fist on top of the smooth parchment that lined her table. "Heresy, Narran? Surely not!"

"Heresy," Narran repeated firmly.

Anel sighed. "Then we must hear your details. If you're right, we will send for Igraine." She gave Enna a reassuring look. "He will be given an opportunity to explain himself.

* * * * *

"Lord Teragrym cannot see you now."

A young Ogre, wearing a tunic with the dragon logo of Teragrym's family, tried to usher Jyrbian out of the small, private waiting chamber. The setting was intimate, lush, the gray stone walls covered by rich hangings, a small, cheery fire crackling in the fireplace, its reflection dancing on the marble of the hearth. Beside the hearth was the stool on which Teragrym had sat in the audience chamber. It seemed like months ago, instead of only four weeks.

Jyrbian brushed at his soiled tunic, at the bloodstains on his sleeves, and wished he'd taken the time to change before reporting to Teragrym. But the closer the group had come on their trek back to Takar, the more urgency he'd felt. Too many people knew what was going on, and Teragrym wasn't going to reward him for information he might pick up in the dining hall.

"Did you tell him how important it is that I see him?" he demanded of the Ogre, shaking free. "Did you tell him I've just come from Khal-Theraxian, and that we were attacked by a band of escaped slaves?"

Not to be brushed off so easily, the younger one smiled politely, bowed, and readjusted his grip on

Jyrbian's elbow. "Yes, of course, I did. But the lord is very busy. Perhaps tomorrow . . . "

Jyrbian gulped the glass of wine he'd snatched from a slave in the hallway on his way to Teragrym's quarters, not caring that he appeared mannerless. The smooth, sweet liquid soothed his dry throat, his agitation.

"I realize the lord is busy, but I have news that I must pass on! Information about Governor Igraine—"

"Not today." The Ogre's pleasant voice disappeared, became as cold as stone. "Lord Teragrym has heard enough of that one."

"What do you mean?"

"Haven't you heard? The council has issued a warrant for the governor's arrest. He has been charged with heresy."

Jyrbian was so surprised that he allowed the aide to push him out the door. Khallayne was waiting in the hallway. Unlike him, she had bathed and changed clothes, her long black hair brushed to a high gloss. She wore a silk tunic and embroidered vestrobe.

She smiled politely, as if she barely knew him, and allowed Teragrym's aide to usher her through the door.

Fury welled up in him beyond his capacity. He could imagine Everlyn slipping through his fingers. His hopes for estate dashed. He threw the wine glass at the wall across from Teragrym's door. Shards rained down upon the floor.

Inside the chamber, Khallayne, pausing as she heard the glass burst, smiled.

"What was that?" Teragrym's aide asked.

"Jyrbian venting his frustration, I would imagine."

Teragrym didn't keep her waiting long.

As he entered, she placed her hands on the floor, palms up and open in the posture of supplication, and bowed low. Only when the lord's shadow had passed over her did she slowly sit up.

Teragrym was seated before her on the stool.

"Lord, I—"

"You have come from Khal-Theraxian," he interrupted.

She hesitated, stammered. For the whole trip back, she'd rehearsed what she would say to him. She wanted what he could teach her, more than ever. She needed his sponsorship more than ever.

The words had been rehearsed over and over again in her head even before she'd seen the bone-white ribbons on the city gates, the funeral colors for the Keeper.

Now she had to struggle to find her voice. "Y—yes. I've b—been to Khal-Theraxian." She struggled to regain her composure. "Some friends were visiting, and I went along. I'm sorry, Lord. Should I have informed you?"

"Tell me what you saw there."

"What I saw—? I don't understand. We saw the estate and the mines. Governor Igraine's—"

"Do not test my patience!" Teragrym snapped. "I believe you know what I mean. What did you see of Igraine's behavior? Was there anything you would deem treasonous?" He hesitated, drawing that last word out, almost as if he expected to trap her.

"Treason—" The word choked her, got lost in the quickening of her breath. "My lord, I . . . " An image of Igraine flashed through her mind, of him in the darkness saying, "Perhaps someday you will be in a position to benefit me." But if she lied to Teragrym and was discovered . . . "I—"

"Did you or did you not discern any treasonous activity?"

"My lord, forgive me. You've startled me with so strong a word. We saw . . . I saw Igraine and his holdings. And I met his family. And he showed us his new methods for increasing production among his slaves."

"And did these methods strike you as treasonous?"

She made her choice. Her allegiance had to go to Igraine. She took a deep breath. "No." The word was out of her mouth before she realized it, irretrievable.

Teragrym nodded, his expression unreadable.

"Lord, about the test. I have something for your consideration."

"Test?"

"You said if I could prove myself worthy, you would consider taking me into your household."

"I could not possibly concern myself with that now." Teragrym stood. "I'm sure you understand. I have simply too much to attend to, with all this going on about Igraine."

"Going on?" She looked at him, stunned, disbelieving. Not interested in the test? How could he say he was not interested?

"Yes. Igraine has been charged with treason and heresy. An envoy and guards have been sent to arrest him and bring him before the council. But surely everything will turn out fine, since you've been to his estate and seen nothing extraordinary."

* * * * *

"Captain." The envoy of the Ruling Council stood on the slope behind the tree cover, but where he could see Khalever, the estate of the governor of Khal-Theraxian. A blanket was draped over his uniform to keep out the dewy chill of the morning.

Not many weeks to go and fall would turn to winter. Already some of the higher mountain passes were impassable. Even at this lower altitude, the mornings and the evenings had grown cold.

There were five guards accompanying him, one from each council member, just enough for protection from the dangers of the trail. Even those five had been hotly debated among the council, with Enna arguing that they could simply send a summons to Igraine. In the end, Narran's report had swayed them. The envoy was glad for the protection.

The captain of the guards strode over to him, carrying two cups of steaming tea. She needed no blanket, for the guards had winter uniforms with heavy cloaks.

He accepted the tea gratefully and wrapped his cold fingers around the metal cup before sipping. "I think it would be better if you remained out of sight and allowed me to go in alone. After all, Igraine is the governor. We should allow him the dignity of obeying without coercion."

The captain, a female Ogre who was half a hand taller than the envoy, shrugged. "This is your mission." She said it as if she didn't envy him a bit.

She took the cup back and walked with the envoy to his horse, then stood watching as he rode away into the woods. The sun was visible on the horizon when she spotted him emerging from the woods and heading toward the long drive that led to Igraine's home.

She went back to her troops, to check that they were faring well after another hard night on the trail. Like her, they were unaccustomed to nights spent in the wild, in the cold, but she was proud of the way they had adapted.

It was late afternoon when one of the sentries came running to her and announced that he had seen the envoy returning along the same road from the house.

"Was Igraine with him?" she asked.

"He was alone, Captain," the young one said breathlessly. "But I'm sure it was him. I recognized his horse."

Sometime later, the horse trotted up the trail with the envoy tied to the saddle, his head slumped backward at an impossible angle. The insignia of the Ruling Council had been ripped from the breast of his uniform.

It took the council guard only four days to make the trip back to Takar. They arrived, exhausted, barely able to sit their horses, and went straight to the council.

A second envoy was dispatched, with a guard of ten with instructions by Narran to take Igraine prisoner. A flurry of arrows took the guard by surprise before they ever left the woods on the border of the estate. One of the first lodged between the eyes of the envoy.

The guard was well trained, fearless, but with no enemy in sight, they had no way to fight. Only six returned to Takar.

Khallayne had spent the days waiting, cautioning

herself to be patient. A week after their return, she
sent a carefully worded note to Teragrym, hinting
that she might be able to break the impasse, but there
had been no response.

Though they had grown friendlier after the slave
attack in the forest, Lyrralt had again ceased speaking to her. He had learned of her visit to Teragrym
from Jyrbian, and accused her of trying to bypass
him, deny him his proper reward.

Jyrbian was surly and unapproachable, speaking
to no one.

So Khallayne played at board and card games
with acquaintances, and wished the whole charade
were over so she could return to Khal-Theraxian and
pick up her studies.

Anxious to get out of the castle, she enthusiasti-
cally joined the majority of the courtiers to attend
one of the last slave races of the season. The day
dawned bright and sunny and unseasonably warm.
Half the city had turned out for the event.

The huge oval stadium was filled with laughing,
cavorting Ogres. The sound of so many packed into
one place was as deafening as the sight of them,
brightly bedecked in all the colors of the rainbow,
was blinding.

Normally, Khallayne would have an invitation
from someone with good seats, but she hadn't
wanted to have to be charming and brilliant, so she
had come alone, choosing to sit in her uncle's reserved area. Though her mother's brother had
bought her place at court, she avoided contact with
the family as much as possible. She hoped her presence would not remind him of the debt.

The horn sounded the first event, and she leaned

forward with the crowd to see the runners bolt out of their blocks. But today the runners appeared lackluster and apathetic. They showed little speed and loped along, obviously not interested in competing with each other.

"Obviously, their trainers didn't adequately explain the inducements," observed the Ogre sitting next to her, a distant cousin in the city for a visit.

Bored, Khallayne fanned herself. "How hard could it be to make them understand?" she responded. "Run or die. Win and live. It's probably just because it's the end of the season. The slaves are always tired toward the last."

The Ogre grunted and sat forward again as the second race was announced.

Khallayne didn't strain to watch.

The second contest was as dull as the first. There was no rivalry. As the slaves crossed the finish line almost side by side, their trainers stepped out of the staging area to acknowledge the crowd. The boos changed to a roar of approval as they saw that the trainers carried whips.

Now Khallayne did ease forward, as the humans were led back from the track toward the posts in the center of the stadium. She felt the surge of excitement that rippled through the spectators. The first crack of whip against flesh was like music, a song of pain which an Ogre could not hear without responding.

Khallayne closed her eyes, then opened them again in surprise as a roar went up from the crowd at the far end of the stadium. Whatever was happening nearest the city gate was obviously more exciting than any slave whipping.

It took only a few moments for news to reach her. Igraine was being brought into the city, to stand before the council.

By the time she understood, the crowd was already pushing toward the high end of the stadium overlooking the main street. She made it to the far aisle and went down the wide steps toward the floor of the stadium. In the dark tunnels that led out to the street, she found almost as much of a melee as above. She wasn't the only one who'd thought to go out on the street for a look.

She pushed her way through the crowd, ignoring the protests as she shoved and jostled and was jostled in turn. She used a little of her magic, giving one a poke here, another a prod of there, discreet but enough to move people out of her way.

She emerged onto the street, into light that blinded her as well as the milling crowd. Igraine's procession was already past. She hesitated, wandering about on the wide walkway beside the street, loathe to head back inside. In doing so, she learned something she would never have guessed had she not been among a crowd of merchants and commoners.

Not everyone, it seemed, supported the council's decision to question Igraine. It was a revelation to her, for she had been raised never to question the rulings of the leaders. How naive she'd been to think she was the only one who supported Igraine!

She collected her horse and started back for the castle immediately. In the stables and yard, even in the hallways, there was almost as much of an uproar as there had been at the stadium. It took only a little detective work to discover that Igraine was being housed as a "guest" in Enna's wing, and just a small bribe allowed her to slip down a small hallway and into the suite of rooms assigned as his quarters.

Igraine was seated before a roaring fire, his hands and booted feet stretched toward the flames. He looked up as she slipped through the door and smiled sadly. "I'd forgotten how drafty the castle can be."

The room had the chill feeling and damp smell of having been unoccupied for a long time. The furnishings were as lavish as anything to be found in the castle, the huge bed piled with blankets, covered trays of food standing on a side table, but still it evoked visions of a cell.

"You shouldn't have come, Khallayne." Igraine stood and accepted her quick bow with an incline of his head.

"I had to come. I had to . . . "

"You had to what, child?" He came forward, caught her cold fingers, and drew her closer to the fire.

"I don't know," she admitted, surprised that she really didn't know why. "I want you to know I told one of the council members that I didn't see anything I regarded as treasonous."

"Thank you." He patted her hand. "It's not treason to try to increase production in one of the state's provinces. It's not treason to try to save your people."

"Then why did you kill the messengers?"

"I didn't." He dropped heavily back into the chair. "My slaves did, with the permission of some of my family. I didn't know until the third one came."

She breathed a sigh of relief. "Then it'll be all right. All you have to do is tell them, and—"

The sadness on his face deepened. "You have understood nothing, have you? Nothing of all that I told you those days in Khal-Theraxian."

Of course, she had, but . . .

"I can't sacrifice my slaves to save myself! If I do, then what I believe is as nothing!"

"But they're only slaves. You can always get more."

Igraine erupted from his chair, his face contorted, and she saw for the first time since she'd met him the strong and terrible Governor of Khal-Theraxian, whose province was the most trouble free in all the mountains.

"The slaves are the innocents in this, despite their killing!" As quickly as it had come, Igraine's temper waned and his sadness returned. Suddenly he looked very old.

"Khallayne, don't you see what our world is becoming? Don't you see that if we don't make changes now, we're doomed?"

He held out his hand for her to come closer. "Our civilization was once vital and innovative. Our citizens were warriors and thieves. We took the best from over the whole continent. Now we do almost nothing for ourselves. Our warriors have grown soft and useless, our people decadent. Our cruelty insists on the suffering of others."

Khallayne dropped to her knees before him, mesmerized by the power of his voice, hypnotized by the sweet reason of his words.

* * * * *

"Igraine, Governor of Khal-Theraxian, you have been charged with treason and heresy, with endangering the lives of your neighbors and friends by inciting the slaves to insurrection."

Khallayne kneeled as before in Igraine's room, only this time, she was squeezed in between Jyrbian and an Ogre female she didn't know. And Igraine was pleading his case before the council.

"It is not treasonous for me to increase the production of my holdings tenfold," he argued. "It is not heretical to treat my slaves with kindness if they work twice as hard."

"And this is the philosophy of 'choice' you espouse?" Narran prompted. "What you call 'free will'?"

"We have grown hard in our ways," Igraine responded, loudly and proudly enough that no one doubted his belief in his words. "We are selfish while espousing order and obedience. Enslaved by our needs. In doing so, we have grown cold and hollow. We decay day by day, and the ugliness that fills begins to show outside."

The audience gasped. Some hissed softly between their teeth, but that didn't stop him.

"It is time we decided for ourselves who we will be and what will be our destiny. We are the firstborn of the gods, the brightest, the best. The most beautiful. Is it not time we lived up to our potential?"

Khallayne shifted imperceptibly. The heat was stifling, the scent of perfumes and bodies thick. She longed for fresh air, a clear head.

Igraine's words, which had seemed so reasonable the day before, in the bald light of a council hearing bore a tinge of the lunatic. Even so, as she looked around, she could see that not all of the others thought him mad. A few, a very few, were gazing at him as she had the day before, enthralled by the power of his voice.

Igraine ended his impassioned speech by turning his back on the council and opening his arms as if he would embrace the whole audience. "I'm sure there are many who agree with me, who believe as I do. Join me. Show your council that we mean no harm."

Khallayne's breath caught in her throat. Several of Igraine's neighbors and family were in the audience, and they stood, joining him before the council.

Igraine's eyes swept the room, urging more to come forward, lingered on her. His scrutiny reminded her of the pain of Lyrralt's healing.

Her muscles tensed, wavering. Just as she started to rise, Jyrbian placed his hand on her forearm. It appeared an innocent gesture, but his fingers bore the weight of his body.

"I think it's going to go very badly for him," Jyrbian whispered, leaning very close, his lips barely moving. "And very badly for any who can't distance themselves from him."

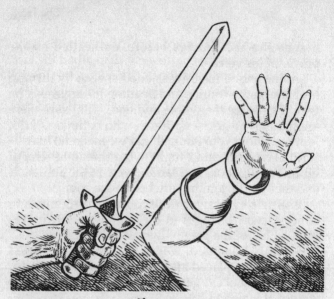

Chapter 8

With Dangers Compassed Round

Khallayne tiptoed into her place a few moments before the judgment was to begin. She craned her neck and peered down the aisle toward the front of the audience hall, where families knelt near the throne platform.

Only the families and allies of the Ruling Council were allowed to kneel in the presence of the king. The rest stood in rows, ranked by order of their importance and heritage. As she did, others in the depths of the audience hall shifted from foot to foot and craned for a glimpse of their sovereign.

That the king was putting in a rare appearance was probably not a good sign for Igraine, she reflected.

The huge chamber looked very different in the light of day, in the midst of controversy, than it had the last time Khallayne had been there. The ceiling was lost in shadow and without the sparkle of candlelight; the walls were once again cold granite that reflected the slightest whisper or scuff of boot.

There was no singing of the History. Khallayne felt a pang of remorse. How odd to begin an official function without the reminder of whence they had come.

Teragrym was still refusing her attempts to see him. Even Lyrralt had relented and talked with her about it. She craned farther out into the aisle, hoping to catch a glimpse of Lyrralt, but she wasn't sure where he was standing.

Her remorse was not enough to make her come forward with the crystallized Song. All Ogres knew the words by heart from hearing it since birth, but the weaving of the intricate melodies, the layer upon layer of meaning, the subtle tonal changes from word to word, sometimes syllable to syllable, were not so easily repeated. Those were locked in the sphere.

The call to come forth and be heard opened the trial.

A stir went through the crowd as the huge doors at the back of the hall opened and the procession began, first clerks and underlings, then lesser nobles. Finally, after a long pause, came the Ruling Council, its members resplendent in their brightly colored tunics, each followed by a standard bearer. Then, after another wait, the king entered, flanked by standard and staff bearers, followed by the largest and most finely attired retinue.

When all had made their way slowly to the throne platform and taken their places, the Noble at Arms advanced with much ceremony up the stairs and bowed to the king.

Khallayne shifted from foot to foot, wishing they would hurry. The floor was cold and bumpy through the soles of her thin dress slippers.

The noble, a thin but broad-shouldered female whose face was lined with age, rapped the steel-capped butt of her staff on the floor three times. "Lord Igraine, Governor of Khal-Theraxian, appear and face your judgment," she sang out in a booming voice.

Khallayne took a deep breath and eased back into her place, shrinking from view. Suddenly, she wished she had not come. Attendance was mandatory, but surely no one would have missed her.

After another long wait, Igraine came slowly down the aisle, his head held high and proud. A gasp went through the room as everyone saw that he didn't walk alone, as those charged with serious crimes normally did. Following him, dressed in their finest, were representatives of the branches of his family, heads of the clans of his neighbors, even some who were from provinces far removed.

Across the aisle and closer to the front of the chamber, she spied Jyrbian pushing through his kinspeople to the aisle. They, like she was, were so shocked at the size of the group behind Igraine that they ignored the abominable behavior.

Khallayne heard the drone of the noble's voice as she read out the formal charges and counter-charges. There were almost fifty Ogres standing with Igraine in an unprecedented show of support. Did they realize this wasn't a council meeting, where they might voice their opinion? The risk of yesterday, of being tainted by association with Igraine, was nothing compared with this public display. If he was found guilty of treason and heresy, by standing with him they would share his sentence also!

She searched the crowd again for Lyrralt. He was nowhere in sight, but Jyrbian still hovered at the edge of the aisle, staring in open-mouthed awe at the backs of Igraine's supporters. As if feeling her gaze, he glanced around at her. Seeing disapproval in the curve of her brows, her lips, he shrugged, raising his palms slightly.

Would this save her from suspicion, this ostentatious display of favor on the part of so many?

The verdict was read by one of the clerks of the council in a voice too low to carry, but his words were picked up in the front and echoed to the back of the chamber, even before the noble could proclaim them.

The judgment.

"Insane . . . "

"Heresy . . . "

"Guilty . . . "

"Guilty . . . "

"Guilty . . . "

Voices rose and fell in shock, in glee and dismay.

Khallayne's head snapped back. She lost her footing momentarily as if the whispers had been a slap at her. Guilty! Guilty! Guilty!

What would happen now?

* * * * *

Fire. Red. Burning. A face loomed before her, twisted and leering, fleshly gnarled with growths, eyes dull and mad. A hand, fingers twisted like stunted twigs, grabbed her shoulder.

Khallayne opened her mouth to scream.

"Khallayne, wake up!"

The dream stopped, shattered into reality. She bit back a cry as she woke to darkness and the scent of Jyrbian. He was leaning over her bed, shaking her awake. With only the barest illumination from the coals in the fireplace, she couldn't see his face, but tension was evident in his voice, in the way his fingers gripped her shoulder.

"Wake up!"

She pushed his hand away, sat up. "What is it? What's wrong?"

"We have to go. Get dressed." He yanked the blankets, barely sparing a glance for her nudity.

She rose quickly and reached for a robe.

"No. Get dressed for traveling. Sturdy clothes, good boots." Jyrbian crossed to her wardrobe and rifled through the items hanging there.

She quickly donned her undergarments, choosing to layer fine silk next to her skin despite his instructions and pulling sturdier linen over that.

Jyrbian tossed things from the closet, sturdy riding pants, a long-sleeved blouse and tunic, a cloak.

"What's happened?" she asked as she donned the clothing.

"Two of Igraine's followers are dead. Officially, while trying to escape during questioning. Unofficially, under the knife of one of the council's interrogators."

"Interrogators?"

"Torturers. They were tortured to death. Executed for their support of Igraine."

Khallayne froze, her fingers tangled in the lacings

of her high riding boots. Tortured. Executed. Suddenly, her fingers found a life of their own, moving swiftly to complete their task. "Where are we going?" she breathed.

"Igraine's people are helping him escape tonight. You're going north with them."

"I don't understand."

"Igraine's people—"

"But why do *we* have to go?" she interrupted. "We didn't stand up with him."

"Lyrralt has seen a list of suspected supporters. Your name is on it. And mine."

She stomped her feet on the floor, as much in frustration and anger as to settle the boots into a comfortable fit. "Where north?"

"Perhaps to Thorad. Or Sancron. Perhaps we'll have to build our own city." His voice was excited.

North. She nodded, swallowing her dread. She had lived her whole life to advance her magic. Now . . . there was no help for it.

"My travel packs are here." She threw the contents of a heavily carved wooden chest onto the floor and tossed a heavy leather saddlebag toward Jyrbian.

He grabbed up the leather pack. "Do you have winter traveling gear? It'll be cold in the northern passes."

"There." She pointed to another chest, under the window. While Jyrbian was occupied stuffing woolen pants and her heavy winter cape into the bags, she packed her hairbrush, perfumes, a few pieces of jewelry, and the one human spellbook she'd never gotten around to destroying. It was very old, the spells very basic, but the bindings, the handwriting, were so beautiful, she'd never burned it.

Jyrbian, the heavily stuffed saddlebags thrown over his shoulder, caught her hand as she slipped the book into the bag. He tilted her wrist until the bare light from the fireplace illuminated the dark red binding, reflected silver highlights off the embossed runes. "Will you teach me?" he asked softly.

Khallayne was astonished by the awe, the hunger in his voice. She started to deny him for all the old reasons, then realized suddenly that now she could do as she pleased. "Why not?"

Jyrbian joined his laughter with hers and, holding her hand, pulled her into the dark corridor. Together they ran lightly toward the stables.

There were others, dark figures who joined them, as they emerged from the building, who slipped from shadow to shadow without making a sound, following Jyrbian's lead.

In the stable and at the southern gate, the bloodied bodies of Ogre guards lay on the ground, their throats cut or the feathered tails of arrows protruding from their bodies. Not one had drawn a weapon. They had all died unaware, without sounding an alarm.

As she and the others galloped out of the courtyard, Khallayne glanced back at the fallen bodies. There was no turning back for any of them.

They rode quickly through the sleeping neighborhoods, taking the side streets and alleys that ran behind the grand homes. Their horses' hooves were muffled with cloth; their identities so obscured by folds of cloak and cape that Khallayne recognized only Tenaj, and her only because of the half-wild stallion that no one else could ride.

Near the trading district, they stopped. Jyrbian

and two others dismounted and quickly snipped the twine that held the cloth on the horses' feet. Following whispered instructions, the group broke off in smaller parties of two and three.

In the nighttime hustle and bustle of the warehouses and taverns, they were barely noticed. Riding between Jyrbian and someone she didn't know, Khallayne kept her hand on her dagger, waiting with tensed muscles for obstacle or interference.

When the alarm flare of the castle whined overhead, it was no surprise. She glanced back over her shoulder and saw the white rush of sparks and fire shoot into the sky over the castle.

Then there was no time left for fear or contemplation. She heard Jyrbian hiss, "Ride!" and she kicked her horse into a run.

Her heart lurched as the animal's hooves slipped on the cobbled street. For a moment, she thought he would go down, then he caught his balance and sped after Jyrbian's stallion. They were heading for the southern gate—the same one the group had used only weeks ago on their trip to Khal-Theraxian.

Hadn't Jyrbian said they would be going north? But behind her she could hear the pounding of hooves as others followed Jyrbian's lead. She let the horse have its head and hoped that Jyrbian knew what he was doing.

Despite the danger of riding so hard in the darkness, they passed the dark stadium, the city gate, without incident. At least now if she fell, it would mean a mouth full of dirt, not that her head would crack open like an egg on the uneven, cobbled streets.

Where the road narrowed and forked up into the

forest, the group of about fifteen stopped, milling about in confusion. She found Lyrralt and Jyrbian arguing with Tenaj and a woman she didn't know.

"—north," Tenaj was saying. "To join up with the others. Won't they expect us to return to Khal-Theraxian?"

"That's the first place they'll send troops," the woman agreed.

"I'm going back to Khal-Theraxian," Jyrbian said, so quietly and with such resolve that it was obvious his mind couldn't be swayed. "But I agree you should head north. All I'm saying is that you should fork back through the forest to the high road. The first thing they'll do is cover all the city gates. And if you cut back around the wall to head north, you'll have to pass the eastern gate."

Lyrralt nodded in agreement. "He's right."

"But can we get through the forest?" Khallayne asked.

"I know a hunting trail," Tenaj said.

Without further argument, they turned south, up into the mountains. They rode hard without pause. Khallayne's horse labored under her, his sides heaving as he climbed the steep trail.

Finally, they reached an intersection in the hunting trail, a mere widening of the distance between thick trees. In unspoken agreement, everyone halted and dismounted.

Khallayne could barely walk. She stumbled to the edge of the trail, sank down and stared up into the gray nothingness of the predawn sky. Someone passed her a waterskin. She gulped from it, water dripping from her chin.

Never in her life could she remember being so

tired, so drained. Slowly she became aware that most of her fellow travelers were equally exhausted, collapsed in tired heaps much as she was, where they had dismounted.

Only Jyrbian and Tenaj were active, moving from horse to horse, running practiced hands over the animals, arguing as they went. Tenaj was trying to convince Jyrbian that he needed to continue on with them, over the ridge and north toward Thorad.

Her bones feeling as if the weight of the mountains were pressing down on them, Khallayne rose and went over to where Lyrralt sat, resting against the ruffled bark of a tree as if his neck would no longer support the weight of his head.

For the first time in weeks, he smiled at her without malice, handing over the skin that drooped from his fingers. It held sweet wine, much better than the tepid water she'd drunk minutes before.

"Why does Jyrbian insist on going to Igraine's estate?" she asked after she'd drunk deeply of the liquid, felt its strength and fire slide down into her throat.

"For a female. Why else?"

* * * * *

It was Everlyn herself, a voluminous shawl swathed over her nightdress, who answered Jyrbian's insistent banging on the door of Khalever. She opened the heavy, carved door barely a crack and stared fearfully out at him, past him to the group of five who sat, still mounted, near the steps.

He smiled at the sight of her. She was so tiny, so delicate, so beautiful. Then he realized, from the way her large eyes were stretched wide and round, that he frightened her by his appearance.

"My lady, forgive me." He sketched a sweeping bow, which, until that moment, he could not remember ever executing without some touch of sarcasm. "I've come on the word of your father, to take you to safety."

"My father!" Everlyn threw the door open wide. "Oh, please, is he safe?"

Jyrbian took in the group of humans and Ogres who huddled in the hallway behind her, their faces white and fearful. "Yes. He's being taken to safety in the north, even as we speak."

The deep silver of her eyes, which had heretofore been as sorrowful, as cold as granite, lit from within. The change was like a glorious sunrise, filling Jyrbian with warmth and light.

Her gladness just as quickly became confusion. "Taken to safety? I don't understand. He isn't coming home?"

Jyrbian started to explain, but the jingling of a bridle, the impatient stamp of a horse, reminded him of the urgency of his mission. "Lady . . . " He took her elbow and guided her back into the house. The hallway was still shadowed by early-morning dimness and cold. "Your father has been judged insane by the Ruling Council."

"Insane! For what?"

The voice was familiar, insolent. It grated on Jyrbian's nerves. He turned and saw Eadamm standing in the doorway of the audience chamber. The slave met his gaze squarely. Another handful of slaves, all dressed as though they worked in the house, stood behind him.

As if she sensed his irritation, Everlyn laid her hand on Jyrbian's arm and led him past Eadamm into the chamber. "Please, Jyrbian, what has happened to my father?"

It was easy to follow her sweet voice, to turn away from the ugly, strutting human and concentrate on her instead. He saw the warning glance she shot the slave. "The council judged him guilty of treason and heresy for his teachings."

Everlyn's deep-green complexion seemed waxy in the dim light. "Treason."

"Yes. But there were many who supported him, and they've fled north with him, to safety. I've come to take you along."

Everlyn's gaze drifted past Jyrbian, in the direction of the group of slaves. "Leave here?" she whispered.

"Everlyn, it's no longer safe here. This is the first place the king's soldiers will look for your father."

The group stared, first at him, then at each other, with slowly dawning comprehension. A female Ogre drifted toward the long windows and peered outside. When she turned back, she nodded grimly to the others. "He's right. We should go."

Only Everlyn wasn't sure. Jyrbian could read indecision in the set of her delicate shoulders, in the glossy dampness pooling at the corners of her eyes.

She crossed to the hearth and took down the bloodstone. Cradling it in her palms, she whispered, "But this is my home."

Before Jyrbian could respond, Eadamm said quietly, firmly, "The lord is right, Lady. You would not be safe. And think what they could do to your father if they held you hostage. He would do whatever they said, even if it meant walking to his death."

Aware of the minutes ticking away while they debated, Jyrbian bit back the harsh words he wanted to fling at the human. If the human could persuade Everlyn, he would allow those transgressions to pass unmentioned for the moment.

Still not convinced, she pressed the large rock to her breast. "They have no right . . . "

"They have every right," Jyrbian said. "This is your father's land by their grace."

"They will attack," Eadamm said. "And these people will die defending you." He gestured toward the gathered Ogres and slaves.

Tears spilled down her cheeks, but she nodded in agreement. "I'll go," she whispered. Still clutching the bloodstone, she motioned for two of the slaves to follow. "I'll get my things. Eadamm, will you come? I have instructions for the others. And we must dispatch messengers to alert our neighbors."

Once her decision was made, Everlyn and her family moved swiftly, efficiently, waking the rest of the household, feeding the children, packing clothing, tools, food, weapons.

By the time all were assembled in front of the manor, his small contingent of four had swelled to fourteen adults and three children, all well mounted. They were as orderly and disciplined as if they'd trained for this day all their lives.

Everlyn guided them around the house, choosing a path through the sea of grain, which she said would take them through the fields and set them much more quickly on the mountain path toward the caves.

As they rounded the back corner of the house, Jyrbian saw movement, frantic activity, in the area of the slave cabins. Women and children with packs of belongings on their backs were disappearing into the tall corn. Along other trails through the waving sea of gold, he saw the flash of morning sun on weapons. He straightened, rising up on his stirrups as he reached to draw his sword.

Everlyn stopped him by catching his reins. "There's no cause for alarm," she said. Something in her voice belied that, a little catch, a breathlessness.

"The slaves are escaping," he exclaimed. "Arming themselves!"

"Yes," she said, and this time the tone was fearful, as if she were a child, defiant and afraid before a parent. She looked back, sadness marring her beautiful face. "They will guard our escape. And as for running away . . . They may go where they wish. I have freed them."

"Freed them!" Dismay, astonishment, and indecision warred within him. It was already too late to turn back, round up the fleeing slaves. There were too many of them, too few Ogres, too little time to waste. Then, suddenly, he realized what she had done. All his emotions gave way to admiration. "By the gods," he told her, reaching out to squeeze her hand, "what a ploy! When the King's Regiment arrives here and finds the slaves have run, they won't even think of coming after us. That was brilliant!"

He spurred his horse and rode to the head of the line. Jyrbian's passage frightened a covey of birds. With raucous cries of protest, they burst from cover and zipped skyward, their brown wings beating in time to his pulse, sending a draft of warm air to caress his face. Glancing back to see that the others were following, he kicked his horse and sped off, imagining that, he, too, had taken wing.

They rode, a ribbon of colorful silks and wool winding through the golden field. Their passage stirred, above the wheat, a cloud of insects as thick as dust, opalescent wings awhir.

Through the fields and into open meadow they rode. Across a swath of river, the water a thin, silver scrim over a bed of white pebbles. Their passage sent up a noisy spray of droplets that sparkled like fire in the morning sun.

Everlyn kept up Jyrbian's pace, pointing out the path through the fields, the places where it was safe to veer off and cut through the meadows.

Up into the mountains they continued, under cover of thick evergreens and oaks, which blotted out the heat and the light. To Jyrbian, the transition from grassy meadow to the hard, packed earth was an assault to his ears. Surely the entire forest boomed with their presence. Once more he took the lead, pushing as fast as he dared on the steep mountain trail. He slowed as they approached the Caves of the Gods, and sent a scout ahead to make sure the area was clear. Finding that it was, he called a halt.

He was the first to touch his feet to the ground, leaping nimbly from the saddle so that he could help Everlyn dismount. She seemed pale and clung to his supportive arm for a moment as she stretched her legs.

"How are you faring, Lady?" He went quickly to his horse and brought back a full wineskin.

She sipped delicately and passed it back. "It's a hard ride."

All around them were groans and gasps, of both

pleasure and pain, as others dismounted. Only the children seemed unaffected, running about, laughing and shouting.

Everlyn's aunt grabbed an older child as they went past. "Care for your mounts first," she ordered angrily. "Then play."

The horses were lathered and still breathing hard. As Jyrbian, too, moved to water his stallion, to rub the animal down and feed him a handful of oats, he realized that the group with which he had begun the trip had doubled in size. There were many crowding into the open area before the cave entrances.

The size of the group had grown again by the time he called the next stop, and with each succeeding stop, until Jyrbian was leading a group easily one hundred strong.

Chapter 9

Battles Lost and Won

The added number didn't slow the group significantly. Two weeks later, at a crossroads high in the mountains to the north of Takar, Jyrbian caught up with the smaller group who'd left Takar with him. Three days later, he led them down into a small dip in the trail, where they joined with the group that had escaped with Igraine.

"I'm not sure where they all came from," Jyrbian said in amazement.

"They're from Khal-Theraxian. From estates that bordered mine," Igraine supplied, seeming not at all surprised at the size of his following. "They're from many districts. From anywhere that the Ogres wanted to embrace a new path."

Everlyn, holding the arm of her father as if she would never again let him go, looked around, spying faces she recognized. "There's Lord Nerrad from Bloten, and Lady Rychal. Her land borders ours on the east. And I think that's most of the Aliehs Clan . . . " She pointed toward a large crowd of mostly young Ogres who looked as if they were on a picnic instead of running for their lives.

Their picnic was interrupted as an Ogre, riding at breakneck speed, tore through their blankets, his horse scattering adults and children and food. The rider sawed viciously on his reins, trying to slow his horse; then the animal reared and stopped.

One of the Aliehs started toward the rider, his scowl evidence of his intentions, but the rider's words stopped him cold.

"King's troops!" He waved back toward the way he'd come. "Coming this way fast!"

"Damned idiot—!" Jyrbian started toward the Ogre, his next words drowned out by the reaction of the crowd, gasps and shouted questions, as they surged forward. A child began to cry, a high, rising wail that was picked up by other children. Jyrbian reached the Ogre and dragged him off his horse.

Another Ogre, almost Jyrbian's height, though not so muscular, reached the two of them and thrust out his hand. Jyrbian remembered seeing him among the crowd at Khalever when they had left the house. "What's the meaning of this?" Jyrbian snarled.

"I'm Butyr, Igraine's nephew," the Ogre told him, trying to catch hold of the newly arrived rider. Jyrbian refused to release his grip and turned, shaking the younger Ogre as he led him, practically on tiptoes, away from the thick of the crowd.

"I sent scouts down the west trail to follow behind us," Butyr said, joining the small circle of Igraine, Everlyn, Lyrralt, Tenaj, and two others Jyrbian didn't know, which quickly surrounded them. Finally Butyr managed to break Jyrbian's grasp on the rider. Jyrbian glared at him. Scouts were a good idea, one that he should have instigated.

Tenaj interrupted. "Did you also tell them to ride back into camp and start a panic?" she snapped.

Butyr's small eyes narrowed dangerously. "Of course I didn't!"

"You said there are troops?" Igraine broke in smoothly, turning to the scout.

The Ogre nodded. His face was pale. "Coming fast. Along our back trail, but they're moving as if they already know we're here."

Butyr shot Jyrbian a look of disgust, as if the situation was all his fault. "They probably had scouts out, too. How far behind are they?" asked Butyr.

"Thirty minutes. Maybe forty. I—I rode as fast as I could."

"How many?" demanded Tenaj.

"I couldn't tell. Fifty, seventy, maybe more. They were coming up the ridge, where the trail is narrow. They're riding two abreast, so I couldn't see the end of the line."

Butyr slapped the Ogre on the shoulder. "Well done, Eilec. You've given us time to set up a defense."

Butyr shouted out the names of several of his cousins, motioning them to come forward.

Jyrbian looked around wildly, trying to see past the milling crowd, to make out the lay of the land. They were in a low place where trails from all four points of the compass descended and crossed.

Butyr squatted and quickly sketched a U-shaped defense in the dirt. "We can send the families on. And disperse everyone who is well versed with sword here and here." He indicated points along the sides of the trail. "Our bowmen should be positioned here."

Jyrbian peered at the nearby crowd. Bowmen? From the way Butyr said it, he half expected to see a troop of smartly dressed fighters, instead of such a weary crowd of refugees. But, yes, he did recall seeing some of Igraine's people with bows slung across their backs. And rare was the Ogre who had not been taught as a child to use a bola for contests. It was considered a skill of the upper class, used to while away summer evenings.

So Butyr's plan had potential, except at this altitude. The forest wasn't dense; the thin, pale-barked trees offered little concealment. Jyrbian tried to remember the paths to the north and west. Didn't one of them climb, then level off, then climb again before it crested? He whispered to Tenaj, and she gazed first north, then west, remembering, then pointed north.

Igraine was nodding as he peered at Butyr's marks in the dirt. With a quick glance at Lyrralt, Jyrbian stepped forward. "The enemy will be attacking from the high ground," he said harshly. "We'll be slaughtered."

Everlyn's face paled. Jyrbian could see her fingers tighten on her father's arm.

Butyr rose slowly and faced Jyrbian, his eyes black with fury. "I suppose you want to ride away as fast as we can," he sneered.

Jyrbian drew himself up. He towered over the

smaller Ogre. Only his brother was as tall among the Ogres who stood listening.

"I only meant that we should withdraw along the north trail, where the ground levels out." Disdainfully, he erased Butyr's plan and drew a new one. "Then we can deploy those with bows here, where the king's troops will be riding uphill. And those with swords can wait behind, for any who are brave enough, or foolhardy enough, to make it through. Remember, the king's troops are mainly an honor guard, trained for ceremonial duties, carrying flags and the like."

"And I suppose you were trained to the sword, Lord Jyrbian," Butyr said.

Before Jyrbian could reply, Igraine stepped in. "It's a good plan, thanks to both of you," he said with heavy emphasis on both. "Everlyn, you get the others to help you start the children on ahead. Jyrbian, you go ahead and choose positions. Butyr will organize everyone into groups."

Jyrbian nodded his agreement and, with a quick bow to Everlyn, strode off.

Lyrralt went with him wordlessly, mounting and following him up the north trail. Jyrbian tossed him the reins and walked to the high point on the trail, looking back down to reconnoiter.

As they stood watching the long line of families and older Ogres go past, Jyrbian asked, "Where's Khallayne? I could use her, there on that rise."

Lyrralt looked at him as if he were crazy, but said simply, "She's gone ahead with the others."

"What's wrong with you, Brother?"

Lyrralt looked at him, then back down the hillside, where their comrades were separating into groups, some with swords already drawn. He could see the flashes of sunlight off the sharpened blades. "Does it disturb you not at all that we're about to fight our king?"

"It's their necks, not ours," Jyrbian said sharply. When Lyrralt didn't respond, he continued, even more harshly, "If you don't want to fight, then go with the children. Stay out of the way."

Lyrralt stiffened, meeting Jyrbian's angry gaze with fury. "I'll fight, Brother. I just don't like it."

Despite his strong words to Lyrralt, as the King's Guard charged up the hill, Jyrbian felt the shock of staring into faces he'd seen at jousting matches, at suppers, at assemblies.

The bowmen proved a success and would have made a rout with sufficient numbers. As it was, there were enough of them to do damage, to delay the enemy, but not enough to stop the inevitable charge up the hill.

Jyrbian met the guard head-on, on foot, a mad courage coursing through him. As he cut the first Ogre from his horse, as his sword met another high in the air, he felt the song of battle in his blood, in his bones. He forgot fear. The enemy was upon him, and he attacked left and right, refusing to give ground, to even step back as he parried. Lyrralt and Tenaj and Butyr were forced to stay by his side or allow him to be overwhelmed. Buoyed by his courage, attracted by his killing frenzy, others joined them, their fierce, exuberant expressions matching his own.

A blade slipped past his defenses and touched his side, but there was no pain. A warm, slick wetness slid down his body, inside his tunic; he felt only joy as he pressed his arm against the wetness and continued to fight. His sword swung in perfect arcs, a beautiful thing to behold, almost poetry in the air.

In sheer numbers, the royal troops outmatched them, but Jyrbian had chosen his spot well. Riding uphill, the King's Guard stood no chance. The ground had turned into bloody mud. The bodies of their fallen comrades crunched underfoot. They gave up and ran, leaving behind a battleground littered with the first casualties of Igraine's War.

Jyrbian raised his arms in jubilation, in thanksgiving. The gods' bloodlust, their blessings, had poured down upon him, upon his troops.

He rode at the head of the troop, still wearing the clothes in which he'd fought, into which his blood and the blood of his enemies had soaked. In the stained, torn silks, he looked like the embodiment of a dark god himself, proud and arrogant, triumphant.

Riding swiftly, they had easily caught up with those they'd sent ahead. The eyes of men and women and children, admiring, grateful, followed Jyrbian as he led his warriors into the camp. He failed to capture the admiration of only one, the one he most wanted.

Her face puckered with worry, Everlyn ran out among the mothers welcoming sons, husbands welcoming wives, children underfoot everywhere, searching frantically for her father. When she found him, standing near Jyrbian, her face broke into a sunny smile.

"Lady," Jyrbian said, bowing. "Would that I might make you smile so."

Flustered, she turned away to greet her father.

Jyrbian determined, at that moment, that he would be whatever he had to be, do whatever was required, to make her pixie face light up for him.

Khallayne's face did light up, for him and for Lyrralt, who was still trailing him, a silent, bad-tempered wraith. She held out her arms to Jyrbian and hugged him close as if she would never let him go, as if they were long-parted lovers. "I was afraid . . . " she whispered, her arms tightening around his shoulders. "I thought I might never see you again."

For a moment, his roguishness rekindled and he pulled her close, swung her easily off her feet even though she was as tall as he. "Did you miss me, then?" he whispered back, turning his head so his breath tickled her neck.

"Terribly," Khallayne laughed, but when she pulled back and turned to Lyrralt, her expression turned serious. "What is it?" she whispered. "Are you injured?"

He looked so tired. She reached for his hands. They were as cold as ice.

Jyrbian snorted and turned on his heel, leaving the two of them staring at each other, hands clasped as if they had shut out the world. He went in search of another healer for the wound in his side. He didn't trust his own brother to heal it properly.

Khallayne spared barely a glance at his retreat. The pain she saw in Lyrralt was greater."Lyrralt?"

His grip on her fingers tightened. "Khallayne, do you know what I've seen?" he whispered, his voice taut. "The end . . . Doom."

She shook her head.

He mumbled barely intelligible words about the fight, about seeing the bodies of Ogres he knew, about blood and bone fragments and swords flashing in the sunlight. Something about the future and runes. Again the word "doom." His fingers twisted in hers.

With a soft cry, she wrenched free.

"Khallayne?" Lyrralt reached to touch her, this time his fingers gentle. "I'm sorry. I didn't mean to frighten you. It's just . . . I just . . . "

"What?"

"Nothing." He turned away, his eyes searching for and finding Igraine. He had to stop the madness soon.

He followed the crowd, which ebbed and flowed around Jyrbian. His brother, now wearing a clean tunic and showing no symptoms of his wound, was arguing to split the group of Igraine's followers, send the families with children on ahead. "We'll keep the warriors behind to guard the rear. I know Takar will not give up so easily."

Lyrralt watched him, suddenly reminded of Jyrbian wearing a soldier's dress uniform, proclaiming that someday there would again be a need for fighters.

Butyr argued against splitting the group. "We've defeated the best the court could send against us. We have nothing to fear at the moment."

They mounted at Igraine's urging, moving on without solving the disagreement. For the next week, while passing through the southernmost part of the Khalkist Mountains north of Takar, Jyrbian and Butyr continued to argue. Split up or separate. Head north or west. Attempt to settle in Thorad, or build a new home of their own.

Igraine, who could have settled all arguments, listened and made no judgment.

They began to climb into the main body of the

mountains. The trails, which had been wide and well traveled, became narrow, rutted for miles on end, then overgrown with roots. The dense undergrowth disappeared, the oaks became conifers, and the land rocky. The nights grew cold. Game, which had been plentiful and had made their nighttime fires smell of rich stew, became sparse.

There was no more arguing. They turned west, working their way toward more hospitable terrain.

Khallayne rode with Lyrralt or Jyrbian as much as she could. Neither were ideal traveling companions. Jyrbian spent his evenings in debate with Butyr or silently sitting at Igraine's campfire, as near Everlyn as he could get.

Lyrralt was withdrawn, uncommunicative, spending his evenings in communion with his god. "I feel as if we're floundering," he said. "Adrift."

"Childish prattle," Jyrbian responded. But Khallayne knew it was more than that. Just as she knew her own power, she sensed Lyrralt's. "Doom," she pressed him, "Why do you say that?"

"Because Hiddukel has told it to me," was all he would say.

Khallayne opened her mouth to ask another question when the horse in front of her reared. Its rider fell backward, an arrow protruding from her chest!

A child screamed. Pandemonium erupted around them. Arrows flew, as thick as bees. Horses stampeded.

Tenaj, who had fallen when the horse ahead of them reared, cried out as the panicked horses almost crushed her.

Jyrbian materialized and, catching a fistful of her tunic, dragged her off the path, away from the skittish horses. An arrow whizzed overhead, and he let her drop to the ground.

"Get down!" he shouted, kicking his horse in the flank. "Everybody, keep low!"

Khallayne yanked her horse in a circle, trying to see who was attacking, and from where. The arrows seemed to be coming from all directions.

The "who" was answered immediately. The man behind her slumped. The Ogre arrow in his forehead sported the brilliant colors of Clan Redienhs.

She ducked lower, clutching her horse's neck. The animal's muscles were trembling under its silky coat. She wanted to scramble into the thick undergrowth that lined the trail, but dared not. Dared not even dismount.

Khallayne could hear Jyrbian's voice, farther away now, shouting orders. She moved toward the sound. To her right she could hear the sing of steel against steel, the shouts of battle, and she knew her people had left the trail, had plunged into the forest to meet their attackers.

Ahead of her on the trail, Jyrbian was in the thickest of the fighting, a dark god of war, terrible and beautiful. With arrows flying through the air around him, he stood in his stirrups. He managed to keep his horse under control with one hand while he signaled with the other, directing archers to cover on the left side of the path, those with swords to dismount and flank the enemy on the right.

Seeing him so much in control, so dauntless, Khallayne lost her fear. She rode into the thick of the fighting. The scent of blood rushed at her, filling her with pure euphoria. The thrill of being able to use magic without restraint wiped out all the sights and sounds.

The power leapt up in her, so voraciously that she didn't even need to use her hands to direct it. Her mind sent it outward, unfocused.

The enemy guardsman who had been nearest Jyrbian had been lifting his bow. He dropped where he stood, his heart burst in his chest. A trickle of blood escaping the corner of his mouth was the only tangible sign of injury.

She felt his death, the sudden explosion of tiny veins, of life-sustaining arteries, as a sickening swelling in the power. She doubled over as the Ogre's death struck her a blow like a fist to the chest. But there was no time to stop and think. She turned, sent the magic outward again, and felt the energy billow as two more fell. And two more.

"Khallayne! Khallayne! There!"

She drew in the power enough to clear her vision. Jyrbian was still standing in his stirrups, bloodied sword held at the ready. Lyrralt was at his side. Jyrbian pointed to her right, into the forest. "There!"

He wheeled his horse around and almost rode down one of his own people to get to her side. "There!" He pointed again. "The archers. Can you get to the archers?"

She stared, but could see only splashes of color, here, there, among the thicket of trees and vine growth. Only the arrows continuing to rain from that direction told her for certain that the enemy was there.

With Lyrralt on one side and Jyrbian on the other, she closed her eyes, envisioned the forest, the undergrowth, the Ogres crouched beneath for cover, rising up to fire an arrow, then dropping back down again.

The power was awakening within her, demanding, thrashing, screaming to be released. She let loose the magic. The forest sprang to life. In the direction Jyrbian had indicated, every vine, blade of grass, every leaf shifted, stretched, moved, became animated.

A male Ogre on Jyrbian's right screamed. Farther down the line of fighting, again and again, the cry was echoed.

For a moment, Jyrbian froze. Every muscle in his body turned to ice. "Khallayne!" His voice cracked, then picked up strength as he saw a vine stir overhead. "Khallayne, control it!"

He didn't know if she heard or not, but the forest turned away from Igraine's people, toward the attackers.

He heard the enemy shout, first surprise, then warning, screams of pain, cries of questioning, terror.

Khallayne sat rigid in her saddle, reins limp in her hands, eyes glazed. Jyrbian looked about. Tenaj was nearby, remounted. "Guard her," he ordered, indicating Khallayne.

He didn't know if it was safe, but he urged his horse forward, off the path, into the forest. Everything was moving, leaves, vines, dead branches, reaching and twisting and killing.

The enemy was caught in its deadly embrace. Vines as thick as his arm wrapped around archers, twining about them. Their bodies were being crushed to pulp.

Farther into the forest lay more horrors, more crushed bodies, bodies impaled on thick branches of living trees. A standard bearer had dropped his staff;

the body beside it was covered with crawling, wriggling leaves.

A vine as thin and dangerous as razorwire dropped down from a branch and struck out at Jyrbian like a snake. Backing away, he slashed at it with his sword. Green ichor spurted from the severed limb. Something hissed. Jyrbian wheeled his horse and kicked it hard.

* * * * *

Bakrell turned from the view of the castle courtyard and the skyline of Takar at midmorning. "Kaede, you can't do this!"

As his sister took clothing from her wardrobe and ferried it to the bed, Bakrell followed her, back and forth.

Traveling packs were laid, already partially filled. Kaede laid another stack of clothing beside what was already there, then gathered another armload from atop a nearby chest before answering. "Why not?"

"Because . . . Because it's crazy. It dangerous, that's why!"

She snorted at him with amusement. "You've grown soft, Bakrell, too accustomed to silks and slaves." She rubbed the brocade lapel of his embroidered vest.

He watched, silent for a moment, as she continued to pull out all she had packed in order to sort through it again. She had, arrayed on the bed, an incredible collection of luxurious as well as sensible belongings, including a bejeweled bracelet worth as much as everything else combined.

"Why would you need this?" He picked up a silky

147

tunic, so soft and delicate it might have been spun by spiders.

Kaede snatched it back, arched an eyebrow. "You never know what you might need. I'm not giving up civilization completely."

"You're really looking forward to this adventure, aren't you? You're not going to mind at all, giving up these creature comforts." He waved his hands to indicate the sumptuous room.

"No, I don't mind." She took a bracelet from him and, eyeing him mischievously, slid it onto her wrist, hiding it inside the cuff of the expensive leather riding jacket.

He considered the packs on the bed only a moment longer, then decided. "All right, I'll go with you."

"What?"

"You can tarry a little longer while I pack. I don't see why we have to sneak away in the middle of the night anyway," he said over his shoulder as he started for the door.

"Perhaps you'd like to leave the castle after a hearty breakfast tomorrow morning, announcing to all within earshot that you're off to join the followers of the heretic Igraine?" she called after him.

He paused at the door, grinned at her, excitement beginning to shine in his eyes. "Don't forget to pack food."

* * * * *

Bedraggled, bloody, beaten, the remnants of the guard of Clan Redienhs rode into the rocky gorge. Afternoon sun beat down on them, reflected warmth back from the red, rocky walls on both sides of the wide trail. In unspoken agreement, they slowed their pace once the group was within the gorge, out of the forest.

Riding near the front of the group, Daria glanced back, making sure her brother was also clear of the trees. She shivered, remembering tree limbs crackling with energetic movement, vines writhing across the ground, reaching for her. In the depths of her worst nightmares, she had never dreamt of such horror!

Raell had stayed near her, once the attack began, even though he was a swordsman and she an archer. He considered himself protecting his younger sister. It had almost cost him his life. When the forest had come alive . . . Despite the warmth of the sun, she pulled her cloak tighter about her shoulders. She clutched the silver clasp, etched with the condor symbol of Sargonnas, at her throat. They were both lucky to be alive.

She was so engrossed, she noticed the agitation in the ranks only when Raell galloped up beside her. "What's going on?" she asked, suddenly noticing the movement ahead.

"Look!" He pointed toward the end of the gorge, at the brightly colored troops coming to meet them, flags with the colors of Clan Signet flying snappily above, one flag in particular, with the logo of the clan leader on it. "Reinforcements!"

Reinforcements. That meant turning back, perhaps another battle. The idea of more fighting didn't bother her. The thought of riding back into the forest did.

* * * * *

The shadow detached itself from high up in the tree and scuttled quickly to the ground, dropping sometimes as much as two feet from branch to branch. The humans on the floor of the hillside gasped each time the girl let go of a handhold, each time she caught. Eadamm grinned as she paused on the last branch, dangling precariously several feet from the ground.

"Stop showing off," he called with pretend gruffness. "Tell me what you see."

She dropped the last ten feet and landed with a bone-jarring thud. "Two or three new companies of Ogres, wearing yellow, with a shiny star here." She sketched a square above her left breast. "What was left of the other group has joined them."

"Clan Signet," Eadamm interjected. "What are they doing?"

She smiled. "Camping."

Eadamm's lips stretched back in a feral grimace. His teeth were white against his dark skin. "We'll attack at dusk."

"I don't see why we should attack at all," Jeb, one of Eadamm's generals, protested. "We're free. We're less than three days' ride from the plains. From home!"

Eadamm resettled a stolen Ogre sword more firmly around his hips. Though some of the others wore stolen Ogre finery, he'd refused to wear even a cloak from his former masters. He wore a blanket, with armholes slashed in it, over his torn and stained slave garments. "And how long do you think you'll be free if we do nothing to stop the Ogres. Perhaps you'd live out your life a free man. But what of our people? If we don't stop the Ogres, they'll just kidnap new slaves and start over."

Jeb peered at him. "You just want to protect your old master!"

Eadamm started to retort, but instead shrugged. "Again, if we don't, how will we ever be secure in our homes? Igraine's followers must persevere. For our safety."

Jeb looked at the plans Eadamm had been sketching in the hard ground. "I don't agree."

"You don't have to stay with us if you don't want to," Eadamm said gently.

Jeb straightened, his hand going to the dagger tucked into his belt before he realized Eadamm meant no offense. For a long moment, he regarded his friend. "I have nowhere to go. But do we have to attack in the dark?"

"It won't be any darker than it was in the mines. Until we're ready for light," he added cryptically.

* * * * *

Eadamm was right. Perhaps to the Ogres, who had not toiled in darkness for years, it was night. To him, even in the wee hours before dawn, that darkest time before sunrise, the craggy canyon in which the Ogre troops had chosen to sleep was plainly visible. The crags and sheer faces of the canyon walls were shadowed and spooky, but the tents of the Ogre troops were outlined sharply.

The blades of Ogre swords flashed in the moonlight as the humans swept down on the camp, pouring into it from both ends, cutting off any chance of retreat. Eadamm's people carried stolen weapons and homemade ones—lovely swords of elven design taken from some rich estate, pikes hand carved from elm wood and capped with hand-hammered metal, axes stolen right out of firewood, hoes and rakes and scythes still smelling of grain fields.

Eadamm led the first charge, riding at the front of his people. The sounds were overpowering; screams of rage and vengeance about to be realized echoed off the canyon walls. It surged in his blood, fueling his battle lust. He met his first opponent, a wild-eyed sentry, and cut him down with one quick slash.

The Ogre response to the attack was sluggish but fierce. Attacked from two sides, they poured out of the tents, leapt from their blankets to meet Eadamm's troops.

Shrieks and death cries filled the air. Sword rang out against sword, pike against pike. Over the din of weapons striking each other, Eadamm could hear an Ogre commander trying to rally his archers. Eadamm wheeled and charged in the direction of the voice. The Ogre had the presence of mind to send an arrow whizzing past Eadamm's ear before he was cut down.

The humans torched the Ogre tents, sending up an eerie light, which cast their shadows, several times enlarged, dancing on the canyon walls.

The Ogres, caught in disarray, rallied quickly, forming pockets of resistance against which the humans battered. They grabbed up shields and pikes and fought back-to-back, protecting the archers, who rained arrows down on the humans. The arrows flew up and out of the circles of Ogres, appearing as if by magic.

Again and again, Eadamm's people rushed the lines, skewered an Ogre here, one there. But again and again, the humans were repelled.

Stragglers, caught too far away to join in the protective circles, fought hand to hand, silhouetted against the flames. Humans picked up bows and quivers of arrows and picked off those Ogres who thought they could climb up the canyon walls to safety.

For sheer ferocity, the humans equaled the larger, better-equipped Ogres. In sheer force, they were no match. For each human killed, Eadamm felt the decimation to his numbers. For each Ogre who fell, another stepped forward to take his place.

He stood in his stirrups and yelled for one of the soldiers on foot to bring him bow and arrow. He lit the feathers from the flames of a burning tent, nocked the arrow quickly, and let it fly. The burning signal sailed in a high arc over the battle. Even before the wildly dancing flames had disappeared from overhead, a bolt of blue sizzled upward into the sky, like lightning in reverse.

Though he was expecting it, the brightness of it blinded Eadamm and panicked his stallion. The big animal reared, pawing in midair. Eadamm felt the momentum of the horse's action toss him backward. He went sailing through the air and landed with a bone-jarring *whump*!

As he gasped for breath, his vision deserted him. Stars danced before his eyes, but whether from the lightning or the fall, he didn't know. Then he could see, figures blurry and indistinct, both atop horses. As he strained to see, the larger figure leapt from his saddle, carrying the smaller one to the ground.

His vision cleared to reveal Jeb and a large Ogre female, locked in a death grip. He tried to stand, to go to Jeb's aid, but his balance was off. He stumbled, went to his knees. Dimly, he was aware when the larger figure lifted a gleaming silver dagger. She lifted it high in the air, then brought it down again and again. The man who had been his second-in-command since the escape from Khalever slumped.

A woman who had escaped from Bloten rushed to Eadamm's side. As she helped him to sit, the lightning sizzled again, lighting the night as brightly as the sun lit the day. The woman, hearing the warning whine of the spell building, covered her eyes.

This time, Eadamm was sure it was the magical lightning of their one human wizard that left spots of color dancing behind his eyelids. He could see barely two feet. Despite the disorientation, he scrambled to his feet and remounted the skittish horse.

All about him, the Ogres were in disarray, blinded and frightened by the magical flash of light. The lines of carefully tied horses had broken loose and were careening through the camp.

Eadamm veered like a madman through a large group of Ogres, cutting a bloody swath through the group. Hacking with his stolen sword, he stabbed and slashed his way through and out of the circle on the other side. Inspired by his bravery, a group of humans plowed through behind him, cutting down their enemy left and right.

For several minutes after the magical lightning, the battle raged around him. Surging through the flames and smoke, the humans pressed their advantage. The Ogres scrambled to regain their defense, but to no avail.

The humans surrounded the few last groups of Ogres and hacked and slashed their way to victory. Until, at last, the mere sight of so many humans, bloodied, was enough to make the few remaining Ogres break formation and run.

The humans gave chase, but Eadamm called them back. "Leave some to carry the tale," he shouted.

Two of Krynn's moons, near to setting, hung low in the sky. It seemed only minutes ago that the battle had begun, rather than more than an hour.

Jeb was dead, pierced through so many times that it seemed the Ogre had been trying to obliterate him rather than just kill. Eadamm knelt at his friend's side and covered his broken body with the fine woolen cloak that had been torn half off him. It was muddied, ripped, stained with the blood of Ogres and Jeb himself.

"We won," Eadamm told his friend. Only then did he notice how quiet the canyon had become.

Chapter 10
Directions from Above

Anel stared at the female Ogre who stood before the Ruling Council. Although every hair was braided and neatly in place, she still appeared harried and frightened.

"The forest killed them?" Anel asked, her voice disbelieving even though she had already heard similar reports from the three guards who had escaped. She glanced at her fellow council members. Their faces were equally stunned.

The warrior nodded. "We were lucky. Our group leader saw the danger, and we managed to pull back, rested, and regrouped. Then, when we were ready to attack again, that's when the humans surprised us. We—We were in the back. We barely escaped with our lives. My brother was . . . Raell . . . " Her voice choked off. "He was one of the unlucky."

Anel nodded in sympathy. "We will sing for your loss." She motioned an aide to step forward and lead the female away. She didn't need to probe the mind of this one. She'd already probed the first three for truth. Except for minor details, this fourth story corroborated the others.

"We must send another company," Teragrym began even before the door had closed. "A stronger, more dedicated one."

"Who do you suggest?" Enna responded acidly. "They have defeated our best. And from where? We need more guards for the estate trails. Two more supply caravans were struck this morning by runaway slaves. And *to* where? Our scouts have died alongside most of the Redienhs warriors."

"Then we must begin conscripting from the common classes. Train harder, faster, better," Teragrym said dryly. "And we must send mages."

Narran flipped open his fingers, sending a jagged flash of light shooting toward the ceiling. It sizzled and disappeared. "Which of us do you suggest, Teragrym?" he asked angrily. "Perhaps you want to send one of your children?"

"We have to fight magic with magic, not swords. I do not prefer to send my family into danger, but what I must do, I will do. As you will." He fixed Narran with a withering glance. "But don't worry. For the moment, I have someone besides you in mind to command a counterstrike."

"Then you may proceed accordingly, Teragrym," Anel said. "Enna, you will institute a program for selecting and training more guards."

* * * * *

Calmness. Serenity. Eight days of safety.

Butyr's young sister had been one of those killed, as well as two sons of the wild Aliehs clan, and five others they couldn't spare, but they had gone on.

The last days had been a healing time, a calming time, though with none of the comforts to which Khallayne had been raised and barely enough food, and that ill cooked.

Her legs aching and belly rumbling, without a home, she had never been happier. Jelindra, a young female Ogre barely a hundred years old, her pale hair still tied with childish ribbons, rode by her side, hanging on Khallayne's words as she taught the young one the incantation for disguise.

"We're close now, Khallayne." Tenaj rode back from the front of the group to interrupt the lesson. Jelindra grimaced with disappointment but obediently rode away, still counting off the lines of the incantation on her fingers.

Khallayne watched her go with a smile. "I think she'll be very good someday. She's very accepting of the power."

"I'd like to learn," Tenaj said very quietly, very shyly. "I've never been very good, but . . . "

Khallayne smiled with pleasure so genuine that the expression lit up her face. "Oh, Tenaj, you have no idea. This is unbelievable. My whole life I've had to hide my magic. Now everyone knows, and instead of being punished, they're asking me to use it more! I'd love to teach you, anything you want to learn."

They both had to gallop to catch up with Lyrralt.

The whole company wanted to go into the city, but they understood the danger involved. Lyrralt had not wanted to go, but had been chosen, along with Tenaj and Khallayne, to check out the city, to spy.

The city of Thorad was as unlike Takar as Lyrralt's father's estate was different from the king's summer home. Like Takar, it was a center for trade, but unlike Takar, it wasn't walled. Built after the Ruling Council had brought peace, the young city had sprung up in the very center of the Khalkists as the hub of the Ogre empire.

It was laid out in the orderly, wagon wheel style of old, its outermost ring consisting mostly of taverns and inns. All the buildings had high, sloping roofs, the better to shed the heavy snows of winter, and the windows had folding wooden shutters that could be closed to shut out the elements. Today, they were all thrown open to let in the warming rays of the unusually warm fall day.

Lyrralt was glad to the see the streets filled with traders, merchants, and travelers. He slowed his horse, wondering which way would be best. They needed information and supplies, but it had to be done without arousing suspicions.

"What do you think?" Tenaj reined in beside him.

"Well, the easiest way to get information in the castle was to sit in the dining hall. I have little familiarity with such places as these." He indicated the rough-looking inns and taverns lining the street. "But I suppose they're the best place to start."

Tenaj nodded agreement, pointing to one across the street.

There were several horses crowded to the hitching rods outside its door. He shrugged and steered his horse toward it. The one Tenaj had chosen was as good as any other.

Inside, the inn was dark, but warm from a crackling fire in a fireplace as large as any in the castle. There were perhaps twenty other guests in the room, mostly at the bar. The tables and chairs in the cramped dining area were gray stone, and as soon as he and Tenaj sat down, Lyrralt understood why the fire was kept hot. The stone leeched the warmth from his body right though his cloak.

An Ogre wearing a huge medallion with the sigil of Hiddukel brought the three travelers some wine without being asked. He bowed to Lyrralt, saying, "You're welcome in my inn, Lord."

Lyrralt relaxed at once, knowing they'd come to the right place. All merchants worshiped Hiddukel, god of ill-gotten gain and greed, but, fearing to insult their customers, who were sponsored by other gods, few did so blatantly. He leaned close so that he could speak without being overheard by the other diners. "With luck, I'll be able to get the information we need out of this one."

Tenaj nodded. "If I stood at the bar, I could listen in on the conversations."

"And I could find another place." Khallayne sipped her wine and made a face. "Preferably someplace with better food and drink."

Lyrralt nodded, motioned them closer. "Listen for anything at all that might tell us what the council is up to. Anything. A large supply order or an inn too full could mean a guard unit on the move. And anything at all about Igraine. How do the citizens feel about him here? What have they heard?

"Most of these people are traders. They travel

most of the year. We might learn of someplace where we could settle. The others wouldn't like to hear of it, but I don't think there's anyplace in the Khalkists where we'll be safe anymore."

"I agree," said a voice behind Lyrralt.

Lyrralt whipped around, his hand automatically slipping inside his robe for his dagger. How had the two who stood staring down at him sneaked up without being detected?

"Who are you?" Tenaj asked suspiciously, her hand also hidden under the table.

"I'm Bakrell. This is my sister, Kaede. We didn't mean to startle you."

"We've been waiting for you." The female Ogre spoke in a sweet voice.

The two, brother and sister, smiled the same smile and took seats on the stone bench on either side of Lyrralt without being invited.

Except for the smile, the two were so different, Khallayne's immediate assumption was that they must have had different fathers. Kaede possessed skin as dark indigo as Jyrbian's and Lyrralt's, eyes so pale a silver that they were almost white. Her brother had medium royal-blue skin, average silver eyes, average build and height. He would have blended into any crowd, from royalty right down to the lowliest shopkeeper. Except for his expression. Despite the smile, he looked at all of them from under his brows with a strange intensity.

She shivered. The temperature felt as though it had dropped ten degrees.

"Waiting for us?"

"Yes. Not you, exactly, but for someone from Takar. For someone traveling with Lord Igraine.

We've heard . . . many things."

"We wanted to know more." Kaede's voice was as light, as beguiling, as her brother's was dark. "We . . . We want to join you. The talk is of nothing else. Of the new life you—Lord Igraine—will build out of the old. I—We want to be a part of it."

Khallayne stared at her through slitted eyes. There was something about her, something she thought she ought to recognize. Had she seen her before somewhere? "You said the mountains aren't safe?"

Bakrell nodded. "We left Takar the week after Lord Igraine escaped. We've been forced to take back trails to avoid the troops."

The two strangers both had their hands on the table in plain sight. Lyrralt relaxed a little, eased his hand out of his robe. "How long have you been here?" He took a sip of his wine.

"Over a week. We knew—well, we hoped someone would come this way. We thought you'd need supplies."

"What we need," Tenaj said, "is information. About Takar."

"The last we heard, the word in Takar is that the Ruling Council is determined that Igraine be caught. We don't know if it's true, but the main trails out of the city are heavily watched."

Tenaj grimaced. "It's what we expected."

"So what do we do now. Live on the plains among the humans?" Khallayne asked, half sarcastically.

Kaede's expression brightened. She turned to her brother. "That would be exciting, wouldn't it?"

"Among the humans?" he asked. "Surely there is a better alternative?"

Khallayne looked at Kaede. "Have we met? I have

the feeling I know you."

"Perhaps you've seen me in the castle. Bakrell and I visited occasionally. I know I've seen you. That's how we knew you were from Takar. I've always admired your unusual beauty. I'm so glad we spotted you. We've been watching the taverns for days."

Kaede sounded sincere. Their story sounded honest. Everything seemed right except for their clothing. They wore simple garb that didn't stand out in the surroundings unless one recognized quality. Khallayne wore the roughest clothes she owned, and the trail was beginning to tell on them. The cloth of Kaede's and Bakrell's tunics and cloaks was the finest material. The clasp at the throat of her cloak was brushed gold, the bands on his wrists polished silver. They seemed unlikely refugees.

"We've been purchasing trail supplies since we got here," Bakrell said. "A little every day, in different places. We thought, if anyone came, it might come in handy."

"I'm sure Igraine will welcome you both." Lyrralt sketched a little bow of welcome.

* * * * *

Several hard days later on the trail, Khallayne's skeptical opinion of the brother and sister still hadn't changed. They did everything that was asked of them, Bakrell haughtily, glancing around to see who might be admiring him. Kaede carried water and started fires as gracefully as if she were at court. But instead of the gaze of many, in just one day, it was obvious she was interested only in the gaze of one person—Jyrbian.

With amusement, Khallayne noted that Jyrbian was as oblivious to Kaede's admiration as Everlyn was to his.

* * * * *

Lyrralt sat well away from the others, behind the curve of a ditch. He uncapped the vial of water he carried always. The flickering fire was barely enough to hold back the encroaching darkness.

The fugitives were camped in a large, open area almost devoid of the dense forest that surrounded them. In the warm glow of the setting sun, the view from the ridge was fabulous, a glorious panorama of the Khalkists, awash in rose and orange and gold.

The History said the bald areas were caused when the gods thumped their fists onto the mountains. But sitting on the ground, with the quietness of the earth seeping into his bones, speaking to his heart, Lyrralt could sense an ancient fire that had burned away the trees, leaving only grass. It seemed a fitting place for his meditations.

As he did each evening, Lyrralt raised his eyes to the heavens, to the constellation of Hiddukel, and whispered a prayer, an entreaty for guidance.

Since the mad flight from Takar, he had been without direction, adrift. Hiddukel had told him nothing since. He knew only that Khallayne was involved in his destiny, and there was doom in the teachings of Igraine. There was also a blindness in the future, something he would not be able to see.

Perhaps tonight guidance would come. Glancing around once more to make sure he was unobserved, Lyrralt slipped his tunic to his waist, exposing his shoulders and arms to the cold night air. The runes glowed white and milky against his skin, mirroring the glow of the stars in the velvet sky.

He waited, lips moving in almost desperate entreaty, praying for guidance and the loving touch of his god.

The inner flesh of his arm tingled, so lightly it might have been only the breeze caressing his flesh. Lyrralt held his breath. Again, the tingle. The sensation was so layered, so complex that it could not be separated, could not be differentiated. Then pain, hunger, rhapsody all vibrated along his nerves.

He wanted to watch, to see the writings that would appear on his flesh, but he could not. The pain, the pleasure, drew his head back, made him take great gulps of air. He could only hold out his arm to the sky and wait for the test to be done.

The stars had moved in the sky by the time Lyrralt was once again conscious. The sensation on his skin had become a mere itch. He hoped the sigils would not be too cryptic, now that he had no experienced priest to guide him.

Or, looking at it another way, he had the highest advisor of all, Hiddukel himself. And with such a guide, how could he fail?

Lyrralt looked down and saw a band of runes encircling his arm, just beneath the one rune that had appeared at Khal-Theraxian. He moved closer to the fire and stirred up the embers until he had some light. His breath caught in his throat.

The symbols could be read easily, even by a beginner. Death. Stealth. Igraine—that symbol he knew already on his arm. And the next one, too, the dead queen—Khallayne. But he couldn't tell what had appeared next to her name. He would have to study it.

For the moment, the ones he could discern were enough to set Lyrralt's head spinning. Getting Igraine away from the protection of Jyrbian and Everlyn wouldn't be easy. But it was necessary.

Igraine had become almost holy to most of the group. Every night, a different group huddled around him at his campfire, clung to his words as if they were bits of wisdom from the gods themselves.

Lyrralt would have to watch and wait and plan. He snuffed out his fire and returned to camp.

* * * * *

They rode north, higher into the mountains to avoid the main trails. Using the back ways slowed them. Somehow more refugees found them, some from Takar, some from Thorad, even a handful from faraway Bloten, and the added numbers slowed them further.

Rain poured from the sky with such ferocity that Tenaj remarked that the gods must surely be weeping. Water dripped from the leaves, cut grooves into the paths, flowed until the travelers had not a thread of dry clothing left.

Each morning Lyrralt woke wet and miserable. He searched the distant mountainside for new landslides. There was always at least one, an ugly scar marring the green slopes, a clay-colored wound where the earth had simply given up and let go. With each slide, he rode more nervously, wondering if the next one would be the one to come down on his head.

The path forked, narrowed to a ledge, and disappeared around a bare cliff face toward a roaring waterfall. To the northeast, the path went around the same cliff, wide and smooth as it meandered toward Thordyn Pass.

They climbed down and gathered around a map, which Jyrbian hunched over and held as tightly against his body as possible to shield it from the rain. It was old, probably inaccurate, but was all they had. This part of the mountains was all bare cliff faces and rocky outcroppings. No one would need a map of it, except thieves and criminals.

Lyrralt peered over his brother's shoulder. The path to the east was nearly twice as long and wound through a narrow valley that would make an excellent spot for ambush, if the tree cover was good.

"I think we should take the west path." Jyrbian folded the map and put it away in his saddlebag.

Lyrralt quickly remounted, his heart beating as loudly as the rain thrummed on the leaves overhead. By the time he was settled, Butyr and Everlyn were arguing for the easier path.

"Jyrbian, it's still raining. That path will be dangerous."

"And least likely to hold an ambush, besides being half the distance," Jyrbian said firmly.

Lyrralt let out his breath, relieved that Jyrbian had the presence of mind to resist Everlyn. He edged his horse toward the narrow path.

The rain had eased to a trickle, coating the trail with a layer of moisture. The rocky path was bare and slick, so narrow that their legs would brush the granite wall. They would be forced to ride single file. And it would be easy for a horse to slip, for the slick hooves to skid, for a rider to tumble down the cliff's side . . .

"What do you think?"

Lyrralt turned to find Igraine beside him. The Ogre was watching him with a solemn, penetrating gaze. Looking at *him*, not the trail, as if he could see deep into his heart.

The hieroglyphs woke on his arm, writhed and itched. "It's very narrow. Slippery and treacherous. But it is shorter, and—"

"Still you favor it?"

"Yes," Lyrralt said, looking away, suddenly sure that Igraine knew what he was planning, knew he was thinking how easy it would be, once they were on the narrow ridge, for Igraine's horse to plunge accidentally over the edge.

"I'm glad you agree, Brother," Jyrbian said as he pushed past, his horse nudging Lyrralt's aside.

Lyrralt looked back and saw Everlyn, Khallayne and Tenaj, and behind them, two of the newcomers, Bakrell and Kaede. Butyr was farther back, scowling, talking with large gestures to one of his cousins.

Two of the Ogres who always loudly supported Jyrbian, who had established themselves as swordmasters, pushed past before Lyrralt could close the gap. "After you, Lord," Lyrralt said when the two were past and motioned courteously for Igraine to precede him.

Chapter 11
Glory and Danger Alike

They rode out onto the ledge.

The fear they all felt was like the gray mist, thick enough to see, to taste. Lyrralt forced himself to concentrate on Igraine's broad back, to watch for an opportunity.

The ledge on which they rode was so narrow that they loosened grit and pebbles from the cliff face with each step of their horses.

No going back.

Lyrralt tore his gaze from Igraine and settled on the immense gulf of open air between him and the ground below.

No going back. The words beat a refrain in his mind.

The roar of the river, the rushing of the waterfall, the pounding of his own heart, made a song to Hiddukel. In tempo to it, he whispered a chant aimed at Igraine and the horse he rode. He urged his horse forward, as close to Igraine's as he dared.

Igraine's horse shied, indication that Lyrralt's chant was working. It whipped its glossy mane back and forth, then stopped, lowering its rump preparatory to rearing. Igraine stiffened, fought against the fear that enveloped him. Somehow, he kept his head, restrained the horse.

Lyrralt chanced releasing his reins and touched his shoulder, drawing on the magic of the runes. He could feel the power flowing through him, out of him, streaming toward the Ogre and beast ahead.

A scream! Lyrralt started, then froze, every muscle in his body seizing up. The magic of the runes died, cut off abruptly.

"Don't stop! Keep moving!" The words echoed, came from somewhere far away, perhaps originating from ahead, perhaps from behind. Perhaps it was Jyrbian's voice. Perhaps his own.

More screams broke through, more than one voice. There was a crack, like a whip striking the cliff face, and pebbles rained down on his back. More screams were followed by a horrible sound of a rider and horse falling, somewhere behind him. The screaming died away and ended abruptly with the sickening, bone-cracking thud of bodies slamming into rock.

Lyrralt's horse, responding to the terror of the other animal, tried to bolt. Its hooves scrabbled for purchase on the path. The rider behind him cried out.

Lyrralt grabbed for the cliff face with one hand, yanked at the reins with the other, tightened his grip on his mount, and prayed for the animal to regain its footing.

The rider behind him cried out again as Lyrralt's horse stumbled backward.

Lyrralt nails tore as he grabbed for an outcropping of rock, a crevice, anything. He kicked out. His fingers found only slick stone. Then he was free, hanging by his fingertips in the air.

His body slammed back into the wall. As breath whooshed out of his lungs, his grip on the sharp rock broke, and he knew momentum was going to carry him over the cliff.

Something—someone—caught him. Strong hands encircled his wrist and yanked him forward. He danced for firm footing, found it, and looked up into Igraine's eyes. His face taut, Igraine held his wrist firmly, held his arm stretched at a painful angle across the backside of his horse, as he tried to control the animal, tried to keep his own precarious balance.

"Don't let go!" Lyrralt gasped.

Igraine gave a single shake of his head and pulled harder, righting himself and steadying the horse with a mighty effort.

Muscles stretched to the breaking point, Lyrralt lowered himself until his feet found the path. He would have fainted but for the pain coursing through his body, but for the steely gray eyes locked with his, holding both of them upright almost by sheer will.

"Slowly . . . " Igraine said tensely, looking back down the trail. "Slowly. Climb up behind me. Now! Climb up!" Igraine pulled on his wounded arm.

Lyrralt gasped as pain shot through his joints.

Behind him, someone screamed. Something slapped against the cliff above him. Pebbles rained down on his back. It was starting all over again!

More screams, more pebbles. A fist-sized rock struck his shoulder. Something hit Igraine, and he let go.

Lyrralt fell back and flattened himself against the granite cliff. Tentacles, ghastly yellow and banded with brown, fleshy rings, were reaching up from beneath the ledge, slithering along the path, searching, tapping the space between riders. When they didn't find anything, first one tentacle, then another, reared back and hammered the wall, sending a shower of pebbles and rocks exploding outward.

As the tentacles returned to their searching, Lyrralt realized he could hear a slavering, gurgling hiss. He reached for his arm, closing his fingers over the runes for strength. He closed his eyes and whispered to Hiddukel, asking for a shield, something to disguise his body from the slithering arms.

A scream louder and more terrible than any before broke his concentration. His eyes snapped open. The tentacles found a victim! As Lyrralt watched, the arms plucked a rider and horse from the ledge and dragged them over and down, out of sight.

The sounds that followed were indescribable. Lyrralt's stomach lurched and would not be denied. Clinging to the cliff, he bent at the knees and vomited over the side.

"We must move. Quickly." Igraine had turned around on his horse, his hand extended.

He seemed to be very far away. The distance from Lyrralt to the back of the horse seemed insurmountable. Lyrralt shook his head. "I can't."

"Can you walk?"

Lyrralt nodded. He stepped, clutched the wall tighter, and inched forward. His feet were numb. One step. Another. Somehow his legs supported him. His arm, though aching, held on to the cliff.

After a moment, Igraine gently urged his horse onward.

Lyrralt dared to look back at the Ogre on the path behind him. They nodded at each other as Lyrralt forced himself to take another step, then another, another.

The rain had started again, drops so huge that he could feel them roll down his neck. They soaked the ledge. Still he forced his legs to carry him on, concentrating on just one step at a time.

It seemed that days passed before the ledge began to widen and he stepped off the shelf. He rushed forward, past Jyrbian, past Igraine, past Khallayne's outstretched hand, past the riders who had stopped ahead of him. He didn't stop until there was solid ground for twenty feet all around him, trees blocking the view down the mountainside. There he fell to his knees and retched helplessly.

When he finally looked up, it was Igraine who had dismounted and was coming to help him, Igraine's hands that held his shoulders, supported his head. Then there were others, supporting his body, someone gently wiping his face with a soft cloth, another Ogre handing him wine to rinse his mouth.

Shamed to his core, he pushed everyone away, stood on his own, and found himself surrounded by concerned faces, Igraine, Everlyn, Khallayne, Tenaj, Everlyn's Aunt Naej.

"I thought we were going to lose you," Igraine

said with a smile, evidence of how pleased he was that they had not.

"I was just ahead," Khallayne said. "I saw your horse go over, and I could tell there was a problem, but I didn't know what happened."

"He saved Lord Igraine!" the Ogre who had been behind Lyrralt on the trail said.

"What!" The word was spoken by a chorus of voices, Lyrralt's among them.

The runes on his arm roused, clamped down, burned. "I didn't—!" Lyrralt protested. He looked at Igraine's face, saw only a serene smile there, instead of irritation for the mistaken idea. "Igraine saved me!"

The mumbling died down. The crowd turned to Igraine, waiting for his response.

"I'd say we saved each other." Igraine clasped Lyrralt on the shoulder.

There were words of approval from the crowd. Some reached out to touch Lyrralt, to pat him, to murmur wordless awe and approbation. He had saved and been saved by Igraine. It was almost as if they felt that by touching him, they touched Igraine and took for themselves a blessing, a charm of protection.

Lyrralt, ignoring the seething runes, was amazed by their warmth.

As the Ogres began to drift back to their horses, ready to move on, Lyrralt looked up.

Jyrbian sat on his horse, looking away toward the horizon, his face dispassionate, expressionless. Lyrralt realized that, of all the hands that had reached out to help him, his own brother's had not been among them.

Jyrbian looked down at him finally and said, "Are you going to stand there all day?" He spurred his horse. The huge animal gave a lurch in Lyrralt's direction, then wheeled and headed up the trail.

* * * * *

"Lyrralt will be one of the ones to go. It's his horse we need to replace." Jyrbian's voice, speaking with the authority of one who knew he would not be disputed, echoed in Lyrralt's thoughts as he and his entourage of fourteen rode into the human settlement.

Since the deaths on the trail, Jyrbian *wasn't* likely to be disputed. His loudest detractor, Butyr, had been the first one dragged from the ledge to gruesome death. Lyrralt, who was exalted for having been saved by the grace of the gods and the intercession of Igraine, hadn't even tried to argue, though he had not wanted to make the trip into Nerat for supplies and information.

The three weeks of travel since the deaths of those on the cliff trail had been long and tedious. Lyrralt had watched, planned, waited for another chance to do his god's bidding, but the opportunity eluded him. Now Igraine was always encircled by a group extolling his brave actions.

Lyrralt himself was sought out, admired. Perhaps, he reflected ruefully, that was why Jyrbian had insisted he lead the group into Nerat. Perhaps Jyrbian didn't want anyone else becoming popular and powerful.

Obviously relishing his leadership of the refugees, Jyrbian was trying to pattern his mannerisms after Igraine.

Lyrralt had watched his brother, day after day,

pulling a mask over his natural cynicism, forcing out calm, gentle words where harsh ones would have been more comfortable on his lips, striving to show a face that would prove worthy of Igraine's approbation . . . and Everlyn's love.

Unfortunately, the latter eluded him. Igraine might smile at Jyrbian and nod approvingly, but his daughter seemed oblivious to Jyrbian, impervious to all his smiles and courtly bows.

As the party rode into Nerat, down the middle of the main street, all human eyes, hostile and cold, turned on them. This burg was nothing like Thorad. It was a poor, dusty collection of unmatched buildings, a few made of stone, some rotting wood, and some apparently made of nothing more than mud and sticks.

Lyrralt and his people were accustomed to humans as slaves, dispirited and harmless, their wills broken, all resistance crushed. These humans didn't appear to be any of those things.

Lyrralt chose a ramshackle building that appeared to be a merchant center and motioned for half his party to accompany him and the other half to remain with the animals.

The inside of the wooden building smelled abominably of human sweat and unclean flesh, of unfinished, weathered wood and mysterious human spices. It was dark, lit by only the light from two dirty windows and lanterns in each corner. The single room was piled with bags and boxes of merchandise, shelves stacked with unmarked earthen containers.

"We don't want your kind in here," a harsh, guttural human voice said from behind the counter, which ran the width of the back of the room. Behind it were more shelves, these containing bottles of ale and wine.

Lyrralt, whose eyes were still adjusting after the noon sun's brightness, could barely make out the lean figure of a male human, fists propped on the bar. The human had long, dark hair curling about his shoulders and shorter hair across his entire face.

Because of the hostility, the outright hate in the human's voice, Kaede, hand on the hilt of her sword, started forward. Lyrralt stopped her unobtrusively.

Igraine and Everlyn had both spoken with him on the trail, warning him of reacting too severely to the hostility they were sure to encounter in Nerat. They had been extremely forceful in their opinion that the humans should be dealt with fairly and respectfully.

Lyrralt said coldly, "We have coin. We require supplies and information. We can pay handsomely. And we offer information in return." Igraine had told him to say that, too.

"I said we don't—" The human who had spoken first began again, his tone even more rude, even louder than before, but another cut him off.

"Turk . . . Let's hear what he has to say." The speaker was taller and leaner than the first human, and even uglier. He had a small circular hat perched on his thin head.

He motioned for the angry human to step back, then turned to the group of Ogres. "We don't get many Ogre *customers*. The only time your kind visits Nerat, it's to steal our children."

Everlyn stepped forward, her palms extended. "Please, we mean no harm. We're not like that. We are . . . " She paused, obviously searching for some way to explain. Finding no single word, she used many, quickly explaining the actions of Eadamm, the philosophy of Igraine, and how they had happened to be on the plains.

The human grunted when she had finished. "Uh. I'd heard something like that. Didn't believe it, though."

"We need horses, five or ten, as many as you can sell us," said Lyrralt. "And supplies. Dried meat, flour, sugar, salt."

"Wine," said Tenaj from behind him.

"And we need to know about the land around here. What lies north? And east?" As he was speaking, Lyrralt pulled money from his pocket, displaying a handful of steel and copper coins.

The human's eyes, which had grown narrow and suspicious at his questions, now glinted. He was no different from an Ogre merchant in that respect. "Get the supplies." He motioned for the one named Turk to bring the items Lyrralt had listed. "There's maybe three horses in the village for sale, I guess. No more."

Turk, who had stomped away to do as he was told, now returned. He slammed a heavy, dusty sack onto the counter, and glared at Lyrralt and Everlyn with such anger in his eyes that Lyrralt would have liked to hack his eyeballs from his head.

He touched the dagger hidden at his waist inside the flowing folds of his cloak. The movement was not lost on the humans.

"Turk was a slave in Thorden," the taller human explained without any hint of apology in his voice. "He has better reason than most to hate your kind. He lost his fingers during his slavery."

As Turk slammed another sack onto the first, he

laid his arms on the top of it. It was true; he had no fingers on his left hand and only two on his right.

"Lost them?" Turk growled and held up his scarred hands, first in the human's face, then waving them toward Everlyn and Lyrralt. "My master"—he spat the word, forming his right hand into a fist—"ate them. While I watched."

Everlyn flushed. Lyrralt shrugged. An Ogre might do as he or she pleased with property. Just the same, he turned away from the sight of the man's missing fingers.

"Get someone else to serve them." Turk slammed his fist into the bag of flour once more before stomping away.

"We'll do it ourselves," Tenaj said softly, moving toward the sacks.

Lyrralt was surprised to see that her face bore the same compassion as Everlyn's.

* * * * *

Khallayne sat on a row of rocks at the edge of the camp and stared at the flat line of the horizon. Even after days of existence on the plains, she wasn't accustomed to the eternal flatness.

A few feet away, Jelindra and Nomryh worked at starting fires and extinguishing them. Jelindra had progressed at an amazing pace, but her brother was having more trouble with the fundamentals of magic.

"No, no, Nomryh," Khallayne admonished. "You're depending too much on the incantation. Try to *feel* it. Try to forget the words and feel the power."

He nodded and bent to a small, cleared space with

a pile of dry grass in the center.

Khallayne went back to gazing at the horizon. For all her life, she'd lived in the mountains, where even the largest valley was ringed with mountains. She found the flatness of the land, the infinity of it stretching away, frightening and fascinating.

She felt what the gods must have felt, looking down on Krynn in the beginning. Away from the camp, with only her two charges and the soft murmuring of the spells for company, she felt small and inconsequential.

"Khallayne?" Jyrbian slid down on the rocks several feet away. "I was watching you work with the children."

"Are you having trouble with your magic?" She patted the rocks closer to her, beckoning him closer.

He nodded, looking so dismayed that she laughed. "It took me two hundred years, Jyrbian. You can't expect to master it in a few weeks."

"I know." He shifted nearer. "It's just that I've come so far . . . "

She understood exactly. "For two hundred years, I tortured human mages, extorting their knowledge from them. But until the battle in the forest, I didn't understand." She turned sideways, drawing her knees up. "Human magic and Ogre magic are vastly different. I didn't realize that I was hampering my own abilities by relying on the human requirements for incantation and spell components."

He was following every word, but she saw that he didn't really comprehend.

"I'm sorry, Jyrbian. I can't explain any better than I already have. You just have to let go. You must trust your own intuition."

She held out her fist and popped her fingers open. Puffballs danced in her palm, like those on the tops of the nearby grasses, except that hers glowed at the center. "Try to *feel* it. I can't tell you any more than that."

He held out his fist, concentrated, and opened his fingers. There was nothing there.

She smiled at his crestfallen expression. It was harder for him than most. The mighty warrior Jyrbian was not accustomed to failure.

"It'll come, Jyrbian. It'll come the way it did for me. And Jelindra."

He was no longer paying her any attention. He was looking eastward, where the line of sky and land was broken by a group of riders on horseback.

"Look!" she called to her students, pointing.

"It's only Lady Everlyn and the others," Nomryh protested.

Khallayne looked at him sternly. "Yes, I believe so, too. But what should we do?"

"Run and alert the sentries. Sound the alarm." He spoke in a tired voice, by rote.

"Very good." Khallayne took pity on them, shooed them away. "Go tell the sentries as you're supposed to. Then go and play for a while before supper. You've done enough for today."

The two hurried away, their energy already renewed.

Jyrbian, too, stood. "I'd better go and see what they've found out." He held out his hand to help her to her feet, but she demurred.

"I think I'll stay a while longer."

The clamor of the camp rose as Lyrralt and his group rode in, leading three new horses loaded with supplies. Everyone came over to see what had been brought back, to hear the news, everyone except for Kaede. She left the camp, a shawl folded over her arm.

Khallayne watched lazily, observing the ebb and flow of the crowd, Kaede's wandering. Kaede roamed far out onto the plain, then bent down.

Khallayne sat up straight and shaded her eyes with her hand. She could see Kaede's arms moving up and down, as though digging.

Kaede must be digging for roots. Some of the Ogre cooks had been experimenting with roots and berries and grasses, looking for something to flavor the monotonous meals. So far, dried meat, boiled and mixed with greens and herbs, still tasted like dried meat.

Still, Khallayne sat there, staring out over the plains, waiting for the golden disk of the sun to slowly drop toward the dark meeting point of land and sky.

The humans attacked at dusk.

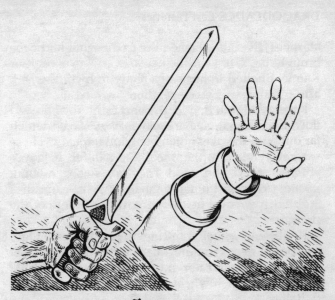

Chapter 12
A Lesson Put to Use

For a moment, Khallayne's mind refused to be drawn away. The violent sounds seemed unreal, far away.

Humans erupted from the grass, screaming and yelling, like fish leaping from beneath the peaceful waters of a pool. The pounding of horses, the screams from camp, the sudden peal of blade against blade, all were background.

Then reality intruded, and Khallayne leapt to her feet with a gasp. Humans were attacking!

She ran, the pumping of her blood thrumming in her ears, fuel to the coursing of the magic. By the time she reached the encampment, the humans were fiercely engaged in hand-to-hand fighting with the

Ogres. They had attacked the east perimeter of the camp.

Power coiled in her belly, ready to be unleashed. The fighting was so close, there seemed no way to set it free without danger to her own.

This was no ragtag band of runaway slaves, wielding homemade weapons and crude spears. These warriors rode into the line of Ogre defense, laying about with axe and mace. They ran, sword in hand. Archers knelt just outside the light of the campfires and let fly arrows feathered with the colors of the prairie.

Khallayne wheeled in time to see a female Ogre run down by a grinning, snarling human on horseback. He crushed her skull with one blow of his heavy mace, then wheeled his mount toward other fighters.

She snatched up the fallen Ogre's sword and ran toward the human. He swung at her, and she felt air whistle past her face. His horse danced sideways, and he jerked it around.

As he charged again, she darted in under his weapon and grabbed his leg, sent magic whooshing out through her fingertips. She had no idea what she was doing. She felt the power, as she had in Khal-Theraxian, as she had in the forest. And as before, the power served her without direction.

The human screamed, fell from his horse, and lay writhing in the dirt, begging for mercy as he died. Without a backward glance, Khallayne threw down the sword.

Another sword sliced through the air. Materializing as if from thin air, Tenaj met the low, whistling swing and deflected it from Khallayne with her sword. Her next movement ripped open the gut of the man, left him standing with his hand pressed to his bleeding stomach, his expression comically surprised. Before Khallayne could say anything, Tenaj had wheeled toward an opening in the line of defenders, blocking to prevent another attacker from slipping through.

Khallayne pivoted. In the thick of the fighting she saw Jyrbian. He was standing his ground, seemingly invincible. Lyrralt fought near him, meeting the human attackers with the same ferocity as his brother.

All around them, the others were rallying to him. She ran toward them. The humans were being driven back!

As Khallayne struck out at the nearest human, Everlyn ran past, weaponless. Khallayne darted to intercept her, past sword thrusts and under swinging axes, but Everlyn reached Jyrbian first. She threw herself between him and the human he was fighting, a husky, hard-muscled human who held his weapon awkwardly because of missing fingers on his sword hand.

Jyrbian dropped his guard, and the human was so surprised at seeing an Ogre throw out her arms to shield him, that he didn't take immediate advantage of the situation.

"Please stop!" Everlyn cried.

"Everlyn! Get out of the way!" He reached out to snatch her aside.

She evaded him, still using her body to protect the human. She reached out and shoved the human who was fighting Lyrralt. The woman warrior was so surprised, she almost dropped her weapon.

Lyrralt, however, didn't. He stepped in, lifting his mace high over his shoulder.

Before he could knock the woman's head from her shoulders, Igraine stopped him. He stepped in front of Lyrralt, raising a hand in front of Lyrralt's mace.

With a glance at her father, Everlyn dropped her arms and said simply, "We have to stop the fighting." Despite the softness of her voice, the words carried to the others.

On both sides, the attacks slowed until, all along the line, humans and Ogres stood warily still, breathing heavily, weapons frozen but held at the ready.

"Please . . . " Everlyn turned to Turk, the human who had shown her his crippled hand in Nerat. "This is not what we came here for. Please, stop the fighting. We mean you no harm."

"Ogres always mean harm!" he snarled, thrusting his maimed hand into her face.

Jyrbian growled as Everlyn closed her fingers over the man's hand, showing him tenderness. Disgusted, Jyrbian reached for Everlyn, but Igraine stepped between them.

"We aren't like that," Everlyn told Turk, meeting his shocked gaze unflinchingly. "That's why we're here, because we—we *choose* not to keep slaves, not to harm others. That's why we've been driven from our homes."

Turk pulled his hand away from her. "You'll not find a welcome here. Too many have died, or worse, at the hands of your kind."

"Then we'll go," Igraine spoke for the first time, laying a hand on his daughter's shoulder. "Put away your arms. Leave us, and tomorrow we'll be on our way. We want no more killing. We want only a place to make a home in peace."

Khallayne looked up and down the line and saw that Igraine's words found support, even among the humans. They had begun to lower their weapons, to stand down from their tense posture. She felt the pressure easing.

Turk looked at Everlyn. "Is this the truth?" he demanded of her. "Will you leave, without further harm to any of my people?"

Before Jyrbian, or any of the dozen or so others who seemed about to answer, could speak, she nodded emphatically. "Yes. I promise."

Turk gestured abruptly, and the humans began to withdraw.

"I'll take your word on this," Turk warned Everlyn, "though I may be crazy to do so. But if you break your word . . . "

Without completing the sentence, he backed away. As quickly, as silently, as they had come, the humans melted back into the plain, taking their fallen with them, leaving behind a band of dazed Ogres. If not for their few dead and wounded, Khallayne could almost believe the fight had never happened.

"What . . . ?" Even Jyrbian, usually so authoritative, so sure of himself, was at a loss.

"What have you done?" Lyrralt asked finally, in a silence so profound that all could hear his words. "Why did you stop the fight? We should have killed them all!"

"Is that what you've learned from my father? Is that who you want to be, after all we've been through?" Everlyn asked with quiet strength.

Obviously struggling to understand, Jyrbian said,

"*They* attacked us."

Kaede appeared at Jyrbian's elbow, a bloody dagger in her hand. "They're humans." If she had said "animals" or "dung," her voice could not have portrayed more disdain, more contempt. "And they attacked us without provocation."

Khallayne remembered that Kaede had left the camp. She tried to remember if she had seen Kaede during the fighting.

"They have *reason* to hate us," Igraine was saying softly, "after all that we have done to them."

Jyrbian opened his mouth to disagree with Igraine, to agree with Kaede. Humans were stupid and savage, good for nothing but slavery. And as for humans who would attempt to kill Ogres . . . his hatred, his lust to kill them boiled over inside. But Everlyn was watching. Sweet, kind, gentle Everlyn, who seemed so fragile that surely his rage could burn her up.

Visibly he controlled his emotions and was rewarded with a smile that warmed his heart. But when he stepped toward her, as usual she turned away.

Kaede put her hand on Jyrbian's, her breast against his arm and gazed up at him with all the heat, the desire, he wished to see in Everlyn's eyes.

He turned away. "We cannot go on this way," he said, facing Igraine.

Khallayne stepped forward. Lyrralt was at her elbow. Bakrell, also, seemed to have appeared from nowhere, clutching a bloody weapon, as his sister had.

Toning his words with respect, Jyrbian said, "Now is the time to speak of the future. We've been running. Now you want us to run again, this time from a pack of puny humans. We could have vanquished them, made slaves of them! Built a new place here."

There was only a minimum of mumbled agreement and much shaking of heads from those around him, but none spoke out. They waited for Igraine to respond.

Everlyn, her face flushed, eyes narrowed, said hotly, "You've learned nothing! Slavery is an evil thing! We can never build—"

Igraine hushed her with a glance. "We must find our own place," he said, softly, then he repeated it in a louder voice for those at the back of the crowd. "And we must build it ourselves. Of our own sweat, not on the misery of others."

"You mean, no slaves?" Lyrralt stared at Igraine in disbelief. The preaching of kindness and generosity in order to increase production from slaves had seemed bad enough. But this . . . !

"Lyrralt. It's wrong to take a person from his home, from his family. It's wrong to lock a man away, take away his freedom." Everlyn touched his arm, as compassionately as she'd touched the human.

Jyrbian's expression changed into one of jealousy and desire.

Lyrralt stared at her as he had stared at Igraine, as if he'd discovered someone, or something, he'd never seen before.

Igraine's persuasive words filled the silence. "If we don't change our ways, we're doomed. Did you—all of you!—not see it in Takar?" He swept his arms wide.

There was murmured assent. "Did you not feel the hopelessness, the uselessness in your lives?" Jyrbian looked around at the crowd, saw the eager faces, the fevered eyes.

Igraine's voice took on a compelling, urgent quality. "Can you not see what our kind will become if we continue on that misbegotten path? Have you ever felt more alive, living as we have these past few weeks, than in all of your miserable lives before?"

He had them now, their hearts and minds. The surge of joy, of faith from his followers, was almost tangible to behold. "We will leave in the morning," he said. "We will find a place of our own, where we can be safe and happy."

The crowd sighed. The Ogres, arms around their loved ones, began to drift away.

Everlyn went with her father, without a glance for Jyrbian, who would have followed her had Lyrralt not caught his arm and pulled him back.

"Is this heresy what he has been preaching all along, about not having slaves?" Lyrralt accused his brother, his glance taking in Khallayne, too.

Jyrbian shrugged, watching Everlyn's disappearing back. "I've been too busy to sit around Igraine's feet like a doting child." He turned away.

The others also walked away, leaving only Khallayne and Bakrell to hear Lyrralt's horrified voice. "This is madness! It was bad enough when he was talking about 'choosing for yourself.' Now he wants you to live as humans live, digging in the dirt for food, building miserable clay huts with your own hands! Don't you even care?"

"Do you? Care, I mean?" Bakrell peered closely into Lyrralt's eyes as if to gauge the sincerity of his answer.

"Well, I don't care," Khallayne said, before Lyrralt could answer.

"You don't care as long as you can practice your heretical magic!"

She met his angry gaze with an expression of equal determination. How long since she'd thought of her magic as a thing to be hidden away? As a wrongness? Any philosophy, heretical or not, was worth the peace and joy and sense of belonging of the past weeks. She shrugged, looking eerily like Jyrbian a moment earlier. "You're right. I don't much care about his philosophy, one way *or* the other."

She turned and walked away, leaving Lyrralt alone with a renewed conviction that he must act soon, whether a good opportunity presented itself or not. He had been looking for a safe moment to kill Igraine, one that would allow him to escape before his deed was discovered. Perhaps he would have to die in the act.

The runes hummed approvingly on his skin.

* * * * *

Fear. The face was there, and it was her own. But it wasn't. The pale sea-green complexion, which had always drawn men to her like bees to honey, was mottled, as splotchy and knotted as tree bark. The black eyes were dull and stupid and humorless. But they were hers.

Screaming woke her. The sound so nearly matched the images of her nightmare that for long moments, Khallayne lay, twisted in her blanket, wrapped in screams that seemed to be her own, except . . .

The screaming went on and on, growing louder then ending abruptly in a silence more terrible than all the noise.

Thinking, at last, that the voice crying out in terror had been Jelindra's and not her own, Khallayne leapt to her feet, stumbling as her blanket caught around her ankles.

Across the campfire Tenaj and Lyrralt each fought free of their blankets, too. Nearer the tent where Igraine slept, Jyrbian tossed off his blankets with a curse that woke more people. "What in the name of Sargonnas is happening now?"

Before anyone could answer, a new scream ripped through the air. Without hesitation, Jyrbian drew his sword and wheeled in the direction of the disturbance. But his sword would be of no use against the thing that had sprung into the air, conjured out of nothing. Or maybe there was more than one. Khallayne wasn't sure.

As Jyrbian charged, slashing with his sword, the cloud that rose into the sky might have been one or twenty creatures. The faces of it changed rapidly. The monster was catlike, snakelike, fanged, black-mawed, a rock, mere mist. There were two, then one, then a mass of them, writhing like snakes streaming from their winter cave into the spring sun.

Jyrbian's sword sank into flesh and mist. An appendage, flickering between long, slithery tentacle and claw-tipped, gnarled horror, reached out and threw Jyrbian backward twenty feet. He landed in a heap and was still.

Khallayne started toward him, and Tenaj grabbed her, hauling her back. "Forget him!"

The creature was smaller now, more solid, more deadly, but still moving slowly, dreamlike, almost loving in its gestures, as it grasped a female Ogre around the neck with its impossibly long fingers.

She tried to scream, but all that came out was gurgling, then abruptly no sound at all.

The cloud creature had gained in substance while the living being had become a flimsy husk, lifeless, no more substantial than paper.

There were new cries from about the camp as more Ogres awakened to find their view of the stars blotted out by the gruesome creature. Lords and ladies who had, weeks before, known a dagger only as a jeweled object to decorate a belt, took up their ceremonial swords and their crude pikes and prepared to fight.

Khallayne knew their courage would do them no good. Hadn't Jyrbian just proved that? She could sense Tenaj collecting her power, could hear the murmured words of a spell forming on the other Ogre's lips. Tenaj was still only learning things Khallayne had practiced as a child, still tentative about the power inside her. Khallayne realized she had to help.

The cloud creature turned on them. Its features were two, three, a dozen frightening faces, shifting until they were one, multiplying again, then melting into something ugly and monstrous and monolithic.

Khallayne tried to close her eyes, tried to concentrate and bring up her own power. She couldn't. She couldn't move a muscle. Even her eyelids refused to budge, to blot out the dreamlike movement, the painfully slow change of features, from one to many. Chameleonlike. Dreamlike.

Tenaj finished her spell, the words to a "banishing" spell hurled at the creature with all the neophyte force she could muster.

The thing wavered in the air, then reared and moved in their direction, all teeth and roaring maw.

It leapt at them, like a snake coiling and striking.

In the instant before it struck, Khallayne perceived its true nature. Fifty feet away, maybe seventy, the tenuous, smokelike tail that tethered the cloud creature to the earth was connected to a sleeping form. In the center of pandemonium, in the middle of the attack, Jelindra slept. The creature issued from her. And it was Jelindra's voice that had wakened Khallayne . . .

Tenaj fell, struck by one of the writhing tentacles. She tried to regain her footing, but was dazed by the blow. She slipped. Her arms refused to support her weight as she tried to push herself back up.

The horrible, half-melted, half-monster face leered at Khallayne. The stench of filth and corruption filled her nostrils. The nearness of the thing freed her tightened muscles.

She flung up her hands, forming a shield to protect herself and Tenaj.

"Do something!" Lyrralt materialized at her side, mace clutched in his fingers. He helped Tenaj to her feet, his tall, strong body bracing her, then grabbed Khallayne's shoulder. "Stop the thing!"

Khallayne tried to tear herself from his steely grasp. The tips of each of his fingers pressed bruises into her flesh. The thing lunged at them again and rebounded off her shield. It struck again and was repelled again. It reared up into the night and screamed, a roar of fury and frustration. It turned on the warriors surrounding it, on Ogres who hadn't the power to shield themselves. It grabbed a young boy and lifted him, screaming and kicking, into the air.

Lyrralt shook Khallayne. "Khallayne! Do something!"

"Jelindra—" she managed to gasp. "Jelindra's nightmare. Wake her." She pointed to the sleeping form, barely visible through the crowd.

At last comprehending, Lyrralt went into action. He leapt campfires, dodged confused, shouting Ogres, made it across the camp, and grabbed the sleeping Jelindra.

His touch was rough and abrupt. In response, the creature writhing in the air above his head roared, spewing fire and noxious smoke. The flame licked at Lyrralt's head and shoulders.

Khallayne surged forward, sure he was about to be immolated. Just as she reached him, the creature disappeared. She blinked, blinked again.

The monster was gone, leaving dark sky and twinkling stars overhead as if nothing had happened. Jelindra was sitting up, clutching her blanket in her fists. Lyrralt, standing above her, mace still clutched in hand, was unharmed.

Then Jelindra screamed, hideously, pitifully.

Khallayne and Lyrralt wheeled in the direction of the child's stare, both expecting to find another monster.

What they saw instead was Celise, Jelindra's mother. She was kneeling on the ground, weeping over the lifeless husk that had been Nomryh.

Chapter 13

Murderous Innocence

"Is Jyrbian all right?" Khallayne asked Lyrralt as she wiped at her forehead wearily.

Jelindra and Celise had been calmed at last, thanks to some wine, a little magic, and Igraine's comforting, soothing words.

Bakrell swaggered up in time to hear her question. "He's making full complaint of an interesting bump on his head. Everlyn is patting his wrist, and my sister is fuming."

Holding her injured arm against her side, Tenaj laughed, a bell-like peal as silvery as her eyes.

Bakrell looked at her with an appraising, appreciative expression that reminded Khallayne of the old

Jyrbian, the one who had wooed her and every other woman at court with rowdy charm and high spirits. Now he had vanished behind a mask of authority, straining for the affection of a woman who paid him no attention.

She felt a moment's pang for that Jyrbian, that by-gone world, then let it pass. Not for a return to that comfortable life would she give up the magic.

The crowd around Jyrbian parted. He walked with a slight limp, his arm around Everlyn's shoulders for support. His expression, beatific, was like nothing Khallayne had ever expected to see on his face.

Whatever the extent of his injuries, at that moment he didn't seem to be suffering much. Just as Bakrell had said, Kaede was holding his elbow for support. Storm clouds in the sky could be no darker than the expression on her face.

"How's Jelindra?" Everlyn asked, looking around for the child.

Khallayne waited until the threesome was within hearing. "She's better. Your father's with them."

"Do you really think she dreamed that monster?" Jyrbian asked, his voice clipped.

"Yes, but you can't hold her responsible. She's only a child, and she's half mad with grief. And no one can control their dreams!"

"If she caused that thing once . . . what do we do in the future?" he asked. "Let her accidentally kill us off one by one?" His voice was less harsh, less accusing, but still bitter.

"I don't know."

"We could take turns at night watching her," Everlyn suggested. "Surely, if it happens again, we can wake her up right away and break the spell."

"Or you can die, sucked dry, like her brother did."

Everlyn slipped from under Jyrbian's arm, her face suddenly distant. "I think I'll check on her."

"What about me?" Jyrbian called after her, his voice playful. Only Lyrralt knew him well enough to sense the disappointment in his tone.

Everlyn smiled back over her shoulder, her long hair tumbling like silk down her back. "Surely you'll manage."

The warmth of her smile made him forget everything. He didn't notice Kaede's expression slipping from troubled to bleak. Without glancing at Kaede, Jyrbian limped toward his bedroll.

With a longing glance at Jyrbian's back, Kaede turned to Bakrell. She motioned for him to stay with the group. He caught her arm and wordlessly held her for a moment.

"Keep them occupied," she whispered.

Reluctantly, he nodded and went back to Khallayne's side as Kaede went to her bedroll for a shawl and a small package.

As Kaede slipped out of camp, she saw that Bakrell was still in the center of the group, drawing their attention with his questions and conversation.

Since the human attack near Nerat, the Ogres had been posting sentries at night. Kaede and Bakrell had taken turns, sitting outside the perimeter of the camp and watching the darkness. But someone could have slipped out—or in.

Kaede pulled the dark shawl over her bright hair and crept away from the camp, heading out onto the plain. Solinari was just rising, offering a pale, cold light on the horizon. She walked through the tall grass, damp with dew, until the fires of the camp were mere twinkles in the distance, until the only sounds were the rustling of grass and the chirp of nightbirds.

She searched until she came to a small rise. Beyond it, she dug a hole and planted the small package. There were no rocks on the plain, as there had been in the mountains, so she marked the place by pulling up all the grass around it for the width of her two hands. Then she set a small spell on it, a beacon for anyone who knew how to search.

Brushing grass and dirt off her pants, she rose and started back to camp. Voices, so nearby that she could understand what they were saying, interrupted the quiet, sibilant whisper of the breeze.

Kaede dropped to the ground, flat on her belly, waiting for the voices to start over. In a moment, a female's soft voice broke the silence.

"I'm here."

An equally soft, male voice answered.

The female's voice again. "Oh, Love, it's you who've come."

This time Kaede recognized it. In spite of the pleasurable tone she'd never heard coloring Everlyn's speech, she knew it was Everlyn's voice! And in a lover's clandestine meeting!

Her heart caught in her throat as the male voice responded. She couldn't hear it well enough to identify it. Praying that it wouldn't be Jyrbian, she raised herself cautiously for a better look.

* * * * *

Bakrell was sitting on her bedroll when Kaede slipped back into camp, waiting for her with a tense expression on his face.

She glanced about, checking that no one appeared overly interested in their conversation before leaning close. "Bakrell, you won't believe what I've discovered about Everlyn!" she whispered.

He looked at her flushed face, at the exhilaration shining in her eyes. Her lips were pulled back in an intense smile. "That's what I wanted to talk to you about, Kaede."

The caution, the disapproval in his voice, dimmed her enthusiasm.

"I was wondering . . . if you haven't forgotten why we came here." He looked first at her, then at his own hands, clasped in his lap.

"What do you mean?"

"Just what I said." He edged closer to her. "I was wondering, considering the way you feel about Jyrbian and all, if you've—"

"I haven't forgotten anything!" Kaede glared at him, slapping away the conciliatory hand he extended. "I've searched and searched, but I'm convinced that Jyrbian is the one. Why do you think I keep running after him?"

Bakrell lifted an eyebrow at her and smiled.

"All right," she admitted. "I do want him for other reasons. What's wrong with that? That only makes it more convincing. I haven't forgotten why I came here, and I resent—"

"Kaede." He stopped her by gently placing his fingers over her mouth. "Slow down. You misunderstand. I wasn't accusing you. I was—I've been thinking. This life really isn't so bad, is it? I mean, it's pretty exciting, and we can do as we please. And I was just thinking maybe we shouldn't cause any trouble . . . "

"I have no intentions of causing trouble," she said sweetly, and pushed him off her blankets.

*　*　*　*　*

Two days later, Kaede waited for Jyrbian near the edge of the camp. He greeted her with a smile, which he regretted the moment her face lit up. She was a beguiling woman, and she had left no doubt about her interest in him. In another life, just a few short weeks ago, he would have been interested in her. But now there was Everlyn, and she eclipsed Kaede the way the sun outshone the stars.

"Jyrbian," she said, her voice as sweet as cream. "I have to talk with you."

The way she said it, he thought talking wasn't what she had in mind. He answered with a word, her name. He eased the warning in his tone with a slight smile.

She reached for him, wrapping her arms around his, pinning them to his sides playfully. Her breasts were soft against his chest, her breath sweet. "I want you."

He stepped back, gentle as he pushed her away. "Kaede, don't. I won't say I'm not tempted, but . . . "

Her expression went from lighthearted and seductive to disappointed and grim. "You think you want her. But she's not what she seems."

"Don't say anything against Everlyn, Kaede," he warned.

"Then ask her yourself! Ask her why she leaves the camp when she thinks everyone is asleep. Ask her who she meets during the night! Ask her . . . "

For the first time since she'd met him, Jyrbian's

fearsome temper frightened her. His face twisted with fury. His fingers bit into the soft flesh of her arms.

"You're hurting me," she whimpered, pushing closer to him.

"Hurting you!" he roared. "I'll kill you!"

"Then kill me!" She went still in his grasp. "Ask her, then kill me if I'm lying. I'll sing my song of death quickly and lie quietly under your sword." She pressed into him harder.

He allowed it. He crushed her to him so hard that the knots in his belt scraped her skin. He twisted his fingers in her hair and yanked her head back.

"Ask her. Unless you're afraid to hear the truth. Unless you're willing to accept her with the scent of a human's hands still fresh on her body."

"What are you saying?" Jyrbian rasped.

"The truth. I've seen things. Before you decide who you want, you should know the truth. Ask her. I'll wait."

Jyrbian looked at her. He stepped back so suddenly that she stumbled. "I'll be back," he almost hissed.

The conviction in her voice didn't waver. "Not to kill me."

"I may kill you either way," he vowed.

He found Everlyn in Igraine's tent, sitting on a camp stool at the makeshift table where Igraine kept his maps. A stub of candle on a piece of bark provided some illumination, warming Everlyn's face with a soft glow. In a shadowed corner Jyrbian could discern a figure underneath a blanket that must be Jelindra, breathing rhythmically.

"Is she sleeping?" he asked.

Everlyn nodded. "You seem better." When he appeared not to understand, she pointed at his leg and said, "You're not limping anymore."

He shrugged, indicating that his injury was of no consequence.

"What's wrong?" She stood and moved closer to him, nearer the flap of the tent, away from the sleeping figure. Still speaking softly, she laid her hand on his arm and repeated the question.

"Everlyn . . . " He almost walked away. For a moment, he thought, I cannot live with knowing. But he had to know. "I have to ask you something. I have to . . . Is there—? I've been told—"

He saw the truth in her eyes, the sadness, the fearful anticipation, even before he could finish the question. He knew the truth of Kaede's words.

"It's true! You are sneaking out of the camp to meet someone."

"Yes." She said it quietly, softly, without any regret.

If she'd a tinge of remorse . . . "Who?"

She shook her head and looked away.

Weeks of watching and waiting washed over him like fever. "Why do you meet in secret like thieves?"

Again she shook her head, but he already knew the answer. "So it's true!" he hissed. "You turn me away, ignore my every smile, refuse the touch of my hand, for a *slave*."

"He's no slave! He's a . . . a being with a heart and a soul, the same as you and me."

Her quick defense, her easy tenderness, fanned his anger. A dagger slid into his belly would have caused no more agony.

"Jyrbian, I'm sorry. I know this is not easy to

explain, but . . . once I knew him . . . I couldn't help it. I couldn't help but love him! I couldn't help but— And now, I don't know what to do." The words began to pour out of her. "I don't know where to turn. We could never live with my people. And his kind hate the Ogres so. They'd never accept me."

Every word was a thorn driven into his heart. Yet, he wanted her to go on, wanted whatever intimacy she was willing to share, wanted to be the one to whom she revealed her heart.

She glanced up, saw his stricken expression, the warring of emotions on his face. "Jyrbian, I'm so sorry. I never meant to hurt you. But he has worn my heart . . . from the day he saved my life . . . "

"Eadamm," he breathed. He remembered the way the slave had spoken to her, that morning in her father's home, the way she had looked at him. He realized that Everlyn would have stayed at Khal-Theraxian if the slave had not advised her to go. He whispered the name again, tasting hatred and jealousy on his tongue.

"Yes," she admitted reluctantly. "He's been following us, protecting us. His people have been harrying the king's troops in the mountain passes. That's why they haven't followed us so far."

He barely heard the last words. She was offering him crumbs. "Do you think you could ever love me?" He saw the answer in her eyes before the whisper had died on his lips. He understood before she murmured a sound.

She lifted her hands slowly and rested them on her belly. "I bear his child."

He reached for her. She stepped into his embrace, resting her forehead on his arm as if putting aside a heavy load. "I don't know what we'll do, where we'll go so that our child can be raised without hatred and pain." He closed his eyes and felt a deathly stillness creep over him, a peacefulness such as he'd never known before.

He moved his hands slowly up her back, feeling the delicate bones, the thin layer of flesh through the silky cloth. His fingers touched her shoulders, slipped tenderly up to her throat.

She made one sound, an ecstasy so exquisite it could barely be discerned, before his fingers closed. She struggled almost not at all.

"Everlyn?" He eased her down gently and smoothed her hair back from her face, straightening the long strands until they fell prettily over her shoulders. "Everlyn?"

So still. So pretty. He placed her hands at her sides, touched her cheek. Her skin was smooth and warm. Her tunic was rumpled around her neck, and as he straightened it, a necklace fell out: a stone wrapped in fine silver wire, hung on a silver chain, shiny and black, shot through with red, and shaped like tear.

He yanked it from her neck, breaking the chain.

A sound, a soft chuckle, disturbed the silence.

He looked up and saw eyes staring at him from the darkness: Jelindra's eyes, wild and mad.

"Get up," he told her. "We're leaving."

The girl obeyed his orders, showing not the least hint of repulsion, though he walked with his arm firmly around her shoulders, so he could stop her if she made a sound.

He led Jelindra through the least populated areas of the camp. Kaede caught up with them at the line where his horse was tethered. "You said you'd come back for me," she said accusingly.

He looked at her as though he'd never seen her before, yet he said, "Get our things."

She stared at him open-mouthed for a moment, then rushed off. By the time he'd readied the horses, she had returned. She carried his bedroll and saddle-bags as well as her own.

The sight of her snapped him back to reality. How long since—? His mind fled from the memory of soft skin against his fingers.

He looked around quickly. Still nobody had noticed them. "Stay here. Watch the girl. If she makes a sound, kill her."

Kaede opened her mouth to question him, but he had already gone back into the camp, slipping silently among the sleeping Ogres.

He found Khallayne easily, quickly. She was buried in her blankets, only the top of her head showing, black hair spilling out onto the ground. He started to shake her awake roughly, then thought better of it and slipped his hand down into the blankets until her soft breath touched his fingers.

The soft skin of her cheek reminded him of another's skin. He stroked her face gently, remembering soft skin and a sweet scent.

Khallayne woke, striking out at his hand. He clamped his fingers over her mouth, leaning down until his lips were against her ear. "Shhh, Khallayne, it's me."

She stopped struggling, and immediately he eased the pressure on her mouth, helped her to sit.

"No need to wake the whole camp," he said easily. "What's wrong?"

"Nothing." He picked up her boots and held them

out. "It's the girl. I need you to come with me."

"Jelindra?" Instantly, she was wide awake. She took the boots and pulled them on. "What's happened?"

"Nothing. She's just—wandered away from camp, and she's frightened. Come with me."

Khallayne stood quickly and grabbed her jacket.

"That way."

As Khallayne started to move, Lyrralt stirred and sat up. His bedroll was only a few feet away. "Jyrbian?"

Jyrbian put a finger to his lips and shushed Lyrralt.

"Jyrbian, what's wrong? Where's Khallayne going?"

Jyrbian gave him a look such as Lyrralt had not seen since Takar, one eyebrow raised high, self-deprecating charm twisting his mouth. "It's none of your *affair*, Brother, if you know what I mean. Go back to sleep."

Jyrbian picked up Khallayne's saddlebags and eased away into the darkness. Khallayne was almost to where he'd left Kaede and Jelindra when he caught up with her.

Kaede and Jelindra were mounted. Kaede was holding the reins to the other horses. The girl appeared even more docile, even more remote, than before.

"What's going on here?" Khallayne wheeled on him.

"We're leaving," he said. "Mount up."

Kaede tossed him his reins, her expression murderous.

"I'm not going anywhere with you, Jyrbian," said Khallayne.

"We don't need her," Kaede jeered.

Jyrbian responded to Khallayne as if Kaede hadn't even spoken. "You don't have to if you don't want to. But if you don't, you'll find her body"—he paused and jerked his thumb in the direction of Jelindra—"left to rot on our trail."

"Why are you doing this? What's happened?"

"It's your choice," he said conversationally. "Her only use to me is as a hostage, to keep you in line. If you're not with me . . . And before you think of casting a spell, are you willing to bet you could take care of both of us before one of us kills her?"

When Khallayne still didn't move, he turned his horse and started to ride away. Kaede followed him, leading Jelindra's horse.

"I wouldn't do that, Jyrbian." Lyrralt's voice came out of the darkness.

Jyrbian spun, his hand moving to his sword, and found himself facing off against his brother and Bakrell.

"Why not?" Jyrbian asked softly. He dropped his hand from his sword hilt, with his palm open and ready, dangling at his side.

"They've found Everlyn."

Jyrbian started at the name. Quickly, he regained his composure. Beyond them, in the lights nearest the tent, he could see agitated movement.

"What's happened to Everlyn?" Khallayne asked.

"She's dead. From the bruises and marks on her body, strangled."

"Jyrbian?" Khallayne stepped forward.

He was reminded of Everlyn, stepping between him and the human at Nerat. The memory seemed etched in blood.

"What happened?" Khallayne asked. Hers was a voice of reason, of conciliation.

"Everlyn was seeing a human male, at night, outside the camp." Kaede also edged forward, her voice brisk, cold.

"Seeing a human?" Lyrralt didn't understand.

"He was her lover." Kaede spat the word as if it were filth.

The others responded with shocked silence.

Before they could react, Jyrbian surged forward and grabbed Khallayne. He yanked her by the back of her tunic, up and over his saddle. Before she could recover her senses, he thumped her across the back of her head and she went limp.

Lyrralt started forward, stopping when Jyrbian reached with one hand for his sword. His horse danced, agitated by the extra weight and the tension around him. "Go back, Brother. Go back to your miserable friends. Don't follow us. Don't—"

"Jyrbian, don't do this." Igraine's voice, choked with grief, interrupted the scene. "There's been enough damage. Don't do anything more."

"You're responsible for this!" Jyrbian retorted, eyeing the silent crowd amassing behind Igraine. "You! Preaching of better ways. But there is only so much we can change while still giving honor to the gods. Still honor our traditions. If you continue this way, the vengeance of the gods will rain upon your heads!"

He glanced at Kaede, the only person in the whole camp who sided with him willingly, and jerked his head in the direction of the mountains. He galloped away, Khallayne hanging limply on his horse.

Kaede started to follow, then stopped and turned

back for a moment, yanking on the reins of Jelindra's horse to control the animal. The child sat astride, much more docile than the horse.

"Bakrell?"

Caught by surprise, Bakrell opened his mouth, then closed it, then opened it again.

"You're not going to stay here? There's no reason anymore. We have what we came for."

She waited, but Bakrell refused to meet her gaze. "No," he said at last.

"You're staying?" Kaede was incredulous, but when he didn't speak to her again, she yanked her horse around and galloped after Jyrbian, leading Khallayne's riderless stallion and the horse on which Jelindra rode.

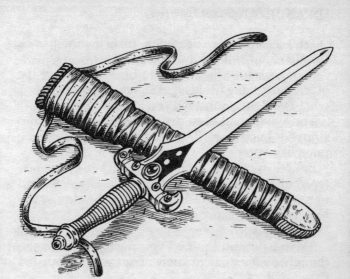

Chapter 14
Vengeance of the Gods

The sound of the four horses, galloping through the dry grass, pounding the earth, sounded across the plain for a long time.

"We have to go after them!"

Tenaj was in favor of pursuit. Several others standing nearby rumbled agreement.

Lyrralt shook his head. "If you chase them in the darkness, they'll kill their hostages for sure. Or you. It would be easy to set an ambush."

Tenaj's hand dropped from its customary set on the pommel of her sword. "Why did they take Khallayne and Jelindra?"

"I don't know."

Igraine, shoulders drooping, turned slowly back toward camp, but Bakrell blocked his way.

"Lord, please." Bakrell fell to his knees before the older Ogre, hung his head in shame. "I must confess what I've done. I must tell you all that I know."

Those who had been drifting back toward camp stopped. Lyrralt and Tenaj moved in closer. Igraine put a hand on Bakrell's shoulder and nodded.

Bakrell swallowed. He began with his gaze fastened on the ground at Igraine's feet. "My sister and I are of the last of the Tallees Clan, the clan of the Keeper of the History of the Ogre."

Lyrralt gasped.

"My sister and I joined you partly because she thought someone here knew about what happened to the History."

"I don't understand," Igraine said solemnly. "I thought the Keeper died a natural death."

"That is what the council allowed everyone to believe. But Kaede believes there was a conspiracy. And she believes the Song is still alive. For our family, the Song has its own special . . . music. She hears it, still."

Bakrell paused, cocking his head as if he, too, were listening to something far off. "I haven't her abilities, but I must say, I agree with her. I think, if the Song were truly gone, there would be a . . . silence."

"Go on," Igraine prompted when Bakrell lapsed into silence.

"The Song drew Kaede here, to someone among us. But she wasn't sure who. Two nights ago, she told me she thought Jyrbian was the culprit."

"So you came here to find the Song," Tenaj said coldly. "Is that all?"

"No. We also came . . . " He mumbled something.
"What?"

Igraine put his hand on Bakrell's chin, tipping it back so he could see his face. "Don't be afraid. No one is going to hurt you now. What is the other reason you joined us?"

Bakrell squared his shoulders. "We came on behalf of the Ruling Council."

A gasp went up from the crowd, and there was a surge forward, but Igraine controlled everybody with a wave of his hand. "Continue."

"Things are very bad in Takar," Bakrell said. "The humans. Escaped slaves are everywhere in the mountains. When we left, there had already been three supply trains attacked and destroyed.

"There were many who didn't approve of how the Ruling Council handled Igraine. They were incensed that an Ogre was punished for consolidating his profits. And they have become even angrier that the council seems powerless to stop the human attacks."

"The council sent out troops to find you. You met the first, and the second, and destroyed them. What you don't know is that they have continued to send reinforcements. As far as I know, from the last communication from our contact, every one of them has been attacked and harried or destroyed. By humans. They thought that you were using humans for soldiers, because there were so many attacks by the escaped slaves, so many coordinated, planned attacks."

"And that's why they sent you?" Igraine asked.

Bakrell nodded. "They wanted information. Kaede volunteered to come."

"But we haven't been in communication with any

groups of slaves," Tenaj protested. "Surely you discovered that weeks ago."

Bakrell started to tell them what Kaede had discovered about Everlyn, and the slaves who'd been guarding their flanks, since after the attacks in the mountains, but he couldn't. Igraine looked old, immensely tired. His eyes were swollen with grief. Bakrell couldn't add to his misery.

"Yes, we did. We realized that immediately. We stayed on, hoping to discover the truth of the lost History. And—" He hesitated. "There's one other thing. Kaede's—that is, *we've*—been relaying messages for a courier, messages to the council, with maps and information on your whereabouts."

There was no response this time, no emotion at all from the broken and grieving refugees. They were stunned.

"We don't know if the messages got through," he said hurriedly. "We don't even know if they were picked up as they were intended to be. We'd just leave them behind, marked in the prearranged way."

Bakrell clutched Igraine's hand. "Please, Lord, the reason I've told you all this is because I have made a decision. I want to stay. The longer we dwelt among you, the more convinced I became that yours is the right way to live. I know I've committed transgressions against you, but I want to stay."

Wearily, Igraine patted his hands. "I can't make that determination, Bakrell. Everyone will have to decide. But for myself, I welcome you. We have all committed crimes and atrocities. We have all suffered."

As if suddenly reminded that Igraine's only child lay cold and dead within the tent, the assembly broke up without any other words, forming into smaller groups. They silently drifted back to the tent at the center of the camp. There they built a pyre for Everlyn's body and sang their songs of sorrow for Igraine.

Bakrell moved among them. Although none spoke to him, none turned away as he helped with the sad tasks.

Lyrralt took his blankets and slipped away, alone, to the edge of the camp, past the lines of horses and the watchful eyes of the sentries.

Tonight. He knew it had to be tonight. Igraine would be left alone with his grief. And Lyrralt would be able to slip into his tent.

The runes throbbed on his shoulder, itched down his arm. He sat alone in the darkness and wished for a moment's numbness, that he might be free of the urging of the runes. He searched for the constellation of Hiddukel in the night sky, but clouds had covered Solinari and blotted out the stars.

In the blackest hours of the morning, he slipped back into camp and into Igraine's tent. The interior was dark; only a single candle was guttering in its own wax, almost dead.

Igraine sat on a mat of thick carpet, his legs crossed, his hands lying on his knees. He didn't look up as Lyrralt entered, but said, "So you've come at last to kill me."

Lyrralt was so surprised, his hand halted in the act of drawing his dagger from inside his robe. "Kill you, Lord?"

Igraine slowly raised his head.

Lyrralt gaped when he saw that Igraine's silver eyes had gone gray.

"Isn't that why you've come? Isn't this what you've planned for, watched for, for weeks?"

Lyrralt shrugged and drew the dagger. So, Igraine knew. Soon he would be dead, and it wouldn't matter anyway. And if he raised the alarm, it would be over before anyone could come. "Yes. That's why I've come."

"You won't stop what is happening, you know. What I've begun is larger than me now. It's larger than any single Ogre."

Despite the tiredness, the defeat in Igraine's voice, Lyrralt felt the pull of persuasion. The runes squirmed, reminding him of his duty. A calmness came over him. "I don't care about what you've begun. Only you."

Igraine nodded. He hadn't made any move to defend himself. Lyrralt shifted the dagger to his left hand and wiped his sweaty palm on his tunic. The runes seemed to wriggle, wormlike, faster and faster. He struggled to maintain the objective in his mind.

"You know you don't *want* to do it, though, don't you?" Igraine asked. "You haven't for some time now. If you had wanted to, you would have done it long ago."

Lyrralt paused in the act of raising the dagger. It didn't matter what Igraine thought. He would soon be dead. "There was never an opportunity. You're always surrounded by admirers, by acolytes."

"There have been plenty of opportunities. You've ignored every one of them until tonight."

Until tonight. Lyrralt lifted the dagger over Igraine, meaning to plunge it downward into his skull. On his arm, the runes felt as if they had caught fire, as if they had grown roots, which were biting deep into his flesh, reaching into the marrow of his bones.

Lyrralt groaned in pain, reared back, and brought the dagger down with all his might! It thudded dully, vibrating as it lodged in the wooden post above Igraine's head.

Pain ripped through his shoulder. He screamed and fell, writhing, spine contorted, onto the mat at Igraine's feet.

Igraine touched his back, his hip, his aching shoulder, and the pain eased. He heard the sound of running feet, the flaps to the tent being shoved open, but he couldn't move.

"Lord?" Tenaj's voice sounded from the entrance. "We heard a scream."

"It's all right." Igraine smiled down at Lyrralt. "It was just a muscle spasm."

Lyrralt sat up slowly and saw several faces peering worriedly through the open flap.

Igraine waved them away. All but Tenaj and Bakrell disappeared.

Those two entered. Bakrell stared at the dagger embedded in the post. He considered the weapon, Igraine, then Lyrralt, then wordlessly he pulled it free and offered it to Igraine.

Igraine took it and passed it back to Lyrralt.

Before Bakrell could comment, Tenaj said, "I want to go after Khallayne and Jelindra."

"And I have told her it is I who should go." Bakrell squatted on the mat beside Lyrralt, facing Igraine. "My sister is partly to blame."

"And it is my friends they've taken."

"They are just as much my friends, Tenaj, though I have not shown them the honor friends deserve," Bakrell said.

"Why you instead of me?"

"Because we'll need you to lead the warriors in Jyrbian's place," Lyrralt told her softly when his wits had returned. "If the council knows where we are, we will need you more than ever. Bakrell should be the one to go." It was only after he'd spoken that he realized what he'd said. He looked to Igraine for permission or censure, but Igraine did as he'd always done when, before, Jyrbian had made some decision of which he approved. He merely smiled.

Bakrell was nodding agreement, too.

"I wouldn't be too pleased," Lyrralt said, rubbing his shoulder as the runes started to dance again. "You're probably riding to certain death, whether you catch Jyrbian or not."

"No. I'll be careful. Maybe we can figure out some way to get a message to the humans who're guarding us. And if I don't catch them before they get to Takar, I can lose myself in the city, where I'll be perfectly safe."

* * * * *

Khallayne woke, groggy. Her neck and the back of her head ached. Her belly hurt, and someone was shaking her so hard, she thought she was going to be sick.

She opened her eyes, and the ground rushed past her eyes with sickening speed. Suddenly, she remembered.

Jyrbian had grabbed her and thrown her across his horse. Then darkness had descended, and she remembered nothing. Until now.

She struggled to hold her head up, to steady it

against the horse's bouncing. She pounded on his leg with her fist and was rewarded with laughter from above.

The horse slowed and broke into a trot, which almost tore her head from her shoulders, then slowed some more and stopped. Jyrbian dragged her up and over the horse until she was on her back, cradled in his strong arms.

"So you're awake?" he asked.

"Where are we going?" Khallayne tried to ask, but her mouth felt as though it were filled with puffballs.

Jyrbian motioned for Kaede. He took the reins of Khallayne's stallion.

"We're riding, my love, into the night." He pushed one of her legs over the saddle of her horse, then lifted her up onto the horse's back. "And remember, if you get any ideas about not keeping up with us, or of getting lost, Jelindra will be staying with us, even if you do not."

He grinned cruelly at her, then kicked his horse into a run. They stopped sometime in the wee hours of the morning, and Kaede tied her wrists and ankles together as she fell asleep, too exhausted, too sick with pain and heartache to resist.

The sun was up, shining in her eyes, when she regained consciousness. She rolled over and buried her face in the crook of her elbow, trying to shut out the sunlight. Darkness descended, and she realized she overheard Kaede talking to Jyrbian.

"Why, Jyrbian?" Kaede was demanding. "Why do we need them? They're just slowing us down."

"It's my decision, that's why," Jyrbian's voice answered.

Khallayne was very alert.

"You asked me to come with you! You want me to help you watch the girl. I think you owe me an explanation!"

"I didn't *ask* you to come," Jyrbian responded, still sounding bored. "And you're free to leave anytime you choose."

Kaede's voice softened, lost its stridency. "I didn't mean it that way. You know I want to be with you. But, I see why they have to come along with us. I don't want—" Her voice died away.

"Well, I do want them with us."

"Buy why?"

"Very well, I'll tell you. If it will satisfy you and stop you from complaining."

Khallayne heard crunching sounds, footsteps on dry grass.

When Jyrbian spoke next, his voice was right above her. "The girl I care nothing for, except to make this one behave. But this one . . . " The toe of his boot grazed her hip. "This one is going to teach me everything she knows about magic."

He slipped his foot under her and shoved hard, turning her over. "Do you hear me, Khallayne? You're going to make me the most powerful Ogre in all of Takar."

He smiled and walked out of her range of vision.

Khallayne sat up slowly, shielding her eyes from the sun. "And what if I refuse?"

He was standing beside Jelindra, who was still asleep, wrapped in a blanket. He touched the girl's head gently with the toe of his boot and looked back at Khallayne. "I don't think you will."

* * * * *

Lyrralt sat on a broken wall and stared around him. After several days of hard riding, they were camped in the ruins of a human city in a small range of low hills. They must be nearing the edge of the plains, he supposed, since the flatness was beginning to be broken by rolling land and small hills.

Bakrell was several days gone. He had ridden back the way they had come with a jaunty wave, leaving Lyrralt with the melancholy feeling that he would never see him again.

What was left of the city around him was sad. The crude, half-standing stone walls gave the impression that they had never stood straight and strong as intended. Perhaps they had been broken and leaning, even when new.

Lyrralt walked through the fallen rock, the piles of dust and rubble and wondered who had lived in the place, and why. There was something about it that reminded him of Bloten. Humans attempting to build an Ogre city? It made no sense. Humans were savages who eked their lives out of the plains. They barely had civilization. Or had they built their own cities and roads, before the Ogres had discovered their usefulness as animals of burden, of hard work?

He was standing on the highest place in the ruin, a small portion of a wall that ran along a ridge, when the rain began.

At first, the downpour was so heavy that it seemed like stars falling from the sky! Burning stars! Stars trailing fiery tails.

The first one hit, not far out on the plains, as he'd thought it would, but nearby, just feet from the sheer drop of the ledge. It was a rain of fire! Pebbles and dirt and rainbow flame exploded upward!

He looked up into the sky and saw more, thousands more fiery spots of light, trailing downward. He shouted a wordless warning to those several feet below him, poking through the ruins. As he pointed, more balls of light hit, sending up gouts of flame.

One of the older cousins of Igraine's clan was standing nearby. A spout of fire curled up and slapped him down. He said, "It's cold," in an unsurprised voice. Then his flesh began to melt, like wax dripping from a candle, and the sound that came from him was an ululation of pain and despair.

As the Ogre fell, a dark, fused mass of flesh and bone, the real horror began. Great balls of the light, feet apart, inches apart, came down! Coldfire it was, sent from the heavens by the gods. Wherever it touched, it burned without flame, burned cold, but with a heat more intense than anything Lyrralt had ever experienced.

Lyrralt leapt down from the wall, landed on the side of his foot, and rolled on the hard ground. He came to his feet running. Where was Igraine? He had to find Igraine.

Another Ogre was hit by the coldfire, and another: Haleyn, who made such beautiful music with his flute, and Issil, who supervised the carrying of live coals from camp to camp, always making sure the Ogres had continued warmth.

One of the children of Igraine's clan, the noisy one, fell. His sister screamed and grabbed him as the fiery ball crashed onto his back, and she, too, was consumed. And Celise, Jelindra's mother, also died shrieking.

He saw Tenaj run, dodging the fiery explosions, dragging two of the children away before they could touch the melted body of their father and become part of his boiling flesh.

He stopped, looked about wildly, and ran again. As he ran, Ogres died all around him. But none of the deadly fire came near enough to touch him. He looked up at the sky. This was no attack of humans or Ogres! No attack even of any kind of magic he recognized.

Reaching inside his tunic, Lyrralt grabbed the medallion that hung around his neck and yanked it so hard that the chain cut into his skin and broke. He clasped it between his palms and shouted—sang!—screamed!—a prayer to the heavens. "Mighty Hiddukel, Great Goddess Takhisis, why have you spared me? So that I might observe death all around me? Have mercy on your children! Show forgiveness and spare us—!"

The silver disc that bore the etched symbol of his god heated up so that he flung it away without thinking. The disc sailed up as he gasped, realizing what he had done.

He grabbed at it. But it exploded. Many-hued brightness erupted, searing his eyes and etching a line like a jagged glyph down his face from eyebrow to chin. He felt the runes on his arms writhe and burn even hotter than the metal.

He screamed and fell back, away from the unbearable pain, trying to escape the agony of his burning flesh. He tore the sleeve from his robe, scraped at his arms, his face.

The pain ended as suddenly as it had begun. The last thing he saw, before darkness overcame him, was the skin of his left arm, unmarked and dark indigo, as unblemished as the day he'd first appeared before his first clerical master.

A peacefulness came over him, covered him like a blanket, like nothing he'd ever known. *This is what it is to die,* he thought. *This quiet, this dark . . .*

Tenaj and Igraine found him. The fiery rain of stars had ended. The fire of the gods had left no wounded, only melted lumps of flesh, no longer recognizable as Ogres.

Lyrralt was sitting, his back against a broken wall of stone, legs crossed comfortably, his hands clasping his unmarked forearms.

His face, his beautiful, finely chiseled face, bore a craggy scar that began at his hairline, dipped to his heavy eyebrows, zagged across his high cheekbone, back across his cheek, and disappeared underneath his chin. It looked like a thunderbolt, molded of silver as bright as the color of his eyes. Except that his eyes were no longer bright silver. They were a shining, opalescent white with no sign of any pupils at all.

"Lyrralt?" Tenaj kneeled beside him, afraid almost to breathe his name, for fear that he would start to scream. Or that she would.

"Lyrralt, are you . . . " What she meant to ask seemed a stupid thing to inquire, with his face disfigured and his eyes so strange.

For a moment, Lyrralt continued to stare, then he stirred, slowly straightening. He reached out, obviously for her hand, but not in the right place.

Igraine took his hand tightly. Tenaj reached across and placed her palm on their joined hands.

Lyrralt fumbled for the linked hands and felt first her fingers, then Igraine's beneath them. He said softly, "I can't see you." And he smiled.

Chapter 15

Blessed with Victory and War

The cool, crisp mountain air felt like home after the alien heat of the plains. Tree branches hung low overhead. The damp, welcoming scent of decay permeated the mulch underfoot.

Jyrbian rode in silence, as he had for days, drawing the scent of rot, the humidity, into his lungs. His despair rode with him.

Khallayne was sullen and withdrawn. Kaede was, for the moment, wise enough to remain silent, for Jyrbian's thoughts were not kind.

The bloodstone seemed warm in his pocket, as if he could feel it against his hip through the layers of cloth. He could still envision it, lying against the smoothness of her throat, the polished black surface of rock, the red veins pulsing through it, pulsing, though blood no longer pulsed in her veins.

Did her human lover know that she was dead? His mouth curled. His fingers clenched into fists; the leather of his reins cut into his palm. He wanted to hit something. He wanted to pound his fists on something until his hands were numb, until his fingertips could not remember the sweet sensation of smooth flesh beneath them.

His horse nickered softly and danced sideways, almost unseating him. He pulled at the reins and tightened his grip on the animal.

"Jyrbian."

He glanced back at Kaede irritably, still tugging as his horse pranced. He saw that her horse, too, was misbehaving, throwing its head up and down.

Immediately alert, Jyrbian signaled for silence. Dismounting, he soothed his mount with gentle hands, then checked his sword, easing it a hand's length in and out of the scabbard twice, just to make sure it was ready to do his bidding. Holding firmly to the reins, keeping the horse's head down, he eased along the trail. With a stealth that spoke of experience, Kaede slid to the ground and followed, leading Jelindra.

Khallayne slid to the ground, too. They knew, as long as Kaede held Jelindra in her thrall, that she would follow them.

The woods had become silent. Gone was the chitter of birds and the rustle of small animals in the undergrowth. The cool, leaf-shaped shadows had become menacing.

Beside the trail, Kaede discovered what was making the horses so restive. Dumped carelessly between the roots of a huge, old tree were what was left of two Ogre guards, a male and a female, wearing uniforms that had probably once been the immaculate white-and-red of the Dalle Clan. The cloth was so stained with blood and dirt, coated with dead leaves and twigs, that it was difficult to know for sure. It seemed as if they had been hacked and battered to death, the bodies dragged off the trail and left for the animals.

"No attempt to hide the bodies," Jyrbian whispered, sliding close to Kaede so that his lips barely made a sound. "Whoever did this didn't care who discovered the evidence."

"Humans!" The word was a hiss, a warning, a curse. Kaede turned away, one hand on her sword hilt, one on her stomach as if she were sick.

Jyrbian knew, however, that she actually clutched the dagger she wore tucked in her belt, hidden beneath the folds of her tunic. He backed carefully away from the bodies and back onto the hard ground of the trail, careful to make as little noise as possible among the leaves and dead twigs.

They were west of Thorad by at least two day's ride. If he remembered correctly, the trail forked ahead, heading east down into a valley and west up into the mountains, bypassing the city. Intuition told him the humans would be to the east, on the more passable trail. Food would be easier to find, and so would prey.

He grinned at Kaede. "Shall we see what lies ahead?"

He glanced back. Khallayne was on foot, leading her stallion, staring at the two guards' bodies with dread fascination. Jelindra was still mounted, staring off into space.

"Can you make her watch the horses?" Jyrbian gestured toward the trees on the opposite side of the trail.

They were very near where the trail came out on a low ridge overlooking the valley.

Kaede spoke for a moment with Jelindra, words Khallayne couldn't hear, and then left her holding the horses. "She'll be all right," Kaede assured Jyrbian.

Crouched low, hidden by scrubby plants and rough, sharp-edged boulders, Jyrbian and Kaede edged through the sparse woods, out to the ridge overlooking the valley. Khallayne followed.

Just clear of the shadows of the forest, where the trail ran along a rocky ridge that circled the valley below, Jyrbian paused, lay down on his belly, and crept to the edge of the crest, keeping his head low.

A troop of Ogres was camped in the curve of a gurgling stream. The camp was orderly. Bedrolls of four to five warriors were laid out neatly around campfires that ringed the field tent. The Ogres were busy cooking. They stood out in the green field, wearing the red-and-white silks of Clan Dalle.

Jyrbian made a sound of disgust. They might as well be painted with targets.

Kaede sidled up beside him, shushed him, and pointed toward the slope to their left.

There, among the thin forest that marched down the hillside, was flitting movement!

Silent shadows weaved in and out among the trees, working their way down to hiding places among the shrubs at the water's edge.

Whoever commanded the company, whoever had chosen such a vulnerable place to camp, deserved to die, to be gutted and left for carrion birds! Unless the approaching humans made noise, they would be upon the guards on two sides of the camp before an alarm was raised.

Kaede tensed, ready to rise and warn her compatriots of the approaching danger. Her sword was already half drawn when Jyrbian grabbed her.

She yanked free of his grasp. "They'll be slaughtered!"

"Wait! Think!" He held her arm. "If you shout now, the humans will melt back into the forest. And we'll be alone up here with them."

"So what do we do?"

Jyrbian grinned, a crooked, thin-lipped expression that made his eyes look as hard as granite. "We go down."

Before she could question him, stop him, he melted back into the shadows.

A moment later, he came crashing past, mounted.

Kaede stared up at him as if he were crazy, then leapt to her feet and followed. Khallayne hesitated a moment.

As Jyrbian reached the edge of the ridge, he drew his sword and held it high over his head. The blade threw out glinting red highlights from the evening sun as he forced his horse to leap down the slope.

The ground was a mixture of dark soil and creekside sand, cut through with gullies of rainwater. The slope was steep, and his horse went down at an angle, sliding, running, falling.

As he reached the level ground, Jyrbian tugged viciously at the reins and sent his horse careening along the edge of the stream, toward the tree line. As he flew past, he noted dark-skinned faces with silver eyes open wide with surprise.

"Humans on your flank!" he shouted. He tore into the woods, into the nearest concentration of humans, and flailed about with his sword. He hit one on the side of the head with the flat of his blade and felt another taste its sharp edge.

The humans had to stand and fight, exposing their positions to the Ogre company.

Jyrbian wheeled his horse among the trees, slashed at a human with a wooden pike, then wheeled back to meet another with a sword. His steel blade sang against inferior metal. He felt as near to ecstasy as could be.

He realized the overwhelming numbers, saw his own death if the sluggish company of Ogres did not respond, then raised his voice in the first, terrible notes of a battle song, a death song.

His foot landed squarely on the chest of a human woman and echoed with a thud and crack. The human emitted a gurgle and fell back. His sword made a welcome whir in the air as he wheeled to meet the next attacker.

Then Kaede was coming to his aid, leading Jelindra into the battle, their horses sending up a spray of sand and pebbles. Her cry of attack made the hair on the back of his neck stand on edge. At last, the Ogres responded to Kaede's battle cry, ran for their weapons, and rushed across the stream to join in the attack.

Jyrbian allowed the first of them to sweep by him, then met the next handful of charging warriors, blocking their path. "That way," he commanded, pointing with his bloody sword. "Into the woods. Flank them."

If there was any hesitation on their part to follow the orders of a complete stranger, he didn't see it. Swords waving, they raced up the hill as he had directed, meeting further waves of humans in the woods.

Quickly, he dispatched others, five here, ten there, any he could commandeer, until the enemy was engaged in a melee all along the stream and through the woods. The Ogre troops might have been slow to respond, but they were making up for it with ferocity.

Three humans fell for every Ogre overcome. Leaping free of his horse, Jyrbian rejoined the fighting for the pure joy of making the odds even heavier. Every human whose throat he slashed, whose belly he stabbed, bore Eadamm's face. He fought and fought harder, mind lost to battle lust.

Finally, he wheeled, sword held before him, and wheeled again, disappointed to find no remaining opponents. Nearby a young female with a short sword was battling a human male with two daggers. Jyrbian stepped into the fray and plunged his sword into the man's chest. As the man slid free of the blade, leaving it coated with his blood, Jyrbian lunged cruelly and cut his throat as well, from ear to ear.

The blood was like an intoxicant. He raised his sword to strike at the body even as it lay, already dead, then Kaede stepped in front of him.

She laid a hand on his trembling arm. "He's dead, Jyrbian. They're all dead. Or running."

For a moment, he stared at her blankly, then the

words penetrated. He looked around. The woods, the shores of the stream, were littered with bodies. The water ran red. It seemed the sky darkened with blood. A heavy, rhythmic wind poured through the clouds, a pounding echoed off the mountainside.

"Let the rest go," Kaede insisted, holding his arm.

Slowly he became aware that his fingers were knotted with pain from gripping his sword, that the heavy, bellowslike sound was not coming from the sky, but from his own lungs. The pounding was the beating of his heart, blood pulsing in his veins.

"Let them go," she repeated in a softer tone, easing the weight of her hand on his arm. "There are troops in the woods who will hunt them."

"Indeed?" said a grating voice behind them. "And I should like to know who thinks himself high enough to order my troops around during battle."

When Jyrbian turned, he automatically adopted a fighting stance.

Several of the Ogres who had surrounded Jyrbian in the heat of the fighting also followed Kaede's example and stepped away from the building confrontation.

The Ogre who faced Jyrbian was obviously the captain of the company. He was tall, though not as tall as Lyrralt, and so slender that he was almost gangly. He wore a fancy version of the red-and-white Dalle uniform, the front so ornamented with citations and ribbons that the cloth barely kept its shape. He had "dandy" written all over him, a soft, pampered member of the high nobility who had probably never set foot away from the court before this life-or-death excursion.

"Ahh." With an exaggerated courtesy, Jyrbian

straightened, bringing his booted heels together with a tap. Though he affected a bow, he never took his eyes from the slender Ogre. "And I should like to know who so stupidly risked the lives of these fine warriors by bivouacking in a place that invites ambush." His voice was like steel and ice.

Anger flared in the captain's eyes. He turned purple with rage. His hand flew to the jeweled hilt of his sword, slid the clean, unbloodied blade from its scabbard.

Jyrbian attacked before the Ogre had a chance to act, but the other parried well. Their blades met high overhead, then lower, at waist level, and locked as the hilts slammed into each other.

With muscles hardened by months of riding and grueling work, Jyrbian was bound to win any test of strength.

Indeed, the captain fell back. One step, two, three, and the growing crowd around them, strangely watchful and silent, flowed with the contest.

Again Jyrbian attacked high, was met, and sent his opponent stumbling backward. He sliced low.

The captain scuttled sideways.

Jyrbian could see the trace of fear in the other man. The other parried, defended, skipped about in desperation to elude the blade that seemed to shimmer in spite of the blood drying on its edge, despite the diminishing light.

Jyrbian reached deftly past his defenses and pricked his opponent's neck, sliced his arm, light cuts that seemed more taunting than harmful. He caught the captain's sword and flipped it neatly out of his hand. With a quick sweep of his foot, he tripped the Ogre.

While the captain lay on the ground, cringing, Jyrbian stepped on his sword and broke the brightly polished blade. Standing over the fallen man, his own sword dangling carelessly so that the tip hovered over the Ogre's chest, Jyrbian said quietly, "I am Jyrbian, of Clan Taika."

He paused, just long enough for the Ogre's eyes to grow large, for him to tremble. Then Jyrbian coldly turned his back and strode away.

The warriors in his path respectfully parted to let him through. Then he heard the whoosh of something fly through the air. He wheeled and crouched low.

The Ogre captain was half sitting, his arm extended, fingers spread. Jyrbian had seen Khallayne in the same posture when she was spellcasting. But this Ogre would cast no more spells.

He was staring stupidly, not at his own hand, but at the dagger protruding from his chest—Kaede's dagger, buried to the hilt.

Kaede stood to Jyrbian's left, her hand still extended. Looking at Jyrbian, her lips curved in a smile. He remembered then that Khallayne had been teaching her magic.

"Apparently," he said, "you've progressed quite nicely in your lessons."

"Now they're *your* troops," she replied.

He looked about at the sweaty, bloody Ogres. He nodded. "And now we're going to win some battles, instead of sitting and waiting for the humans to come and slaughter us."

A shout of victory, of celebration, went up around him.

*　*　*　*　*

Khallayne had been left behind when Kaede had gone crashing down the slope, dragging Jelindra along with her. Her horse had almost thrown her.

Kaede was about to join the fighting when Khallayne caught up with her and tore Jelindra's reins from Kaede's saddle. Kaede had barely paused before turning her attention to the battle.

Khallayne took Jelindra into the valley, away from the worst of the fighting. Jelindra was dazed, caught up in some spell. She tried to get away. Khallayne rode her down, caught her by the back of her tunic, and held on as the girl kicked and screamed. Khallayne slid to the ground, still gripping Jelindra's tunic.

"Jelindra! Jelindra, stop it! Let me talk to you!"

Jelindra kicked her, tried to run.

Khallayne tackled the girl, brought her down hard. When Jelindra rolled over and tried to fight back, she slapped her. "Stop fighting me!" Khallayne shouted.

Jelindra collapsed into sobs. "Please, let me go! Please, Khallayne, let me go. She keeps the thoughts away. Please let me go."

"What are you talking about?"

The fighting had grown fierce near the stream. Khallayne held Jelindra's face against her shoulder and watched the Ogre company sending the humans fleeing back into the forest. Their chance to escape would soon vanish if they didn't leave now.

"She lets me forget," Jelindra cried, pushing away from Khallayne. Her childish voice rose to a piercing scream. "She lets me forget Nomryh! She lets me forget that I killed him!"

Khallayne sat stupefied as the girl jumped up and

ran back toward the group of Ogres who were congregating at the stream, toward Kaede.

She witnessed the end of the fight between Jyrbian and the Ogre captain. She saw Kaede send the dagger flying. Then she saw Jyrbian look around for her and send a handful of guards trotting across the field toward her. She sat on the cold ground and waited for them.

* * * * *

Jyrbian claimed the tent of the dead leader. No one disputed his right.

Kaede stood for a moment at the door, surveying the small room created by canvas walls. It housed a cot, which appeared fairly comfortable, a chest, and a small folding table. The table bore neatly folded squares of thick paper, obviously maps, which the Ogre captain had not seen fit to consult.

Jyrbian unbuckled his sword and laid it on the table, then sat on the edge of the cot and loosened the laces of his boots.

"You made the mistake of turning your back on him," she said finally, part statement, part question.

He eased one boot off and stretched his foot out in front of him before planting it on the carpet. "You were there."

She smiled at his confidence in her, at the appreciation in his gaze, and remembered with pleasure flinging her dagger and feeling the power of her magic send it to its target.

"Where're Khallayne and the girl?" Jyrbian asked.

"The girl came back to me," Kaede said smugly. "I'll assign guards to keep them under watch, but she won't stray."

"No. I want them in here." He removed the other boot.

Kaede's expression went from joyous to disappointed, but she turned to follow his orders.

"But not now." He reached out and caught her before she could take a step, caught the front of her tunic and used his grip to pull her close. With one arm around her, he tugged on the material again, and one of the carved bone buttons popped off.

He tugged again, harder, and thread snapped as two more buttons flew. As she reached for the front of the tunic to unbutton it rather than ruin it, he yanked more buttons off. "Never mind. You'll need a new uniform for our return to Takar anyway."

* * * * *

They rode into Takar at the head of the company, flags held high, symbolizing their victory.

The warriors' uniforms had been altered as much as possible, stripes and decorations torn off. They all wore, as did Jyrbian, the crescent symbol of Sargonnas, God of Destruction and Vengeance, fashioned from the bones of their enemy. They were no longer of the Dalle Clan. They were Jyrbian's.

The pageantry of the warriors drew a crowd of onlookers as they rode through the streets, stirring cheers.

Kaede was breathtaking in her red-and-white silks, her long, silver hair pulled back and braided warrior style.

Khallayne and Jelindra rode behind them, flanked by guards. Jelindra was swallowed up in her warrior tunic. Khallayne wore hers carelessly, showing her disdain.

Jyrbian proudly wore the same clothes he was wearing when he had left Takar, now bloodstained and well used. He'd cut his long hair to just above shoulder length and gathered it at the nape of his neck. His sword lay across his back.

The crowd responded to him, to the power they felt in him. They cheered and ran alongside the troops to keep him in sight.

Riding beside him, Kaede felt like laughing, and did so as the cobbled streets grew crowded and boisterous.

Chapter 16
Song of the Island Home

Jyrbian faced the Ruling Council as dirty and bloody as the last time he'd stood before one of them. But this time, they were the ones who needed something, and he was the one in a position to bestow favors.

Kaede stood to his right. Jelindra was behind her, and Khallayne stood farthest away, back against the door.

The five members of the Ruling Council seemed smaller somehow, aged by the weeks that had gone by. Jyrbian stood, tall and proud, and did not perform the requisite bow. "I've come to offer my services as leader of all the troops of Takar."

They glanced at each other, but before Anel, the

leader, could respond, Jyrbian continued. "My proposal is this. I will consolidate the guards of the clans, and I will turn them into one army. I will reclaim the mountains from the humans. My army will make all the roads safe, as well as the passes and estates. My army will put the slaves back to work, where they belong."

He took a step closer to the platform on which the five council members knelt and lowered his voice. "And when I have done that, my army will track down the heretic Igraine and his treasonous followers and bring them all back to stand trial for their crimes."

He heard Khallayne's soft gasp, but paid it no attention.

Without glancing at the others, Anel smiled and nodded to Jyrbian. "This plan you propose is indeed ambitious, Lord. We shall take it under serious advisement, of course. I'm sure you realize we'd like to discuss it first and hear the report of our agent." Anel glanced at Kaede. "We—"

"Of course, I understand, Lady," he interrupted smoothly. "But you must also understand, of course, that I will do these things with or without your approval."

The gasps this time were from the council, and Teragrym and Enna both half rose, ready to challenge him.

Jyrbian waved them back down. "With you or without you. It is your choice."

He left the audience chamber as abruptly as he had come, Kaede, Jelindra and Khallayne trailing in his wake. He spoke to the first Ogre he encountered in the hall.

"Who are you?" he demanded.

The Ogre, a male about Jyrbian's age, but much smaller and paler, had obviously heard of their arrival. "I'm Ginde, Lord Jyrbian, general aide to the council," he said nervously.

"Well, now, you're my aide," Jyrbian said brusquely.

The Ogre gulped, looking first at the door to the chamber, then at Kaede, then back at Jyrbian. "Yes, Sire."

"I'll be wanting new quarters. The larger ones on the southern side of the building will do nicely."

Jyrbian started off down the hall, the aide dancing alongside him, trying to catch his attention.

"But, Lord, those are occupied by—"

"I don't care. Have them *unoccupied*. Now. And I'll want my troops quartered in the section the king's troops used to occupy," Jyrbian said, banging open the door to the dining hall.

The room was half filled, busy for midafternoon, and the conversations died away as everyone looked at Jyrbian.

"I'll be wanting all new things," he said over his shoulder. "I left nothing behind of any importance. You can put Khallayne in my old apartment. And give Jelindra Lyrralt's old room for the time being."

Kaede nodded, leaving him at the door of the dining hall, motioning for the two of them to follow her. Jelindra obeyed with alacrity, Khallayne sullenly.

There were guards everywhere, at corners and doors where there had never been guards in the castle for as long as Khallayne could remember. And very few slaves, most of whom were wall-eyed and cowed.

They passed a small woman slave carrying a tray,

and she recoiled against the wall as if she expected to be struck as Kaede brushed by her.

Had the slaves always been so afraid of them? Had they always walked with bowed heads and cringed at the slightest sound of a raised voice? Khallayne glanced back at the woman, but kept walking.

"In here." Kaede held open the door to Lyrralt's old apartment and waited for Jelindra. As soon as the girl was inside, Kaede pulled the door closed and locked it, tucking the key inside her jacket.

Khallayne heard Jelindra scream.

"Kaede—!" She wheeled toward Jelindra's door, then toward the rooms that would be hers—Jyrbian's old apartment. The door was already closing behind Kaede. Khallayne surged forward, realizing that, now that Jelindra was safely locked away, Kaede had released the spell that had bound the child's memory.

Khallayne banged the door open, slamming it into the wall.

Kaede looked up from a chest set against the far wall, her eyes narrowed, dangerous, as she waited for Khallayne to speak.

"Looking for something?"

Kaede stood and allowed the lid of the chest to bang shut. "Evidence."

"Of what?" Khallayne pulled her jacket close against the chill in the room. It smelled damp and musty, of being closed up for weeks. Without moving a muscle, she lit the half-burned logs in the fireplace.

Kaede didn't blink. "Of the Song of History."

"The what?" Khallayne covered her quick intake

of breath by turning toward the crackling fire and holding out her hands. Every ounce of her willpower was required to not look at the window, at the sill, to see if Jyrbian's collection of crystals still stood there.

"The Song of the History of the Ogre."

"I don't understand," Khallayne lied, pretending to examine the figurines on the mantel. Surreptitiously, she glanced at Kaede in the mirror that hung above the fireplace.

Kaede had the door to the wardrobe open and was fingering Jyrbian's clothes. "Bakrell and I are the last of the Clan of the Keeper."

"I thought the Keeper was the last."

"My mother was not born in a sanctified marriage, but we are blood nonetheless!" Kaede said the last fiercely, as if daring Khallayne to deny it.

When Khallayne said nothing, Kaede continued, "I've never felt the Song was dead. Never. There would be a silence in me if it were gone."

"So . . . where is it?"

Kaede looked frustrated. She went to the center of the room and turned slowly, eyes closed tightly, as if sampling the air. She sighed. "I don't know. But I feel it strongest when I'm with Jyrbian."

Khallayne nodded. "Why haven't you just asked him?"

Kaede grinned. "Obviously you don't know Jyrbian as well as I thought you did. If he knew I really wanted it, he'd never give it to me."

The room was beginning to warm. Khallayne slipped off the heavy riding jacket and tossed it across a chair. "If you know what kind of Ogre he is, I don't see why you follow him."

Kaede laughed mirthlessly. "Obviously, you really *don't* know him." She was still laughing as she left the room without bothering to lock Khallayne in.

Khallayne ran on light feet to the door and opened it just a crack. She could hear Kaede's laughter dwindling as she strode down the hall.

She retrieved her jacket and forced herself to wait several more minutes before venturing out into the hall.

A guard was stationed at the intersection of the corridor at the other end of the hall, and she straightened as Khallayne emerged. Khallayne concentrated, striking with a mental blow, right above her eyes, as hard as she could.

The guard dropped with a clatter of sword.

Khallayne held her breath. She waited for someone to come to the guard's aid, but the hallways remained silent. She pressed her face against the heavy carving on the door, but there was no sound coming from Jelindra's rooms. "Jelindra?" She called softly.

No answer.

She was afraid of what the girl might have done when all the memories, of her nightmare and the death of her brother, were unmasked and given back to her.

Khallayne breathed deeply, forced herself to control her fear. She concentrated as she hadn't concentrated since the battle in the forest, drawing power from inside.

She had intended to blow the door off its hinges, to blast it into tiny pieces, but at the last moment, she changed the spell. Made it something delicate and precise. She slipped it into the keyhole in the door, into the tiny passages in which the key fit. *Click.*

Click. Click.

The door swung open with just the tiniest pressure.

"Jelindra?" Her voice was soft, as delicate as the spell.

The room was in darkness, even colder than hers, but she was loathe to light it with magic. She bumped into the bed and felt across the uneven surface until she touched Jelindra's hair, spilling out over a pillow. "Jelindra?"

A tiny sob escaped the bundle of blankets.

"Jelindra. It's me. I've come to take you out of here."

The girl sat up and folded herself into Khallayne's arms, erupting in a torrent of tears. "She gave it all back, Khallayne. She gave it all back. After she promised! She made me remember it all."

Khallayne held her for a moment, then pulled back the covers. "You knew you couldn't forget forever, didn't you?"

Jelindra tried to pull away.

"She takes away the good memories, too. And you don't want to lose those, do you?

Jelindra began to cry again, but she shook her head. "No, I don't. It's just that—it's just that it hurts so much. And I'm afraid."

"I know. I am, too. But it'll get better. I promise." Khallayne held out her hand. "Come on. We're leaving." Jelindra took it and allowed herself to be pulled up and out of the room.

Khallayne led her through passages remembered from another lifetime. The walls were familiar, the rooms they passed likewise, but they seemed to belong to a past unconnected with her own. The guards they passed, one after another, were also

245

from another life altogether. Khallayne disabled the first two, then after that, used a "sleep" spell to save energy.

They reached the stables without arousing any suspicions. Jelindra was breathing hard, but moving with quick steps. With another blow, Khallayne incapacitated the stable guard. She waved away the slave working in the stalls, and he shrank fearfully into the shadows.

Khallayne led their horses from the stalls, grabbed blankets and saddles, talking as she did so. "Jelindra, listen to me, okay? And try to remember all this. If we're separated—"

Jelindra started, tears welling up in her eyes, and Khallayne wasted precious minutes calming her. "Just listen. I'll be right behind you, okay? But in case something happens, ride for the western gate. Okay? Get away from the city, but stay on the main trail. I'll come that way as soon as I can. Okay?"

Jelindra nodded and vaulted onto the back of her horse. "The west gate. I'll wait for you."

They started out of the courtyard, riding slowly in the watery winter sunlight. Khallayne would have preferred the darkness of night to cover their movements. She magically muffled the sound of their horse's hooves slightly, hoping nobody would hear them.

The gates of the courtyard loomed overhead, casting a shadow over the cobblestones. She breathed a sigh of relief. They were going to make it.

Suddenly, a cry of alarm went up from the castle. She glanced back and saw Jyrbian, standing at the top of the steps, pointing at her.

"Stop them!" he shouted. "Don't let them get

away!"

Khallayne slapped the rump of Jelindra's horse. "Go!" she screamed. "Run!"

The horse leapt forward and streaked through the gate, Jelindra bent low over its back. Khallayne wheeled to face Jyrbian.

Guards poured from the castle and from the exercise yard behind the courtyard, running for the stables. If they reached their horses, they would catch Jelindra for sure!

Power hummed along her nerves. She cast it out, slamming the doors to the stables, fusing the hinges. The guards beat against the doors, then turned and headed toward her.

She spoke a word, a simple word, and a wall of fire sprang up to meet them. The guards fell back.

An arrow whizzed past her, far off to the side. She heard Jyrbian scream, "Don't hurt her! I want her alive!"

She could see him, through a haze of heat, gesturing at the guards. His lips were moving in spell casting, and she felt the power of the fire waver. She breathed the wall of flame higher.

She wheeled her horse again, turning toward the city. The animal, frightened by the fire, scrabbled for purchase on the cobblestones, almost fell, then righted himself. The gate flashed past as he leapt forward. She was clear! She was free!

Something smote her, something like a giant hand. It jarred her teeth, jolted her muscles, then lifted her up off her horse and dropped her with skull-crushing force. She cried out, braced for the impact.

At the last moment, something equally powerful cushioned the fall so that only her back was bruised, her breath knocked out of her.

Dazed, she sat up. Clattering feet were right behind her, but it wasn't too late to buy more time for Jelindra. She came to her feet, ready to fight.

The two guards in front drew bows, nocked arrows, and dropped to their knees.

"Gently," Jyrbian called, striding down the hill toward her. "Gently." He was smiling, waving the guards away as he moved forward.

"Khallayne." When he reached her, he motioned the guards away and walked right up to her. He clasped her shoulders in his big hands. "Thank you."

She jerked away from his grasp. "For what?"

"I understand." His smile grew even wider. "When you ran, I tried to stop you, but the words wouldn't come. But then the spell did, from inside, just like you said it would."

He tilted his head back, face to the sky, and laughed. "Now there's nothing I can't do!"

* * * * *

Shadows moved. Stars as bright as gems burned holes in the black sky and twinkled so brightly that Bakrell thought he could hear them singing a song of fire and darkness that tinkled like chimes. The night seemed full of rustling movement.

He rode easily, humming to himself for company. Two warriors had ridden with him, but as they had neared the mountains, he had sent them back. Tenaj would be angry. If he ever saw her again, he was sure she would have a few choice phrases, but he also felt he would be safer alone.

The mountains loomed, a blot in the sky, casting a long, dark shadow out on the plains. In the next hour, he would be in the foothills.

He kicked his horse to a canter. He watched for any sign of human or Ogre encampment, listened for warnings in the hooting and calling of the night-birds, of the rustling of animals in the grass.

He chose the most direct route he knew, a trail almost straight up into the Khalkists, riding into rain as soon as he left the rolling foothills behind. The drizzle made pleasantly pattering sounds on the leaves, dripped down the back of his neck, and plastered his clothes to his skin.

It was miserable in the higher elevations. The mountains smoked, a phenomenon Bakrell had heard about but never seen. It seemed the bluish smoke from dozens of campfires spiraled up through the lush foliage and blended into the blue-gray sky. It was quite beautiful, and he hoped to never see it again, if it meant being this cold and wet.

After days of travel, he still had seen no Ogre parties, which both relieved and puzzled him. Had the council given up their pursuit? He was sitting at the edge of the forest, staring at the city of Thorad, when he came up with an idea.

Maybe he could find an inn near the edge of the town. He was so cold and miserable that he was willing to risk it for one night of comfort, of sleeping on a surface that didn't squish.

With no walls like those that protected most of the older cities, Thorad had been an easy target for human attacks. At the wide road that was the main entrance on the east side, barricades marked where attacks had been met. Bags filled with earth, huge timbers, even barroom tables filled the gaps. Buildings bore charred facades.

As Bakrell rode in, a few Ogres eyed him with suspicion, unease, and downright hostility. He had never seen such Ogres as these! They looked as bad off as Igraine's people. In fact, refugees were exactly what they appeared to be, families with belongings piled in two-wheel carts, farmers with packs slung on their backs, all as wet and miserable as he.

He chose the inn where he and Kaede had stayed before. The public room was empty save for two Ogres huddled near the fire in the dining area. The innkeeper, whom Bakrell remembered, was behind the bar, polishing the shiny surface of the old wood.

It was then that Bakrell realized what made the city seem truly strange and empty. There were no slaves! He hesitated, thinking back, and could not remember seeing one human face in the streets.

"Come on in, stranger," said the innkeeper.

The two at the fire looked up at him warily, but quickly went back to their mugs when he nodded at them.

The innkeeper placed a mug of steaming tea before him as Bakrell climbed onto a stool. "Berry and bark," he offered as explanation when Bakrell sniffed it. "All we've got."

Bakrell wrapped his fingers around the mug and took a sip. The brew was weak and bitter, but the warmth of it felt like the finest whiskey. "I'd drink plain water and be as happy as if it were wine, as long as it's hot."

"Been traveling?" There was suspicion in his tone, under the nonchalance.

Bakrell nodded. "It's been miserable, with all the

rain. I need a room for the night."

"You can have your pick if you've got the price."

"I have money." Bakrell dug into his cloak and pulled out a soggy purse. Coins clinked as he counted them out on the bar.

Instead of the gleam Bakrell had expected, the innkeeper's face showed disappointment. "Better than nothing," he said. "Rather have food, or candles. Or wine."

"I have—" In his mind, Bakrell went over the items he was carrying on his horse. He had no candles, and he wasn't willing to give up his two skins of wine. "I have dried meat," he offered finally. "And salt."

The innkeeper's face brightened. "Salt? You can have a room for a whole turning of the moons!"

"It's in a pack on my horse, outside."

"Outside! You can't be leaving something valuable like that outside. It'll be gone before you can blink." The innkeeper rushed to the door behind the bar and shouted for someone to go and get Bakrell's horse. "And bring the bags in here!"

Bakrell sat back, his fingers closed on the warm mug.

The innkeeper narrowed his eyes. "Where is it you said you're from? Have I seen you around here before?"

"I stayed here in the fall. My sister and I. We were waiting for . . . someone."

The Ogre's eyes narrowed as he considered Bakrell. "I remember a young one with a sister sharp as a whip. He was pretty useless-looking, though, decked out in fine clothes. Not like you."

Bakrell smiled sadly. "No, I guess I don't look

much like that."

"Them two, they were heading out onto the plains, looking for Igraine." The innkeeper spat on the floor as soon as he said the name. "And may they find him, too. Heretic bastard!"

Bakrell nodded, then sipped thoughtfully at his drink.

"He's the cause of all this, him and his ideas about slavery." He waved his arms about, indicating the empty room. "Me with no slaves to work the place. Not that it matters. Got no customers anyway. Half the population doesn't even have homes anymore."

"I saw all the people outside. They looked like they're on the move."

As the innkeeper continued to speak, he became more agitated. "City's not safe. No walls. The humans ride in and do whatever they want and ride back out again before the guard even rouses itself."

"Where will they all go?" Bakrell was beginning to be sorry he'd ventured into Thorad, information or not.

"Humans'll slaughter most of them on the trails. Damn fools don't know what it's like out there. Think they'll be better off running away. Others'll starve when they get to Takar and Bloten and find they're not wanted there either."

"But surely they'd be welcome in Takar. The Ruling Council—"

"Ruling Council! Pahhh!" He spat again, with as much animosity as when he'd spoken of Igraine. "They're sitting behind those walls, safe and warm. Don't care if their own starve. Why would they want any more?"

Bakrell sighed heavily, pushing his cup toward the

Ogre for a refill. "How did things get so bad, so fast?" he whispered. He felt, suddenly, a desperation to find Khallayne and Jelindra and get away from the mountains as quickly as possible.

* * * * *

Lyrralt stood on the shore, digging his bare feet into the sand. The breeze off the water was bitterly cold. The sand was cold between his toes, and grainy.

Reaching the Courrain Ocean, the great body of water to the north of the continent, had been a joyful moment. They had been camping nearby for almost a week, and many of the Ogres still ventured down to the beach despite the cold. They had spread out in small family encampments all along the seaside, among the sandy, grassy hills.

Children played near the water's edge, laughing and shouting, mixing their voices with the cries of the seabirds and noise of the surf. He heard all, saw nothing.

"You shouldn't be walking around without your shoes," Tenaj called cheerily, crunching her way across the sand toward him. Igraine was with her, just back from a trip into Schall, a human city two days to the west. Lyrralt recognized him from his scent.

"How was your trip?"

The smile on Igraine's face vanished.

Tenaj tucked her arm through Lyrralt's, but waited for Igraine to speak. Igraine grimaced. "Disappointing. I'm afraid the reputations of our brethren have preceded us. We were most unwelcome. I've brought plenty of supplies, but I think we need to move on soon."

"Before the humans decide to attack?" Lyrralt guessed.

"Yes."

"Is there no place where we can be safe?" Tenaj asked, her voice suddenly depressed. "I'm tired of running. I'm tired of always looking over my shoulder."

"Perhaps there is a place." Lyrralt turned her toward the ocean. "In Schall, were there sailing vessels?" he asked Igraine.

"Yes. I saw sails near the waterfront."

"Large enough to carry us? All of us?"

"I don't know."

Tenaj was trembling. "Where?" she whispered. "Where would we go?"

Lyrralt pointed out over the water.

"How do you know this, Lyrralt?" Igraine's voice was caught by the wind and tossed back to him so that it seemed to come from very far away.

"There's an island somewhere to the north. It's . . . It's calling me."

Igraine turned into the ocean breeze, feeling the salt spray on his face. He tried to quiet his thoughts, putting away the worries of caring for so many Ogres, feeding them, sheltering them, keeping them alive. Yet he heard no song, no call from across the ocean waves. As always, when he allowed the mask of day-to-day worries to fall away, he felt only grief, the overwhelming sorrow and loneliness that had permeated his soul since Everlyn's death, a heartache almost too strong to bear.

* * * * *

Darkness, dank and dripping. Scuttling of claws on stone, somewhere in the shadows. Light from a smoky, oily torch, showing flashes of moldy walls, of grayed, chewed lengths of bone.

There were doors, recessed, so thick and heavy that they might never open. One door was open, and Khallayne backed away from it, instinctively knowing that she didn't want to know what lay out of range of her torchlight.

She was in the dungeons beneath the castle. The guard who had come for her volunteered no information, and he responding to her questions with only, "I'm following Lord Jyrbian's orders."

Lord Jyrbian. Lord Jyrbian had, so far, been as good as his word. He had organized the troops. He and Kaede had drilled them until they were ready to drop, then Kaede had drilled them more. made them fight each other with pikes, with swords, with fat maces, like the humans used, on foot and on horseback. And they loved him for it. The first supply train guarded by his troops had come through unscathed, and now everybody loved him.

Khallayne and the guard passed a deep doorway, and in the flash of torchlight she saw an unidentifiable mass, disintegrating cloth that might have been a pile of rags, or might have been a body. A lump of clothes, flesh all but gone, with wispy blond hair sticking up like straw.

She gasped softly, drew back. Had this always been here, this suffocating, dark place, below the rooms where she danced, ate, made love?

"In here, Lady," he said, stopping before a door,

deep-set in granite. "Lord Jyrbian is waiting."

She froze, suddenly sure that if she went through the door, she would never leave the cell alive. She would spend the rest of her life eating unidentifiable food passed through a slit, living in the darkness until her skin was leeched of all color, her mind of all sanity.

The door swung inward, and yellow light spilled into the corridor. The warm air that came rushing out hinted at a scent musky yet somehow familiar. After the chilly dampness, the light and warmth pouring through the door should have been welcome.

It wasn't. Her intuition told her so.

Jyrbian was just inside the door. His lips were moving, but she couldn't hear the words.

The power. The power in the room. She sensed the seething of the magic, the darkness despite its brightness. An aura greenish and ugly, stronger than any she'd ever seen, enveloped Jyrbian.

The guard pushed her hard in the small of her back. Inside the room, the din of the spell was even worse. Her own power crawled in her veins, wanting to respond, to protect, but she fought it down. She'd never felt anything like it, not even the magic that flowed about the Ruling Council. Such malevolence! Such evil!

Then she saw what—who—Jyrbian had brought her to see. Hand to her mouth to stifle a cry of anguish, she took a step forward.

Bakrell was tied to a slab of stone in the middle of the floor, its surface angled. He was naked, muscles bulging. His mouth stretched wide, teeth bared in a silent mask of anguish.

"I'm sure you remember Bakrell," Jyrbian said

smoothly. As he spoke, the aura of power around him ebbed and diminished.

Bakrell made a pitiful sound, an animal whimper. Except for the trickle of blood that oozed from the corner of his mouth, he might have been sleeping. Or dead.

Khallayne maintained her composure. She dug her toes into the soles of her boots, feeling the coldness of the floor. Fought to keep her face impassive because she sensed her safety and Bakrell's life depended on it. She fought and lost. There was no way she could conceal her horror, her disgust, her nausea.

"I know him," she choked out, horrified when her voice stirred him, made him open his eyes.

Jyrbian straightened, made some small gesture she noted only at the periphery of her vision, and the putrescence that was his power poured back into the room.

Bakrell's body contorted, straining at his bonds with such ferocity that it seemed he burst. And just as suddenly, slumped pathetically.

"Jyrbian, please . . . " Although every inch of her skin crawled with revulsion, Khallayne held out a hand to him. "Why are you doing this?"

Jyrbian took her hand, drew her close enough that he could put a hand on her shoulder. "Because it pleases me." He turned toward his captive and asked, "Doesn't it please you, too?"

Bakrell's eyes were dull, the shine of life gone from them, and she knew he was dying. She'd seen too many, fallen in battle, their lives draining away, not to recognize the signs. Gaze locked with Bakrell's, she whispered, "Jyrbian, please don't do this. I'll do whatever you want."

"My dear, you have nothing left that I want. He, however, has information that might lessen his suffering, should he choose to share it." His fingers tightened on her shoulder, then eased off into a caress.

She couldn't stop the shiver of repulsion that ran down her spine. "What?"

"The location of Igraine's camp."

The greenish light, the malevolent power, leapt again. Bakrell's body arched up off the stone. Jyrbian grabbed Khallayne as she tried to do something, grabbing her around the waist with strength she hadn't known he possessed.

"Bakrell, if you know, tell him!" she cried.

Bakrell didn't respond. His body pushed up off the stone, held for long moments, then dropped. His eyes rolled up in his head.

"If you know, tell him! He'll kill you!"

Bakrell simply shook his head. No.

Irritated, Jyrbian flicked his fingers.

Bakrell's body spasmed. His muscles bunched as if they would rip through his skin. He screamed. And screamed. The sound reverberated around the small room, echoing, stabbing her ears, her heart, like daggers driven into her skull. So loud, so tortured a sound, that it persisted in her mind even after Bakrell went silent.

Jyrbian released her. He went to Bakrell, touched him as gently as a lover. "Don't you want the pain to be over? Don't you want this to end? All you have to do is tell me. Just tell me where I can find Igraine. I know you know where they were going. How else were you going to take Khallayne and Jelindra back?"

Unable to speak, Bakrell rolled his head back and forth. Back and forth. No.

His dull eyes stared out through swollen lids at Khallayne. For a moment, just a moment, there was recognition in his face. Horror. Understanding. "Forgive me," he rasped, his voice a blood-filled whisper. With effort, he rolled his head back until Jyrbian was in his vision. "You won't hurt her?" he rasped, and when Jyrbian agreed, whispered, "Near Schall. On the shore."

His eyes slid shut. His head rolled heavily to the side. His chest heaved, then settled, and didn't rise again.

For a moment, the silence in the room was overwhelming. With a triumphant malevolence, Jyrbian turned to the guard in the doorway. "Take a company immediately. Start tonight. Bring Igraine back to me, dead or alive. But the humans who guard him I want alive."

The Ogre saluted smartly, disappearing into the dark corridor.

When his footfalls had died away, Jyrbian turned to Khallayne. "Allow me to escort you back to your apartment."

Chapter 17
Drawing Near to Dust

Sunlight pierced deep into the clear blue waters of the Courrain Ocean. As she often did in the mornings, the Xocli paused, her large, flat tail moving lazily in the current, and turned one of her three heads to watch the return of her fellow sea creatures, riding the warming beams of light down from the surface.

A stately leaffish drifted by; the rippling fins for which it was named gamboled like ornaments, waving a warm good morning.

The nightly, vertical migration had begun at dusk. Tiny fish, too small for the Xocli to actually see, rose, seeking food. Slowly, the small fish that fed on the tiny ones followed, and the larger creatures followed them in turn. Nighttime in the depths of the Courrain Ocean was a totally different world than the day.

She watched the nightly dance and the morning return, though the Xocli didn't rise with nightfall, not unless there was a voice, calling to her—as one called to her this morning, faintly and dimly.

The caller was not nearby, perhaps not even on the water, but she could feel the call of its sadness; the sorrow touched her core. Motioning to her children, she set out across the ocean floor, allowing the current to pull her along, take her where it would. There was no hurry. The melancholy of the caller would tell her when to rise.

One of her heads snapped up a larval shrimp floating on a sea leaf that sparkled like sequins. The tiny morsel made her hungry for more. She opened her three mouths and gulped in water, enjoying the rush of it through the gills on her necks.

Spectral light played across the gossamer, transparent mantle that shielded the organs in the Xocli's necks and torso. Streaming along behind her, the little ones, the children, frolicked in and out of the beams of sunlight, diving below the reef and popping back out above or behind it.

The children ranged wide, then circled back to her as she turned. Not only was she avoiding the colder area north of the reef, where a vent in the ocean floor sent inky fluid smoking toward the surface, but the melancholy from the surface was stronger, singing in her bones, a siren song that could not be ignored.

The young were miniature copies of her: three heads sitting atop long necks, golden scales and fins rippling with all the colors of the ocean. The transparency of their young skin, their developing mantles, made them difficult to see against the reef, save for the brightness of their eyes.

She felt, rather than heard, the cry of one of the children. Turning back rapidly, she counted. One, two, three, against the reef. Another out on the floor, examining a miniature "chimney," the beginnings of a vent, from which pale particles drifted upward. Another, still farther away, swam lazily. That left one unaccounted for, the one who was bugling in pain and fear.

The cry was coming from the north, from the vent. Ordering the others to stay away, she darted toward the sound. She twined her three long, thick necks and swam with her three heads nose-to-nose. Gone was the lazy, panoramic view of the underwater as she homed in on the pleas.

Visibility narrowed as she approached the vent. The smoky black fluid that spewed from the vent clouded the water until almost no sunlight penetrated. She swam by feel, following the vibration of her child. Its pitiful cries were weakening, moment by moment.

She bugled her distress, and a mere whimper was the only response from the lost one. She circled in the cloudy darkness. Just when she thought she would never find the little one, she saw it, its back closer to the reef than she had thought, trapped in the waving tentacles of a giant tube worm.

The tube worms were not maneuvering creatures. They lived out their lives attached to the reef or a boulder, unable to chase after their prey. They shot stinging tentacles into the current to capture their food, then dragged the stunned, hapless creature back in a deadly embrace.

The little one was mewling weakly. Held immobile in the grasp of the huge tentacles, it was drowning. The Xocli swept in toward it, screeching a cry of warning, of distress and challenge.

The tube worm, stupid and sluggish when feeding, was quick when it sensed prey. The stinging tentacles darted out and latched onto the tender flesh at the base of her necks.

Pain like the bite of hundreds of tiny teeth shot through her nervous system. She squealed and kicked backward with her large pectoral fin. Her weight and the power tore her loose, leaving her flesh on the barbed tentacles. She darted in again. And again the tube worm pricked her, pumping its venom into her veins.

She tore loose again, tearing several of the tubes from the base this time. She felt the whisper of the mindless creature's anger conveyed through the water. She surged in once more, spreading her three necks as far as they would go, as wide, attacking from three different directions.

Ignoring her pain, she attacked. Again and again. Tireless. Desperate. She besieged the tube worm from above, below, charged in, a direct frontal assault. She tore off pieces of the ugly, writing tentacles, snapped whole clumps from the base.

The tube worm met her assault on all sides, spraying out a thick, noxious white poison in addition to the stinging tentacles. The Xocli backed away, blinded, bleeding, defeated. Her little one moved no more in the grasp of the tube worm. Its ululations stilled forever.

She reared back and sounded her distress, her

grief. Her anguish was so great, it almost overwhelmed the calls from the surface. With one last glance back at the remains of her child, she swam upward, signaling for the other children to attend her.

She shot upward, heeding the siren call from above, feeding on the misery of the caller, drawing it into herself.

Added to her own sorrow, the emotion was overpowering. She gave vent to her pain. Anguish became fury, building inside her to a fever pitch, until the Xocli that broke the surface of the ocean, rising up into the air, was crazed with rage.

The tiny ships pitched on the ocean's surface below her. And she drank in the fear and pain of the tiny beings that clung to the decks. She sucked in the anesthetizing, exhilarating emotions.

* * * * *

Water, blue-gray and endless, stretched as far as the eye could see, merging with the sky. Rippling in the cold sunshine, it looked like melted glass.

They were north of the continent of Ansalon, far west of the Khalkists. Nearby were islands, called the Dragon Isles, the human captain assured them, some of them large enough to support a colony of Ogres.

"How much farther?" Tenaj called to Lyrralt, who sat in the shade of the upper deck, his back braced against the bulkhead. She strode across the rolling deck, stepping over those lolling in the sun with the ease of many days aboard ship, and squatted down next to him. "How much longer?"

He smiled, turning his sightless eyes toward her. "Not much longer. Can't you hear it?"

She cocked her head. "Yes." She drew the word out in a sibilant hiss. And she did hear something, as they all were beginning to, a siren call, drawing them across the water. "But it's still so faint. I can't tell if it's near or far."

"It's near," said someone behind her. "Very near."

"It better be," another voice growled.

Tenaj stalked back to the bow. That was the problem with being packed on the ship so close with so many others. There was no privacy. The smaller ship, which sailed behind them, was probably even worse.

Igraine came up beside her, laid a hand on her shoulder. "Feeling crowded?" he asked quietly.

As always, Tenaj was surprised at how well he read her mind and ashamed to have harbored such unworthy thoughts. "I know I should be grateful," she admitted contritely. "We were lucky to find a captain willing to take us all at once." Lucky to find a human whose greed appreciated the coin they could pay.

"We're lucky to be here, all healthy." Igraine said it ruefully, for he had been one of the few who had taken seasick the first few days out. Then very quietly, very sadly, he whispered, "I wish Everlyn could have seen the new home."

Tenaj looked at him in surprise. It was the first time she'd heard him mention Everlyn since the killing.

Igraine wasn't the same leader who had left Takar. His daughter's death had drained all the life from him, leaving a male who seemed diminished, his silver hair and eyes now a drab gray. But his voice still carried the authority to move mountains.

She squeezed his hand sympathetically, turned her face to the wind, and stared out at the sea. Just as Igraine started to speak, she drew a sharp breath and leaned forward, over the railing.

"Do you see the island?"

"No." She shook her head, pushed away his hand. "No." What she saw was a pattern in the water, a whirling pattern that wasn't natural. She cupped her hands around her mouth and shouted to the captain, trying to make her voice heard above the billowing of the sails. "Something's ahead!"

The captain pantomimed that he couldn't make out her words. Shielding his eyes, he peered ahead, then abruptly grabbed the wheel of the ship and strained to change direction, shouting orders to his men.

The ship pitched as it turned, groaning in the water.

Tenaj grabbed Igraine and hustled him toward the bulkhead, toward the stairs and belowdecks. "Everyone get below!" she shouted.

Everyone had already risen in alarm, and when the ship had turned about, sending up a plume of water, they'd scattered.

Igraine gasped. Screams broke out across the deck, and Tenaj turned just in time to see something raise its head, a golden snout breaking through the surface, water sheeting off its rippling skin. It was beautiful and horrible, she thought, a creature cast in transparent, pearlescent gold, with the scales of a fish and eyes as red as rubies.

Another head broke the surface beside it, then another, three of them, huge, mantled necks bulging, glistening. They reared back, sending air whistling past her ears, her hair whipping into her eyes.

The captain was yelling something unintelligible. Ogres were shouting, running. Igraine was the one pushing her now. She bumped into Lyrralt, standing with his back braced against the bulkhead.

"Brace! Brace!" the captain was shouting.

The creatures were surging forward, churning white froth in their wake, their huge blunt heads lowered for battering. She had only a moment to think, to act, before the creatures bashed into the side of the ship. Surely its timbers couldn't withstand the tremendous blow!

Tenaj threw up her hands, making a shield with every ounce of magical power at her disposal. The monsters' heads struck the invisible shield with such force that she felt the tremor. One of the heads crashed past and rammed the ship.

The ship rocked with the impact, pitching wildly back and forth. Wood groaned and splintered, threatening to give way. The blow threw Tenaj to the deck. Her head struck the planks. She rolled onto her back, dazed, and saw the sea monsters preparing to ram again.

She pushed to her knees, muttering under her breath the words to another spell, hoping to strengthen it.

An instant later, Igraine was there beside her, and Lyrralt, helping her to stand. Then others, crowding in close, added the strength of their own magic to hers.

The creatures attacked again, coming up hard against the invisible shield. Bugling in fury and frustration, the creature reared back, rising up another fifty feet into the sky, and attacked again. It struck a blow that tossed them all to the decks as if they weighed nothing. The shield shook with the force of the blow, but held.

From behind them, a cheer went up. Anticipating the creatures' next attack, Tenaj shouted, "Concentrate!" There was another shout as Lyrralt grabbed her. "They're going!"

A human sailor went running past, and Igraine grabbed him. "What are they?" he demanded.

"Not they. It! A Xocli. It's trying to feed its young! We're the food."

"It's heading for the other ship," Tenaj said dully. She ran toward the railing, waving her arms and shouting as she went, hoping to distract the creature.

It sailed past, half submerged. As she reached the end of the deck, she cast a spell with all her might. Something like a thunderbolt sizzled through the air and fell short. She threw fireballs, one, then two, more. They flew through the air, but fell short.

By her side, Igraine also cast a spell, and something hit the water very near the monsters, sending a geyser high into the air.

The Xocli swam on toward the smaller ship.

"There's no one on that ship with the power to stop it," Tenaj said, her voice defeated. The ones who were more advanced in magic and spellcasting had sailed together, hoping to spend their time on board learning from each other.

She watched numbly as the creature repeated its performance with the smaller ship, ramming it repeatedly. She saw bodies fall into the water, heard thrashing and screaming, then stillness. On her ship, there was moaning and songs of sorrow.

The smaller ship tipped over on its side, like a toy in a pond. Bodies slid off the deck, scrabbling to hold on. Something beneath the water tore at the Ogres as they hit the water. Still the creature butted its golden heads against the ship. Again and again.

Tenaj tore loose from Igraine and ran back up to the captain. "Go back!" she screamed. She scrambled up the ladder to the upper deck. "Go back! We've got to help them!"

"We can't." The human met her gaze squarely. "It would sink us, too."

"Doesn't matter," said his second mate gruffly, pointing. "It's going."

Tenaj turned. The sea monster was sailing away, gracefully, beautifully, gradually disappearing beneath the water as it moved.

The second ship was still afloat, but listing badly to the right. Starboard, she corrected herself.

As they watched, signal flags slid up the mast. "Taking on water," the captain translated. "Able to sail, though. Signal them back. We'll fall in beside. Help out as best we can."

Tenaj insisted they circle close and check the water for survivors, but she knew it was useless, even as the captain acquiesced.

How many lost?

She went back down the ladder to her place at the bow. The people behind her on deck were subdued now, crying softly, speculating in whispers as to who among their friends and family was lost.

Igraine joined her, then Lyrralt. The sun set. Still she stayed, watching the black water ahead, lit by Solinari so that it sparkled like diamonds. The wind grew colder. The stars came out.

She was still standing there when the lookout shouted. "Land!"

She looked this way and that, then realized it was right in front of her. The blackness she'd taken for starless sky was an island.

A large island.

Igraine and Lyrralt joined her once more, pushing through the Ogres who had crowded up from below deck.

For a moment, Igraine stared at the black finger of land on the horizon. Then he spoke quietly. "We will be called the Irda, Children of the Stars, Watchers of the Darkness. As we have found our way to this place, we will make our own way into the future." For the first time since Everlyn's death, he felt hope and peace and a wonderful calmness in his heart.

* * * * *

Khallayne sat for days, silent and uncommunicative. She ate when food was put before her, slept when a slave led her to bed. She shivered when the room was cold, sweated when she sat too near the fire.

She hurt. Her teeth, her skin, her fingers. Her muscles, her eyes. Everything ached, and for days, a sound, even the tiniest one, made her cringe. But she knew all that would pass. Her aches would recede, and her ears would return to normal. She wasn't so sure about her sanity.

It was all hazy, like an early morning high in the mountains when the clouds haven't lifted and the air hangs heavily moisture laden and nothing has sharp edges.

"Why are you keeping her alive?" Kaede's voice, tinged with jealousy, broke through the haze.

"Because it amuses me," Jyrbian's voice answered, his despicable voice as smooth as silk.

She watched it all as she would have watched a play, waiting for her heart to wake up and tell her she was alive. The thing that made her look, listen, made her at last return to the world of angry whispers, was a scream, the scream of a dying man.

"So," a voice said from near the window. "You are going to wake up." The voice didn't sound very pleased with the prospect.

Slowly, Khallayne sat up. She spotted Kaede standing at the window, a crystal from Jyrbian's collection held in her palm.

Bakrell's death came back to her. "Bakrell . . . " she choked out.

Kaede put the crystal back onto its bronze stand and turned toward her. "Ummm. I always thought you liked my brother a little more than you let on. No doubt he's one of Igraine's most loyal followers by now. He never did anything halfheartedly."

She didn't know! Khallayne understood immediately. Jyrbian hadn't told her. She opened her mouth to tell her, to let the anger and pain come pouring out. But she didn't. That revelation might be something she could put to good use, later.

With effort, Khallayne pushed her legs over the edge of the bed and pulled herself up. Wobbly and weak, she made her way toward her scant wardrobe. "What does Jyrbian want with me?"

Kaede shrugged, but Jyrbian answered her from the door. He was dressed beautifully in a red uniform, brimming with good health. "There might still be a few spells I don't know."

She leaned her head against the door of the wardrobe. "You'll have to kill me," Khallayne said quietly. Then with growing vehemence, she added, "I'll die before I'll ever teach you another thing!"

He shrugged as if it didn't matter.

And it didn't. What miserly, little spells could Khallayne teach him when he already knew how to torture someone to death without leaving a single mark on the body? When she glanced at Kaede, standing in the light pouring through the window, her fingers moving lazily over the crystals from Jyrbian's collection, she suddenly knew there was one spell to teach. And she knew, even before Kaede gasped, that he *would* kill her, if necessary, trying to wrest the secret from her.

At that moment, Kaede snatched up the crystal, her mouth open wide in disbelief, holding it up to the light. The clear, round ball was filled with a curling ribbon of smoke. Sunlight streamed through the crystal, creating a dancing rainbow of light.

"The History!" Kaede gasped, holding it close to her ear. "The History. Jyrbian, how did you get it?"

Jyrbian was as perplexed as Khallayne was horrified.

"What are you talking about?" He held out his hand, but she refused to give him the crystal. He wrested it from her hand, repeating his question.

"It's the History. The Song of the Keeper! It's *in* there. How did you get it?"

"Are you sure?" He held the sphere up to his ear, then up to the light. "That's ridiculous! How could that be?"

"I can hear it! Give it to me. It's mine! Someone stole it from the Keeper. She wasn't sick. She was murdered!"

He held it higher, out of her reach, pushed away

her grasping hands. Before Kaede could stop him, he'd strode to Khallayne, thrust it into her hand.

Round and smooth and cool. Khallayne's fingers closed around the sphere. She recognized the tingle of life. She carried it, cradled, to the fire and held it up.

"You did this," Jyrbian said with absolute certainty. "Lyrralt said something the day the Keeper took sick, something cryptic, about singing for his fortune, the same day he was so angry with you. But he alone never had the knowledge to do this, so you must have helped him. How?"

Yes, the Song was still in there. She could feel it, the way Kaede could hear it. "No. I didn't do it." She lied. Khallayne handed the crystal back to him. "I don't feel anything but a piece of glass."

Jyrbian regarded her for a moment. "Try to remember," he said sweetly. "Perhaps it'll come back to you. Before I have to jog your memory, the way I had to jog . . . someone else's." He thrust the crystal back into her hands.

Kaede cried out in protest. "It's mine! You can't—"

One glance from Jyrbian silenced her, and she followed him from the room with murderous eyes.

Khallayne carried the sphere to the bed. Propped up on pillows, buried in warm quilts, she placed the crystal in her lap and stared at it, trying to remember the night it all happened, trying to remember the spell and how it had felt and the way it had all worked together.

Then, when she thought she remembered the ribbony darkness and the flow of the Song from the Old One's lips, she reached out with her power. In her mind, she tapped the crystal ball.

And the sphere opened. The Song flowed out,

around and about her hands, through her fingers, a music beyond description, so bittersweet that tears clouded her vision, a song about a world that would soon vanish forever. A beautiful, glittering world like an apple with a worm of decay in it.

She was lost in the Song, unable to follow the music, when she heard cheers, the uproar of something in the courtyard below. She leapt to her feet and ran to the window.

In the courtyard below, she could see a crowd of troops, all milling about, shouting, crying out greetings and congratulations. She thought she saw Jyrbian, resplendent in dress uniform, marching through the crowd of men and horses. Then she saw the reason for all the noise.

The crowd of troops surrounded a group of prisoners, chained together around a wagon on which a lone prisoner stood, chained and tied: Eadamm, the human leader for whom Jyrbian had been searching like a madman.

* * * * *

Jyrbian forgot everything—the History, Kaede's angry entreaties, and the tantalizing spell Khallayne would surrender to him, sooner or later.

Hundreds of humans, old and young, had descended into Jyrbian's dungeons and not returned. They had died, screaming and begging for mercy, or so far gone into insanity that they could not even cry out. As he had destroyed each of them, it had been Eadamm's likeness he saw on their savage human faces, Eadamm he wished he were killing.

Now he would have that pleasure.

Jyrbian strode through the throng of Ogres and humans who had crowded into the courtyard, pushing them out of his way. He climbed up onto the wagon and faced the human he hated above all else. "What a pity you can die only once," he told the man, disappointed when the slave maintained his composure.

He searched the crowd for the captain of the troop that had brought the human in, motioning the man forward. "Where did you find him? Was he guarding Igraine's people, as I thought?"

"No, Lord. As far as I know, the others have not been found. He was captured near Persopholus. We think he was directing the siege of the city."

"And the battle?"

"We won, Sire." The captain pulled himself up proudly. "The humans were slaughtered."

Jyrbian grinned with pleasure and leaned down to clap the Ogre on the shoulder. "And did you find anything valuable on him?" He jerked his head in the direction of Eadamm.

"Yes, Sire, just as you said. My warriors brought it to me." The captain reached into his tunic and drew out a pile of silver chain attached to a charm, wrapped in silver wire.

From his tunic Jyrbian pulled out another charm just like it. The bloodstone he'd taken from Everlyn's neck. He held them both up wordlessly for the slave to see.

Eadamm lunged at him, his lips pulled back, teeth exposed like a feral animal. The chains wrapped around his body held as Eadamm strained against them uselessly.

A beatific smile on his face, Jyrbian climbed down

from the wagon. He found Kaede in his bedroom. She was barely dressed, her hair long and loose, her perfume heavy and heady, seductive.

"You've heard?"

She nodded, proffering a glass of wine. "His death must be spectacular. It must be an example to others."

A slow, candied smile creased his lips. His mind was already beginning to ferment with ideas, with images. His smile grew wider, eyes wandering over her body. He took a step toward her, saw her answering smile and the heat in her eyes . . .

* * * * *

Khallayne barely heard the noise of the crowd as she mounted her horse and followed the others out through the courtyard and into the city. The sun was bright on the cobblestones and glinted on the gray stone walls.

She rode behind Jyrbian, fear in her throat. "Only a parade," he had said, smiling a smile as guileless as a child. "In honor of the capture of the humans. You really shouldn't miss it." She had played along, eager to get out of the castle, hopeful of a chance to escape.

Now they traveled slowly, regally, down the curving switchbacks that led into the city streets, and along the wide avenues toward the coliseum. All along the route, Ogres lined the streets, waiting for the entertainment, drinking, buying food from vendors who worked the crowd. Khallayne felt a terrible foreboding about the event for which the whole city had turned out.

The streets outside the coliseum were lined with

platforms, viewing stands draped with satin in the colors of all the powerful clans. Jyrbian's was nearest the center, in the shade of the looming coliseum. Only the Ruling Council's was better positioned.

Kaede was already on the stand, resplendent in an emerald gown with matching jewels at ears and throat. But when she saw that Khallayne sat at Jyrbian's right, she frowned and turned away. Jyrbian dismounted and led Khallayne up the stairs.

The Ruling Council arrived. Anel looked across the banister and bowed to Jyrbian. There was a buffet table, laden with delicacies, at the back of the viewing stand, and someone thrust a bronze goblet filled with deep red wine into Khallayne's hand.

Music began, the high, trilling sound of a flute. Other instruments joined in, adding their melodies. Drums. Cymbals. Bells. Another flute. Twining their light, playful sounds.

The light seemed to dim, as if the sun had gone behind a dark cloud. Khallayne shivered, blinked her eyes to clear them, and found the light as bright as before. She clutched her goblet tighter to keep her fingers from trembling and peered down the street, as everyone around was doing. All except Jyrbian, who stood straight, stared straight ahead.

First to appear were the children. Ogre children, dressed in white with ribbons of every color, strewing flowers in the street as they danced, laughed, played, and shouted.

Behind them were the flute players, more musicians, more children. Young women and men tossed flowers to friends in the crowd. Troops, smartly dressed in their best, swords shining in the light, followed, then more children, older ones, all so filled with a gaiety that it struck Khallayne as false.

Then came the captured slaves, naked, barefoot, oiled as if they were on display for the auction block. They were bound together with chains that shone as bright as the soldiers' swords.

The crowd cheered and clapped the same as they had for the dancing children.

Through it all, Jyrbian displayed a ghastly smile. "You don't want to miss this," he said, taking her arm gently.

More troops marched out of the coliseum. These were on foot, though from their uniforms it was obvious they were officers, higher in rank than those who had come before. They walked in perfect rows, in perfect step, shoulders thrust back proudly.

As they drew near, Jyrbian's fingers tightened on her arm.

Three figures walked in the center of the rows of officers—one stumbling, almost carried by the two who walked at his side.

That one was Eadamm. His wrists were bound in front, and his legs streaked with bright red. He had been hamstrung, the heavy tendons cut just above the knee.

Khallayne cried out. The goblet of wine fell from her fingers, flashing in the sunlight. Jyrbian held her against him, forcing her to stand where she was. When the goblet hit the street below, it made not a sound.

Khallayne looked down and saw that, while Jyrbian held her in a tight grip with one hand, with the other he held Kaede's fingers, lightly, gently stroking them. "Eadamm will be paraded every day for six days," Jyrbian was saying. "One day for each of the six months since the rebellion. Then he will be publicly executed."

He looked down at her and smiled before turning back to the spectacle, his eyes following Eadamm's every step.

And Khallayne saw that his face, which had once rivaled hers for beauty, now had become twisted and ugly, like his soul.

* * * * *

Two.
Three.
Four.
Five.
Six.

Each day, Jyrbian sent a new dress to Khallayne's apartment, each more elegant than the last.

Each day, he sent two burly guards, well versed in magic, to escort her. They broke through her wards. They carried her when she resisted.

Each day, Jyrbian sat astride his horse in the courtyard and watched as they brought her out and lifted her into the saddle of her horse beside him.

"Why do you slap and kick when you could destroy them with a simple magical thought?" he asked, amused.

"Kill them because they blindly follow your orders?" she asked. "That would make me just like you."

Each day, he laughed as he led her down the mountain into the festive streets.

Each day, he stood beside her and held her arm and forced her to watch Eadamm's humiliation,

Eadamm's torture.

On the seventh day, it was late afternoon before a slave came with the tunic and embroidered vest she had worn all those many nights ago, at the party where she'd looked at Jyrbian with lust and anticipation.

The castle had been rumbling with parties and celebrations all day. The execution was soon, she knew. And she knew Jyrbian would force her to watch, but she could feel nothing but relief that it would soon be over. At least Eadamm would be beyond Jyrbian's reach, beyond pain.

The late afternoon sun shone brightly in the courtyard, making the cobblestones so warm that she could feel them through her boots.

Jyrbian was waiting for her as always, as was Kaede. She mounted without being prompted, but held back on the reins until Jyrbian turned back to her. "Why do I have to go to this?" she asked quietly.

He smiled and chided her, "Khallayne, you were here for the beginning. You can't miss the end."

The end was even more bizarre than what had gone before.

The coliseum was packed and surrounded by hundreds of Ogres who couldn't get in. They wouldn't have made it through the crowd without Jyrbian's guards opening a path. The mood was ugly; there were mutterings and complaints because there wasn't space for everybody.

Jyrbian and his entourage rode under the heavy stone arch into the coliseum. The sounds of the crowd muted. The whole coliseum became strangely quiet. They dismounted and were escorted to Jyrbian's box, a private chamber that opened onto a huge balcony overlooking the stadium field. It was only then that she understood.

All around them, in other special boxes, were courtiers, packed into seats, hanging over the balconies, calling to each other and laughing.

To her horror, the majority of the seats were filled with slaves. They were interspersed with guards who brandished swords and pikes and bows.

The entertainment began. Dancers and jugglers and acrobats. Smartly trained horses and smartly trained soldiers went through their paces. Troops marched and saluted with perfect precision. Magicians magicked, pulling flowers out of thin air and juggling fireballs.

The Ogres clapped and cheered and drank. The slaves sat silently.

Then great torches were lit, and the real entertainment, what all the Ogres had come to see, began.

Eadamm was brought into the center of the coliseum.

Every slave in the place sat forward.

Shackles were attached to his arms with great ceremony. Horses backed into their traces.

Khallayne turned away. Jyrbian didn't notice. His eyes were glued to the tableau, fists tapping his thighs. Kaede stood near him, brushing his arm, but he was unaware of her.

Khallayne saw Anel, in the center box, raise a red square of cloth, saw it fall, felt the sudden hush, heard sounds so horrible, she knew she would never be able to wipe them from her mind again. Whips cracked. Something creaked and snapped. Something tore.

She clapped her hands to her ears to shut out the

raucous, frenzied cheering. Tears streamed down her face.

There was another burst of cheers, higher and louder than the first, then another, and she thought, "It's over. It's over."

Eadamm had been drawn and quartered.

Then came a sound like nothing she'd ever heard in her life, like nothing she would ever hear again. It was dim at first, but building, surging, a hum that became a song that became a fire that became an explosion, rage and fear and horror too long suppressed, pain too long endured.

The slaves were rising up. The sound was their fury, all of them, as if someone had passed a signal. They were turning on their masters, on their guards.

Chapter 18

Ending and Beginning

Kaede screamed. Jyrbian shouted orders.

Though she knew, from his gestures, that he was marshalling his guards to rush them to safety, Khallayne didn't care. Now was her chance to escape!

She moved quickly, catching up her long skirts and pushing through the confused, frightened crowd toward the door. Guards were trying to block any attack. Their backs were to her.

She looked around. The drop to the ground was over three times her height. But then she would be on the field.

In the box next to Jyrbian's, on the opposite side of the Ruling Council, there were fewer guards, more courtiers. Pandemonium. The box itself was lower to the ground. If she jumped, then the ground was only perhaps ten feet away.

She climbed onto a chair, kicking food and porcelain out of her way. For a moment, she wasn't sure she could manage it. Then she heard Jyrbian shout her name, and she pushed.

She reached out as she fell. Her fingers caught on the rough stone, scraping, tearing nails and palms. Her body slammed into the wall. Her breath whooshed out of her, and she let go.

She fell the rest of the way and hit the ground hard. Stars danced before her eyes, and she felt sharp jabs of pain lancing on her left side. She rolled onto her back, gasping for breath. Above her, staring down, she could make out Jyrbian face. And Kaede's.

She rolled to her hands and knees. She pushed up to her feet and stood. With a glance to make sure she wasn't being pursued, she slipped out from between the boxes and looked for an exit.

Most of the slaves had jumped from the stands onto the field and fled toward the city gate. Many were still in the stands, and what they were doing to their owners, to the guards, made her whimper. She hugged the wall, aiming for an exit. A few yards away was the tunnel used to transport slaves and animals onto the field.

She edged around the corner into the darkened tunnel and came face-to-face with a slave, a human whose head barely came up to her shoulders. He had carrot-orange hair and mean, little eyes twisted with hate, and blood spattered across the front of his ragged shirt.

He grinned at her, a Jyrbian grin, all teeth and

loathing. He was carrying a stick, perhaps a piece of a lance or pike, jagged on both ends where it had been broken. In the darkness, it looked as if it had blood on it.

Before she could react, a woman's voice interrupted the rise of the club.

"Stop!" A small slave woman ran toward them out of the darkness. "Not this one," she told the man, stepping between Khallayne and her attacker.

He shoved her away and raised his club. "All Ogres die!" he snarled.

The slave grabbed a stick of wood and swung it, hitting the male squarely in the back of the head with a sickening thump.

"This way," the human said without a glance for the crumpled man, jerking her head toward the dark tunnel.

Before she could turn, Khallayne caught her arm. "Laie?" There was no one else it could be. The kitchen slave who had helped her the night she and Lyrralt had taken the History, now thinner, harsher around the eyes, but with the same straw-colored hair and bluer-than-blue eyes.

The slave looked at her, a strange expression in her eyes. Khallayne felt guilty. The female obviously knew her. Why else had she saved her? "Laie, thank you."

The slave looked around her, checking to see that no one observed them. "Hurry." She turned and ran back down the dark tunnel.

Without any hesitation, Khallayne followed. With her longer stride, she caught up easily and followed Laie almost to the end of the tunnel, then through two turns and three different corridors.

Twice they were almost seen by other slaves, but each time they were able to slip back into the shadows, behind a door, until the danger was past. And once, Khallayne had time to work her spell of "distraction," so the running slaves passed them by.

At last, they came out into the street, into a city gone mad. The last of the sun had faded, and night should have settled over the city, but the city was in flames. The sky was filled with an orange glow that threw shadows so long they stretched across the street. Buildings on either side of the coliseum had flames spouting from their windows. The street was littered with debris and bodies. Screams and wild laughter echoed off the walls of the houses.

How could it all have happened so fast? Khallayne stared into the sky. Would there be anything left standing when the sun came up?

"We have to go!" Laie caught her sleeve. She led the way up the street, dodging other slaves carrying weapons, walking around lumps in the road that were crumpled and broken and gleaming red.

One of the broken bodies that littered the walks seemed to writhe into something alive as they passed it. Khallayne saw it first, felt it. She caught Laie and yanked her away.

"What is it?"

Khallayne knelt and stared at the writhing thing. She could feel the malevolence of it, the power that still clung to it. "I don't know. A spell gone awry, maybe. Just don't touch it. And watch for others. Let's get out of here."

Laie nodded, but this time let Khallayne led.

Khallayne saw two other things that seemed wrong to her. A thing, similar to the one they'd passed, clung to a brick wall. And a body that was so badly damaged, it had to be dead, still moved and crawled, reaching out for them.

They found an alley filled with barrels and boxes and crouched in the shadows while figures ran past not five feet away.

"I have to go to the castle. There's something there I must retrieve." She was free, out of Jyrbian's grasp. Her common sense screamed at her to run, but she'd left the crystal—the History of the Ogre, laid out from the beginning of time—in the castle. She had forgotten it once. She didn't want to make the mistake of leaving it behind again.

Laie looked at her as though she were crazy. "Back into the castle? I can't go there."

"I know. I understand. But I have to."

Laie nodded, turned away.

"Why?" Khallayne blurted out. "Why did you save me?"

The blue eyes stared at her. "I owed you a life. I've paid it back."

Khallayne nodded. "Thank you." She was almost to the end of the alley when she impulsively turned. "Laie, if you can make it out of the mountains, head northeast. There are human towns there, humans who aren't afraid of the Ogres, who fight and live good lives."

Then she turned around and walked away rapidly, not looking back.

The castle was strangely empty, strangely dark, though there were candles everywhere, on the floor and window ledges and tables, as if the Ogres who were still there were attempting to expel the darkness.

They, not the humans, were the scurriers now, carrying their own belongings, packs stuffed with food, as they prepared to flee.

No one gave her a second glance as she strode rapidly through the halls. They were all too intent on saving themselves.

The apartment in which she'd dwelt for the past weeks was brightly lit, the door standing open in welcome. She knew who would be waiting for her inside.

Jyrbian was by the fireplace. He wore a fresh uniform. His hair was combed, not a strand out of place. He leaned, one arm draped across the mantel, as casually as if she had stopped by for an evening visit.

Khallayne didn't see Kaede, standing by the window ledge where the sphere was concealed, until she was already through the doorway.

Kaede smiled cruelly when she saw Khallayne's glance. "I didn't expect we would ever see you again," she said dryly.

"Oh, I knew she'd be back," Jyrbian said easily.

Khallayne looked at him, surprised. Then she saw what he held in his hand, casually rolling it in his palm: the crystal sphere.

His movements might be indifferent, his voice bland, but his face was taut, the skin stretched over the muscles. His eyes were a tarnished metal gray, heavy lidded, and completely mad.

"You still haven't told me how you did it."

Khallayne's eyes followed the crystal.

"Please, Jyrbian," she said softly.

Jyrbian threw back his head and laughed, low-pitched and filled with madness.

She took a step toward him, sensed Kaede take

one toward her. "Please, Jyrbian, let me have the sphere. You have no use for it here. Takar is gone forever. But it doesn't have to be forgotten. All that we were doesn't have to be forgotten."

"You want it to take back to Igraine?" He held it out teasingly.

"To our people, not to Igraine."

He grinned, his teeth gleaming. "You do know where they are? You knew all along."

She shook her head. "No, but I'll find them. Somehow."

"Tell me." He held out the sphere. "A trade. The History for the location. For my curiosity."

Her intuition said run. Now, quickly. No more conversation. Just feet moving, one in front of the other. Quickly.

"No. You'll just kill me, the way you killed Bakrell."

Kaede made a muffled noise at the mention of her brother's name. She stepped forward.

Laughter was bubbling out of Jyrbian once again. The laughter erupted, demented, maniacal. Jyrbian held the globe out to her, cupped between his palms and, as she stepped forward, smashed it, crushed it in his bare hands.

With shards of crystal and blood dripping from his hands, he regarded her.

"How could you?" Kaede screamed. "That was mine! Mine! You've destroyed it, as you've destroyed Bakrell!"

Jyrbian sidestepped her, continued his stalking of Khallayne, but Kaede jumped in front of him again. "Tell me why you killed my brother!" she screamed in his face.

"He murdered him for no reason," Khallayne said. "He died in the dungeons of this castle." Khallayne backed away quickly as Jyrbian swept Kaede aside effortlessly.

With a scream, Kaede rushed him. He backhanded her casually, sending her sprawling on the floor. Her head hit a chair.

Magic seethed in the pit of Khallayne's stomach, reminding her of flames. Fire. Now. It had to be now. She closed her eyes, a dangerous thing to do, but it helped focus the power.

She felt Jyrbian tense, ready to leap, and she cast the power outward with all her strength. Coldfire. She had no idea where the spell came from. It was intuition by now.

The bluish orange flames leapt toward Jyrbian, enfolded him. He screamed in rage and twisted within the field of flame, shouted out words of an incantation, a prayer for protection from his god. Flames weakened, sputtered; still she concentrated, putting all her knowledge, her fear, her pain, into maintaining the spell. He stumbled, staggered, clutching his brow.

Then, incredibly, Kaede was standing, adding her force to the fire.

Jyrbian turned on Kaede, reaching out through the wall of flame. He grabbed her shoulder, pulled her close, into the fire with him.

Khallayne cried out. Kaede convulsed, her body arching in pain. Jyrbian's fingers dug into her throat.

Khallayne fell to her knees, sweat and tears mixing on her face. She balled her fists into her stomach and doubled over with the effort of maintaining her attack. Kneeling on the floor, she could feel the broken shards digging into her knees and cutting into her palms. She gathered the pieces up into her hands. A residue of magic still clung to them, an echo of power and song.

Jyrbian dropped Kaede, abandoning her bruised body, and turned his attention to Khallayne.

Khallayne rose to meet him, the pieces of crystal in her fingers, met him with fury for what was lost— the city, the Ogre civilization, the Song of History.

Unable to defeat the flames that surrounded him, he reached through them. A lamp exploded. Something large fell behind her. The window, the beautiful, etched glass window, exploded inward, sending glass arcing toward the ceiling.

Behind him, Kaede climbed slowly to her feet, almost unable to walk. Khallayne couldn't understand her, but her lips were moving as she stumbled toward Jyrbian.

He turned his attack on her. Something leapt toward Kaede. She took the blow full-force in the chest, but kept moving, walking toward him, leaning forward as though into a blizzard-strength wind.

Too late, he realized what she was doing. He tried to back away, but Kaede reached out for him. She stepped into the fire of Khallayne's spell, bringing with her whatever spell it was she'd been casting, and turning the power of his own attack back on him.

"Go!" she whispered to Khallayne. "Go!"

Khallayne ran as things in the room erupted into flame, as the rocks and crystals on the window ledge began to explode.

In the doorway, she paused to look back, seeing only Jyrbian's face, the face she'd once thought the most beautiful in all of Takar, twisted with hate.

She wheeled and ran down the corridors, down the stairs, and out into night, into the cool air. But she could still hear Jyrbian's voice, twisted, demented, inside her head, screaming.

Run! Run! There is no place on all of Krynn where the Ogres will not find you, where the gods will not find you!

* * * * *

Her horse had been left at the coliseum, so she took Jyrbian's big stallion. He stood in his stall, still saddled.

Khallayne galloped down into Takar, back into the flames, automatically heading for the west gate. To get back to the plains, she'd have to take a different route than before, toward Bloten. The passes northward would already be snowed in.

The streets were almost empty. Most of the houses and buildings showed damage, but the worst of the fires still burned brightly to the east, nearer the coliseum.

No one bothered her. No guards challenged her as she galloped through the gates and out onto the wide road leading out of Takar.

She almost didn't hear her name being called out over the pounding of the horse's hooves. She looked back and saw a small figure in rough clothing running down the shoulder of the road, waving her arms, cloak streaming out behind.

Jelindra! She pulled hard on the reins, bringing the horse to a stop. She was sure Jelindra would be gone by now! She slid to the ground. Jelindra almost knocked her off her feet as she threw her arms around her.

"Oh, Khallayne, I though you'd never come!"

Khallayne hugged her just as tightly. "I thought I wouldn't either. I can't believe you're still here."

Jelindra appeared healthy, though her face was dirty and her hair full of twigs. "I told you I'd wait," she said. "I hid in the woods, and I watched the road every day. Then I saw the fires, and I thought you weren't going to come!" She threw her arms around Khallayne again.

Khallayne hugged her back. "Well, I'm here now. Let's go home."

Nodding, Jelindra stepped back, wiping away tears and streaking dirt across her cheeks. "How will we find them?"

Khallayne shrugged. "I don't know. But we'll manage somehow."

* * * * *

The two stood on the deck of the huge ship and leaned against the rail.

Beneath Khallayne's feet, the ancient timbers of the deck creaked. Above her head, the canvas sails snapped and billowed in the wind. And all sounds were underlined with the soothing motion of the ship slicing through the ocean, smooth, relaxing, as lulling as going back to the womb.

Khallayne leaned far out, feeling the sting of salt spray on her cheeks and forehead, the splintery oak beneath her fingers as she gripped the rail. Would the island be there? Would their people be safe? In Schall they'd lost the last trace of them, but a sailor had told an incredible story of a group of people called the Irda, beautiful people who'd gone away to

293

live on an island—an island that had called to them.

Khallayne, too, heard the song on the wind. It was a sound more beautiful than any Ogre voice, high and pure like crystal chimes, more beautiful than the voice in the sphere.

The bright, silvery light of Solinari sparkled on the featureless water, as far as they could see. But there was no island yet. No finger of land to mar the perfect beauty of the moonlight on the black-silk water.

Bare feet gripping the wooden deck, Jelindra ran to the other side of the boat and hung over the rail, but that way, too, was water, dappled with moonlight. Jelindra ran back to Khallayne.

Water and moonlight seemed unbroken to the horizon. Jelindra slumped against the rail where moments before she'd eagerly leaned across. "What do we do now?" she asked. "If there isn't an island . . . "

"It has to be there!" Khallayne thumped the railing with her fists. Her heart wouldn't contemplate otherwise. "I can hear it."

Jelindra cocked her head. "Yes," she agreed. "I can hear it. Let's go!"

Before Khallayne could stop her, she'd slipped down the rope ladder to the little boat they'd prepared earlier in the evening and started to untie the rope mooring it to the ship.

Khallayne climbed down into the boat. "Are you sure? You know, if you're wrong, we'll die!"

"We're not wrong," said Jelindra firmly.

The little boat slowed and pivoted as the ocean took it, slipping away from the ship with the current. They had committed themselves. Noisily, Jelindra dipped an oar into the water. The boat responded, and she stroked again.

The boat shot forward. Khallayne dug into the water again and again, matching her strokes to Jelindra's, aiming the craft toward where she thought, hoped, *believed*, the island should be.

She rowed until her arms ached, until her shoulders burned with fire, until the pain almost drowned out the song of the land, until she couldn't move the wooden oar anymore and it hung over the edge of the boat.

Then, suddenly, as if a fog had lifted, the island was before them. A dark silhouette loomed up to block out the gorgeous sky.

Laughing, crying, Jelindra reached back to hug Khallayne, then began to row faster.

The pain forgotten, Khallayne pulled with her oar, sliding it so deeply into the water that she was dipping her fingers, until she felt the boat scrape bottom.

Then she slid into the cold water and pulled the boat by a rope. It seemed to take forever. Jelindra joined her, adding her insubstantial weight to the rope.

The boat scraped sand, and they left it, running the rest of the way, until warm, dry sand was beneath their feet.

Khallayne dropped to her knees, dug her fingers into the gritty sand. She pressed it to her face and felt the grains stick to the furrows that tears had left on her cheeks.

"Home, Jelindra! We're home!" She threw handfuls of sand into the air, then covered her eyes when the ocean breeze blew it back in her face.

"Khallayne . . . "

The fear in Jelindra's voice ended Khallayne's celebration. She saw that someone was coming toward them.

Blinking against the sand that coated her lashes, she stood and took a tentative step toward the figure, partially hidden in shadows at the edge of the trees. "Who's there? I'm Khallayne. I've come to find Igraine . . . "

Lyrralt! It had to be Lyrralt. She knew the way he moved, the way he stepped, his scent on the salt breeze.

The figure moved forward cautiously, too small, too slight, to be an Ogre. "Khallayne?" The light caught the soft hair, the canted eyes of an elf.

Khallayne froze.

Jelindra's cry shattered the stillness of the night.

Khallayne stepped in front of the girl, reaching back to protect her, to comfort her, and the figure said her name again, no longer in question, but in joyous greeting.

It dawned on her. An elf had said her name! A male, tall and slender, with the features of an elf— only with Lyrralt's voice.

Before their eyes, he transformed. It was a shape-shifting, like the appearance of the island, magical, miraculous. The lithe elf became Lyrralt, tall and strong and broad of shoulder, sapphire skin gleaming in the light of Solinari, silver hair as bright as the moon. And sightless now, forever.

"Forgive me," Lyrralt said, holding out his arms to them. "Forgive me, but I had to be sure."

Khallayne ran to him, threw her arms around him. A moment later, Jelindra threw herself bodily against them, joining their circle.

He shivered, held them closer.

"How did you do it?" she asked. "For a minute, I thought you were an elf!"

Laughing, he released them. "The gods have touched us, Khallayne, blessed us with a gift beyond believing, beyond—beyond—"

"Stop." She touched her fingers to his mouth to stop his excited, confusing words, felt the warmth of his breath under her fingers, and something else. The scar. She turned him in the moonlight and saw the jagged mark running the length of his face. "Start slowly. Tell us everything."

In response, he ran his fingers across her face, as if reassuring himself about the Ogres who stood beside him. He brushed sand from Jelindra's hair. In a serene tone, he explained, "Last month, at the High Sanction of Solinari, the gods touched us. In the night, they touched us with peace, with calm. And when we woke, we could change."

"Change?"

"Shapechange, as you saw me a moment before. I can assume the shape of another being. We all can. Do you realize what that means?" His voice rose excitedly. "It means that we never have to be afraid again. We never have to run again. We will always have the perfect disguise. Even if the island is discovered, no one will ever know who we are!"

"The island! Why couldn't we *see* the island?" Jelindra demanded.

He paused, smiling shyly. "It's my spell, a spell of hiding, but we all work to maintain it."

Khallayne could hardly dare to believe it. There was simply too much information, too fast. Gifts from the gods. Everyone's magical ability, powerful enough to hide an island? And Lyrralt, blind, scarred and using magic?

"Khallayne?" He caught her hand.

"It's so much to take in," she whispered. "So much."

The sadness in her voice, in her face, registered. "What is it? Tell me," Lyrralt asked.

She caught his hands in hers. "There's so much, I hardly know where to begin . . . "

"Jyrbian?"

"Dead, I think," she whispered, hoping it was true. She hoped there was no way he could have survived Kaede's fire, for she never wanted to think of Jyrbian alive as she had last seen him. "Bakrell, too. And Kaede."

"And Takar burned," Jelindra piped in.

Khallayne nodded. "We looked back, just before we left the west road. It was like a smoking cinder. The whole city . . . "

"The others will want to hear."

Epilogue
The Book of the Irda

The Keeper of the history of the Irda stood on the hillside, surrounded by her people, assisted by friends and love ones, though she was as young and strong as the saplings that grew nearby. She had seen the world of her childhood pass on, had seen the sacred History of her people destroyed, but still she smiled, because of the Gift that she would give to all her people.

She held up the book, the Gift of the gods, and in a voice as pure and clear, as bright and beautiful as sunshine, spoke the beginning of the words written within, the words that wove the History of the World, of the Ogres, firstborn of the gods.

This I have salvaged out of the destruction. The music is gone forever, as is the beauty of the Ogres, but the words are preserved for all to read.

We are the Irda, firstborn of the gods.

The High God looked down upon the chaos and bid the god Reorx to forge the universe with his mighty hammer. From the forge of the gods, our world was wrought and the gods played here, as children gambol in a field.

In the sculpting of the world, sparks flew from the anvil and settled in the skies, danced in the heavens. The sparks were spirits with voices like starshine. They shone as the gods themselves, for they were pieces of the gods themselves.

The gods saw the spirits and wanted them for themselves, and they battled over them, striking mighty blows upon the world. The High God looked down upon the destruction and was angry with his children. In the heat of his anger, he decreed that each of the triumvirate of the gods, Evil, Neutral and Good, could gift the spirits with one legacy, and afterward, must allow the spirits to go free.

The gods of Light gave the spirits bodies, that they might master their world. The Dark gods offered weakness and want, that the spirits might learn greed and corruption. The gods of Gray, the Shadow gods, gave the spirits free will, that they might shape their own lives.

And so, the races were born.

From the gods of Evil came the Ogres, firstborn of the world. Gifted with immortality and untold beauty, the Ogres chose the lofty mountains as their home.

From the gods of Goodness and Light came the elves, graceful and regal and good, who sought the enchanted forests and hid themselves away to live in harmony with the land.

Those of the Middle, the Gray gods, brought forth the humans. They were short lived and brutish, but they had the capacity to both destroy and love. To them were left the grassy plains.

The Ogres set themselves above to rule the other children of the world, but the elves were too placid, too good to make suitable slaves. The Ogres turned to the humans to build their castles and their cities and their roads. On the bones of humans, the Ogres built a civilization.

Like stars in the sky, the watchers of the darkness were the mighty Ogres, building a nation of order and discipline. But their hungers consumed them, their greed and desire made them weak and ugly, and their appetites devoured them.

The humans rebelled against their cruelty and vengeance, and the Ogres fell from the grace of the gods.

Igraine, governor of a mighty province, learned from the humans the most precious gift of all. He learned of choice, of choosing between right and wrong. He learned from the humans the gift the gods had given, the ability to destroy and to love and the potential to choose between.

He gathered about him the Irda, the Children of the Stars, his friends and family, those who believed his vision, and they fled the mountains. Through hardships they traveled, finding a new home, Anaiatha, among the Dragon Isles.

The Ogres are no more. They will disappear back into the chaos from which the world was made.

But the Irda will continue, in goodness and strength, firstborn of the gods, chosen of the gods.

And this History, the Irdanaith, the Book of the Stars, will continue. I write it for all the Irda to see and study, that we may never make the mistakes of our ancestors, that the History will never be lost.

DRAGONS
of
SUMMER
FLAME

**An Excerpt
From a Work in Progress
by
Margaret Weis and Tracy Hickman**

Chapter One
Be Warned . . .

It was hot that morning, damnably hot.

Far too hot for late spring on Ansalon. Almost as hot as midsummer. The two knights, seated in the boat's stern, were sweaty and miserable in their heavy steel armor; they looked with envy at the nearly naked men plying the boat's oars. When the boat neared shore, the knights were first out, jumping into the shallow water, laving the water onto their reddening faces and sunburned necks. But the water was not particularly refreshing.

"Like wading in hot soup," one of the knights grumbled, splashing ashore. Even as he spoke, he scrutinized the shoreline carefully, eyeing bush and tree and dune for signs of life.

"More like blood," said his comrade. "Think of it as wading in the blood of our enemies, the enemies of our Queen. Do you see anything?"

"No," the other replied. He waved his hand, then, without looking back, heard the sound of men leaping into the water, their harsh laughter and conversation in their uncouth, guttural language.

One of the knights turned around. "Bring that boat to shore," he said, unnecessarily, for the men had already picked up the heavy boat and were running with it through the shallow water. Grinning, they dumped the boat on the sand beach and looked to the knight for further orders.

He mopped his forehead, marveled at their strength, and—not for the first time—thanked Queen Takhisis that these barbarians were on their side. The brutes, they were known as. Not the true name of their race. The name, their name for themselves, was unpronounceable, and so the knights who led the barbarians had begun calling them by the shortened version: brute.

The name suited the barbarians well. They came from the east, from a continent that few people on Ansalon knew existed. Every one of the men stood well over six feet; some were as tall as seven. Their bodies were as bulky and muscular as humans, but their movements were as swift and graceful as elves. Their ears were pointed like those of the elves, but their faces were heavily bearded like humans or dwarves. They were as strong as dwarves and loved battle as well as dwarves did. They fought fiercely, were loyal to those who commanded them, and, outside of a few grotesque customs such as cutting off various parts of the body of a dead enemy to keep as trophies, the brutes were ideal foot soldiers.

"Let the captain know we've arrived safely and that we've encountered no resistance," said the knight to his comrade. "We'll leave a couple of men here with the boat and move inland."

The other knight nodded. Taking a red silk pennant from his belt, he unfurled it, held it above his head, and waved it slowly three times. An answering flutter of red came from the enormous black, dragon-prowed ship anchored some distance away. This was a scouting mission, not an invasion. Orders had been quite clear on that point.

The knights sent out their patrols, dispatching some to range up and down the beach, sending others farther inland. This done, the two knights moved thankfully to the meager shadow cast by a squat and misshapen tree. Two of the brutes stood guard. The knights remained wary and watchful, even as they rested. Seating themselves, they drank sparingly of the fresh water they'd brought with them. One of them grimaced.

"The damn stuff's hot."

"You left the waterskin sitting in the sun. Of course it's hot."

"Where the devil was I supposed to put it? There was no shade on that cursed boat. I don't think there's any shade left in the whole blasted world. I don't like this place at all. I get a queer feeling about this island, like it's magicked or something."

"I know what you mean," agreed his comrade somberly. He kept glancing about, back into the trees, up and down the beach. All that could be seen were the brutes, and they were certainly not bothered by any ominous feelings. But then they were barbarians. "We were warned not to come here, you know."

"What?" The other knight looked astonished. "I didn't know. Who told you that?"

"Brightblade. He had it from Lord Ariakan himself."

"Brightblade should know. He's on Ariakan's staff. The lord's his sponsor." The knight appeared nervous and asked softly, "Such information's not secret, is it?"

The other knight appeared amused. "You don't know Steele Brightblade very well if you think he would break any oath or pass along any information he was told to keep to himself. He'd sooner let his tongue be ripped out by red-hot tongs. No, Lord Ariakan discussed this openly with all the regimental commanders before deciding to proceed."

The knight shrugged. Picking up a handful of small rocks, he began tossing them idly into the water. "The Gray Robes started it all. Some sort of augury revealed the location of this island and that it was inhabited by large numbers of people."

"So who warned us not to come?"

"The Gray Robes. The same augury that told them of this island also warned them not to come near it. They tried to persuade Ariakan to leave well enough alone. Said that this place could mean disaster."

The other knight frowned, then glanced around with growing unease. "Then why were we sent?"

"The upcoming invasion of Ansalon. Lord Ariakan felt this move was necessary to protect his flanks. The Gray Robes couldn't say exactly what sort of threat this island represented. Nor could they say specifically that the disaster would be caused by our landing on the island. As Lord Ariakan pointed out, perhaps disaster would come even if we didn't do anything. And so he decided to follow the old dwarven dictum, 'It is better to go looking for the dragon than have the dragon come looking for you.'"

"Good thinking," his companion agreed. "If there is an army of elves on this island, it's better that we deal with them now. Not that it seems likely."

He gestured at the wide stretches of sand beach, at the dunes covered with some sort of grayish-green grass, and, farther inland, a forest of the ugly, misshapen trees. "Elves wouldn't live in a place like this."

"Neither would dwarves. Minotaurs would have attacked us by now. Kender would have walked off with the boat *and* our armor. Gnomes would have met us with some sort of demon-driven fish-catching machine. Humans like us are the only race foolish enough to live in such a wretched place," the knight concluded cheerfully. He picked up another handful of rocks.

"It could be a rogue band of draconians or hobgoblins. Ogres even. Escaped twenty-some years ago, after the War of the Lance. Fled north, across the sea, to avoid capture by the Solamnic Knights."

"Yes, but they'd be on our side," his companion answered. "And our wizards wouldn't have their robes in a knot over it. . . . Ah, here come our scouts, back to report. Now we'll find out."

The knights rose to their feet. The brutes who had been sent into the island's interior hurried forward to meet their leaders. The barbarians were grinning hugely. Their nearly naked bodies glistened with sweat. The blue paint with which they covered themselves, and which was supposed to possess some sort of magical properties said to cause arrows to bounce right off them, ran down their muscular bodies in rivulets. Long scalp locks, decorated with colorful feathers, bounced on their backs as they loped easily over the sand dunes.

The two knights exchanged glances, relaxed.

"What did you find?" the knight asked the leader, a gigantic red-haired fellow who towered over both knights and could have probably picked up each of them and held them over his head. He regarded both knights with unbounded reverence and respect.

"Men," answered the brute. They were quick to learn and had adapted easily to the Common language spoken by most of the various races of Krynn. Unfortunately, to the brutes, all people not of their race were known as "men."

The brute lowered his hand near the ground to indicate small men, which might mean dwarves but was more probably children. He moved it to waist height, which most likely indicated women. This the brute confirmed by cupping two hands over his own breast and wiggling his hips. His men laughed and nudged each other.

"Men, women, and children," said the knight. "Many men? Lots of men? Big buildings? Walls? Cities?"

The brutes apparently thought this was hilarious, for they all burst into raucous laughter.

"What did you find?" said the knight sharply, scowling. "Stop the nonsense."

The brutes sobered rapidly.

"Many men," said the leader, "but no walls. Houses." He made a face, shrugged, shook his head, and added something in his own language."

"What does that mean?" asked the knight of his comrade.

"Something to do with dogs," said the other, who had led brutes before and had started picking up some of their language. "I think he means that these men live in houses only dogs would live in."

Several of the brutes now began walking about stoop-shouldered, swinging their arms around their knees and grunting. Then they all straightened up, looked at each other, and laughed again.

"What in the name of our Dark Majesty are they doing now?" the knight demanded.

"Beats me," said his comrade. "I think we should go have a look for ourselves." He drew his sword partway out of its black leather scabbard. "Danger?" he asked the brute. "We need steel?"

The brute laughed again. Taking his own short sword—the brutes fought with two, long and short, as well as bow and arrows—he thrust it into the tree and turned his back on it.

The knight, reassured, returned his sword to its scabbard. The two followed their guides deeper into the forest.

They did not go far before they came to the village. They entered a cleared area among the trees.

Despite the antics of the brutes, the knights were completely unprepared for what they saw.

"By Hiddukel," one said in a low voice to the other. " 'Men' is too strong a term. *Are* these men? Or are they beasts?"

"They're men," said the other, staring around slowly, amazed. "But such men as we're told walked Krynn during the Age of Twilight. Look! Their tools are made of wood. They carry wooden spears, and crude ones at that."

"Wooden-tipped, not stone," said the other. "Mud huts for houses. Clay cooking pots. Not a piece of steel or iron in sight. What a pitiable lot! I can't see how they could be much danger, unless it's from filth. By the smell, they haven't bathed since the Age of Twilight either."

"Ugly bunch. More like apes than men. Don't laugh. Look stern and threatening."

Several of the male humans—if human they were; it was difficult to tell beneath the animal hides they wore—crept up to the knights. The "man-beasts" walked bent over, their arms swinging at their sides, knuckles almost dragging on the ground. Their heads were covered with long, shaggy hair; unkempt beards almost completely hid their faces. They bobbed and shuffled and gazed at the knights in openmouthed awe. One of the man-beasts actually drew near enough to reach out a grimy hand to touch the black, shining armor.

A brute moved to interpose his own massive body in front of the knight.

The knight waved the brute off and drew his sword. The steel flashed in the sunlight. Turning to one of the trees, which, with their twisted limbs and gnarled trunks, resembled the people who lived beneath them, the knight raised his sword and sliced off a limb with one swift stroke.

The man-beast dropped to his knees and groveled in the dirt, making piteous blubbering sounds.

"I think I'm going to vomit," said the knight to his comrade. "Gully dwarves wouldn't associate with this lot."

"You're right there." The knight looked around. "Between us, you and I could wipe out the entire tribe."

"We'd never be able to clean the stench off our swords," said the other.

"What should we do? Kill them?"

"Small honor in it. These wretches obviously aren't any threat to us. Our orders were to find out who or what was inhabiting the island, then return. For all we know, these people may be the favorites of some god, who might be angered if we harmed them. Perhaps that is what the Gray Robes meant by disaster."

"I don't know," said the other knight dubiously. "I can't imagine any god treating his favorites like this."

"Morgion, perhaps," said the other, with a wry grin.

The knight grunted. "Well, we've certainly done no

harm just by looking. The Gray Robes can't fault us for that. Send out the brutes to scout the rest of the island. According to the reports from the dragons, it's not very big. Let's go back to the shore. I need some fresh air."

The two knights sat in the shade of the tree, talking of the upcoming invasion of Ansalon, discussing the vast armada of black dragon-prowed ships, manned by minotaurs, that was speeding its way across the Courrain Ocean, bearing thousands and thousands more barbarian warriors. All was nearly ready for the invasion, which would take place on Summer's Eve.

The knights of Takhisis did not know precisely where they were attacking; such information was kept secret. But they had no doubt of victory. This time the Dark Queen would succeed. This time her armies would be victorious. This time she knew the secret to victory.

The brutes returned within a few hours and made their report. The isle was not large. The brutes found no other people. The tribe of man-beasts had all slunk off fearfully and were hiding, cowering, in their mud huts until the strange beings left.

The knights returned to their shore boat. The brutes pushed it off the sand, leaped in, and grabbed the oars. The boat skimmed across the surface of the water, heading for the black ship that flew the multicolored flag of the five-headed dragon.

They left behind an empty, deserted beach. Or so it appeared.

But their leaving was noted, as their coming had been.

Fr. Edward Lee Looney

a Rosary Litany

Renewing a Pious Custom

Fl✿res Mariae Publishing

May help us!
Fr. Edward
Looney

A Rosary Litany
Renewing a Pious Custom
Fr. Edward Lee Looney

Cover images: Robert Hill, Murals by Jericho and Shutterstock.com
Cover and book design: Flores Mariae Publishing Design Department

Imprimatur granted on January 25, 2016 by
The Most Reverend David L. Ricken, DD, JCL

Nihil Obstat: Very Reverend John W. Girotti, JCL

For information regarding permission, write to:
Flores MariaePublishing
Attention: Permissions Dept.
4806 South 40th Street
Phoenix, AZ 85040

ISBN 978-1-61956-526-5

First Edition March 2016
10 9 8 7 6 5 4 3 2 1

Published and printed in the United States of America by Flores Mariae Publishing an imprint of Vesuvius Press Incorporated.

♻ Text printed on 30% post-consumer waste recycled paper.

THE RATIONALE BEHIND
A Rosary Litany

The rosary, popularized by the sons of St. Dominic, has been a devotion of the Christian faithful for centuries. Unfortunately in the third millennium, many people have become dissatisfied with the rosary as a form of meditation and prayer, viewing it as old-fashioned and outdated.

The rosary itself is scriptural by nature, containing the Our Father and the angelic salutation (Hail Mary) in addition to the mysteries being rooted in Sacred Scripture. Moreover, the rosary has been called a compendium to the Gospel as it leads us through the life of Jesus and Mary. In it, Mary leads us to reflect on the life of the savior, from His birth, through His public ministry, to His passion, death, and resurrection.

The rhythm of the rosary is not repetitive as some may contend; rather the repetition lends itself to meditation. As we pray each of the decades, we get lost in the reflection of the mystery. Thus, the repetition of the Hail Mary allows the mystery to consume the devotee.

Perhaps in our technological era which is consumed by noise, people are no longer able to be still for twenty minutes and bring themselves into the presence of God and reflect. It has become difficult to meditate on one thing for a short amount of time because our thoughts are fleeting and the worries of life distract us. That is why in recent years rosary devotional books have been written–in order to assist in the meditative and contemplative aspect of the rosary.

This small devotional book, *A Rosary Litany*, reintroduces the Christian faithful to an old custom of praying the rosary. St. Louis Grignion de Montfort in *The Secret of the Rosary* proposed for devotional purposes the addition of a meditative element to the Hail Mary prayer. Paul VI in *Marialis Cultus* and John Paul II in *Rosarium Virginis Mariae* also encouraged this devotion. These additional phrases guide and focus the meditation of the mystery within the context of the Hail Mary.

In each decade of *A Rosary Litany*, the De Montfort

suggestion is provided, in addition to several other invocations which could be inserted after the name of Jesus or Mary. When prayed in succession, the rosary becomes litany–like, on account of the varied invocations.

HOW TO USE
A ROSARY LITANY

St. Louis de Montfort encouraged the addition of one phrase and is listed separate from the ten other phrases proposed by this book for directed meditation. If one would like to use the St. Louis de Montfort suggestion, simply omit one of the ten listed. Also, it should be noted that the Luminous Mysteries were added by John Paul II, so there is no suggested phrase from St. Louis de Montfort. Some mysteries contain additional invocations which could be used as alternatives to the ones enumerated.

Some invocations are written in the style using the word "who." These invocations could be rephrased at the discretion of the devotee. "Thy womb Jesus, who met John the Baptist," could be modified to "thy womb Jesus, meeting John the Baptist." Or "thy womb Jesus, who prayed all might be one" could be modified to "thy womb Jesus, praying all might be one."

Here are three different ways *A Rosary Litany* could be used:

1. All ten invocations for each mystery could be used during the recitation of the rosary. In this way the devotion truly becomes litany-like. When praying each of the ten Hail Mary's, insert the "litany invocation" after "thy womb Jesus" or "Mother of God." In some cases the Marian reference modifies "Holy Mary, Mother of God."

2. A person could choose to use one or two of the phrases at one time thereby spreading the phrases over a few week period. The repetition of a specific phrase over and over again makes it resonate within the prayerful meditation. In one sense the invocation becomes an earnest plea or desire. It is possible that while using *A Rosary Litany* a certain invocation may become your favorite and you will use it every time when reflecting on the mystery.

3. John Paul II recommended this practice for the public recitation of the rosary. If using an invocation that follows Jesus' name, the prayer

leader would pray the first part and everyone else the second. When using an invocation following Mary's name, the group should pray the first half of the Hail Mary and the prayer leader would conclude the prayer adding the invocation after Mary's name.

Let us pray that this small rosary devotional book can help to renew devotion to Our Lady's rosary for it is a tried and true devotion of our faith.

From the Popes

Paul VI

As a Gospel prayer, centered on the mystery of the redemptive Incarnation, the Rosary is therefore a prayer with a clearly Christological orientation. Its most characteristic element, in fact, the litany-like succession of Hail Mary's, becomes in itself an unceasing praise of Christ, who is the ultimate object both of the angel's announcement and of the greeting of the mother of John the Baptist: "Blessed is the fruit of your womb" (Lk. 1:42). We would go further and say that the succession of Hail Mary's constitutes the warp on which is woven the contemplation of the mysteries. The Jesus that each Hail Mary recalls is the same Jesus whom the succession of the mysteries proposes to us-now as the Son of God, now as the Son of the Virgin-at His birth in a stable at Bethlehem, at His presentation by His Mother in the Temple, as a youth full of zeal for His Father's affairs, as the Redeemer in agony in the garden, scourged and crowned with thorns, carrying the cross and dying on Calvary, risen from the dead and ascended to the glory of the

Father to send forth the gift of the Spirit. **As is well known, at one time there was a custom, still preserved in certain places, of adding to the name of Jesus in each Hail Mary reference to the mystery being contemplated. And this was done precisely in order to help contemplation and to make the mind and the voice act in unison.**

—Paul VI, *Marialis Cultus*, paragraph 46.
(Emphasis added)

JOHN PAUL II

The centre of gravity in the Hail Mary, the hinge as it were which joins its two parts, is the name of Jesus. Sometimes, in hurried recitation, this centre of gravity can be overlooked, and with it the connection to the mystery of Christ being contemplated. Yet it is precisely the emphasis given to the name of Jesus and to his mystery that is the sign of a meaningful and fruitful recitation of the Rosary. Pope Paul VI drew attention, in his Apostolic Exhortation *Marialis Cultus*, to the custom in certain regions of highlighting the name of Christ by the addition of a clause referring to the mystery being contemplated. **This is a praiseworthy custom, especially during public** recitation. **It gives forceful expression to our faith in Christ, directed to the different moments of the Redeemer's life. It is at once a profession of faith and an aid in concentrating our meditation, since it facilitates the process of assimilation to the mystery of Christ inherent in the repetition of the Hail Mary.** When we repeat the name of Jesus — the only name given to us by which we may hope for salvation (cf. Acts 4:12) — in close association with the name of his Blessed Mother, almost as if it were done at her suggestion, we set out on a path of assimilation meant to help us enter more deeply into the life of Christ.

—John Paul II, *Rosarium Virginis Mariae*,
paragraph 33 (Emphasis added).

Joyful Mysteries
Traditionally prayed on Mondays and Saturdays

1. Annunciation

De Montfort Suggestion: **Jesus incarnate**

1. thy womb Jesus, **announced by the angel Gabriel**, Holy Mary, Mother of God, pray for us sinners…

2. thy womb Jesus, **conceived by the Holy Spirit**, Holy Mary, Mother of God, pray for us sinners…

3. thy womb Jesus, **Son of the Most High**, Holy Mary, Mother of God, pray for us sinners…

4. thy womb Jesus, **ruler of the House of Jacob**, Holy Mary, Mother of God, pray for us sinners…

5. thy womb Jesus, **whose kingdom will have no end**, Holy Mary, Mother of God, pray for us sinners…

6.	thy womb Jesus, Holy Mary, Mother of God, **spouse of the Holy Spirit**, pray for us sinners…

7.	thy womb Jesus, Holy Mary, Mother of God, **chosen by God**, pray for us sinners…

8.	thy womb Jesus, Holy Mary, Mother of God, **handmaid of The Lord**, pray for us sinners…

9.	thy womb Jesus, Holy Mary, Mother of God, **overshadowed by the Holy Spirit**, pray for us sinners…

10.	thy womb Jesus, Holy Mary, Mother of God, **Ark of the New Covenant**, pray for us sinners…

ALTERNATIVE INVOCATIONS:
—thy womb Jesus, **dwelling in the womb of the Virgin**, Holy Mary, Mother of God, pray for us sinners…

—thy womb Jesus, Holy Mary, Mother of God, **betrothed to Joseph**, pray for us sinners…

—thy womb Jesus, Holy Mary, Mother of God, **who pondered the angel's greeting**, pray for us sinners…

2. VISITATION OF MARY TO ELIZABETH

De Montfort Suggestion: **Jesus sanctifying**

1. thy womb Jesus, Holy Mary, Mother of God, **who went in haste to visit Elizabeth**, pray for us sinners…

2. thy womb Jesus, **who met John the Baptist**, Holy Mary, Mother of God, pray for us…

3. thy womb Jesus, **the cause of John's joy**, Holy Mary, Mother of God, pray for us sinners…

4. thy womb Jesus, **recognized as Lord by Elizabeth**, Holy Mary, Mother of God, pray for us sinners…

5. thy womb Jesus, Holy Mary, Mother of God, **woman of charity**, pray for us sinners…

6. thy womb Jesus, Holy Mary, Mother of God, **proclaimed blessed by Elizabeth**, pray for us sinners…

7. thy womb Jesus, Holy Mary, Mother **of our Lord and** God, pray for us sinners…

8. thy womb Jesus, Holy Mary, Mother of God, **who believed what was spoken to her**, pray for us sinners…

9. thy womb Jesus, Holy Mary, Mother of God, **who magnified The Lord**, pray for us sinners…

10. thy womb Jesus, Holy Mary, Mother of God, **who remained with Elizabeth three months**, pray for us sinners…

3. BIRTH OF JESUS

De Montfort Suggestion: **Jesus born in poverty**

1. thy womb Jesus, **born for us in Bethlehem**, Holy Mary, Mother of God, pray for us sinners…

2. thy womb Jesus, **who is Emmanuel**, Holy Mary, Mother of God, pray for us sinners…

3. thy womb Jesus, **son of God and son of Mary**, Holy Mary, Mother of God, pray for us sinners…

4. thy womb Jesus, **wrapped in swaddling clothes**, Holy Mary, Mother of God, pray for us sinners…

5. thy womb Jesus, **laid in a manger**, Holy Mary, Mother of God, pray for us sinners…

6. thy womb Jesus, **visited by shepherds and magi**, Holy Mary, Mother of God, pray for us sinners…

7. thy womb Jesus, **born to save us from our sins**, Holy Mary, Mother of God, pray for us sinners…

8. thy womb Jesus, Holy Mary, Mother of God, **who held the child Jesus**, pray for us sinners…

9. thy womb Jesus, Holy Mary, Mother of God, **whose womb bore the Son of God**, pray for us sinners…

10. thy womb Jesus, Holy Mary, Mother of God, **who nursed the child Jesus**, pray for us sinners…

ALTERNATIVE INVOCATION
—thy womb Jesus, Holy Mary, Mother of God, **ever virgin**, pray for us sinners…

ADDITIONAL INVOCATIONS INSPIRED BY THE GOSPEL OF JOHN CHAPTER 1

—thy womb Jesus, **Word made flesh**, Holy Mary, Mother of God, pray for us sinners…

—thy womb Jesus, **who made His dwelling among us**, Holy Mary, Mother of God, pray for us sinners…

—thy womb Jesus, **who was full of grace and truth**, Holy Mary, Mother of God, pray for us sinners…

—thy womb Jesus, **from whom we have all received grace in place of grace**, Holy Mary, Mother of God, pray for us sinners…

—thy womb Jesus, **who is the Light that shines in darkness**, Holy Mary, Mother of God, pray for us sinners…

—thy womb Jesus, **who is the True Light, which enlightens everyone**, Holy Mary, Mother of God, pray for us sinners…

4. PRESENTATION IN THE TEMPLE

De Montfort Suggestion: **Jesus sacrificed**

1. thy womb Jesus, **presented in the temple**, Holy Mary, Mother of God, pray for us sinners…

2. thy womb Jesus, **offered to the Father**, Holy Mary, Mother of God, pray for us sinners…

3. thy womb Jesus, **the fulfillment of Simeon's mission**, Holy Mary, Mother of God, pray for us sinners…

4. thy womb Jesus, **the light of revelation**, Holy Mary, Mother of God, pray for us sinners…

5. thy womb Jesus, **destined for the fall and rise of many**, Holy Mary, Mother of God, pray for us sinners…

6. thy womb Jesus, **a sign of contradiction**, Holy Mary, Mother of God, pray for us sinners…

7. thy womb Jesus, **proclaimed to others by the prophetess Anna**, Holy Mary, Mother of God, pray for us sinners…

8. thy womb Jesus, Holy Mary, Mother of God, **whose heart was pierced by a sword**, pray for us sinners…

9. thy womb Jesus, Holy Mary, Mother of God, **the contemplating Virgin**, pray for us sinners…

10. thy womb Jesus, Holy Mary, Mother of God, **who was purified**, pray for us sinners…

5. FINDING IN THE TEMPLE

De Montfort Suggestion: **Jesus, Saint among saints**

1. thy womb Jesus, **who accompanied His parents to the temple**, Holy Mary, Mother of God, pray for us sinners…

2. thy womb Jesus, **who remained behind in Jerusalem**, Holy Mary, Mother of God, pray for us sinners…

3. thy womb Jesus, **who was found in the temple**, Holy Mary, Mother of God, pray for us sinners…

4. thy womb Jesus, **who was sitting among the teachers**, Holy Mary, Mother of God, pray for us sinners…

5. thy womb Jesus, **who asked questions of the rabbis**, Holy Mary, Mother of God, pray for us sinners…

6. thy womb Jesus, **who was about His Father's business**, Holy Mary, Mother of God, pray for us sinners…

7. thy womb Jesus, Holy Mary, Mother of God, **who searched for Jesus**, pray for us sinners…

8. thy womb Jesus, Holy Mary, Mother of God, **worried for her son**, pray for us sinners…

9. thy womb Jesus, Holy Mary, Mother of God, **who asked why have you done this to us**, pray for us sinners…

10. thy womb Jesus, Holy Mary, Mother of God, **who kept these things in her heart**, pray for us sinners…

ALTERNATIVE INVOCATIONS
—thy womb Jesus, **obedient to His family in Nazareth**, Holy Mary, Mother of God, pray for us sinners…

—thy womb Jesus, Holy Mary, Mother of God, **puzzled by Jesus' response**, pray for us sinners…

LUMINOUS MYSTERIES
Traditionally Prayed on Thursdays

1. BAPTISM IN THE RIVER JORDAN

1. thy womb Jesus, **baptized by John**, Holy Mary, Mother of God, pray for us sinners…

2. thy womb Jesus, **who entered the River Jordan**, Holy Mary, Mother of God, pray for us sinners…

3. thy womb Jesus, **who must increase in us**, Holy Mary, Mother of God, pray for us sinners…

4. thy womb Jesus, **on whom a dove descended**, Holy Mary, Mother of God, pray for us sinners…

5. thy womb Jesus, **in whom the Father is well pleased**, Holy Mary, Mother of God, pray for us sinners…

6. thy womb Jesus, **the Beloved Son**, Holy Mary, Mother of God, pray for us sinners…

7. thy womb Jesus, **who is the one mightier than John**, Holy Mary, Mother of God, pray for us sinners…

8. thy womb Jesus, **who will baptize with the Holy Spirit and fire**, Holy Mary, Mother of God, pray for us sinners…

9. thy womb Jesus, **who sent His disciples to baptize**, Holy Mary, Mother of God, pray for us sinners…

10. thy womb Jesus, **who is the Living Water**, Holy Mary, Mother of God, pray for us sinners…

ALTERNATIVE INVOCATIONS EMPHASIZING JESUS' TEMPTATION IN THE DESERT

—thy womb Jesus, **who was led by the Spirit**, Holy Mary, Mother of God, pray for us sinners…

—thy womb Jesus, **who fasted and prayed**, Holy Mary, Mother of God, pray for us sinners…

—thy womb Jesus, **who triumphed over the Devil and His temptations**, Holy Mary, Mother of God, pray for us sinners…

2. Wedding Feast at Cana

1. thy womb Jesus, **invited to the Wedding Feast**, Holy Mary, Mother of God, pray for us sinners...

2. thy womb Jesus, **who learned of the wine shortage from Mary**, Holy Mary, Mother of God, pray for us sinners...

3. thy womb Jesus, **whose hour had not yet come**, Holy Mary, Mother of God, pray for us sinners...

4. thy womb Jesus, **who commanded the servants to bring six jars of water**, Holy Mary, Mother of God, pray for us sinners...

5. thy womb Jesus, **who turned water into wine**, Holy Mary, Mother of God, pray for us sinners...

6. thy womb Jesus, **in whom His disciples began to believe**, Holy Mary, Mother of God, pray for us sinners...

 24

7.   thy womb Jesus, **who performed the first of His signs at Cana**, Holy Mary, Mother of God, pray for us sinners…

8.   thy womb Jesus, Holy Mary, Mother of God, **attentive to the needs of others**, pray for us sinners…

9.   thy womb Jesus, Holy Mary, Mother of God, **who interceded for the couple**, pray for us sinners…

10. thy womb Jesus, Holy Mary, Mother of God, **who said do whatever he tells you**, pray for us sinners…

ALTERNATIVE INVOCATION
—thy womb Jesus, Holy Mary, Mother of God, **the Attentive Virgin**, pray for us sinners…

3. PROCLAMATION OF THE KINGDOM

1. thy womb Jesus, **who proclaimed the kingdom**, Holy Mary, Mother of God, pray for us sinners...

2. thy womb Jesus, **who calls us to repentance**, Holy Mary, Mother of God, pray for us sinners...

3. thy womb Jesus, **who taught His disciples how to pray**, Holy Mary, Mother of God, pray for us sinners...

4. thy womb Jesus, **who taught us to forgive others**, Holy Mary, Mother of God, pray for us sinners...

5. thy womb Jesus, **who proclaimed the Beatitudes**, Holy Mary, Mother of God, pray for us sinners...

6. thy womb Jesus, **who came not to abolish the Law**, Holy Mary, Mother of God, pray for us sinners…

7. thy womb Jesus, **the fulfillment of the Law**, Holy Mary, Mother of God, pray for us sinners…

8. thy womb Jesus, **who forgives our sins**, Holy Mary, Mother of God, pray for us sinners…

9. thy womb Jesus, **who inaugurated His ministry of mercy**, Holy Mary, Mother of God, pray for us sinners…

10. thy womb Jesus, **who shows us the way to the Father**, Holy Mary, Mother of God, pray for us sinners…

ALTERNATIVE INVOCATION:
—thy womb Jesus, **teach us how to pray**, Holy Mary, Mother of God, pray for us sinners…

4. TRANSFIGURATION

1. thy womb Jesus, **who ascended Mount Tabor**, Holy Mary, Mother of God, pray for us sinners…

2. thy womb Jesus, **accompanied by Peter, James, and John**, Holy Mary, Mother of God, pray for us sinners…

3. thy womb Jesus, **whom it is good to be with**, Holy Mary, Mother of God, pray for us sinners…

4. thy womb Jesus, **transfigured before His disciples**, Holy Mary, Mother of God, pray for us sinners…

5. thy womb Jesus, **whose face was as radiant as the sun**, Holy Mary, Mother of God, pray for us sinners…

6. thy womb Jesus, **the beloved Son**, Holy Mary, Mother of God, pray for us sinners…

7. thy womb Jesus, **whom we should listen to**, Holy Mary, Mother of God, pray for us sinners…

8. thy womb Jesus, **who instructed the disciples to rise and not be afraid**, Holy Mary, Mother of God, pray for us sinners…

9. thy womb Jesus, **the Son of Man who will suffer**, Holy Mary, Mother of God, pray for us sinners…

10. thy womb Jesus, **the fulfillment of the Law and the Prophets**, Holy Mary, Mother of God, pray for us sinners…

ALTERNATIVE INVOCATION
—thy womb Jesus, **appearing with Moses and Elijah**, Holy Mary, Mother of God, pray for us sinners…

5. INSTITUTION OF THE HOLY EUCHARIST

1. thy womb Jesus, **who instituted the Eucharist**, Holy Mary, Mother of God, pray for us sinners…

2. thy womb Jesus, **present in the Eucharist**, Holy Mary, Mother of God, pray for us sinners…

3. thy womb Jesus, **the living bread come down from heaven**, Holy Mary, Mother of God, pray for us sinners…

4. thy womb Jesus, **true food and true drink**, Holy Mary, Mother of God, pray for us sinners…

5. thy womb Jesus, **who took, broke, blessed, and gave the bread to His disciples**, Holy Mary, Mother of God, pray for us sinners…

6. thy womb Jesus, **whose blood is the New Covenant**, Holy Mary, Mother of God, pray for us sinners…

7. thy womb Jesus, **who promises eternal life**, Holy Mary, Mother of God, pray for us sinners…

8. thy womb Jesus, **who instructed us to do this in memory of Him**, Holy Mary, Mother of God, pray for us sinners…

9. thy womb Jesus, Holy Mary, Mother of God, **Ark of the New Covenant**, pray for us sinners…

10. thy womb Jesus, Holy Mary, Mother of God, **and Mother of the Eucharist**, pray for us sinners…

Alternative Invocation
—thy womb Jesus, **present body, blood, soul, and divinity**, Holy Mary, Mother of God, pray for us sinners…

SORROWFUL MYSTERIES
Traditionally Prayed on Tuesdays and Fridays

1. AGONY IN THE GARDEN

De Montfort Suggestion: **Jesus in His agony**

1. thy womb Jesus, **agonizing in the Garden**, Holy Mary, Mother of God, pray for us sinners…

2. thy womb Jesus, **praying in the Garden**, Holy Mary, Mother of God, pray for us sinners…

3. thy womb Jesus, **who prayed they all may be one**, Holy Mary, Mother of God, pray for us sinners…

4. thy womb Jesus, **who prayed that this cup might pass**, Holy Mary, Mother of God, pray for us sinners…

5. thy womb Jesus, **whose sweat became like drops of blood**, Holy Mary, Mother of God, pray for us sinners…

6.   thy womb Jesus, **who said watch and pray**, Holy Mary, Mother of God, pray for us sinners…

7.   thy womb Jesus, **who found the apostles asleep**, Holy Mary, Mother of God, pray for us sinners…

8.   thy womb Jesus, **whose hour had arrived**, Holy Mary, Mother of God, pray for us sinners…

9.   thy womb Jesus, **betrayed by Judas**, Holy Mary, Mother of God, pray for us sinners…

10. thy womb Jesus, **arrested in the Garden**, Holy Mary, Mother of God, pray for us sinners…

ALTERNATIVE INVOCATIONS

—thy womb Jesus, Holy Mary, Mother of God, **the Sorrowful Mother**, pray for us sinners...

—thy womb Jesus, **who prayed to His Father**, Holy Mary, Mother of God, pray for us sinners...

—thy womb Jesus, **who prayed three times**, Holy Mary, Mother of God, pray for us sinners...

2. SCOURGING AT THE PILLAR

De Montfort Suggestion: **Jesus scourged**

1. thy womb Jesus, **scourged at the pillar**, Holy Mary, Mother of God, pray for us sinners…

2. thy womb Jesus, **beaten and bruised**, Holy Mary, Mother of God, pray for us sinners…

3. thy womb Jesus, **scourged for our offenses**, Holy Mary, Mother of God, pray for us sinners…

4. thy womb Jesus, **chained to the pillar**, Holy Mary, Mother of God, pray for us sinners…

5. thy womb Jesus, **who was in excruciating pain**, Holy Mary, Mother of God, pray for us sinners…

6. thy womb Jesus, **bruised by a reed**, Holy Mary, Mother of God, pray for us sinners…

7. thy womb Jesus, **who was spat upon**, Holy Mary, Mother of God, pray for us sinners…

8. thy womb Jesus, **stripped of His clothes**, Holy Mary, Mother of God, pray for us sinners...

9. thy womb Jesus, **clothed in purple garments**, Holy Mary, Mother of God, pray for us sinners...

10. thy womb Jesus, Holy Mary, Mother of God, **the Sorrowful Mother**, pray for us sinners...

3. CROWNING WITH THORNS

De Montfort Suggestion: **Jesus crowned with thorns**

1. thy womb Jesus, **crowned with thorns**, Holy Mary, Mother of God, pray for us sinners…

2. thy womb Jesus, **King of the Jews**, Holy Mary, Mother of God, pray for us sinners…

3. thy womb Jesus, **King of Kings**, Holy Mary, Mother of God, pray for us sinners…

4. thy womb Jesus, **mocked by the soldiers**, Holy Mary, Mother of God, pray for us sinners…

5. thy womb Jesus, **bleeding from His wounds**, Holy Mary, Mother of God, pray for us sinners…

6. thy womb Jesus, **in excruciating pain**, Holy Mary, Mother of God, pray for us sinners…

7. thy womb Jesus, **Lord of Lords**, Holy Mary, Mother of God, pray for us sinners…

8. thy womb Jesus, **the Suffering Servant**, Holy Mary, Mother of God, pray for us sinners…

9. thy womb Jesus, Holy Mary, Mother of God, **weeping for her son**, pray for us sinners…

10. thy womb Jesus, Holy Mary, Mother of God, **the Sorrowful Mother**, pray for us sinners…

ALTERNATIVE INVOCATIONS

—thy womb Jesus, **who was handed over to Pilate**, Holy Mary, Mother of God, pray for us sinners…

—thy womb Jesus, **who was humiliated for our offenses**, Holy Mary, Mother of God, pray for us sinners…

—thy womb Jesus, **who was rejected by His own people**, Holy Mary, Mother of God, pray for us sinners…

—thy womb Jesus, **behold the Man**, Holy Mary, Mother of God, pray for us sinners…

—thy womb Jesus, **in whom Pilate could find no guilt**, Holy Mary, Mother of God, pray for us sinners…

4. CARRYING OF THE CROSS

De Montfort Suggestion: **Jesus carrying His Cross**

1. thy womb Jesus, **who carried His cross**, Holy Mary, Mother of God, pray for us sinners…

2. thy womb Jesus, **who fell three times**, Holy Mary, Mother of God, pray for us sinners…

3. thy womb Jesus, **who met His mother**, Holy Mary, Mother of God, pray for us sinners…

4. thy womb Jesus, **helped by Simon of Cyrene**, Holy Mary, Mother of God, pray for us sinners…

5. thy womb Jesus, **whose face was wiped by Veronica**, Holy Mary, Mother of God, pray for us sinners…

6. thy womb Jesus, **who consoled the women of Jerusalem**, Holy Mary, Mother of God, pray for us sinners…

7. thy womb Jesus, **stripped of His garments**, Holy Mary, Mother of God, pray for us sinners…

8. thy womb Jesus, **nailed to the cross**, Holy Mary, Mother of God, pray for us sinners…

9. thy womb Jesus, **lifted above the earth**, Holy Mary, Mother of God, pray for us sinners…

10. thy womb Jesus, Holy Mary, Mother of God, **the Sorrowful Mother**, pray for us sinners…

5. CRUCIFIXION

De Montfort Suggestion: **Jesus crucified**

1. thy womb Jesus, **crucified for our offenses**, Holy Mary, Mother of God, pray for us sinners…

2. thy womb Jesus, **who thirsts**, Holy Mary, Mother of God, pray for us sinners…

3. thy womb Jesus, **who forgave His transgressors**, Holy Mary, Mother of God, pray for us sinners…

4. thy womb Jesus, **who promised the Kingdom to the good thief**, Holy Mary, Mother of God, pray for us sinners…

5. thy womb Jesus, **who entrusted Mary to John**, Holy Mary, Mother of God, pray for us sinners…

6. thy womb Jesus, **who breathed His last**, Holy Mary, Mother of God, pray for us sinners…

7. thy womb Jesus, **pierced in the side**, Holy Mary, Mother of God, pray for us sinners.

8. thy womb Jesus, **from whom blood and water flowed**, Holy Mary, Mother of God, pray for us sinners…

9. thy womb Jesus, Holy Mary, Mother of God, **standing at the foot of the cross**, pray for us sinners…

10. thy womb Jesus, Holy Mary, Mother of God, **who held the body of Jesus**, pray for us sinners…

ADDITIONAL INVOCATIONS

—thy womb Jesus, **hanging from the tree**, Holy Mary, Mother of God, pray for us sinners…

—thy womb Jesus, Holy Mary, Mother of God, **the Sorrowful Mother**, pray for us sinners…

—thy womb Jesus, Holy Mary, **the Desolate** Mother of God, pray for us sinners…

GLORIOUS MYSTERIES
Traditionally Prayed on Sundays and Wednesdays

1. RESURRECTION

De Montfort Suggestion: **Jesus risen from the dead**

1. thy womb Jesus, **risen from the dead**, Holy Mary, Mother of God, pray for us sinners...

2. thy womb Jesus, **whose tomb was empty**, Holy Mary, Mother of God, pray for us sinners...

3. thy womb Jesus, **who defeated death**, Holy Mary, Mother of God, pray for us sinners...

4. thy womb Jesus, **who appeared to Mary Magdalene**, Holy Mary, Mother of God, pray for us sinners...

5. thy womb Jesus, **who revealed himself on the road to Emmaus**, Holy Mary, Mother of God, pray for us sinners...

6. thy womb Jesus, **who entered through the locked door**, Holy Mary, Mother of God, pray for us sinners...

7. thy womb Jesus, **whom Thomas doubted**, Holy Mary, Mother of God, pray for us sinners...

8. thy womb Jesus, **who fed His disciples**, Holy Mary, Mother of God, pray for us sinners...

9. thy womb Jesus, **who asked Peter, "Do you love me?"** Holy Mary, Mother of God, pray for us sinners...

10. thy womb Jesus, Holy Mary, Mother of God, **the rejoicing mother**, pray for us sinners...

ALTERNATIVE INVOCATION
—thy womb Jesus, **whose garments were found in the tomb**, Holy Mary, Mother of God, pray for us sinners...

2. ASCENSION

De Montfort Suggestion: **Jesus ascending to Heaven**

1. thy womb Jesus, **who ascended into Heaven**, Holy Mary, Mother of God, pray for us sinners…

2. thy womb Jesus, **who promised to send the advocate**, Holy Mary, Mother of God, pray for us sinners…

3. thy womb Jesus, **who lifted our human nature into Heaven**, Holy Mary, Mother of God, pray for us sinners…

4. thy womb Jesus, **who spent forty days with the disciples**, Holy Mary, Mother of God, pray for us sinners…

5. thy womb Jesus, **taken up by a cloud**, Holy Mary, Mother of God, pray for us sinners…

6. thy womb Jesus, **who made the disciples His witnesses**, Holy Mary, Mother of God, pray for us sinners…

7.   thy womb Jesus, **who blessed the disciples**, Holy Mary, Mother of God, pray for us sinners…

8.   thy womb Jesus, **who gave the great commission**, Holy Mary, Mother of God, pray for us sinners…

9.   thy womb Jesus, **seated at the right hand of the Father**, Holy Mary, Mother of God, pray for us sinners…

10. thy womb Jesus, Holy Mary, Mother of God, **witness to the Ascension**, pray for us sinners…

ALTERNATIVE INVOCATION
—thy womb Jesus, **who must go in order to send the Holy Spirit**, Holy Mary, Mother of God, pray for us sinners…

3. PENTECOST

De Montfort Suggestion: **Jesus filling Thee with the Holy Spirit**

1. thy womb Jesus, **who sent the Holy Spirit on the fiftieth day**, Holy Mary, Mother of God, pray for us sinners…

2. thy womb Jesus, **who promised to send the Holy Spirit**, Holy Mary, Mother of God, pray for us sinners…

3. thy womb Jesus, **who breathed on the Apostles**, Holy Mary, Mother of God, pray for us sinners…

4. thy womb Jesus, **giver of gifts**, Holy Mary, Mother of God, pray for us sinners…

5. thy womb Jesus, **send us the Spirit to renew the face of the earth**, Holy Mary, Mother of God, pray for us sinners…

6. thy womb Jesus, Holy Mary, Mother of God, **who joined the apostles in the Upper Room**, pray for us sinners…

7. thy womb Jesus, Holy Mary, Mother of God, **present at Pentecost**, pray for us sinners…

8. thy womb Jesus, Holy Mary, Mother of God, **who persevered in prayer with the disciples**, pray for us sinners…

9. thy womb Jesus, Holy Mary, Mother of God, **on whom the Holy Spirit descended at the Annunciation**, pray for us sinners…

10. thy womb Jesus, Holy Mary, Mother of God, **Spouse of the Holy Spirit**, pray for us sinners…

ADDITIONAL INVOCATION
—thy womb Jesus, **who said he had to ascend before the advocate could come**, Holy Mary, Mother of God, pray for us sinners…

4. Assumption of the Blessed Virgin Mary

De Montfort Suggestion: **Jesus raising Thee up**

1. thy womb Jesus, **who assumed His Mother into Heaven**, Holy Mary, Mother of God, pray for us sinners…

2. thy womb Jesus, Holy Mary, Mother of God, **highly favored lady**, pray for us sinners..

3. thy womb Jesus, Holy Mary, Mother of God, **who fell asleep**, pray for us sinners…

4. thy womb Jesus, Holy Mary, Mother of God, **assumed into Heaven**, pray for us sinners…

5. thy womb Jesus, Holy Mary, Mother of God, **assumed body and soul**, pray for us sinners…

6. thy womb Jesus, Holy Mary, Mother of God, **unblemished in all ways**, pray for us sinners…

7. thy womb Jesus, Holy Mary, Mother of God, **who did not experience the corruption of the tomb**, pray for us sinners…

8. thy womb Jesus, Holy Mary, Mother of God, **the glory of Jerusalem**, pray for us sinners…

9. thy womb Jesus, Holy Mary, Mother of God, **splendid boast of our race**, pray for us sinners…

10. thy womb Jesus, Holy Mary, Mother of God, **image of the Church**, pray for us sinners…

5. CORONATION OF MARY

De Montfort Suggestion: **Jesus crowning Thee**

1. thy womb Jesus, **King of the Universe**, Holy Mary, Mother of God, pray for us sinners…

2. thy womb Jesus, **who crowned His mother**, Holy Mary, Mother of God, pray for us sinners…

3. thy womb Jesus, Holy Mary, Mother of God, **reigning with Her Son**, pray for us sinners…

4. thy womb Jesus, Holy Mary, Mother of God, **the Queen Mother**, pray for us sinners…

5. thy womb Jesus, Holy Mary, Mother of God, **the majestic Queen**, pray for us sinners…

6. thy womb Jesus, Holy Mary, Mother of God, **Queen of Heaven and Earth**, pray for us sinners…

7. thy womb Jesus, Holy Mary, Mother of God, **Queen of Peace**, pray for us sinners…

8. thy womb Jesus, Holy Mary, Mother of God, **Queen of Families**, pray for us sinners…

9. thy womb Jesus, Holy Mary, Mother of God, **Queen of the Holy Rosary**, pray for us sinners…

10. thy womb Jesus, Holy Mary, Mother of God, **Queen of the Clergy**, pray for us sinners…

ADDITIONAL INVOCATIONS
—thy womb Jesus, Holy Mary, Mother of God, **Queen of Apostles**, pray for us sinners…

—thy womb Jesus, Holy Mary, Mother of God, **Queen of Prophets**, pray for us sinners…

—thy womb Jesus, Holy Mary, Mother of God, **Queen of Saints**, pray for us sinners…

—thy womb Jesus, Holy Mary, Mother of God, **Queen of Martyrs**, pray for us sinners…

ABOUT THE AUTHOR

Fr. Edward Lee Looney was ordained a priest for the Diocese of Green Bay on June 6, 2015. At a young age, he fostered a devotion to the Blessed Mother, which comes alive in his writings. Fr. Looney is a member of the Mariological Society of America and publishes regularly in theological journals and the blogosphere. His most recent works include *A Novena to the Queen of Heaven*, *Our Lady of Good Help*, and two prayer cards, *A Prayer After Communion for the Conversion of Sinners* and the *Litany to Our Lady of Good Help*. To learn more, visit his website: http://www.edwardlooney.com

PRAISE FOR
A ROSARY LITANY

Fr. Edward Looney was a student of mine at Mundelein Seminary. I have long recognized his intelligence, his prayerfulness, and his great love for the Mother of God. All of these qualities are on abundant display in this moving devotional, which can only help to deepen your spiritual life and your relationship to Mary.

—Bishop Robert Barron

In A Rosary Litany: Renewing a Pious Custom *Fr. Looney has done the Church a great service by retrieving an ancient and honorable method for praying the rosary in a more meditative manner. For centuries the rosary has been referred to as a "mini-catechism" and a "summary of the Gospel" and this little devotional book is a treasure that will greatly aid us in contemplating the sacred mysteries in a more profound way!*

—Fr. Donald Calloway, MIC, STL
Author of *Rosary Gems: Daily Wisdom on the Holy Rosary*

What a beautiful little devotional! This book will help you to grow closer to Our Lord and our Lady, through this method of the rosary. Read this book and use it in your daily prayer and discover the power and love of our Blessed Mother! I highly recommend it!

—Fr. Larry Richards

"THE SCHOOL OF MARY!" This was Saint John Paul II's simple yet profound description of the Holy Rosary. In the same spirit Fr. Edward Looney offers us this devotional book that can help us to "pray the Gospel," guided by our Holy Mother. Through A Rosary Litany, Father Looney revives a way of praying the Rosary that we have forgotten in America, that highlights the Scriptures to come to know Jesus with Mary. This is a fine and practical help for us to pray more deeply.

—Rev. James H. Phalan, CSC
Latin American Regional Coordinator,
The Family Rosary

Whether you're a rosary pro or a reluctant pray-er, A Rosary Litany *will be an indispensable guide for helping you grow closer to Jesus through Mary.*

—Sarah Reinhard, author and blogger,
SnoringScholar.com

In this age of spiritual crisis, people are in need of encountering Jesus Christ. The rosary is a timeless way of achieving such an encounter. Reflection on the mysteries of the rosary is the very soul of praying this simple but profound and powerful prayer. Through Fr. Edward Looney's new book A Rosary Litany, *the mysteries of the rosary come alive and a personal relationship with Christ springs forth. The story of redemption through Jesus Christ is not relegated just to a historical moment in the past, but continues to be applied in our daily life.* A Rosary Litany *provides nourishment to ensure this in the present moment.*

—Dick Boldin, Cofounder and Director of the
Rosary Evangelization Apostolate